The CASTLE KEEPERS

Also by Aimie K. Runyan

A Bakery in Paris (available August 2023)

The School for German Brides

Across the Winding River

Girls on the Line

Daughters of the Night Sky

Promised to the Crown

Duty to the Crown

Also by J'nell Ciesielski

To Free the Stars (A Jack and Ivy Novel, available August 2023)

The Brilliance of Stars (A Jack and Ivy Novel)

The Ice Swan

Beauty Among Ruins

The Socialite

Among the Poppies

The Songbird and the Spy

Also by Rachel McMillan

The Mozart Code

The London Restoration

Murder in the City of Liberty (A Van Buren and DeLuca Mystery)

Murder at the Flamingo (A Van Buren and DeLuca Mystery)

The
CASTLE
KEEPERS

AIMIE K. RUNYAN
J'NELL CIESIELSKI
RACHEL MCMILLAN

HARPER MUSE

The Castle Keepers

Copyright © 2023 Aimie K. Runyan, J'nell Ciesielski, Rachel McMillan

Published by Harper Muse, an imprint of HarperCollins Focus LLC.

Published in association with William K. Jensen Literary Agency, 119 Bampton Court, Eugene, Oregon 97404.

This book is a work of fiction. The characters, incidents, and dialogue are drawn from the authors' imagination and are not to be construed as real. Any resemblance to actual events or persons, living or dead, is entirely coincidental.

Any internet addresses (websites, blogs, etc.) in this book are offered as a resource. They are not intended in any way to be or imply an endorsement by HarperCollins Focus LLC, nor does HarperCollins Focus LLC vouch for the content of these sites for the life of this book.

Library of Congress Cataloging-in-Publication Data

Names: Runyan, Aimie K., author. | Ciesielski, J'nell, author. | McMillan, Rachel, 1981- author.
Title: The castle keepers / Aimie K. Runyan, J'nell Ciesielski, Rachel McMillan.
Description: Nashville : Harper Muse, 2023. | Summary: "From three beloved authors comes a collection of stories that examines questions of healing, legacy, and love against the rich backdrop of a historical castle--and its adjoining poison garden"-- Provided by publisher.
Identifiers: LCCN 2022056827 (print) | LCCN 2022056828 (ebook) | ISBN 9780785265320 (paperback) | ISBN 9780785264910 (epub) | ISBN 9780785264972
Subjects: LCGFT: Fiction.
Classification: LCC PS3618.U5667 C37 2023 (print) | LCC PS3618.U5667 (ebook) | DDC 813/.6--dc23/eng/20230104
LC record available at https://lccn.loc.gov/2022056827
LC ebook record available at https://lccn.loc.gov/2022056828

Printed in the United States of America

23 24 25 26 27 LBC 5 4 3 2 1

THE TRUTH KEEPERS

1870

CHAPTER 1 ——————————————

~*RULE No. 1*~

All the world's a stage, and all the men
and women merely players.
—William Shakespeare

New York City
February 1870

Beatrice examined her reflection in the mirror, and though she didn't risk her mother's ire by commenting on her own appearance, she knew she was ready to take the stage for one of the most important performances of her life.

Daddy wore his best tailcoat with mercifully fewer complaints than usual. For this, Beatrice offered silent thanks. She didn't need her father's grumbling and her mother's resultant henpecking to rile her nerves. Her sweet-natured father's grousing was a way of flirting with Mama, but Beatrice found it exasperating when it happened at important moments.

Tonight they would dine at the home of Caroline Astor. Mrs. William Backhouse Astor, the single most influential person in all of New York society. And Beatrice, if she ever wanted admittance to Mrs. Astor's good graces, would have to be flawless. Her hope was that if she played the part well enough, she just might secure a proposal from Thomas Graham.

Thomas, who actually watched plays when he went to the theater rather than attending purely so he could be seen by those who mattered.

Thomas, who was the only company that felt superior to the company of her beloved journal, a pen, and a roaring fire in her bedroom.

Thomas, whose piercing gaze made her stomach wobble and her breath stop in her throat with the merest glance.

Thomas, who had spent a great deal of social capital to secure this all-important invitation in hopes of advancing Beatrice and her family in society. Beatrice hoped it was so his parents could have no objection to their forming an attachment beyond seeing each other at social events and in the gathering areas at the theater once or twice a week.

Thomas, who would be the great compromise: a position to please her mother and the potential for the honest-to-goodness love match Beatrice longed for but had never hoped to aspire to.

Until Thomas.

Befitting the event, Beatrice and her mother dressed in fine silks and tasteful jewels. Their ruffled bustle skirts were like sugary confections—flowing masterpieces of fabric, rather than meringue— that seemed to defy the very laws of nature. Their restrictive bodices defied nature as well, molding the shape of the wearer into the feminine ideal. Their hair was just as elaborate—a massive tower of braids and curls that took the skill of a sculptor to achieve. Their money was so new, it was practically fresh from the printer's, but Mama knew full well how to spend it.

"You don't think you'd do better to wear a bit of color, kitten?" Daddy eyed Beatrice's cream gown with delicate gold beading. Mama's was a lovely shade of royal blue with silver embroidery that accentuated the blue in her eyes, but the matrons tended to wear more vibrant colors than their daughters. Beatrice guessed the object was to make the eligible ladies look more like brides, so they wore shades as close to white as they dared on a day other than their wedding day. Creams, ivories, silvers, pale golds, and yellows. Occasionally a shell pink or a featherlight blue—anything to imply innocence and purity. "Why not one like the green you wore yesterday? Or that nice red one from last week? You look a treat, but I do like a punch of color."

"Those are afternoon dresses, Morris." Mama tucked her arm in his and patted his gloved hand. "The young ladies tend to wear more muted colors for evening attire."

"Drab, if you ask me," Daddy said. "But I suppose my opinion is the least important on the subject."

Sarah Holbrook looked indulgently at her husband and prodded the party out the door. She barked a few orders to Robinson, the much-put-upon lady's maid who looked after Mama and occasionally Beatrice.

Beatrice remained silent, knowing her mother's tone with the staff earned her clucking tongues from the more refined of their acquaintances who always gave the guise of magnanimity to those in their employ. Mama mistakenly thought that kindness to the staff was a sign of familiarity that would make her seem common.

Mama was the classic American beauty with honey-blonde hair, sapphire-blue eyes, and perfect, even features, while Beatrice was too tall and her hair was too deep a chocolate brown to be fashionable. Thankfully it was abundant enough for the latest hairstyles. And no one could deny Beatrice's complexion was as enviable as her mother's. Beatrice's gray eyes with flecks of blue, she had to admit, were a source of pride.

Daddy was of humble birth, having been born to tenant farmers and lured west by the temptation of the California gold rush. He was one of the lucky few who hit the mother lode, and luckier still to have married Mama. She had pressed him to invest the money in railroads rather than squandering it on fleeting luxuries. The investments were a booming success, and by the time Beatrice was three, they moved from their lavish home in San Francisco to New York so they could make their mark on society. More than anything in the world, Mama wanted to leave behind the memory of her impoverished beginnings and find true acceptance in the most elite circles of New York.

Mama had told Beatrice—on the rare occasions she was willing to speak about her girlhood—how poor they'd been. How cast out she'd felt. She'd read about New York in magazines and dreamed of going there and being welcomed by the finest families. It was never Beatrice's dream, or Daddy's, to become pillars of New York society, but Mama had made it their chief aim in life nonetheless. It was as though admittance to balls and fine dinners would somehow erase the years of privation.

"Your opinion matters a great deal, Daddy," Beatrice assured him. "I wouldn't dare pick a riding ensemble without consulting you."

Daddy rewarded her with a kiss on the forehead. For whatever refinements he lacked, he was as skilled a sportsman as any in New York's elite circles. The Holbrooks only lacked the luck, socially speaking, of people like the Fishes and Astors who came from old, established fortunes. They were, to use Caroline Astor's term, *arrivistes*. But Daddy had taught Beatrice how to ride when she was barely able to walk, and he'd always gifted her with lovely riding habits in hopes that she wouldn't lose interest in their mutual pastime. There was no danger of that, but she let him indulge her anyway.

Daddy kept up jovial small talk on the ride to the Astors', but Beatrice was too busy swallowing back bile to give him more than a cursory response. Every social outing brought her nerves to the brink of their limits. It grew worse and worse as each engagement carried increasingly more importance in advancing the family's social position and improving Beatrice's marital prospects. And as the stakes grew, Mama became more and more overbearing where Beatrice was concerned. Each *clip-clop* of the horses' hooves sent her stomach churning, and she could do no more than concentrate on her next breath if she was to arrive at the Astor home with her wits intact.

Mama hissed a few reminders about decorum at Daddy, who, as always, took them in indulgent stride.

They were ushered inside by the butler and found the orderly receiving line moving efficiently. Mrs. Astor greeted them with the same formality tempered with the barest trace of warm cordiality she extended to everyone. Caroline Astor was, of course, the most splendidly dressed woman in the room. She wouldn't have stood for anything else. Beatrice had seen the pictures of the social maven as a young woman when she'd been fresh like dew on a rose. It was hard to reconcile that image with the formidable woman who stood before them. She wore a gown of steel silk (and a gaze to match) that would have overpowered a lesser woman, but there wasn't a gown in existence that would have dared to overpower *the* Caroline Astor.

The simple truth was that the keys to the gates of New York society resided squarely in the Astor matriarch's pocket, and she clenched them tight, admitting precious few to her fashionable inner circles.

Beatrice escaped the receiving line without incident and saw Thomas. He had a flute of champagne in hand and was deep in conversation with some Astor relation Beatrice didn't know who always wore an expression of vague boredom but who seemed pleased enough to be in Thomas's lively company.

Thomas looked up and his eyes locked with hers. He'd noticed her glancing in his direction. A faux pas. She didn't play coy and pretend she hadn't seen him but rather nodded in his direction, allowed a delicate smile to pull at her lips, and continued to scan the room.

She wanted to stare into the deep-brown pools of his eyes. His irises flecked with gold caught even the least glimmer of light and could hold her captive for hours. She wanted nothing more than to run her fingers through his thick black hair, but she could not let him know this. She couldn't be aloof, for no man wanted to waste his time with a woman who couldn't be won, but nor could she be too effusive.

Mama often called it a game of cat and mouse, and her mother wasn't wrong. It was made all the more challenging when the mouse had to keep the hunt exciting when she wanted nothing more than to be caught.

In mere seconds Thomas appeared by her side. As in many great plays, the truths weren't in the words spoken but rather in the ones left unsaid.

"So lovely to see you here at last, Miss Holbrook," he said. *I'm so glad Jack was able to weasel an invitation out of the old windbag.*

"Thank you, Mr. Graham. I was delighted at the invitation. Making new acquaintances is one of the true joys in life, is it not?" *I never thought she'd ask us. She's a miserable old crone, isn't she?*

"Mrs. Astor is the finest hostess New York has ever seen. You're in for a treat." *She's a nightmare.* "You'll do me the honor of allowing me to introduce you and your parents to the room, won't you?" *I desperately want to show you off.*

"Of course, we'd be glad to meet your friends." *That's precisely why I'm here.*

For twenty minutes Thomas escorted Beatrice from guest to guest, introducing her as though she were an important dignitary come all the way from the other side of the globe to spend the evening in their company. He radiated pride as her hand rested in the crook of his arm. She had to work hard to keep her smile from being too broad and her expression too animated when he was in such proximity.

A man might not be able to sense when a woman was too enthusiastic about him, but one had to be more guarded with the mothers. They were far more observant than their husbands and sons, even if they led the men to believe otherwise in order to puff up their egos.

"I'm afraid we're to dine on opposite sides of the room," Thomas said as the dinner chime sounded, the regret in his voice ringing sincere. "I'd very much hoped to talk to you in more detail about the performance of *Hamlet* from last week. I thought your take on the performance was quite insightful."

"We shall simply have to delay that pleasure for another time, then." Beatrice rewarded him with a genuine smile.

He returned the gesture and bent low to her ear when he thought no one was looking. "You look positively sublime, my sweet."

His words were spoken so softly, she wasn't sure if she'd imagined them. His breath was warm against her ear, and she could smell the heady tinge of champagne on his lips. Had they been alone, she would not have been able to resist brushing her own against them to taste it for herself.

She prided herself in keeping a serene countenance, but to keep the color from her cheeks in such a moment was beyond even her greatest attempts at self-control.

Mrs. Astor's dinners were, as one might expect, the epitome of Knickerbocker graciousness. There was no unnecessary affectation beyond the gleaming, polished silver candelabra and fine china. The house was grand enough, the food elegant enough, to stand for themselves.

Daddy was seated near William Astor, the patriarch of the family, which was a particular honor. Why the family had been given such an attention, Beatrice didn't know for certain, but she was sure

Thomas had used his Astor ties to encourage Lina Astor to pay them special attention that night. It was, after all, an audition.

Thomas, though seated several tables away, saw where Beatrice and her family were situated and nodded his approval to her. Beatrice gave herself a reprieve of her rule about daydreaming while in public and took a few seconds to imagine a crowd like this one assembled for her wedding to Thomas. She pictured the starched white table-cloths and sparkling crystal. What would her mother insist upon for the gown? Satin? Silk? Perhaps velvet if they were married in winter.

Mama cleared her throat and Beatrice snapped back to attention. *How does she know?* It was a constant wonder to her. Mama seemed to have an otherworldly knack for knowing when her daughter's attention wandered.

The food was served by attentive footmen. Dazzling arrays of oysters served as the hors d'oeuvre. Scalloped, fried, broiled— prepared in any way the Astors' chef could contrive.

Beatrice took one of each sort of oyster, knowing that sampling each offering would be the polite thing to do. The only option she wasn't keen on trying was the raw one, so she decided to try it first. She summoned her courage and tipped the shell so the contents would slip into her mouth as she saw the others do. It tasted positively foul and smelled vaguely of sulphur, but she managed to swallow without making a face. A mercy, since Mama was watching her discreetly as she held a conversation with a Mrs. Twombly. The stylish matron held Mama enraptured with her discussion of her recent trip to France and England with her husband and two daughters.

For the next three hours Beatrice absorbed the conversation, partaking just enough that she didn't appear dull or overly timid. Her nerves were quaking like spindly tree branches in the wind, but she was confident it didn't show too badly. She hoped it was just enough to make her appear charmingly demure. If her mother noticed her disquiet, Beatrice would be treated to a lecture about self-control later. There was no convincing Mama that her constant critiques only made Beatrice's anxious nature hover even closer to the surface.

She ate a few more of the oysters, all of which tasted much better for being cooked, no matter the method. Then the footmen came forth every half hour or so with mutton and barley consommé, chicken breasts, beef filets, foie gras, and several kinds of salads. Each was a work of art in miniature. Perfectly seasoned, perfectly presented. Caroline Astor never would have stood for less.

Beatrice took only small portions of each but was already reaching her limit of comfort, owing to the restrictive steel boning in her corset. A footman set a plate of delicate candied fruits and petit fours before her. There wasn't a French pâtissier in existence who wouldn't have looked at the arrangement with pride. She took a small bite of one of the petit fours—this one was a miniature lemon cake topped with a tiny violet made from sugar. The first seconds after it touched her tongue were pure bliss, but then the sugar became unbearably cloying.

Dread filled Beatrice when she realized she was going to be ill. One of the oysters must have gone bad, and Beatrice was going to suffer for it.

The nausea hit suddenly and with the force of one of the nor'easters that took New York to its knees. Sweat beaded on Beatrice's forehead and she began to shake.

"Mama, I fear I am quite unwell." Beatrice tried to keep her tone as low as she could without being so rude as to whisper.

Mama studied Beatrice's face, which must have been chartreuse with nausea. "Have some water, dear. I'm sure that will right you."

Beatrice raised the etched-crystal water goblet to her lips but was overcome before she could swallow even a drop of the cool water.

"Control yourself," Mama hissed before she could reel the words back into her mouth.

"Please excuse me," Beatrice mumbled, standing from her place and rushing toward the door with a napkin held to her mouth. One of Caroline Astor's fine linen napkins. Beatrice prayed she could escape before the contents of her stomach made an untimely exit, but the wobble in her knees didn't inspire confidence.

She'd nearly made it to the door when she tripped over the hem of her skirt and splayed flat on the marble floor. She didn't dare look up to put faces with the snickers she could hear from the nearby tables. She summoned every ounce of her strength to scramble up and find the nearest obliging plant in the hallway in which to empty her stomach. Trying though she might to keep the sounds of her retching quiet, she was certain every Astor for miles could hear her defiling of what was likely a priceless Ming urn or some such museum-worthy *objet d'art*.

In that moment there was nothing Beatrice wanted more than for the curtain to come down on this scene and for all to forget her performance that night. She knew in her heart there would never be another.

CHAPTER 2

If you don't know your lines,
speak as though you do.

MAYFAIR DISTRICT, LONDON, ENGLAND
MAY 1870

The glint of the crystals hanging from the chandeliers in Lady Millbourne's ballroom danced in the glow of candlelight as elegantly as any of the dancers beneath them. Beatrice was wearing one of the ball gowns her mother had helped design. It was a lovely plum-colored organza that complemented her complexion, and the bodice boasted elaborate beading and a sweep train that made her feel as regal as the queen herself. Her coiffure was a well-organized riot of chestnut pin curls that had taken Robinson ages to put in place.

Lady Millbourne had the outrageous fortune to marry an earl. Most of the New York ladies who came to marry for titles were lucky to end up with a baronet or even a mere peer of the realm. Luckily, Lady Millbourne remembered her days as Lucy Twombly and had been fond of Beatrice before her ascent in society. The countess agreed to serve as Beatrice's mentor in London society, and it was a boon Beatrice would need desperately.

As her entrée to Caroline Astor's inner circles had been an unqualified disaster, London's *ton* was to be her triumph. One embarrassment in front of the elite of New York society and not two weeks later, Beatrice and her parents were on a steamship to Paris, where they spent several fortunes at Worth's atelier before heading to London for the season. Trading one elite social group for another, with the hope of a fresh start, they hadn't time to waste, for the tale of her embarrassment hadn't yet made it across the Atlantic. But it wouldn't be long before it did.

Beatrice carefully sipped champagne at Lady Millbourne's elbow as she was introduced to so many lords and ladies, she felt like she would never remember them all, though it was imperative that she did. For some reason, Beatrice felt somewhat more at ease. Perhaps because this wasn't *her* society; the one she'd been raised to conquer. The one she had failed—miserably—to win over. But here she had the advantage of being a novelty. And having a large fortune that could be quite useful to some baron or viscount in need of shoring up his estate.

Mama was embroiled in conversation with one of the senior matrons in attendance, but Beatrice felt her mother's eyes trailing her the entire time. Heavens, what she wouldn't have given to be free from her mother's stares. At times she felt like an actress constantly dogged by her worst critic. It made her bone weary. Beatrice knew her mother hated to let Lady Millbourne take over the duty of chaperone that night, but it was a necessary part of the game they were playing.

Lady Millbourne presented her to a middle-aged man, dressed finer than the others. "Your Highness, may I present Miss Beatrice Holbrook of New York. Miss Holbrook, His Royal Highness, the Prince of Wales."

Beatrice dipped into a low curtsy before the man, who otherwise looked as unremarkable as any other man who had entered his forties or fifties. He was balding and given to fat around the middle, but he possessed a charm she'd scarcely encountered before. Though people were chatting in small groups or pairs, there was the sense that everyone had one eye on the prince and wished for nothing more than to please him. They deferred to him as everyone in New York deferred to Caroline Astor. No one else's opinion mattered more.

"The charming Miss Holbrook. I've been looking so forward to meeting you since Lady Millbourne told me of your arrival. Tell me, does London meet with your approval after all the hustle and bustle of New York?"

"It far exceeds it, Your Highness. I've never met a more charming people in my life." He needn't know how limited her experience was, but the statement was true enough. Beatrice had been too young to remember her time in San Francisco before she and her parents left. She felt well rid of New York and had seen little of Paris outside of Worth's atelier.

"I hope your visit will prove satisfactory, Miss Holbrook. And be of some duration."

"Thank you so much, Your Highness."

He inclined his head and moved to chat with another.

"Well done, my dear Miss Holbrook. A good first impression," Lady Millbourne said when they were out of earshot. "I wager he finds you interesting enough to keep around for the season."

"Thank heaven." Beatrice dropped her shoulders by a few inches.

"Indeed, my dear. Now we've only to get you in front of Baron Chatsworth. I think he's just the thing for you. What a handsome couple the pair of you would make. Why don't you excuse me for a moment and I'll see where he might be."

Beatrice nodded and her hostess walked off in a swoosh of taffeta.

Beatrice inconspicuously walked to the edge of the ballroom to await Lady Millbourne's return. Mama was still deeply engrossed in her conversation and had moved off into one of the quieter side rooms reserved for the purpose. Beatrice drew in a deep breath, knowing that, at least for a few moments, her mother wasn't watching—rather, scrutinizing—her every move. Beatrice didn't see her father anywhere, so it seemed prudent to stand to the side and feign interest in watching those who were engaged in dancing.

As Beatrice was absorbed in the swirls of silks and satins on the dance floor, she felt a cold splash on her front that came from someone bumping her from the right.

"I am so terribly sorry!" a hushed voice exclaimed. A tall, dark-haired man blushed furiously, holding an empty champagne flute in one hand and leaning heavily on a cane. He looked far too young to need such a device. What might have caused the injury that made its use so necessary?

A ball of ice formed in her stomach. "My mother is going to murder me" was all Beatrice managed to say. Her mother, who had never been indulgent before the incident at the Astors', had been merciless in her speeches about flawless comportment in the days before this ball. And for all that, Beatrice had failed. She would have to go home and miss the opportunity of meeting the baron. This wasn't a disaster of the same magnitude as the night at the Astors', but one whisper implying that Beatrice was stealing away due to fragile health or some such could be harmful enough to her prospects.

She exited to the hallway without taking her leave of the man to inspect the damage in one of the large mirrors. She was fairly well drenched, but at least he'd been drinking champagne and not claret.

"Is there any way I can be of some assistance?" the man from the ballroom asked. She'd tried not to notice the sound of his footsteps punctuated with the *clack* as the metal tip of his wooden cane made contact with the marble floors.

Just go away, she wanted to mutter. "No, sir. All shall be well. Thank you. But there's nothing to be done for my dress. I'll have to fetch my parents and go home."

"Please, let me see what can be done. Surely one of the maids can be of service."

"Don't go to any trouble, please." Beatrice knew the color was high in her cheeks, and she was afraid she'd start shaking if he didn't leave her in peace.

"I couldn't bear to be responsible for ruining your evening. I insist. Come with me."

There in the hall, memories of her disastrous dinner at the Astors' flooded her brain, and suddenly Beatrice found her breath trapped in her lungs and she couldn't exhale.

"You're unwell," the gentleman said.

A stone bench stood in the hallway, and he motioned for her to sit. They were alone and unchaperoned. If they were discovered, this would be her undoing, but as the corridor began to grow hazy around the edges, she had little choice but to sit and risk public ridicule.

"Just breathe, Miss . . ."

"Holbrook," she managed to supply as she expelled the stale air in her lungs and exchanged it for fresh. If she was going to be the laughingstock of London because of this man and be forced to return to New York in disgrace, he might as well know her name.

"Do you need a doctor?" he asked, though he seemed relieved that she was able to speak.

"No." She shook her head. "I don't know what came over me."

It was a lie. She knew exactly what had caused her to panic, and the fear of being cast out of London as well as New York had been too much to bear. Where else was left? Paris? She could hardly imagine charming the French elite with her schoolroom French.

"I'd wager you have a war wound yourself," he said, wobbling his cane.

"War wound?" She stared at the patterns made by the veins in the marble floor to steady herself.

"India," he said by way of explanation. The rebellion. She'd read about it in the papers, but it seemed like such a far-flung thing she hadn't paid it much heed. "I expect you didn't have to go so far."

"New York. Caroline Astor's dining room."

"I'll take India any time over that viper's nest." His lips pulled up at the corners.

"You have the measure of it then," she said, weakly able to return the smile.

"I'm so sorry I've dredged up bad memories for you. I feel like a cad."

"It wasn't your fault," Beatrice said, grateful that the room was finally coming back into focus. "It was an accident."

"Accidents have a nasty way of haunting a person. But I am glad you're willing to overlook it."

Beatrice nodded. She'd been away and unchaperoned for quite some time now and had regained enough control over herself to know how serious her absence was.

"I need to get back before I'm missed," she said. "Lady Millbourne is probably frantic already."

"Yes, yes. Let's see you cleaned up first though. It won't take but a moment." He led her to the servants' hall with the familiarity of one who knew the house. Or perhaps one who knew all great houses. "And then if your absence is noticed, a maid will vouch for us if anyone thinks we've been up to mischief."

Beatrice's stomach sank. If anyone noticed she was missing and pressed the matter, she might already be ruined.

When they reached the servants' hall, every staff member immediately stood still upon seeing them. "You'll excuse us, but Miss Holbrook here has been the victim of my clumsiness." He addressed the room full of black-clad servants who were all standing with drink trays or awaiting their next orders, depending on their function in the household. "Would one of you be so kind as to help us?"

A maid whisked her away, blotting the stain with instructions to have a maid wash it with a mixture of vinegar, lemon juice, and water later that night. The maid didn't want to send a guest out onto the dance floor smelling of salad dressing, and Beatrice was grateful for the forethought. Within minutes Beatrice was fit to be seen in public again. She thanked the maid profusely and wondered where she'd learned her trade so expertly.

"You look right as rain." The gentleman glanced at Beatrice's gown when she returned. "Let me escort you back."

Beatrice nodded and accepted his arm. He led her back to the ballroom, looking as though he were searching for words but could find none.

"There you are, Miss Holbrook!" Lady Millbourne said. "I couldn't imagine where you'd gotten to."

"The fault is mine, Lady Millbourne. I'm sorry I deprived you of your guest." The gentleman bowed and departed before she could speak.

"What on earth were you doing with Lord Alnwick?" Lady Millbourne asked.

"Lord Alnwick?" Beatrice wrinkled her brow. "He didn't even introduce himself."

"I'm not terribly surprised. He's not known for being particularly ebullient. I'm surprised he's here, to be honest with you. He's Charles Alnwick, styled Earl Alnwick, the future Marquess of Northridge," she confirmed. "You address him as Lord Alnwick. Aside from the prince, there isn't a soul here with a title to match his."

Beatrice's eyes scanned the dance floor for him and did not find him. Lady Millbourne noticed Beatrice's gaze and clucked, "It's a shame he's so aloof."

"Aloof?" He'd seemed uncommonly kind, if a bit reserved. One of the more amiable people she'd met since arriving in London.

"Some unpleasant rumors too. I wouldn't set my sights on him if I were you."

"As you say," Beatrice assured her. But there was something unforthcoming about the way Lady Millbourne spoke that betrayed there was a great deal she wasn't revealing.

CHAPTER 3 —————————————

~RULE No. 3~

Never be afraid to accept a larger role.
You can learn the lines as you go.

It seems you were quite the success, kitten," Daddy said as he glanced over the society column at breakfast three days later. "You were mentioned prominently and several times. Very well done."

"Indeed." Mama placed her teacup crisply on its saucer. "The party went off well enough for you. Now if only the next encounter with your Baron Chatsworth is productive, we may have made some real progress. And so soon too. I can't deny that I'm impressed, Beatrice."

"Thank you, Mother." Beatrice held back the rancor that threatened to leap off the tip of her tongue. It was as though she were so used to offering censure that Beatrice's mother could hardly find the words for praise.

Lady Millbourne had indeed introduced Beatrice to the baron at the ball, and he'd been an attentive companion for several dances. Beatrice could sense he was interested in courting her, but she wasn't fully convinced of her own enthusiasm for his suit. He was convivial enough, but nothing about him truly gripped Beatrice's attention.

"Wear your lavender organza this afternoon," Mama continued. "Lady Millbourne seemed to think he would call today."

"Very well. I might as well change now." The gown was lovely and would suit her complexion, though she'd have preferred to choose her own. Robinson entered at that moment, some mending in a basket under her arm. "Excellent timing. I'll need you for a few moments before you get to that."

"Actually, miss, you have a guest. I've shown him to the parlor. I wasn't sure what else to do."

"It's not even ten in the morning," Mama said. "Why on earth would the baron call so early?"

"It wasn't the baron, ma'am. It was a Lord Alnwitch, I believe."

"Lord Alnwick, do you mean?" Beatrice asked.

"That's the one," Robinson replied.

"Who is this coming to call?" Mama asked. "And practically at the crack of dawn."

Daddy rolled his eyes. "My God, woman. It's almost midday. I remember when you couldn't sleep past seven. I don't care how many years I've spent with this lot; I'll never get used to the hours you keep. Waking when the day's half done and going to bed at dawn. It isn't natural."

"Oh, Morris. I do wish you wouldn't say such nonsense." Mama fiddled with her napkin. She scanned the room as though she were worried Caroline Astor had placed spies to overhear Daddy speaking with longing of the days before his social ascent.

"He's Earl Alnwick, heir to the Marquess of Northridge," Beatrice said. "We were introduced last evening."

She omitted that they *technically* hadn't been introduced. And the manner of their meeting too. It would be one less reason for her mother to chide her.

"Marquess?" Mama sat up straighter. "My heavens. Well, I suppose you'll have to go in like that. We can't keep him waiting.

Robinson, see what you can do with her hair." Mama continued to hiss orders at the staff to prepare refreshments for the earl while Robinson sprang into action and whipped Beatrice's long chestnut braid into a low twist. Beatrice was wearing a simple white cotton two-piece dress with printed pink rosebuds. Something suitable for breakfast with her parents, or perhaps an early afternoon spent sewing with intimate companions, but little else. But there was nothing for it. Beatrice would have to cross right by the parlor to change. It would be less of a spectacle for him to see her as she was.

He was staring into the fire and stood in a hurry when she entered the room. Robinson followed, having been ordered to act as chaperone, and settled in the corner with her mending.

"What an unexpected pleasure, Lord Alnwick." Beatrice crossed the room to offer her hand.

"I'm so sorry to push in so early. Only, I was in the area and wanted to see you before your usual parade of visitors comes calling."

"Well now, you have me intrigued, sir. Do sit down." Beatrice gestured to the sofa where he'd been sitting.

"My dear Miss Holbrook, let me get straight to the point. I gathered from the soiree the other evening that Lady Millbourne has set her cap on Baron Chatsworth for you?"

"Lord Alnwick, I don't think it would be proper for me to admit to anything of that sort. I don't know what you've been told about American women, but we're not wholly without discretion."

"I'm so terribly sorry. I'm not much at niceties, much to my mother's chagrin, as you might expect. I just wish, very kindly, to ask you to be very cautious with your dealings with the baron. And Lady Millbourne, too, for that matter. The baron spent half the evening at the soiree playing—and losing—at cards. A fantastic sum, I've no doubt. And he's run up considerable gambling debts with my brother, John, as well. I'm not one to pass judgment on a gentleman who places a wager or plays a few rounds of cards for a diversion, but it seems this is a regular habit of his."

"Oh, how awful," Beatrice said. "What a waste of resources."

"Especially as it seems he hasn't much skill at cards, nor the good luck to redeem his losses."

Beatrice giggled despite herself. "An unfortunate combination. You also caution me against Lady Millbourne. What could be the matter there?"

"I know she's taken up the mantle as a bit of a matchmaker for American heiresses looking for titled husbands. Unfortunately, her motives are often self-serving. In the case of Baron Chatsworth, I'd be shocked if he hasn't asked her to find him a wealthy American so he can pay off his debts in exchange for a portion of the dowry. Lord Millbourne's estate is in dire need of shoring up as well."

"These are serious accusations. But I thank you for putting me on my guard."

"Consider it thanks for not losing your temper with me when I nearly ruined your gown," Lord Alnwick said. "If you had the volatile American disposition my compatriots jest about, I'd have been in dire straits. I appreciated your restraint."

"I overreacted exceedingly in the moment." Beatrice cast her eyes downward at the shameful memory. "Indeed, I'm surprised you risked your life in coming here, as churlish as I was. I assure you, I'm not usually the sort to fly into a rage over a quarter glass of champagne spilled on a gown."

"No, but if it had been a full glass, now then . . ." He shook his head.

"Well, a duel would be the only appropriate response in that case. You can't expect us to leave our honor undefended."

"Certainly not," he agreed, his expression sober. "And I would have deserved my comeuppance."

"So long as we're in agreement." Beatrice smiled.

"All joking aside, Miss Holbrook. Do be careful. Don't let the prestige of a title blind you to the faults of the man who holds it. I imagine there will be many men who will court you whose intentions aren't as pure as they seem. And many of them are more talented than actors on the stage."

Beatrice concealed a smirk. He couldn't know that she viewed her life as one long stage play. Whether it was a drama or a farce depended on the day.

"I'll be cautious," she promised. "And you're kind to be so concerned."

"I'd hate to think of one as lovely and kind as you falling prey to such scheming."

"You speak as though you've been in my company for much longer than you have, sir."

"One doesn't need more than a moment in your company to know that you're lovely. As for your kindness, I was able to hear the way you spoke to the housemaid at the Millbournes'. I observed the way you interacted with people at the party. Your kindness is evident, Miss Holbrook."

"I hope you're right, Lord Alnwick. I can imagine no better compliment." Heat rose in her cheeks. She wasn't used to being heaped with praise beyond a flippant word or two about her appearance from her father. But despite the foreignness of it, she didn't feel uncomfortable in Lord Alnwick's presence. She felt rather more at ease than she had expected to, and she rather liked the sensation of breathing freely.

"I was wondering if you might consider allowing me to call on you again. I know that the demands on your time must be many."

"I would like that immensely. I should very much like the opportunity to get to know you better."

A smile spread across his face. He wasn't an overly handsome man, but the smile improved his countenance by leaps and bounds.

"My day has been made, Miss Holbrook. And now I shall leave you to yours."

He bowed his way out of the room, and Mama entered as soon as the door snapped shut.

"Well, what on earth was that, Beatrice?" Mama took the seat Lord Alnwick had just vacated. "I heard Lady Millbourne say he was rather an odd duck. And he was abominably rude to show up here so early."

"Not such an odd duck, I don't think, Mama. But most assuredly a bigger fish."

Beatrice smiled to herself. Even her mother would be delighted. Victory was so close she could almost grasp it in her very fingers. Her marriage had been the thing she'd spent her whole life building toward, and she was about to make a social leap beyond her wildest dreams. What would it be like to finally be married? Would she be able to breathe freely as mistress of her own home, out from under her mother's constant chiding? She'd spent so much time considering the match, she'd spent precious little considering her life afterward.

Her mother had thought the best Beatrice could do was a baron or one of the lesser landed gentry. She had been persuaded of this, rather convincingly, by Lady Millbourne. Beatrice would have been pressed to accept and be grateful for the union. But now, Beatrice would make a social coup to which no one in their circles would have aspired. She would become the Marchioness of Northridge one day, and her mother would never again dictate the way she lived.

———◆———◆———

Though Mama was worried about crossing Lady Millbourne, she had sense enough not to keep Beatrice from keeping company with Lord Alnwick. While Lady Millbourne was their sponsor for the season, an engagement to Lord Alnwick would render her superfluous—and Beatrice's social inferior. They'd been invited to so many balls, dinner parties, masques, and other such lavish social gatherings, Beatrice could scarce keep track of them all. If Mama worked up the temerity to ask the hostess, with as much nonchalance as she could muster, if Lord Alnwick would be in attendance, the answer was always the same—the invitation had been extended (for who could risk offending the earl and his family), but they had received no reply and expected none.

But he was there. Always.

Beatrice would see him in the ballroom as she entered. He'd either be in conversation with a gray-haired old man and looking dour about it or else off on the side of the room, quietly observing the proceedings while sipping from a glass of claret.

According to the whispers of the other young ladies, he had the reputation of having a rather sullen disposition, but Beatrice reasoned he was merely shy. But to watch him in moments like these, it was clear he looked as comfortable in a ballroom as he would at the gallows. He was an observer of the festivities rather than a participant in them. But despite his reluctance to mingle in society, he was there. And he asked her, without fail, to dance the customary two—but never more than two—dances.

Then Beatrice would catch his eye, and for a moment, his face would brighten. He was *happy* to see her. He was willing to endure events he could not have enjoyed less, merely for the sake of seeing her. Or at least she assumed such, given that he rarely danced with another lady and spent most of the rest of the evening in idle chatter with the other gentlemen.

Either his estate truly needed an infusion of money, as so many estates did these days, or he genuinely wanted to spend time with her.

She was willing to allow that both could be true. And though Beatrice kept her heart in check, vowing never to let anyone hurt her as Thomas had done, she was genuinely happy that he seemed to like her.

Like. Such a tepid word.

But it wasn't nothing. It was a spark that could one day be kindled into something larger. Perhaps not a raging inferno, but a comfortable blaze. The kind one could curl up beside with a good book. It was likely because he cared so little for the rules of polite society. Not that he was above them; he simply didn't care at all. It was honest. He had no desire to take his role in the crass theatrical production in which she'd been raised to perform. She imagined the possibility of a life with him and felt a sense of peace that she'd not known before.

The evening of a ball hosted by some duke or another whom Beatrice would never remember, Lord Alnwick was bold enough to lean down and take the liberty of whispering in her ear. "Would you care for some air? I can scarce draw breath in here it's so crowded."

"Of course," Beatrice replied. He escorted her to the verandah, away from the crush of the dance floor. It was the closest they could have to privacy, given the constraints of society.

Two other couples strolled on the massive verandah, each pair keeping a respectable distance from the other so as not to overhear their murmurings. The ladies stood as close to the gentlemen as decorum would allow, sometimes testing the limits of propriety. One could be sure there were always prying eyes, which ensured that nothing untoward happened. They would also be the first to spread the news if something did.

But there was an art to assuring a suitor that a lady was not without warmth. In moments such as these, allowing him to stand just a few inches too close conveyed far more meaning than words. Few men wanted to face the prospect of a cold marriage.

"You look so lovely," Lord Alnwick said when they were finally alone. There was a slight tremor in his voice that somehow served to soothe Beatrice's own nerves. She wore one of the many gowns she'd acquired in Paris. A confection in mother-of-pearl silk with a daring sweep of pink fabric roses. Her dark-chocolate-brown hair was swept upward in an elaborate coiffeur with dozens of pin curls. It had taken Robinson over an hour to construct it, and Beatrice didn't look forward to the uncomfortable process of removing the pins later that night. She wore only the barest hint of rouge on her lips and cheeks and a trace of scent she'd procured during her weeks in France. "But then again, you always do."

"Thank you." *It cost my father a fortune for me to look like this, not to mention three hours with a lady's maid to make it happen. And it was all for you, so I hope you appreciate it.* "You're too kind."

"I'm horrid at small talk," he said, staring off into the gardens barely visible under the cloak of night. "I'd sooner spend an hour discussing the prime minister's latest speech before Parliament, but I hardly know how to direct the conversation with a lady."

"The same as you would with a gentleman, I expect. Truly, you needn't feel nervous around me, Lord Alnwick."

"I've been schooled in the rules of polite society since I could toddle in the nursery room, but I'm never at ease here." He gestured back to the ballroom.

"In truth, I know little of what's expected in British society, so you could convince me that almost anything was correct. I could lecture you for several hours about the expected comportment in Caroline Astor's drawing room, but London is another world altogether."

"It's just as well. I am not meant for London. Not really. My heart is always at Leedswick."

"Tell me about your home," Beatrice encouraged. "Is it very beautiful?"

"The most magnificent estate in England, as far as I'm concerned. It's nearly seven hundred years old and surrounded by battlements.

The gardens are some of the finest in the land. It looks out onto the River Aln and was a glorious place to grow up. You'll have to forgive my boastfulness, but when it comes to Leedswick Castle, I am incapable of my usual temperance."

He spoke with a wistfulness that Beatrice envied. There wasn't a place on earth she cared for with such devotion. She adored the family home in Newport, but her father had purchased it just fifteen years prior. Lord Alnwick's family had generations of history at Leedswick. It was no mystery why his roots ran so deep there. The place was ancient and likely in need of modernization, which was where the need for Beatrice came in. She wasn't so naïve as to think otherwise.

"That's as it should be. Leedswick is your birthright, and you ought to be proud of it." Beatrice recognized the timidity in his expression and decided to offer some encouragement. "I hope I shall have the occasion to see it one day, Lord Alnwick. From the sound of it, I shall never see England properly until I see Leedswick."

"I hope you will have occasion to spend a great deal of time at Leedswick, Miss Holbrook." He finally looked back to her. His expression changed, somehow both serious and hopeful. "We haven't known each other long, but I think you know me well enough to know I'm simply not capable of some of the social niceties expected from men of my station. I don't think it bothers you as much as it would a girl from one of our families."

"No," Beatrice admitted. "I find your candor refreshing. I've an abhorrence for artifice that makes me ill-equipped for good society. But I've been hammered into the mold and try to do my best." As she spoke the words, she realized how true they were. She had to imagine herself as an actress to be able to stomach the lot of it.

"I promise you, if New York society was challenging for you, mixing in London society for the rest of your days will be a nightmare. I don't envy you."

"I haven't much choice, have I?" Beatrice retorted. "I'm here because I must marry, and here I will stay, flitting about society until I do so, or embarrass myself so completely that I have to return to New York in disgrace." *Even deeper disgrace.* But she didn't dare voice that thought. She couldn't bear to think of all of London knowing her misfortune. Part of her wanted to tell him the whole saga, but she'd trusted a man once before, and she still felt the sting of the results. Charles might be the kindest man in England, but she couldn't find it within her to be perfectly candid just yet.

"Unhappy alternative, isn't it? I could offer you a better one. That is, I hope you'll find it to be preferable to going home with your head cast down."

"Oh?" Beatrice turned to him, fixing her gaze on his profile.

"You could marry me." He stared down at his hands gripping the railing of the verandah.

"I beg your pardon?" Beatrice felt light-headed. She'd been hoping her encounters with Lord Alnwick would come to this, but it still felt somehow unexpected. She was on the verge of her social triumph and could only picture all the things that could spoil it. Making some slip of the tongue. Tripping over his cane. Catching cold and appearing frail.

She forced herself to push the thoughts from her head and focus on Lord Alnwick, though his face was fuzzy for all her garbled, fatalistic thoughts.

"Marry me, Miss Holbrook," he repeated, finally turning to look at her. His expression was earnest, as though discussing a business venture instead of a marriage. Perhaps it was more appropriate than an insincere attempt at romance. "You'll put an end to your season here in London far earlier than expected. And when you return to New York to visit, your title as Countess Alnwick and future Marchioness of Northridge will be the envy of every Astor, Livingston, and Goelet in the whole of the city."

"You'll forgive my shock," Beatrice replied. "I just hadn't expected . . ."

"I know, I know. I'm bungling this horribly, but I promise I will endeavor to make you happy, which is as much as any prospective bridegroom can offer his bride. And it will be a match beyond even your mother's lofty expectations. I do hope you'll consider it. I don't need an answer straightaway."

Are you asking me for my fortune? Do you care for me at all, beyond my father's money and my pleasing face? Beatrice longed to ask these questions but didn't dare. She didn't fully want to know the answers to them. So many questions were circling in her brain, she all but clung to the railing of the verandah to steady herself. There was, however, one certainty to which she could moor herself: Lord Alnwick had made her the best offer she could ever hope to receive.

"You needn't wait," Beatrice said. "Lord Alnwick, I accept."

He reached up to her face and tucked a loose curl behind her ear. A remarkably familiar gesture, but Beatrice found it wasn't unwelcome.

"I cannot tell you how happy I am." Color suffused his cheeks. "I could never picture myself married, though I knew it was my duty."

"Whyever not?" Beatrice asked. "You're a man with everything to recommend him to a lady. Noble birth, university educated, good fortune. You couldn't possibly have imagined you'd spend the rest of your days alone. Why now? Why me?"

"Why does any man propose to a lady? Because she is comely and he thinks she will make him a suitable wife."

Beatrice resisted the urge to snort with derision. "I can't say we've known each other long, Lord Alnwick, but I think I know you well enough to know that you're not a man to make such a monumental decision on such trite grounds."

"Perhaps you're right. But it isn't customary for a gentleman to be so forthcoming with a lady he is courting."

"I don't think either of us is overly fond of bending to custom, are we?" Beatrice added, "I should hope you would think well enough of me to be forthcoming whether you were courting me or no."

His eyes drifted to some point off in the distance for a moment, then returned to her. "I'm an outsider, my dear Miss Holbrook. But luckily for me, so are you. You'll be able to understand me a little better, and I you. What's more, there's something more to you than many of the ladies of my acquaintance. Wit, though I can't say all the ladies here are without brains. Something deeper. An understanding of human character that is rare to find. I couldn't help but try to win your hand, though I never thought I'd be successful."

"Well, Lord Alnwick, if I do possess a deeper 'understanding of human character' as you say, then you may take my acceptance as the greatest of compliments." She smiled as the tension of the moment ebbed into a gentler sensation of joy.

"A point I hadn't considered, but a valid one." He smiled in turn. "And a compliment of which I will strive to be worthy."

CHAPTER 4 ————————————

Showtime is no time to lose your nerve.

Beatrice and Mama had designed the gown at Worth's during their stay in Paris before they'd gone up to London. It was crafted from the most elegant silk satin the color of a fresh magnolia petal. The bodice was adorned with imitation seed pearls, which were becoming incredibly popular at the Worth atelier, intricate embroidery, and machine-made lace using the newest techniques. The skirt was ample with a flowing ruffled sweep train attached at the waist. It had been created for the most significant day in Beatrice's life. The day she would play the role she'd been rehearsing for her entire life. A bride on her wedding day.

And it had been made before Beatrice had even met her bridegroom.

That spring, Daddy had joked that they were dooming the enterprise to failure by selecting a gown before selecting a man for the job. Before she'd even officially entered the marriage market. Beatrice wondered if there wasn't something to her father's superstitions—counting chickens and all that—but Mama would not see her daughter married in a dress from a lesser London designer. Or worse, something ready-made and hastily tailored to suit at the last moment.

No, they had gone to London with a singular motive—to see Beatrice married off to the highest-ranking man who would have her. There was no reason, in Mama's mind, to go to London unprepared for their desired outcome. And all the better since their engagement was of almost no duration. Just enough time to procure a special license and for Lord Alnwick to send word to Leedswick.

Charles had no desire for a large spectacle of a wedding, and Beatrice longed only to have her objective attained. It would mean her mother's main ambition for the past twenty-one years had been met and Beatrice would be free. Charles's family had chosen not to take the long trek up to London from Northumberland for the occasion, but did send a rather terse telegram wishing them well.

And so, on the morning of Beatrice's nuptials, Robinson helped Beatrice into the gown, styled her hair, and affixed the veil that had been specially made for her to wear on her wedding day, whether the groom had been Earl Alnwick, Baron Chatsworth, or any of the men Mama might have thrown her way.

Beatrice studied her reflection in the mirror. If she was meant to play a part, at least her costume was a resplendent one.

"How lovely," Mama breathed, having just entered the room without knocking. "I've pictured this day a million times, and you've exceeded my wildest dreams."

But what of mine? Beatrice wanted to ask. But her dreams were of little consequence to anyone else. So much so that she'd spared little energy on forming her own. All she'd hoped for was some measure of happiness in the life her mother had shoved at her. She might grow to love Charles in time, but even if she did not, she would strive to find contentment in her situation.

"Thank you, Mama," Beatrice managed to say. Her throat was parched, and it was an effort just to part her lips.

"Oh, my dear, I hope you won't be one of those weeping brides. I always find that tiresome. I do hope you'll be able to master yourself."

"Of course, Mama," Beatrice said with a touch more confidence. Robinson appeared at her side with a small glass of cold water, which Beatrice accepted and consumed in short order.

"You've made an excellent match, my dear. New York will be buzzing about it for years to come." Mama took in Beatrice's full ensemble.

"It's only too bad I won't be there to hear all the buzzing. It seems a shallow victory to win the admiration of a society from which I'll be long removed."

"Oh. Well, yes. But I'll be sure to send you any of the good write-ups from the papers by post," Mama promised.

The buzz had never been for Beatrice's benefit anyway. It had all been to make Mama feel like she truly belonged to the upper echelon of society she'd coveted for decades. The Astors might even welcome them back after this, and in Mama's mind, that was worth marrying off her only child and leaving her an ocean away.

They were to be married at St. George's on Hanover Square at half ten in the morning. Mama thought it was a terribly unfashionable hour. As the groom's family wouldn't be in attendance, the guest list would be limited to just a handful of their closest friends. Mama was horribly disappointed that the wedding would not be a grandiose affair to rival Lucy Twombly's gala event, but even for all this, she wouldn't risk the union by pressing for a more lavish wedding. Beatrice, in truth, was happy for the haste. This was a performance for which she didn't mind having a limited audience.

"Time's a-wastin', kitten," Daddy announced at the door. "The carriage is waiting."

Beatrice walked over to her father and accepted his proffered arm. "You do look a treat," Daddy said, echoing the words he'd used before they'd gone to the disastrous dinner at the Astors'. That there would be no oysters served at any point this day was more than a small comfort to Beatrice.

"You're sure you're ready for this? You wouldn't rather come home and go riding with your old man? There'd be a dandy new habit for you if you did."

"Morris, don't speak such nonsense," hissed Mama. She was likely terrified Beatrice would take him up on the offer.

"I have given my word, Daddy." Beatrice kissed his cheek. "And what is a Holbrook who doesn't keep her word?"

"Not much of one." He nodded. "So I suppose it's to church with you?"

"Yes, but we'll ride again sometime. You'll have your pick of the stables at Leedswick," she promised.

"I'll hold you to that," he said, patting her hand on the way to the carriage with Mama trailing a pace behind them.

Beatrice knew it would be a miracle if either of her parents came to Leedswick. Not even for the pleasure of meeting their grandchildren when the time came. Mama's life was too enmeshed in New York society to leave it, and Daddy had never been excessively fond of travel. If she was ever to see them again, she'd have to be the one to make the crossing. And for this, as in all things, she would be dependent on Charles's whims.

Thankfully, Beatrice sensed he wasn't a man much given to whimsy, and she trusted her instincts that told her he would care for her far better than most men would.

+———+

Charles stood, stoic and handsome, at the altar in a charcoal morning coat and gray trousers. The massive pipe organ behind him seemed to soar to the heavens. He didn't smile, but he did seem pleased to be there. Beatrice struggled to keep her countenance serene and hoped she met with at least some measure of success.

And in shorter than the space of a waltz, they were man and wife.

The culmination of her life's ambition was at hand. And though she felt a twinge of dread, wondering what was next, she felt the lightness of having reached this milestone. And there was nothing, nothing her mother could fault her for now.

They returned to her parents' rented house in Mayfair and had a sumptuous wedding breakfast, all orchestrated by Mama, and done as lavishly as she could. Beatrice felt she could hardly see the food on the table for all the flowers her mother had placed there, which was rather a feat since the table all but groaned under the weight of the numerous platters of food.

"The finest breakfast I've had in longer than I can recall," Charles declared. Though of course he sought to please his mother-in-law, there was an earnestness in his tone that resonated in Beatrice. She was so used to overblown flattery, the sincerity of Charles's words felt jarring.

"Only the best for our Bea," Daddy proclaimed, then beamed at Charles. "And I hope that includes her choice of husband."

"I will spend the rest of my life endeavoring to meet that standard, sir."

"That's a good lad," Daddy said.

"And we know Beatrice will be a credit to you and your family, Lord Alnwick," Mama said. "It's only a shame we won't be here to help her get settled. I am sure we'd be of some use to her."

"We've been over this, dear. Bea needs time to figure this out on her own. She'll be fine, woman. And I've got business to oversee in New York."

Mama blanched at the mention of Daddy's work, knowing that no gentleman in England would admit to a profession, but held her silence. She'd railed against Daddy to stay. To go to the north of

England with Beatrice and Charles to "help" Beatrice as she settled into her life as Lady Alnwick. Likely she wanted to imagine herself terribly important while she chided Beatrice over non-offenses until she went mad. But Daddy, knowing she needed a reprieve from her mother, intervened. Beatrice had never loved him more.

"But so soon," Mama continued. "I thought we might stay another week or more at least."

"I was able to get the tickets for tomorrow morning, and I don't want to risk a rough crossing by waiting any longer," Daddy reminded her.

"You'll all be welcome to Leedswick," Charles said. He barely knew his parents-in-law and had no way of knowing how unlikely they were to accept his hospitality. "I'm sure Beatrice will miss you terribly."

Beatrice.

She was almost certain it was the first time he'd used her Christian name, and the familiarity of the sound of it on his lips made her shiver despite the warmth of the room. With dread or thrill, she wasn't certain. It was a reminder that she was now and forever irrevocably joined to a man she'd known only a few weeks. If she'd made a terrible misjudgment of his character, she'd live with that mistake the rest of her days.

It wasn't long before the meal concluded and the small assembly of their friends departed. Robinson helped Beatrice out of her gown and into a smart afternoon dress and had the wedding gown placed in the last of her trunks. The rest of her things had already been sent to Charles's town house where the newlyweds would spend the night before heading to Leedswick the following morning.

Mama and Daddy's staff had flung themselves into the task of packing for their return home. By this time the following day, they would be on their way back to New York. For all the frustration Beatrice had felt with her mother and for all the times she had to keep from rolling her eyes at her father's antics, usually designed to irritate his wife, to know that she might never sleep under the same roof as they caused an ache deep in her chest.

"I'm proud of you, kitten." Daddy kissed her cheek.

"I made it all the way down the aisle and didn't trip once," she said with a wink.

"I do hope you'll be happy. You'll write to your old man and let him know how you're getting along?"

"Of course, Daddy." Beatrice wrapped him in an embrace.

"Don't speak nonsense. Naturally she'll be happy." Mama kissed the air above Beatrice's cheeks. "She has everything she wants. Everything she's worked for."

Everything you told me I had to want. Beatrice wanted to toss those words back at her mother but decided not to spoil their last moments together. Part of her wished she'd had some freedom in her youth to explore her own desires and interests. Wished she'd had the freedom to become better acquainted with herself.

When the carriage pulled away from her parents' lodgings, she felt a sting pricking at the corners of her eyes as the wheels ground their way over the cobblestones.

+———+

For the rest of her wedding day, Beatrice felt as useful as a paper parasol in a blizzard. The staff were scurrying about, preparing for the trek north the following morning, and Charles holed up in his study, attending to business of some sort. She wanted to be of use, but she knew she'd merely be in the way of the maids and footmen if she tried. Charles had given orders, and she was better off leaving them to be executed by the people who knew how the house was run.

In the end she found a tome in the small library the town house boasted and attempted to amuse herself until Charles emerged again.

She didn't see him until dinner, which was an exquisite meal given the harried state of the staff. He was charming throughout the meal, though perhaps somewhat preoccupied. Beatrice herself felt it difficult to focus on the conversation, thinking about what would be expected of her that night.

Dessert, a lovely apple-and-cream gelatin that had been set in an elaborate mold and topped with sugar-paste rose petals, had been cleared away and the moment was upon her. She tried not to appear too nervous. Her mother had flatly refused to explain what happened between husband and wife in the bedchamber, somehow thinking ignorance was more fashionable.

"Young ladies of good breeding let their husbands explain their duties to them. If you enter the married state knowing too much, he may think the less of you for it."

Beatrice had refused to accept this maxim and had bribed Robinson—handsomely—to explain how things were done, but by the end of their hurried chat, Beatrice felt like she didn't understand married love much better than she had before. Robinson, Beatrice supposed, was no expert on the topic, but it was preferable to know a little more than nothing before she submitted to Charles.

"I suppose I ought to escort you upstairs," Charles said. "It's been a taxing day, I am sure."

Taxing day. Not the way Beatrice would have hoped to describe her wedding day. Joyous. Blissful. Enchanting. Not *taxing*.

Beatrice affixed the smile she'd been instructed would be the most valuable piece in her trousseau and took Charles's arm. She took even breaths and tried to enjoy the companionable silence as they ascended to the gallery and their rooms. The *clunk* of his cane against the marble floor punctuated her thoughts.

"I believe this is where they've installed you for the evening." Charles stopped in front of the graceful set of rooms reserved for the lady of the house. "Of course, there isn't much use for it now, but you'll have to let me know if you wish any changes to be made before we come back for the season next year. When Father next comes to take his seat in Parliament, I'd like to be in town."

Beatrice nodded. She'd read that as a peer of the realm, the Marquess of Northridge would have a seat in the House of Lords for as long as he lived. In the time since her family had decided to make the crossing, she'd done what she could to learn about the country that was to become her own. Though she feared there was much she had to learn that could not be found in books. "Of course." She looked down and willed the heat not to rise in her cheeks. "I-I imagine you'd like to come in?"

Her heart fluttered. She knew, at least in vague terms, what was expected of her. It was a sacred part of her duty as a wife and a vital part of ensuring Charles's legacy. She felt both the twinge of anticipation in her core and the grip of nerves around her chest. She desperately wanted to please him. She hoped that if she were able to make him happy in this, it would be a pathway to marital harmony. She was trying to convince herself she'd be happier keeping love out of the equation, but an amicable—and productive—marriage would be a good outcome for all.

Charles stared over her shoulder a moment, then cleared his throat. "Darling, the voyage north will be tiring and we're to leave at an ungodly hour. I think it might be best that you retire and get as much rest as you can. You'll want to be at your best when you meet my family."

There was something foreboding about his tone when he mentioned his family, and Beatrice's stomach sank. It had all happened so quickly; she didn't have the time to consider that his family might not be welcoming of an American interloper.

"Truly, I'm not tired," she protested. Perhaps Charles wouldn't like her speaking so freely, but she had a duty to fulfill, and she would not be accused of shirking it. And, in truth, she longed for the diversion of children. She would not be the lady of the house when they moved to Leedswick. Charles's mother would still be at the helm of the ship, perhaps for many years to come.

Beatrice had spent her entire life to that point preparing to marry, and with that goal now met, she saw an endless landscape of vacant hours stretching before her. She hoped that if they started a family soon, she'd have the time to be a loving influence on her children before the demands of the estate claimed so much of her attention.

"But I am afraid I am. Good night, Beatrice." He brushed a light kiss across her cheekbone. "I'll have one of the maids come up to attend to you."

Beatrice retreated to her room and stared at her reflection in the vanity mirror. She saw nothing out of sorts beyond the tears welling in her eyes. Yes, she'd met her goal. Her mother's goal, anyway. But there was an emptiness to it all that enveloped her and weighed on her shoulders.

She'd pictured her wedding night more times than she could count.

But she'd never pictured spending it alone.

CHAPTER 5

LEEDSWICK CASTLE, NORTHRIDGE, ENGLAND

The train ride from London seemed to take an eternity and the carriage ride from the station to the castle even longer. The silence between Beatrice and Charles wasn't companionable—it was stifling. Beatrice tried to hide her disappointment at the previous night's outcome, but she feared she wasn't being entirely successful.

"You're not nervous, are you, my dear?" Charles finally asked.

"I feel like a mouse on its way to be introduced to a family of ravenous cats, if I'm being completely honest." Her hands were knitted in her lap, and she'd given up any pretense of hiding her nerves as she stared through the window at the trees, which became thicker the closer they got to the castle.

Though her marriage was solemnized and the family had precious little recourse if they disapproved of her, these were still the people who would determine whether her life was peaceful or miserable.

"I wish I could reassure you that your fears are unfounded, but I admit they have claws and fangs enough between them. I cannot say how they feel about you or this marriage, but it might be prudent for you not to expect a warm welcome. I do hope they will become more agreeable in time. But if they do not, you and I will manage as best we can in each other's company." He patted her hand tenderly.

Where had that tenderness been last night?

"You put my heart at ease, my lord," she said wryly.

"I wish I could offer you platitudes, but I find myself incapable when those words, no matter how kindly meant, are closer to lies than euphemisms."

"That's to your credit, even if it does nothing for my churning stomach. But never mind. We'll be able to assess the situation soon enough and will know better how to act."

"You speak like a general going into battle rather than a woman going to meet her family-in-law. I wish it didn't have to be so."

"From your account of things, the two have more than a little in common in this case. And every general must strategize. Tell me, who should I fear most? Your mother or your father?"

"I should think both, though Mama hasn't the politician's tact that Papa has. It makes her seem more vicious than he is, though I'm not sure it's true. Though were I you, I'd keep my eye on John. He's the real schemer of the bunch."

"Your younger brother?"

"Yes. And he's never forgiven me for the heinous offense I committed of being born first."

"Seems like that would be the typical lot of a younger brother in England," Beatrice said. "At least in America we can spread our wealth among our children. I would think it breeds less resentment."

"So spoken like an only child." Charles laughed for the first time since their ascent into the north. It seemed to take fifteen years off his usually solemn countenance. "Would that I'd been born with your good fortune."

"It was a lonely way to grow up," she confessed. "I always dreamed of having younger sisters so I could braid their hair and teach them little things. And younger brothers so I could train them up to be far more interesting than the rest of the young men of my acquaintance."

"So the young men of New York bored you? Is that why you came to seek your matrimonial fate abroad?"

Thomas's face emerged in her memory in a flicker. His wedding photos had made the papers in London as well as New York, and she'd forced herself to look at all of them and read every syllable put to print. No, not all of the men had bored her. But she hoped the subject of Thomas and the awful dinner would never come up in conversation.

"Mostly, yes," she said. "But in the end, I found that I'd have an easier time finding someone agreeable here than by trying to chum up with the Astors. Our money was too new to really enter their good graces. You'll forgive such blunt talk, I hope."

"I hope that you'll always be direct with me. We're man and wife now, and I think it's always better if a couple can converse openly."

Beatrice nodded but didn't reply. His manner of speaking was open when they were alone, but he'd not told her why he chose not to share her bed the night before. If he valued open discourse, it was clearly with a few limitations.

It was still a shock when she remembered he was her husband. She was no longer a Holbrook; she was an Alnwick. Countess Alnwick, the future Marchioness of Northridge at that. But despite the title, she felt no grander than she had as the incredibly fortunate daughter of a gold miner with good sense and a smidgeon of fore-sight. Perhaps she'd thought the union would transform her into a true noblewoman just as her father's money had been transformed from new to old, but it seemed money was easier to legitimize than people.

The castle came into view suddenly and spectacularly as they turned a bend in the road. It was far more than a grand house on an extensive property. It was a fortress from a bygone age that had become a monolith lording over the marquisate. Though some of the stones were crumbling, it looked like the marquess was not an indifferent caretaker. The maintenance of such a place would require a fortune—perhaps several—and it was clear that some repairs had been deferred until more money filled the coffers. The grounds were well kept but overgrown, and it was only from travel weariness that Beatrice was able to resist the urge to hop from the carriage and ramble in the gardens that seemed to outstrip Versailles as far as size but encapsulated the rugged wilderness of the north.

"You're taken by the gardens, I see," Charles observed, as her eyes never wavered from the expansive grounds.

"Quite. They look delightful to get lost in."

"How poetic of you. The Marchioness of Northridge traditionally oversees the gardens. That's been the case since the fifth marchioness, two hundred years ago."

Beatrice arched a brow. "Interesting that it became a tradition instead of each generation deciding for themselves."

"Welcome to England, my dear. Most of it seems to be rooted in superstition. The fifth marchioness was jealous of the grounds. Her husband, the marquess, was obsessed with creating the most lavish gardens in all of England, and it seems he neglected his wife to do so. He died young, and she acted as steward until her son was of age. In order to protect her daughter-in-law from the same lonely fate, she took over caring for the gardens and passed the duty on to the female line so it wouldn't happen again."

"It's a good thing none of the women became as obsessed as the fifth marquess," Beatrice said.

"Well, they would all be daughters-in-law to the marchioness, wouldn't they? It wouldn't bear the same weight of responsibility as something she inherited in her own right."

"Too true." Beatrice nodded. "So caring for the gardens will be one of my duties as marchioness?"

"If you wish it to be. In some cases I have no qualms about dispensing with traditions that no longer serve us. Overseeing the gardens has not been one of Mama's favorite chores, nor is she fond of the expense of it. She'd rather use the money to entertain and have an army of staff."

"I won't mind it," Beatrice said. "These gardens deserve a devoted caretaker." And it would give her something to do. Especially before children came.

Charles took Beatrice's hand and pressed her knuckles to his lips as they pulled to a stop before the main door. Whether it was a show of affection or to brace her against the coming torrent, she knew not. She was annoyed at the flutter in her gut, wishing she was a better master of herself.

"You are lovely, you know," he said as though he were commenting on something as obvious as the weather they stood in. But something earnest in his expression gave her pause. The sort that would make it impossible for her to keep him at arm's length to protect her heart. But she collected her thoughts and gave him a winning smile. Perhaps he would not be so tired this night.

She wished she were immune to the tugging of her heartstrings, but she could not help but feel a sort of softness where he was concerned. He seemed so very much in need of tenderness, she found herself risking her heart, just as she'd done with Thomas. It was foolish. It was the path to a second heartbreak.

She vowed to keep those feelings in check. She wouldn't be made a fool of again.

A footman came to the carriage to assist her, and she stepped down onto soil that had belonged to Charles's family since time immemorial. Far from the land she knew and all she'd ever called home. Though she'd been in England for many weeks, she was just now coming to terms with the permanence of her stay.

The Marquess and Marchioness of Northridge along with Lord John awaited the newlyweds' arrival in the library. Tea was brought up by a butler, who looked as stiff as his starched shirt, as soon as they settled on a small settee opposite the massive scarlet damask–covered sofa where Beatrice's new family-in-law perched like birds of prey.

"So you are the American who found her way into my son's affections, are you?" the marquess said by way of greeting.

"I hope that's the case," Beatrice said affably, patting Charles on the knee.

"Very much so," Charles affirmed.

"And here we'd thought for years that our Charles wasn't cut out for marriage. You've restored all our faith in miracles, Miss Holbrook." John winked as he took a sip of his tea.

"Lady Alnwick," Charles corrected. "She is my wife."

"Of course. We're all just adjusting to the idea, brother dear. You'll have to excuse the occasional lapse."

"Must I?" Charles sat taller beside her as he stiffened in indignation.

"Now, boys, that's quite enough," the marchioness chided. "We mustn't show our tempers in front of our guest."

Charles looked as though he wanted to rebuke her, but he swallowed it back. Despite having married into the family, Beatrice was still viewed as an outsider, but that wasn't surprising. She'd married into the family before God and man, but they'd never clapped eyes on her before.

"I should think Beatrice would suffice," she said, trying, like her mother-in-law, to make peace. She trembled under the marchioness's gaze but refused to be cowed. "We are family, after all."

The marchioness shot Beatrice a withering look so brief that she couldn't be sure she hadn't imagined it.

While the marquess was a squat man and otherwise unremarkable to look at, the marchioness had clearly been a great beauty in her time. Her hair had softened to silver, and she wore a dress in the same hue to accentuate it and to set off her piercing blue eyes. She didn't try to mask the advancing of years like so many women did but embraced the inevitability. The effect was far more graceful than the obstinate clinging to youth.

She had clearly learned lessons from what she'd witnessed. She turned her gaze on Beatrice, appraising. "Well, my dear. We know next to nothing about you. Tell us about yourself."

"I was born in San Francisco and raised in New York." Beatrice set her teacup aside and immediately regretted having no occupation for her hands. "But my parents come from California. Not far from San Francisco."

"How exotic," the marquess said as though speaking of a parrot from the Amazon. "I suspect you'll find things very different here."

"In some respects, sir, but not all." Snobbery was just as alive in the drawing rooms in New York as it was in Northridge. The marquess looked doubtful but did not challenge her.

"Well, we'll have to see you settled. I hear you haven't brought a lady's maid?" the marchioness asked.

"No. We thought about taking one on for me before the voyage, but we couldn't find any likely young women who were willing to settle overseas. It would be rather hard, I would think. My mother's maid was more than able to help us both while we were abroad, but Mama wouldn't have spared her for anything in the world, not even for me." Beatrice didn't add that Mama didn't want the bother of hiring a girl in London only to find she wasn't willing to move to wherever Beatrice settled.

"Good help is never easy to find." The marchioness breathed a knowing sigh. She turned to the butler, who had been standing still as a statue waiting for orders since the tea had been poured. "Foster, will you have Mrs. Nichols place an advertisement for someone suitable when you go back downstairs?"

"Of course, your ladyship. Though if I might be so bold, Jane the housemaid has been eager to advance. She's been working with Miss Sutcliffe at odd times to learn the skills of a lady's maid."

"It might be worth a trial," the marchioness said, stirring her tea. "Finding a new housemaid will be a lot less trouble."

"Indeed," Foster said. "We have eager girls from Birchwick enquiring regularly."

"Very well. Send Jane to Lady Alnwick's room to unpack her things. She can dress her for dinner this evening and we'll proceed from there." The marchioness paused and gazed at Beatrice. "If that suits you, of course."

"Very well, I should think," Beatrice replied. "I'm of the opinion promotions should happen from within the household whenever possible. I shall look forward to giving Jane the chance."

Foster met her eye and nodded his approval. At least someone seemed to approve of her, if only when it came to staff changes.

From the marchioness's expression, it was apparent that Beatrice would have to do far more to win over the rest of the family.

CHAPTER 6 ────────────────

There would be no show without
capable stagehands.

You'll have to instruct me as to how you like things done," Jane
said as she laid out Beatrice's ensemble for dinner. "How you
like your hair styled. How you take your tea. What time to bring up
your breakfast tray. Don't hesitate to ask for a thing."

Though it was meant to be a quiet dinner *en famille*, Jane had
suggested one of her smarter evening gowns for the occasion. It was a
lovely frock of emerald satin with a black lace overlay, which Beatrice
had thought perfect for the theater or a night in London. She wondered if the dress wasn't a bit extravagant for the occasion, but she
decided to defer to the girl's judgment. It would be a good test to see
if she could be trusted.

"You're very kind, Jane. I'm grateful to you."

Beatrice sat in a padded velvet chair in the corner of the room
with a cup of tea and excellent butter biscuits Jane had brought up
unsolicited after her afternoon nap. She'd anticipated her mistress's
need after her long voyage and the added strain of meeting her new

family. Beatrice was impressed, though she should act as if it were merely expected of an attentive servant.

"I mean to make a good lady's maid to you, milady. It's a chance for me, I won't deny it, and I'll do my level best to make the most of it."

"I've no doubt you will." Beatrice set her teacup back on the saucer with a barely audible *clink* as she'd practiced so many times. "You seem a very quick study."

"One has to be. If you want to please the family, you have to remember all the little things. Lord Northridge takes his tea with more sugar than you can imagine. Lady Northridge loves cream in hers but only takes it on Sundays as a treat to keep her figure trim."

Beatrice nodded, knowing that was only the barest sampling of the details Jane had filed away in her brain. Jane, like every other young woman in the employ of the Alnwick house, was efficient in movement and soft of voice.

"Tell me, Jane, are you happy here?"

"Of course I am," she replied automatically. It was the only appropriate answer to such a question, especially to a new member of the family.

"What I mean to ask is, do you find the marquess and marchioness to be kind employers? I find it's a far better gauge of the family's character than anything else I could ask." Trying to assess the honor of the Alnwick family after marrying into it was the quintessential example of shutting the barn door after the horses had gotten out, but she found herself compelled to ask nonetheless.

Jane nodded sagely. "You're not wrong there, milady. I would say Lord and Lady Northridge are as fair-minded and just employers as one might find."

Beatrice saw plainly that she was biting back a critique but knew better than to press. It wouldn't do to make her nervous now and discourage her from making confidences later. "I'm glad to hear it. I hope you shall find me the same."

"Of course, milady. Shall we see to your hair?" Jane seemed eager to change the bent of the conversation.

Perhaps Beatrice had pried a little much for a first interview, but she was keenly interested in opening discourse with Jane. She understood, in ways that her mother had not, that servants, rather than newspapers and gossip rags, were the true source of news in society. And within a great house such as this one, having an ally among their ranks was indispensable.

Mama had come from nothing and always feared that becoming too familiar with the servant class would somehow make her appear more common. The effect was quite the reverse. People noticed Mama's terse nature toward her own staff and that of others and considered it a sign of ill breeding. Beatrice compensated for her mother's lack of gentility by being overly gracious toward servants when her mother wasn't near enough to deride her for being too friendly.

Jane brushed Beatrice's dark-chocolate-brown hair until it lay in glistening waves down the middle of her back. She moved to several angles to consider her new mistress's hair. "Nothing too elaborate, I think," Jane murmured. "You don't need too much frippery. Up with a few curls to frame the face and a few to trail your neck. Just a hint of sparkle with some of your haircombs I saw while I was unpacking your things."

She opened Beatrice's jewel case and removed a pair of diamond combs Daddy had given her on the occasion of her eighteenth birthday. They were small and intricate and caught the glint of the candlelight magnificently. They were one of the few mementos Daddy had chosen for Beatrice without Mama's interference and were all the more precious for it.

"That sounds perfect," Beatrice said.

Jane's hands moved with admirable dexterity and conceived an elegant hairstyle that Beatrice felt suited her far better than the elaborate creations her mother had insisted upon. Womanly but youthful.

Paired with the dress, she would have been one of the most elegant women in Caroline Astor's dining room. If she was lucky, it would be just enough to pass muster in Lady Northridge's.

"Thank you, Jane." Beatrice admired her reflection. "You're talented."

Jane looked down and muttered, "That's kind of you, milady."

It was clear Jane wasn't used to being praised, and Beatrice determined in that moment to accustom her to the practice. It was evident that she'd worked and studied hard and deserved to know her efforts were noticed and appreciated.

The dinner trumpet sounded, much to Beatrice's surprise. She'd expected a gong, as was customary in such homes, but Jane explained it was a family eccentricity that far predated the current marquess. Beatrice descended the stairs to find Charles at the foot of them. He offered her a small smile and his arm to escort her to the dining room.

"You look lovely," he whispered.

"Your family will approve?" She let her nerves show for a moment.

"Their approval doesn't matter," he said, his eyes skimming over her with rapt interest. "But they cannot find fault with your appearance tonight, that much is certain."

"A relief." Beatrice exhaled more dramatically than she'd intended. Though she'd tried to give the impression she was unflappable, his parents and brother had her in more turmoil than she was willing to admit to herself. And she'd pleased Charles. That meant even more. He gazed at her so keenly that she felt a hope that tonight they might be able to celebrate their wedding properly. Perhaps he'd been waiting for Leedswick. It was a sacred place to him, after all.

"Don't let them bother you. I've made my choice, and there is nothing they can do about it now. If they have brains in their heads, they will be grateful for your presence in our lives."

Because the estate needed money. It was always about the money.

There was hardly an estate in England that wasn't in need of an infusion of cash, and Beatrice was now well aware that Leedswick was among them. But she still hoped that the money was just one of the virtues that had attracted Charles to her.

But none of it mattered. With her money she and Charles could modernize the estate and make it more prosperous than ever. Not for their sakes but for the tenants and people in their employ. It would give her a purpose. Procuring a good marriage had been the sole focus of her life until just a few days ago. She'd need something else to fill her days now.

Beatrice swallowed back her reservations and walked forward.

He might have married her for the money, but she'd married him for his title, after all.

Lord Northridge might have been the head of the household, but in the dining room, Lady Northridge was sovereign. Though Lord Northridge sat at the head of the table and Lady Northridge at the foot, everyone moved in a way that deferred authority to her. Each bow of a footman, each movement of a fork, every syllable spoken was done to please her ladyship. Beatrice surveyed the table, pleased beyond measure to see no sign of oysters anywhere.

"Not hungry after your travels?" Lady Northridge directed her gaze at Beatrice, who was so absorbed in watching her mother-in-law holding court over the table she'd yet to raise her fork to her lips. "Curious after such an exerting day."

"Perhaps more tired than she is hungry," Lord Northridge interjected. Beatrice now understood what Charles had said about his father having more of the politician's tact than his mother.

"Rather both, but the two sensations seem to be warring against each other at the moment, and I can't decide which to oblige," Beatrice admitted.

"Always hunger," Lord Northridge pronounced as solemnly as

if he were addressing Parliament. "If one does not eat, one's sleep will be fitful."

"I find it dreadful to go to bed on a full stomach," Lady Northridge said archly. "I lie awake all night with indigestion."

"Hence, you understand my struggle," Beatrice said. "You're both right."

A polite titter of laughter rang over the table. Beatrice smiled, hoping she'd succeeded in lightening the moment.

"Your wife is quite the diplomat, brother. She'll serve you well." John took a long draught from his glass of claret. His tone made it clear that he was not issuing a compliment.

Charles, seemingly impervious to his brother's scathing tone, replied earnestly, "Indeed. Despite the haste of our courtship, you'll find I didn't choose haphazardly. A treasure like Beatrice wouldn't have stayed on the marriage market long, and I had to be decisive."

A pretty compliment, indeed. Though she wasn't sure if he was sincere. Or if he was, perhaps he valued her as a prize, an ornament to be won and displayed and nothing of more substance.

"So you say, Charles," Lady Northridge said. "But since you have broached the topic, I don't see why you felt the need to procure a special license. The speed of your courtship will raise eyebrows. I hope you've prepared for that."

"Beatrice and I did not want to wait the month out because we saw no utility in waiting. And it's not as though we ran off to Gretna Green. And people will talk, they always do, so I see no reason to concern myself with the state of anyone's eyebrows." Charles stabbed a stalk of asparagus.

"Don't forget yourself, boy," Lord Northridge said. "You won't do the name any favors by losing friends."

"Quite right," John quipped. "Little is more important than friends and connections, you know."

"Oh yes," Charles spat out. "We know John has legions of friends. In every gambling hall in England."

"Now, Charles, this is no way to speak in front of a guest," his mother snapped for the second time that day. "And I'll not have you spreading falsehoods about your brother."

"She's not a guest; she's my wife. But you have my apologies. I'd never want to spread untruths. I'm sure John has racked up gambling debts far beyond our shores during his extensive travels. Beatrice, if you've had enough to eat, let's retire."

She nodded and allowed the footman to pull her chair backward. She took Charles's arm and had to jog to keep pace with him.

"I'm sorry. I should have better prepared you for them," Charles said. "I'd hoped company manners would help temper their usual rancor, but apparently they have decided to forgo such formalities."

"I'm not sure whether I should be flattered or insulted." These were things for which her mother had never prepared her. She'd spent her entire childhood being molded to become a model bride, but little effort was spent to discuss how to make a place for herself as a wife and part of a new family. The truth was likely that Mama had planned to be a more integral part of her daughter's life, socializing together in New York and basking in her daughter's social successes, but now there was an ocean between them. For better or worse. Likely both.

"Nor am I." He paused at the top of the landing and pinched his fingers to the bridge of his nose, exhaling loudly. "Have you had enough to eat? I can have a tray brought to you."

"I'll be fine." She'd be able to have Jane sneak something small from the kitchen rather than have a full meal brought to her. The last thing she wanted was to add chatter among the servants about her being burdensome to the scuttlebutt about their leaving the meal early.

"I am ever so sorry," Charles said. "I mean to make you happy here. Truly."

"You can't help their disposition." Beatrice looked up to him and offered a small smile. "Don't worry about me. You chose an American, and we're made of hardy stock."

"I'm afraid your mettle will be tested over the next months. Brace yourself the best you can."

"Of course," she said.

They stopped in front of the door to her suite of rooms. She saw no flicker of intention in his eyes, though she was certain he wouldn't be the sort to be overly forward about his desires. "Will you . . . ? That is . . . should I ring for Jane, or did you think to join me?"

Charles glanced at the door and back to her. "My dear, I think you've endured enough for one night. Sleep well, and I shall see you in the morning." He bent down and placed a chaste kiss on her forehead before retreating to his own suite of rooms.

She pulled the bell for Jane, and as she waited, Beatrice couldn't help but wonder what she'd done to disappoint him.

CHAPTER 7 ——————————————

~RULE No. 7~

Stage fright is natural, but never let it show onstage.

Beatrice was to have tea with the marchioness that afternoon—alone. The prospect had Beatrice pacing the floor of her new suite. It was a lovely space with plush rugs and beautiful rosewood furniture that had been polished until it shone like marble under stage lights. The fires were always lit, there were gas lamps in abundance, but the space was frigid, no matter the temperature outside.

Jane explained it was because the stones retained the cold, damp northern air. Beatrice imagined it had more to do with the cold nature of the inhabitants, but offhanded comments made to staff in weak moments had their way of making it to the wrong ears. So holding back her criticisms seemed wise.

Jane selected a flowing tea gown, a delicate affair in rosebud, from among Bea's vast trousseau. The tea gowns she'd had made at Worth's were some of Beatrice's favorite pieces in her collection. Though just as lavish as some of her formal afternoon gowns, tea gowns were as loose and airy as dressing gowns but perfectly acceptable to wear for receiving an afternoon visitor or taking tea at home. Their chief virtue was they were meant to be worn without a corset. The freedom to breathe unrestricted was something Beatrice was coming to appreciate and was a sensation she had rarely experienced in day wear since she was sixteen years old. Beatrice fervently hoped more fashion would follow suit.

They decided on accessories together and fussed with Beatrice's hair until Jane insisted that with any more meddling it might all fall out.

"I wouldn't worry if I were you." Jane spoke in low tones as she straightened the bed linens. "You've already married him. What can she do to you?"

"She's a powerful woman." Beatrice cast a final glance at herself in the mirror. "I know her type. I can't say what she might do to me if she truly disapproves of me, but I have too much respect for my own mortality to find out."

"You *are* smart," Jane said with a shake of her head. "The staff all says so, and they've all seen enough people come and go from this place to be able to judge a person."

"I take that as the most gracious of compliments. Looks fade. Intelligence lasts a little longer."

"You should take it as one. My sister worked here before I did, and she said that it would take an intelligent woman to survive here with Lady Northridge still in residence. I think she's met her match in you, milady."

Beatrice sighed. "I suppose I must go down to face her."

"Indeed, you must." Jane opened the door out to the hallway. "Just remember, all she can do is try to frighten you. It won't work if you don't let her."

"Quite right." Beatrice squared her shoulders. "Chin up and all that." She walked down the stairs to Lady Northridge's private library, wishing very much that she had the confidence she'd displayed for

Jane. In truth, it was all she could do to keep from shaking as she entered the room.

There Lady Northridge sat, stiff as an English oak on the edge of her red velvet chair. She had a book in hand, but Beatrice somehow doubted that she'd been reading. The marchioness's air seemed far too preoccupied for serious study. Beatrice took a furtive glance at the spine. *The English Flower Garden* by William Robinson. Likely research for maintenance of her gardens.

Beatrice considered asking the marchioness's thoughts about the topic, curious to find out if the book was indeed a prop, but Lady Northridge would find the gesture impertinent.

"I find great pleasure in books as well," Beatrice said instead, motioning to the book in her mother-in-law's hand. "Perhaps we can discuss our favorites from time to time."

"You'll find, my *dear*, that as Marchioness of Northridge, I have precious little time for idle conversation. You will find it true yourself, if you take your duties as Countess Alnwick half as seriously as you ought." The endearment came off her tongue laced with poison.

Beatrice's spine shivered at the tone her mother-in-law used. Clearly Lady Northridge was not new to the art of intimidation, and though Beatrice felt ice in her veins just being in the same room, she admired her mettle. The marchioness wasn't the meek English matron Beatrice had perhaps foolishly expected to find in a mother-in-law before she'd been introduced into English society.

"Naturally I do," Beatrice replied. "There is much good to be done for the people in the marquisate. I hope to help Charles usher the area into an era of unprecedented prosperity."

Beatrice felt certain the magnanimous speech was precisely the sort of thing her new mother-in-law would want to hear. Of course, Charles had been so occupied with his father since their return to Leedswick that she only saw him at dinner—when she was fortunate. He still chose to keep his rooms apart from hers. A discussion of this ambition had yet to transpire between the couple, but she hoped very much that he'd be amenable to her taking an active role in the estate.

Beatrice took a sip from the teacup that had been wordlessly placed on the side table for her by a maid who moved so deftly she was a blur of black dress and white apron. Tea. She didn't mind it, but she found it to be a wishy-washy sort of drink. Too flavorful to be water, not flavorful enough to be coffee. How she longed for a strong cup of American coffee, black as night, just as Daddy took it. But she tried to forget those little American comforts and learn the ways of the English.

"Yes, yes. But your first duty, you must remember, is to this family. There is nothing more sacred than the honor of the Alnwick name. This family has earned its spot among the finest families in England without a stain on its honor, and I won't see it blemished while I am at the helm."

"Begging your pardon, but isn't the marquess 'at the helm,' so to speak?"

"How much you have to learn. The marquess may run the estate, but the marchioness must protect appearances when it comes to the family. She must promote the family's interests at court and elsewhere. She must be the moral force behind the whole enterprise, else it would all fall into mayhem."

"I see. It seems quite a massive responsibility."

"I cannot begin to explain the weight of it to one who has not borne it."

"I can only hope I will learn to be equal to it." For a moment Beatrice broke character and rubbed her damp palms on her dress. She stopped herself immediately as soon as she realized the nervous tic.

"I don't see how. If you had been born to a family like ours, you would have been trained for it. Groomed from infancy to fill the role with grace, honor, and dignity."

"And that, Lady Northridge, is what I *will* do."

"We shall see in due course. But I warn you, my *dear*, if you bring the slightest stain to this family name, the consequences will be dire."

✦ —————— ✦

Beatrice walked the halls of Leedswick Castle, trying to absorb her mother-in-law's words:

"If you bring the slightest stain to this family name, the consequences will be dire."

The marchioness was not a woman to make an idle threat. If Beatrice stepped out of line, her mother-in-law would make certain she paid the price for it. And the marchioness wasn't one for half measures. Beatrice had the distinct feeling that the lady of the house was well practiced in the art of revenge, and she had no desire to be the firsthand recipient of her talents.

The castle felt oppressive in its size in that moment, the echo of her footsteps on the stone floor of the corridor deafening. Beatrice felt exposed, vulnerable, like a fox pursued by a pack of highly skilled hounds ready to go in for the kill. She wanted nothing more than to hide away in her rooms, but that would be of no help to Charles. She needed to make an effort to be part of the family and to learn her role as future marchioness, and she could not do so in isolation.

Beatrice had wondered about his solemn, self-effacing manner when they had first met. Usually men of rank and breeding were full of pride and pomp, but it was now clear that his family had hammered all of that out of him.

"You seem lost in thought, sister dear," a voice called from behind her.

John. Of course he'd mastered the art of walking stealthily on the stone floor. She glanced down to see if he'd removed his shoes to stalk her like a cat but saw his shining black boots in place.

Satin slippers. She'd send Jane into town for soft-soled slippers to wear indoors. Beatrice might not have the grace to walk soundlessly on the stone floor with hard-soled shoes, but she could find her way around the limitation. Like every other performance, it just required the proper costume.

"Do I?" Beatrice said, unable to think of anything more clever. "I've just had tea with your mother."

"Ah, a tea with Mama leaves one with enough to ponder for a few months in most cases."

"I'm beginning to see that." Though she suspected John's knowledge came secondhand from hearing his mother dress down others. She surmised the marchioness rarely had a harsh word for her younger son.

"I do hope you're adjusting well. I expect it's a lot to take in. Things are quite different over here than across the pond."

"That they are." Beatrice nodded. "Have you been to America?"

"No, though it's an appealing prospect. Lots of opportunity for men like me." Enmity laced his tone like poison laced a glass of wine.

"Men like you?"

"Second sons. The ones who have precious little to stay for here. Your country was founded by those of us forced into the red or the black by the order of our birth."

"The red or the black?"

"Not surprising that you haven't read Stendhal. Red, the army. Black, the clergy. The red coat or the black cassock. Those are usually the choices for the younger brothers in England."

"You seem resentful of your lot in life."

"You'll find most people are. Though it *is* a bit hyperbolic to think my lot is all that unfortunate, I must admit. One can always pursue a respectable career as a solicitor or a doctor. New opportunities arise for men in my station every day. Of course it's not the same as running an estate and carrying on the family legacy."

"I've only known you a short while, but I sense you're the resourceful sort. You'll find success in whatever path you choose."

"Kind words. Clearly you're cut from the same cloth, or you wouldn't have aspired to such an advantageous match. There must be enough rich cowboys and steel barons to go 'round, but you wanted more than money. You wanted respectability."

"Or my parents did."

"Oh, now there we find common ground, don't we?" John said. "Always striving to live up to our parents' expectations. Always falling short. One of the few blessings of being a 'spare,' the parents spend all their energies on their firstborn. I'll never disappoint them to the degree Charles is capable."

"I am an only child, so I carry the burden of being the sole recipient of my parents' attentions."

"My condolences. It puts my own woes into perspective. Thank you for that."

"You'll forgive me, but you don't seem to care for your brother very much. He's such a good-natured man, I struggle to understand why. He doesn't seem to lord over you or act unfairly. What's more, he seems the sort to ensure that you are well cared for when he takes the reins."

"That's it, isn't it? He's insufferably gracious. And it will be his undoing. To follow in our father's footsteps, to be a peer of the realm, to manage this estate and keep it profitable will take a ruthlessness that Charles simply doesn't have."

"You make it sound a rather brutish business."

"If you think it's anything less, you're horribly mistaken, sister dear. But I expect even your parents sheltered you from the worst aspects of human nature."

"Oh, *brother dear*, if you think that's true, you clearly know little of the New York marriage market. Or London's, for that matter. And I assure you I was sheltered from nothing in that sphere."

"Touché. At least you have some wits about you. I didn't imagine Charles being able to woo anyone with much spirit in them, but I suppose that the title and estate make up for whatever defects of personality he may have."

"I fear you underestimate him," Beatrice said. "He is an intelligent and worthy man. Even more important, he's a good one. But I do feel sorry for him on one account."

John arched a questioning brow in response.

"It seems you'll never forgive him for the unpardonable slight he committed against you. Being born first," Beatrice said, quoting Charles's quip from their carriage ride to Leedswick.

"Alas, no. There's no way for him to make amends, apart from jumping into the Thames. And even then, he'd leave behind the taint of scandal . . . more than he already has."

With this he spun on the ball of his foot and continued back toward the main corridor of the house, leaving naught but questions in his wake.

Beatrice stood transfixed to the spot, pondering the exchange with John. No doubt he was angling for something. No doubt he had schemes aplenty percolating in his brain. She sensed that no one who got in the way of those plans would be safe. And he intimated that Charles had known his share of scandal. The possibilities, each worse than the last, swirled in the darkest corners of her consciousness.

"Are you all right, milady?" a voice asked behind her.

Beatrice tensed for a moment before placing the voice. Jane had emerged into the hallway, carrying a tea tray.

"Oh, Jane. Yes, fine."

"I brought this up for you. If you were having tea with her ladyship, you didn't have much in the way of tea."

"You made a good guess." She resumed the path to her rooms with Jane falling in step beside her.

"More than a guess. I've seen more than one tea tray left full when Lady Northridge is in high dudgeon."

They arrived at Beatrice's rooms, and she opened the door so Jane could pass through. She set the tray on Beatrice's writing table and smoothed her apron.

"High dudgeon?" Beatrice asked. "Is it as bad as that?"

"It doesn't take much to set her there." Jane stuck her head out into the hall to ensure it was vacant, then shut the door behind her.

"I thought she'd be pleased that Charles made a match that would shore up the estate. That would allow for needed improvements and provide for the future."

"If I may be honest with you, I think she was hoping Lord Charles would never marry and leave the estate to Lord John. You've spoiled her plans."

"What a loving mother. And his brother doesn't think any better of him. We had a nice chat in the hallway before you happened upon me," Beatrice said and gave in, breathing the sigh that had been weighing on her chest.

Jane looked highly uncomfortable at the mention of John but busied her hands filling a teacup for Beatrice.

"I'm glad you've come, Lady Alnwick. I've been here for several years, and I've never seen Lord Alnwick with such a spring in his step." Her face blanched when she realized the impropriety of her choice of words.

Beatrice nearly choked on her tea trying to stifle a laugh.

"I beg your pardon. I really meant no disrespect."

"Oh, I know, Jane. Please don't fret." Beatrice set down her teacup and laced her fingers in her lap. "But you might make up for the transgression with a bit of information on the subject. You see, I've not had the heart to ask him myself how he was injured."

"He's a proud man," Jane agreed. "He probably wouldn't want to talk about it. He came home injured from the war. He fought in

India and came back barely able to walk. This was five years ago? His soldier-servant, a well-liked lad from the village of Birchwick by the name of Francis Dawson, didn't make it home. The war hurt more than his leg if you ask me. He was never exactly a gadabout, but the war changed him. He was even quieter and more serious than before."

"War is a hard business. I can imagine he saw things we couldn't conjure up in our worst nightmares."

"True enough. It was after he came home that things really soured between Lord John and Lord Alnwick. Lord John used his brother's absence to set their parents against him. And when Lord Alnwick came home injured and a bit sullen, it only fueled the fire."

"How awful. A poor way to treat a son and brother who just returned from serving his country," Beatrice said. Charles's reserve made more sense to her now. He'd had five long years coping with his injuries and the trauma of his service, not to mention nearly as long as persona non grata in the village and even among his family.

"Too right. My brother was there, too, and never came home. My sister was working here when Lord Alnwick returned. She knew him better than I did, as she was the one who cleaned his rooms. She noticed the changes in him straightaway."

"And why is your sister not here any longer? Did she marry?"

"No, milady. She moved on," Jane said, a cloud passing over her face.

"Hopefully to better things."

"Indeed, milady. But you'll promise me never to tell his lordship who told you about his leg?"

"Sacred, I assure you."

"He's a good man, milady. And he cares more for this estate and the people running it than anyone else in the family. I don't know what's wrong with the rest of the family that they can't see his merits for themselves."

"Some people are blind to the things they don't want to see." Beatrice realized that her new family would never see the good in Charles that she did. And while she grieved that they would never acknowledge him for who he was, it made her admire him all the more for never wavering in his dedication to be the man he knew he needed to be.

CHAPTER 8

~RULE No. 8~

Study the lines for the roles you wish to play.

NORTHRIDGE, ENGLAND
AUGUST 1870

The summer weather had yet to cede its way to the gloom of the northern climes, but Beatrice had been warned that the halcyon days would soon be at an end, so she took the chance to stroll about the gardens before winter kept her bound to her icy prison. The grounds were more extensive than she'd ever seen, and she delighted in wandering through the once-manicured beds and artfully trimmed shrubs that had been left to grow unruly from lack of care.

Nothing so lush existed in New York or even Newport. As the heels of her boots sank into the fertile earth, Beatrice felt there was something good and healthy about the sensation. She longed to remove her boots and let her feet feel the rich soil between her toes, but it would mean a mess for Jane, who would be left to scrub the mud from inside the shoes once she returned to the castle.

For a few moments Beatrice raised her face to the sunshine. No proper Englishwoman would do such a thing, risking her complexion to the harsh rays of the sun, but Beatrice was *not* a proper Englishwoman, as her new family never ceased to remind her.

"They told me I'd find you out here." Charles approached from behind her, his limp a bit more pronounced than usual.

The corners of her mouth turned upward at the sight of him. Despite the coldness of the rest of the family, he didn't make her feel ill at ease. He was the only one who made her feel welcome at all. At least she could take some small security in that, but the infrequency of their interactions made this a cold comfort.

"With all the dire warnings of the winters here, I thought it would be wise to take in the sun while I can."

"You're right to heed their warnings. I don't think the winters here are what you're used to."

"New York can have its share of storms, to be sure. We were always glad for the warmth of Newport in the summer to bolster us for the rest of the year. But I suspect something is unrelenting about the winters here that I haven't seen before."

"I'll take you to Newport next summer to recover." Charles offered Beatrice his arm. She accepted and found she enjoyed the sensation of his warmth at her side. "I suspect you'll be rather home-sick by then."

Beatrice looked at him and longed to squeeze his hand. But would he be put off by the gesture? He was so thoughtful and kind, she had to think he didn't just hold her in high esteem but regarded her with affection too. Despite this, he had yet to come to her rooms. If she was not expecting a child in the new year, questions would emerge. Questions that would not be directed at Charles. The man was never to blame in these matters, even when there was reason to believe otherwise. To question a man's ability to sire a child was to question his very manhood. To question a woman's ability to bear an heir was to question her very worth. The latter, Beatrice was finding, was a far less dire offense.

"That would be wonderful but quite an expense. Perhaps the money would be better spent on the estate." She scanned the gardens, which were lovely but clearly suffered from inexpert care. She also noticed the crumbling stones of the main building and the areas where the roof had been haphazardly patched. The servants' quarters would leak horribly once the rains came. What was more, the idea of her mother parading her around New York like a prizewinning pony was as appealing as another helping of Caroline Astor's oysters.

"Your selflessness does you credit, but I refuse to see your entire fortune swallowed up by the estate, no matter what Father might want. I won't allow one single green American dollar to be spent on the estate until it is our own. I made sure of that much in the agreements with your father. I won't see you impoverished to save the family from past folly."

Beatrice hadn't been made privy to most of the details of her wedding contract, beyond her generous annual dress allowance that was hers to spend. She hadn't expected to be. These negotiations were made without a bride's input, despite their direct effects on her well-being. To know that her husband had been so thoughtful in his provisions lit a hearth fire in her core. To know that her father-in-law saw her as a source of income to be exploited made her furious. To know that her own father would have left enough leeway for that exploitation to be possible was an incredible disappointment. Charles alone had been the one to ensure the protection of her dowry.

She thought of the few times he'd brushed a kiss on her cheek and wished she had the temerity to steal a kiss herself. If only to spark the same warmth within him. He'd been without warmth for so long, he deserved to feel some kindness in his life.

"These gardens are enchanting," Beatrice said at length.

"They aren't what they should be. Mother has little interest in them. If she had the budget to keep them as grand as the gardens at Versailles, she might be more interested in the task."

"That seems an accurate assessment, from what I know of her." Beatrice instantly regretted the words. The marchioness hadn't been welcoming to her, but Charles might have a strong enough sense of filial duty that he wouldn't appreciate her commentary.

"I'm sorry she's not kinder," Charles said. Not kinder to *her*. Just . . . kinder. "I hope you're not too unhappy here. And I've been so horribly busy with Father that I've been inattentive and left you to your own devices. It's beastly of me."

"I can't expect you to keep me company all the time, dearest." She tried on the endearment. "I'm managing well enough." She didn't voice her disappointment—and her worry—about his absence from her rooms. There could be any number of reasons for his reticence in that area. Perhaps he was unwell. Perhaps his wounded leg troubled him more than he let on. Perhaps he was as nervous as she was.

Perhaps she simply wasn't what he'd hoped for. Just as she wasn't what Thomas had hoped for either. Perhaps, as her mother would have had her believe, there was something fundamentally wanting about her.

She tried to banish that last pernicious thought from her mind. Charles chose her. He was an earl and would be a marquess. If he hadn't fancied her, he could have found any number of wealthy American heiresses who would have suited him better.

But she couldn't banish the worry entirely.

"Perhaps your mother would allow me to take over the responsibility now," Beatrice said. "It would take a duty she finds irksome off her shoulders and would give me something to do that would be of use to the estate."

Charles paused, pensive. "I don't know how she would feel about the offer. She might consider it a slight against her ability to manage things. But it would be for the best. As things stand, she leaves the care of them to the household staff who aren't trained as gardeners, and I'm certain they resent the extra work."

Beatrice doubted very seriously whether any other member of the family spared much thought for the workload of the staff. Just like horses in the stables, they had to be prepared to ride for as long as their masters bid them to. Beatrice had seen more than one cook and lady's maid leave her mother's employ for the same reason. To run an estate in the same manner wasn't sustainable. Charles was the only one with the head to run this place.

"I can see that," Beatrice said. "But I do long for something to do to make myself useful to you."

"Your presence alone is of more use than you know." Charles caressed her hand so briefly, she might have imagined it. "And regardless of what Mother might desire, one day the care of these gardens—this house—*will* pass to you. From the great hall and servants' quarters to the rose gardens and tulip beds, right down to the belladonna and hemlock."

Beatrice arched an eyebrow. "Belladonna and hemlock? Aren't those rather dangerous?"

"Oh yes, the fifth marchioness kept a poison garden, and it's become a bit of a tradition. Some say she was a bit mad, but back in her time, some of the ingredients were useful in medications. Or for keeping unwanted dinner guests to a minimum."

Beatrice let out a throaty laugh for perhaps the first time since she'd arrived in England. "No, I can well imagine that no one would have come to Leedswick without a warm invitation from the fifth marchioness."

"I believe there is an old adage about it being better to be feared than loved. It seems she understood that lesson rather well."

The couple shared a bout of laughter, and when Charles turned to Beatrice, for just one moment she thought he might lower his lips to hers. But as quickly as she imagined it, his attention was diverted by the sounds of servants chattering up ahead as they trimmed back hedges and pruned weathered leaves.

Walking briskly down the path from the house, Lady Alnwick descended upon the servants and appeared to give a few orders, though she was too far away for either Beatrice or Charles to make out what she said. A maid approached the marchioness several moments later with a basket brimming with cascades of blue flowers on long stems. The marchioness accepted the basket without so much as a nod and retreated to the castle.

"Is it usual for the marchioness to come to the garden herself?" Beatrice asked. "Wouldn't she be more likely to send someone?"

"Oh, Father has a penchant for bluebells. She's been known to make an arrangement of them when they come in season as a treat for him. I expect she considers herself quite the country girl while she's getting her hands dirty."

Beatrice looked at Charles. "I *don't* mind getting my hands dirty," she said. And she meant it. Now that she was married, she had to find a purpose for the next phase of her life, and helping turn the estate back into a viable enterprise seemed a worthy one. "I mean to help you in running the estate when it's our turn. And not just these gardens, though I'll see them tended as they ought to be. I can bear many things, but being idle isn't one of them."

Just then, the marquess's voice boomed across the expanse of the garden. Charles was being called away.

"I appreciate that sentiment more than I can express." Charles brushed a kiss on her cheek so softly, it might have been the breeze from the wings of a butterfly.

Beatrice, once again, was left alone, but she felt less aimless than before. She would make herself equal to what she'd promised Charles. She placed one determined foot in front of the other and decided she would read every book in the marquess's library that would help her learn the intricacies of estate management. And though it was a small thing, she'd begin with every tome they had on gardens. If that would be her domain at present, she'd make the gardens the finest in all of England.

She thought of the kiss they'd almost shared, dismayed that it had been interrupted. Why was he so reluctant? Was she repulsive to him, or was something amiss with him? Did it have to do with the scandal John had mentioned? The thought of it had plagued her since John alluded to it, which she was certain was his plan. She wanted to push it from her thoughts, but the more she tried, the harder it was to dismiss.

CHAPTER 9

Beware of unscrupulous understudies.

For two weeks Beatrice buried herself in the study of the gardens, though she did so as covertly as possible so as not to stir the marchioness's ire. Beatrice scoured every text in the library on the care and maintenance of gardens in general as well as histories written of the castle gardens themselves. The fifth marchioness had kept extensive records, detailing every plant she'd selected for the garden, where they were planted, when they bloomed or bore fruit, what sort of care they needed, how they fared in the estate's rocky soils, and every change she made to the composition during her twenty years as caretaker.

But they were more than just dry horticultural records. She included long passages about her rambles in the garden, how she delighted in the coming of the spring flowers. How the bustle of autumn harvest in the orchards filled her with a sense of purpose, though of course she wasn't the one to be toiling in the fields.

Beatrice sensed the gardens were an escape for the fifth marchioness, Lady Elizabeth Alnwick. She never made an outward complaint, seeming very aware of the comfort of her situation compared to so many others she saw in her daily life, but there was a melancholy in her words that Beatrice could not ignore. Lady Elizabeth almost never mentioned her husband in her passages, other than the rare times he decided to take a turn with her in the gardens to inspect her handiwork. Beatrice saw no love, no passion, no sign of joy for anything but her small garden that was overshadowed by her husband's extensive grounds.

Likely because it was the only domain of her life over which Lady Elizabeth had any measure of control.

A frisson of fear skittered down her spine that the same fate could well be her own. She didn't want to be relegated to insignificance, though she would have little choice in the matter if that was what Charles chose for her. Their infrequent exchanges were cordial, and each night she waited for a knock at her door, but none came.

She considered dropping hints, at least indicating her willingness to perform her duty, but she worried that any prodding would cause him to retreat even further into himself. Worse, she worried about an outright rejection. She would have to find a way to coax him, gently, into married life, but she was completely without ideas to bring about that outcome.

So she found her solace in the library.

During the day the library was inconvenient, as it was the marchioness's preferred room in which to take tea, so Beatrice felt a little self-conscious using the space. She would grab a tome and retreat to her own sitting room to read in peace. But at night, after she was certain Charles wasn't coming for her, she would creep downstairs and spread the books out on the massive English oak table that was probably five centuries old with a storied life. She could sprawl in her chair, clad in her loose nightgown and a woolen shawl without the constraints of corsets and prying eyes. She could jump from volume to volume and study for as long as she desired. She did force herself to retire before too late so she wouldn't appear sluggish and withdrawn the next day, but she lived for the quiet hours of the night.

Charles, busy with his father and the estate, was unaware of the depth of her study. But wanting to be encouraging of her interests, he gave her a green cloth journal in which to take notes. She found herself making detailed commentaries and reflecting on the wisdom in the books she'd read, the plans for improvements she wanted to make, and her musings about the fifth marchioness and her writings.

"My, my. How studious we are this evening," said a baritone voice from the doorway. John.

Beatrice pulled her shawl tight around her shoulders. "I had no idea I'd be bothering anyone here," she replied.

"Not at all. I'd have never known you were here, save for the candle glow under the door. I thought Father might be toiling over the ledgers, and I was going to offer him a few moments of conversation to lighten his spirits."

"Thoughtful of you," Beatrice said.

John's eyes were sharp, and she wanted nothing more than to be free of his gaze. As much as it pained her, she'd have to give up her long nights in the library and take the books to her sitting room so she wouldn't run the risk of being discovered by him again. Something about him made her feel as though she were a small fawn and he a wolf. She couldn't abide the sensation of feeling hunted.

"I am, no matter what Charles might say on the matter. And I had thought, sister dear, that you would be in bed at this hour. Or else enjoying my brother's company."

Heat rose in her cheeks and she dropped her gaze for a moment before realizing she'd betrayed the truth.

"Oh, so that's it. My brother isn't warming your bed, so you comfort yourself with books. What a shame. You're too lovely to be trapped in such a cold marriage. And it's foolish on his part. He's in want of an heir. Perhaps his little war injuries left him . . . incapable.

How embarrassing. I could, of course, come to his aid if you ever have need. He'd never whisper a word to anyone. Imagine the shame."

"The shame of what?" A deeper voice sounded behind John.

Her shoulders sagged with relief as Charles emerged from the shadows of the corridor into the library.

"It seems none of us can sleep well tonight, can we? How curious. I was just having a little tête-à-tête with my new sister. It seems strange that a bride would be alone in the middle of the night so soon after being married. One would worry that her husband was inattentive . . . or uninterested . . . in his poor bride. I was merely consoling the dear."

"You bastard," Charles growled. He took a step closer to John, and her breath lodged itself in her chest. If the servants caught wind and chose to spread the word in Birchwick, a midnight brawl between the brothers would reflect badly on them all, but particularly Beatrice. Even if she didn't deal a single blow.

Before Charles could act upon his anger, an almighty scream rang out from the gallery.

The three of them ran from the library and out into the foyer to see what the commotion was about. Within a couple of moments several maids and footmen and the butler himself thundered down from the attics and across the gallery, for once forgetting their decorous march and sprinting in the direction of the master bedrooms.

Charles dashed up the stairs first, John hard on his heels, Beatrice a length behind him. When they reached the wing of rooms where the marquess and marchioness kept quarters, a number of the staff were gathered outside the door of the marquess's bedchamber. Their murmurs fell to silence when the three of them approached. A few held their arms crossed over their chests, eyes downcast. Others' faces were ashen. They all looked stricken.

"What's the matter?" Charles demanded.

The door to the marquess's chambers flew open, and the

marchioness, clad in an opulent bedgown and her hair still perfectly coiffed, stood in the open doorway. She looked ready to receive the queen herself, save for the chalky color of her cheeks.

"The marquess has died," she announced to those assembled at large. "Summon help."

"The marquess has died," John repeated, then slid his gaze to his brother, his eyes narrowed. "Long live the marquess."

CHAPTER 10 ———————————————

~*RULE NO. 10*~

The production may be in chaos, but
the audience should never know.

The family doctor was summoned, an affable, gangly man by
the name of Fielding who had served the marquess and his
family for the entirety of his career. He wasn't a coroner or a medical examiner, but he was the best that could be found in the middle
of the night in such a remote part of the country. He was in the
marquess's chambers, examining the body while the family was left
to wait.

Charles, John, Beatrice, and the marchioness—dowager
marchioness now—were gathered in the library, still in their nightclothes, their dressing gowns hastily donned to give them protection
from the chill in the room that had little to do with the brisk autumn
night. The men stood by the fire and took thoughtful draughts from
crystal tumblers filled with unhealthy quantities of scotch, while the
women sat on the dais and sipped sherry. Though not overly fond
of spirits, Beatrice found a bit of comfort in the warming tingle of
the fortified wine. Charles had acted as barkeeper, not wanting the

servants to overhear what any of the family might say in such an unguarded moment.

It was some time before the doctor entered the library to speak with the family, and he appeared nearly as haggard as they. He accepted the scotch Charles offered before taking a seat in one of the armchairs when invited by the dowager.

"In my preliminary investigation, it would appear the marquess has died of an apoplexy or angina pectoris—a stoppage of the heart. Not exactly common in a man as young and seemingly robust as Lord Northridge, but not unheard of either."

The marquess had been in his early sixties, and while he was not given to depriving himself at mealtimes, he wasn't corpulent beyond the scope of men of easy circumstances at such an age. They'd all expected he'd live another ten to twenty years. Perhaps more if luck had been on the marquess's side. But clearly it had not been.

"It makes no sense to me, Dr. Fielding," John said. "He had no signs of being in poor health. Had you noticed anything, Mama?"

"Nothing out of the ordinary. He was not a young man, but I hadn't any real cause for concern."

"There is something off about this whole business," John said. "A man like Father doesn't simply drop dead."

"Well, clearly he did, John," his mother chastened, glancing from her son to the doctor, then back to her son again. She was worried about scandal, Beatrice recognized. She didn't want John being so candid in front of the doctor.

"Can you tell me how he was discovered, Lady Northridge?" The doctor took a sip from his tumbler. "One of the servants came upon him?"

"No, I found him." She looked distant, staring beyond the doctor's head rather than at him. "I went to ask him about a shooting luncheon we'd been invited to at the Weatherbys' estate. I'd forgotten to ask him this afternoon and wanted to write our response to post in the morning. I thought he'd be awake reading his book in bed as he's wont to do when he retires early. I thought he'd fallen asleep while reading. He had a book on his chest and looked so peaceful. I went to move the book to his night table when I realized—" The dowager dabbed her handkerchief to the corners of her eyes, unable to finish her sentence.

"Doctor, clearly these questions are too much for my mother to cope with in her present condition. Are they really necessary?" Charles asked.

"Unfortunately, I am of the same mind as Lord John. The marquess had been in vigorous health as recently as a month ago when I treated him for hay fever. I would like to summon the coroner to do a proper examination. Advances have been made in that field that far outstrip my own abilities. My focus has, understandably, been treating the living."

"Of course," Charles said. "Summon whomever you require at daybreak. Send to London if you see fit. The estate will bear the expense."

"Very good, Lord Alnwick. Lord Northridge, rather. My apologies."

Charles waved his hand in dismissal. More than one tongue would trip over his new title, and it was the least of the family's concerns in that moment.

When the doctor's carriage had been called, the family remained ensconced in the library.

"What on earth do you mean allowing the doctor to summon some common charlatan to examine your father?" the dowager demanded. "Have you no sense of dignity? No respect for the sanctity of his memory?"

"What I have, Mother, is a healthy respect for the power of idle gossip. If anyone questions the circumstances of Father's death, if the good doctor himself is not convinced that Father died of natural causes, then we must allow the examination to take place. Either we will find that Father did indeed die of natural causes, and we can put the rumors to rest. Or—"

"Or what, brother?" John growled, folding his arms over his chest.

"We find that Father's death was no accident, and we act accordingly."

"Act accordingly?" the dowager asked.

"Allow the authorities to do their duty. If Father did not die from an apoplexy or a stoppage of the heart, it stands to reason that someone killed him." Charles drained his glass.

"And the murderer is among us," John supplied.

"Indeed." Charles gave his brother a hard stare before he set the tumbler on the side table with a decisive *clink* of crystal against wood. "And with that in mind, John, I'll ask you to escort Mother to her rooms and I'll take Beatrice to hers. We'd all do well to be on guard."

John offered no protestation and offered his arm to his mother, who readily accepted. Beatrice doubted her mother-in-law would sleep that night but would likely welcome the comfort of isolation. When they departed, Charles offered his arm to Beatrice, who had remained largely silent as the events unfolded.

"How do you fare, my dear?"

"I hardly know what to think," Beatrice confessed. "I barely knew your father, but he seemed a vital, healthy man."

"I know," Charles said grimly. "Beatrice, I want you to prepare yourself. Whatever the outcome of the investigation is, there will be talk. We can hope it won't be a full-scale scandal, but it may well be. You're the marchioness now, and eyes will be focused on you. I never thought you'd face so harsh a test so soon after your arrival, but these are the circumstances laid at our door. I'm counting on you to uphold the family honor while we weather this crisis."

"If a crisis it turns out to be," Beatrice said. They had reached her bedroom door and they stood outside it. "It might turn out the doctor's original analysis was correct and the marquess suffered an unfortunate medical mishap."

"And I pray that's the case. But my very gut tells me we must prepare for the worst."

"I wish you'd let me comfort you," Beatrice said. "You could . . . come inside."

"Beatrice, I know . . . I know things haven't been as they should. But now is not the time to link yourself to this family even more irrevocably than you have."

"We're married, Charles. I think we crossed the Rubicon then, don't you?"

"Darling, you know as well as I do that if our marriage remains as it is, you have an out. You can file for annulment on the grounds that I didn't perform my duty. I won't take that from you now." He crossed his arms over his chest as though bracing himself against Beatrice and her affections.

"That's not what I want." Beatrice's voice quavered despite the resolve in her heart. "I do not make vows I don't intend to keep."

"And you are all the more admirable for it. But you must understand, Beatrice. Given the situation, an annulment may be the only thing to save you from ruin. I think you fail to realize that if my father's postmortem becomes a murder investigation, I will become the primary suspect. If I am tried for murder, your only hope of living a scandal-free life is to be rid of me."

"But you didn't murder your father," she said with certainty.

"The truth is of little consequence in these matters, darling. The look of the thing can inflict the same damage as if I'd shot him in broad daylight. I will not take you down with me."

"Charles, none of this makes sense. Your father died this night. You've been keeping me at arm's length for all the months we've been married. Explain yourself." She had reached the point of her patience and shoved an accusatory finger into his shoulder. "I'm not so naïve as to think that ours was a love match, but I do know you hold me in some regard. Enough that you must know within yourself that I'm entitled to the truth."

"Indeed you are." He lowered his voice. "I couldn't have known that my father was going to die, but I knew my brother would try to do something to see the estate entailed upon him rather than me. I knew my mother would likely help him in his pursuit. I knew our marriage would be a catalyst for the plot. By marrying a woman of means, I've taken another step toward molding myself into a suitable heir. John had long dreamed that I would simply die young and childless so he could secure his succession."

"Then shouldn't you do everything in your power to secure *your* lineage? If I were with child, it would dash John's hopes and he could find some other flight of fancy. It seems like he's the sort whose attentions are easily diverted."

"Delaying the consummation of the marriage was the only way I could think of to protect you. If I do not claim my due as your husband, you'll be free to have the marriage annulled and remarry. I won't see you a social pariah on my account."

"You can't possibly think such a thing will be necessary."

"Darling, I think you underestimate John and Mama's desire to hold the estate. If they could find any way to toss us out, they would spare no thought for a child born of our union. I couldn't bear to see you and our innocent child disinherited and without the title and estate I promised you our child would have. Even if we produced a strong line of healthy heirs and John was unable to sire a single sickly whelp, the two of them would rather see the line pass to some distant cousin than to me."

The blood drained from Beatrice's face. "I had no idea why they were so cold to us, but now it all comes together. How wretched of them."

Charles nodded. "Mama has puffed up John for years to believe he's the more suitable heir to the estate and will hear nothing else. She's blind to his faults and won't hear a word spoken against him. Father tried to be more judicious, but he'd been bullied by Mama and John for so long, he couldn't help but begin to see their side of things."

"What a ruthless family. Do you think John . . . ?"

"I wouldn't dare accuse him without proof, but there is no doubt that he has motive," Charles said, his face ashen. "They are ruthless, the pair of them. And I will not leave you to their mercies. Until all is settled, I will not visit your bedchamber, Beatrice. I will not see your fortune squandered by my brother, nor will I be hanged knowing I've left you unprotected."

"You will not hang."

"Don't speak a wish as though it were a certainty. But I will hope the truth of the matter will out in due course."

"So you had no intention of making me your wife—properly— until you inherit?" Beatrice asked. She couldn't bring herself to look him in the face.

"I was pressuring Father into formalizing his succession on paper. Making a written promise that the estate would pass to me and our future children and not to John. I wanted some assurance that if your dowry was to be used for the estate, then we would have some legal guarantees. If he had agreed to make the terms of his will clear on the matter . . ."

"But he didn't?"

"I'd like to think he was on the point of it," Charles said. "I hope, truly, that he saw that you and I were the future this estate deserves. I married you under the premise that you would become Marchioness of Northridge, and I will not bind you to a marriage that provides you with less than what was promised."

"I don't give a single damn about titles, Charles. No matter what my intention was when I came to England."

"I know, my dear." He rubbed his mouth, deep in thought, and returned his eyes to her. "There is something I would ask of you, Beatrice," he said in low tones. "If I am taken in for questioning, and I am almost certain I will be, do not let Mother and John take over the running of things. You are the Marchioness of Northridge, and if you cede your place—our place—it will seem like an admission of guilt. Run the estate as though there is no doubt in your mind of my innocence."

"That will be quite simple. For I have none."

Charles bent and brushed Beatrice's lips with a kiss. Sweetness tinged with regret lingered there. He opened the door to her rooms and closed it behind her, remaining alone in the corridor. Her back to the door, she slid to the floor and buried her head in her knees. She allowed the tears to flow but kept her sobs in check.

The way Charles spoke, it seemed inevitable that the inquiries would find something amiss with the marquess's death and that Charles would be implicated. She had to find a way to protect her husband, knowing that the dowager and Lord John would do nothing to save Charles if it made way for John's ascension to the proverbial throne. It would be preferable that the scandal be kept as quiet as possible, but perhaps they were willing to pass the reins to John even if it made the family notorious.

It wouldn't be the first time such a thing happened in a grand family. She doubted it would be the last.

Knowing she wouldn't be able to sleep, Beatrice took the tome of common English garden plants she'd pilfered from the library and did what she could to focus on the words on the page. She wouldn't give in to her worry and grief just yet. The best thing she could do for Charles was to carry on performing the duties that were expected of her as though the marquess's death were simply a tragic and untimely misfortune.

She would carry on as Marchioness of Northridge.

And she would carry on as such until the police escorted her from the castle in chains, if that was what was required.

CHAPTER 11 ———————————

~RULE No. 11~

Never let the understudy play your part
if you don't want to risk losing it.

Charles's prediction that blame would land itself at his door proved to be prescient, and in short order too. Charles was called to London one week later. The evidence that the marquess had been poisoned was strong enough that he would face a formal inquiry, though Charles was the chief suspect only by virtue of his being next in line to inherit. A solicitor came to collect him, and Beatrice could do nothing but watch as valets scrambled to pack his trunk and help him into his overcoat.

"You mustn't worry too much, your ladyship," Charles's solicitor said. "Even in the seemingly likely event that the coroner concludes that the late marquess fell victim to foul play, it will be exceedingly difficult for the courts to prove that your husband had a hand in it."

"Difficult, but not impossible." Beatrice folded her arms around her middle, a shield against the awful news that kept coming.

"You know him to be innocent, my lady. And I like to believe the truth will out. This is not a trial, remember. He's merely being held for questioning. I assure you he'll be kept quite comfortable."

"But won't these inquiries make him infamous throughout London? And the whole of England after that?" Beatrice tried, in vain, to keep the panic from her voice. Any scandal would be grist for the dowager's rumor mill. Ammunition to keep the marquisate from the son who was fit to run it.

"Quite the reverse, ma'am. It should remove the stain of doubt from his character once he is exonerated. Which we both know he will be."

Beatrice nodded her comprehension but didn't find the solace in Mr. Perkins's words that he'd hoped to offer her.

Before Charles's departure, she thrust a brown leather journal in his hands. "The journal you gave me has been great company when I had none other. Take this with you and find solace in it as you add your thoughts."

He bent and kissed her with an intensity he'd not shared with her before. It was the first time she'd been kissed in earnest, and her heart fluttered despite the gravity of the situation. "Remember your promise to me, darling" was all he was able to say, his voice strained against the words.

"I am the Marchioness of Northridge, and this is my home." Beatrice conjured the image of courage for his sake. He nodded and left, the solicitor pinned to his side.

Beatrice had no doubt that the solicitor meant what he'd said, but she wasn't able to fully persuade herself that he wasn't filling her with false hope.

When the carriage had taken Charles away to London, Beatrice felt more alone and terrified than at any moment since she'd left New York. She wasn't sure she'd ever felt this sort of isolation—verging on despair—before. She was daunted at the prospect of a single night without Charles's presence in the castle, let alone an absence of a fortnight. There was comfort in knowing he was in the adjacent rooms in the marquess's quarters, even if he didn't venture into hers.

Beatrice stretched out on her bed, hoping to rest her eyes before the evening meal. Though she wasn't sure how she'd summon the will to eat, she was to dine with the dowager and Lord John that night. Though they ought to have been her greatest allies in the midst of the scandal, Beatrice knew it was quite the reverse. They would capitalize on any doubt about Charles's innocence for their own benefit.

She would have worried for her own safety, but she alone posed no threat to them. Charles was safer in London than here with his family of pit vipers. Beatrice hoped they were smart enough to realize that if anything happened to her while Charles was away, the scandal would be theirs entirely.

As cold and calculating as Sarah Holbrook was, Beatrice couldn't imagine her mother being so unfeeling toward her own child.

A knock sounded at the door, quickly followed by Jane's entry to the room.

"Heavens, is it half seven already? I must have dozed off, or been so lost in thought I was as good as." Beatrice sat up in bed and rubbed her eyes, hoping she wouldn't appear thickheaded at the dinner table.

"Half six, your ladyship. The marchioness, that is, the dowager marchioness gave instructions just now that dinner is to be at seven. She wishes to retire early. She also made a number of changes to the menu for the week. Mrs. Pelham is rather cross, I'm afraid."

The cook's temper was legendary, and Beatrice expected she did not view the dowager and her daughter-in-law's spat with much patience. "I imagine she is. When, pray tell, did the dowager issue this order?"

"Not long ago, milady. The kitchens are scrambling to get it ready since you'd told us to keep to the usual schedule."

Beatrice fought the urge to hurl her silver-plated hairbrush at the closed window, but she restrained herself. She might soon begrudge the expense of a new hairbrush, let alone the cost of one of the massive windows if she faced a long and costly legal battle. It was just as Charles predicted—his mother and John were trying to usurp them. It would start in the dining room and quickly spread far beyond. Beatrice regained mastery of herself, and this time felt no fear about issuing orders.

"And so we shall. If the *dowager* marchioness wishes to dine early, she may have a tray sent to her rooms. It has been a trying time for us all, and I won't begrudge her some much-needed rest. She will not, however, upset the order of things here, disrupt my staff, and countermand my orders. You will go to the kitchens and assure them that they can proceed as planned. And have her maid inform the dowager that she may join us at eight or dine alone in her rooms whenever she chooses."

"Very good, milady." Jane bobbed in a shallow curtsy.

"And, Jane, you might let it be known downstairs that I have no wish to personally remind anyone of who sets the dining schedule at Leedswick. I know a change in command is awkward, but I hope the staff will take this little blunder as a valuable lesson. If that lesson is learned, we need never speak of it again."

A glimmer of a smile crossed Jane's lips. "Very good, milady."

Beatrice resisted the urge to fling herself back into bed, knowing rest would elude her were she to attempt it again. She had taken the fifth marchioness's diaries to her room, hoping she might find some comfort in them between slogging through dry legal texts that offered very little in the way of useful information that might help her secure Charles's freedom. She didn't have much confidence that the late marquess's impressive collection of legal tomes would have anything she might use in Charles's defense, but reading them gave her something to do, which felt a little better than being utterly useless.

If nothing else, if she kept digging her way through all the hundreds of the late marquess's books, she'd be prepared to sit exams to become a barrister herself. If such a thing were legal, which, as she confirmed in one of the many texts, it was not.

Jane returned at the appointed hour, and though it would just be a private family dinner of two or three, Beatrice dressed as she would have done were they expecting important company. She would not let the dowager or Lord John think she would let standards slip.

The dinner trumpet would sound at eight and under no one else's order but her own.

As she walked to the dining room, the short sweep train of her sapphire-blue evening gown dragged the marble floors like a blue taffeta wave going back out to sea with every step she took. The dowager and John were already seated in the dining room, though neither had been served. The dowager was not in her usual spot, which the staff now reserved for Beatrice.

She smiled inwardly. A victory.

A harried-looking footman seemed ready to bolt from the room and was greatly relieved at the arrival of his new mistress. She nodded to him, and he scurried away to give the order for the food to be brought up from the kitchens.

"I don't know who you think you are, but—" the dowager began.

"No, I am quite certain of who I am. I am Lady Beatrice Alnwick, Marchioness of Northridge and mistress of Leedswick Castle. Which, as you're well aware, means I am charged with a great many duties. Among them is setting menus and arranging the dining schedule. I trust your maid conveyed my message."

"Indeed, she did. And I'll not have a presumptuous upstart girl from heaven knows where flitting around my home acting like queen of the manor while my foolhardy son languishes in prison."

"Lord Northridge is not in prison. And I am not *acting* like queen of the manor in *your* home. It is Charles's home and mine. I *am* queen here, whether you are too ill-bred to pass on the reins to Charles or not."

John set his glass down with a loud *thunk* on the gleaming wood of the table. "Watch your tone with my mother, you American trollop. The time may soon come when you will depend very heavily on my benevolence, and this behavior won't win you favors with me."

"God spare me from the day when I have to ask you, of all people on this earth, for a favor. I'm not sure I'd be able to bear the shame of it."

"The shame you feel on that score may be the least of your concerns once the results of the inquiry are made public, sister dear." He sneered. "And when that day comes, the only credit to Charles's name will be his imprudent marriage to you. He may die on the gallows and you may be forced to skulk back to America in disgrace, but at least your dirty American money will be in the family coffers to shore up the estate."

Beatrice cocked her head and offered an ironic smile. He didn't know. He didn't know the pains Charles had taken to protect her. John didn't know because he would never care enough about a prospective bride to spare a thought for her best interests. She could tell them the truth—that regardless of the outcome of the inquiry, they would never see a brass penny of her fortune—but she decided to keep those cards close to her chest.

Beatrice felt a tremor in her hands, but she refused to indulge it. She had to give her mother-in-law and brother-in-law the performance they deserved, even though she wanted nothing more than to hide away in a guest room somewhere and wait for Charles's return. If she wanted to secure his legacy as marquess, she had to stand her ground as marchioness in his stead.

"Be that as it may, until the law says otherwise, I am Marchioness of Northridge, and I will not allow you to usurp my position, nor that of my husband. And if you have any quarrel with that, *Mother,*

I suggest that you consider it time to set up your residence at the dower house. And you, *brother dear*, may find your way to your town house in Belgravia or a charming hut in the Australian Outback for all I care."

"How dare you!" the dowager said, shaking with rage. "Have you no respect for rank and privilege? Have you no sensibility of your own insolence?"

"I suppose one might say it's the American in me. I wasn't raised to bow and scrape when an earl or a duke comes into the room. Though I am sure it must be hard for you. You're so used to everyone genuflecting before you, you haven't the slightest idea how it is to live without being venerated for being born lucky. In America one actually has to accomplish something to receive that level of groveling."

As soon as the words were out of Beatrice's mouth, she knew it was a lie. Caroline Astor was treated with the deference of a queen, and she did little more with her time than host parties, dress well, and use her resources extravagantly. She pontificated about the proper comportment in "good" society, and every socially ambitious ear turned to her when she spoke. Not because her opinions on the subject were in any way better, but because she had enough money to make the rules everyone else had to follow.

The difference was, in England, the rules had been set for centuries. And even an impoverished duke was still a duke and commanded respect. If the Astors lost their fortune, Beatrice mused, their standing in society wouldn't last much longer than their line of credit at A. T. Stewart's.

The rules were different, but so utterly the same.

The dowager rose from the table wordlessly, tossed her linen napkin on the table, and retreated to her rooms. Whether to retire for the evening or to pack for her departure to the dower house, Beatrice didn't know, but it was a victory. It was a declaration that Beatrice wouldn't step aside and let Charles's inheritance be swindled from him. She was doing as she promised and hoped Charles would be proud of her efforts.

"You think you're clever, don't you?" John cast aside his fork, glaring at her. "Enjoy your moment, sister dear, for it won't last long. The rumor mill will have been churning since my brother was escorted away. He'll be ruined, no matter the outcome of the inquiry. And you by association."

"So you say, John." Beatrice dared to address him without title or courtesy. "But for as long as my moment lasts, you're not welcome in this house. I want you out before breakfast tomorrow."

He pushed his chair away and stalked out of the room without a backward glance.

Beatrice took a sip of the dry white wine that one of the footmen had poured with the first course that had lain forgotten on the table. Her hands shook, but no one was there to observe the nerves she'd barely been able to conceal when John and the dowager were present. She didn't have to hide now, so she didn't bother expending the energy.

Heaven knew she would need it in the days ahead. She would have to close the castle—once she was certain her mother-in-law and brother-in-law had left the premises and were established elsewhere—and go to London. If rumors were flying about Charles, she would hear them spoken to her face and right them herself.

CHAPTER 12 ———————————

~RULE No. 12~

If you don't know your lines, improvise.

Beatrice readied the household for her leaving for London a week later. Most of the staff would stay behind, but Jane and a small contingent would accompany her. The butler seemed only too happy with the order that the dowager and Lord John shouldn't be given admittance to the house. If either claimed to have mislaid a personal object, the staff would find and return it in due course. The less noble part of Beatrice wished she'd been able to see the dowager in high dudgeon, but hearing Foster's retelling of the events when she had been evicted was almost as good as witnessing them herself. Beatrice had pegged the butler as loyal to the dowager and her causes, but it seemed his loyalty was to whomever held the house and the title, which would serve Beatrice well. As long as she was able to keep the title from John's clutches.

And the best chance of doing that, Beatrice was convinced, was to go to London and stand by her husband's side in his time of need. She booked first class tickets for herself and second class for Jane, Mrs. Pelham the cook, a couple of junior housemaids, and a footman who might be of use in the London house. They would have to change trains in Alnmouth, and she was grateful to have a small entourage with her if she could not have Charles.

It would take most of the day to reach London, and she spent most of it second-guessing every decision she'd made. But despite Charles's assurances that he would be well, despite his insistence that he needed her to stay at Leedswick for the sake of appearances, she knew it was his way of shielding her in case things went poorly. He had a rosier view than she of what her prospects might be if they had to annul the marriage. He imagined the fashionable neighborhoods of Mayfair and Belgravia in London would open up to her as soon as annulment papers were signed and she was free of him. Perhaps he thought her lovely face and sweet disposition would cause all of London society to welcome her back into the fold. He assumed they'd be willing to forget her connection to him and treat her as a prized debutante. Or perhaps he thought she'd return to New York, where her time overseas would give her a mystique that might make her more eligible in the marriage market.

In either case, he was wrong. The *ton* would shun her, and Caroline Astor's privileged inner circles had closed their doors on her the moment she'd gotten on the bad side of a foul oyster all those months ago.

It seemed a lifetime ago.

The family house in Mayfair was decorated every bit as tastefully as Leedswick Castle. Soft robin's-egg-blue walls with gleaming white trim, polished mahogany doors and furniture throughout with lines as graceful as a ballet dancer's. On the walls hung artwork that was probably more than a hundred years old and that could fetch a fortune, but beyond being pleasant to look at, it had no real meaning to Beatrice. The skeleton crew that cared for the place in the family's absence had been frantically preparing for their new mistress's arrival, given the short notice they'd had to ready the house. They seemed grateful for the additional help Beatrice had brought with her to help run things while she was in residence.

"Milady, might I ask what your plans are?" Jane asked as she helped Beatrice from her traveling gown.

Beatrice rubbed her temples and exhaled. She loved travel, but the incessant rattling for hours on end paired with her mounting anxieties regarding Charles's welfare had brought her to the end of her endurance.

"Well, I trust you've drawn a bath hot enough that we can use it to smelt into new shoes for the horses later. Then once I've scrubbed off the dirt from the train, I'll want the best supper Mrs. Pelham can conjure up. Preferably with a hearty red wine and a chocolate dessert that is too decadent to be good for me. Then once I'm clean and well fed, I will sleep. Then I'll consider the next steps. Over breakfast served with a vat of coffee. Not tea."

"That sounds like a good plan, milady." Jane set aside Beatrice's brown wool traveling jacket. "Though I hope you won't do anything risky. London can be a very dangerous town, especially to gentlewomen, and it's not only the pickpockets and ruffians you need to watch out for."

"I appreciate your concern, Jane, and I promise to be prudent."

"Thank you, milady." She bustled about, drawing the bath. Then she left her mistress to soak in silence, for which Beatrice was grateful. Jane did raise an important question: Now that Beatrice was in London, what was she to do? Her aim was to support Charles and to see him exonerated if she could. But how? Her only thought had been to get to London, and she hadn't spared much time for scheming what she would do afterward. But it was of no consequence. She was better off in London where she could enact a strategy at once—as soon as one came to her.

In that moment London seemed vast and cold. Friendless. Her parents were long since back in New York. Her courtship had been of such short duration, she'd hardly had the chance to *meet* anyone, let alone to make friends and allies. She didn't even know where Charles was being detained, though she suspected that sending a footman to enquire at the family solicitor's office would yield that information readily. It wasn't much, but it was a place to start.

Beatrice tried not to let the silence in the dining room disturb her as she took her meal, but she found herself shuddering with every echo and unexpected creak of a distant floorboard from dinner until she crawled into bed.

She had to find a way to free Charles. The prospect of facing the world alone was unbearable, but worse, the prospect of facing it without him was unthinkable.

＋———＋

The following morning, after Beatrice had breakfast and consumed the vast quantity of coffee she'd requested, she did feel better. The staff might have looked askance at her choice of beverage, but there was no use in pretending she wasn't American. She was happy to take tea in the afternoon. It was a perfectly delightful beverage, especially when prepared with the expertise of Jane or Mrs. Pelham, but mornings were no place for the elegance of tea. A love of bold, black coffee, fashionable or not, was a trait she'd inherited from her father. She'd tried until now to forgo her revivifying morning cup while in England, but no more. She'd spent so much time molding herself to play the role of her lifetime, she'd sacrificed so much of herself, she hardly recognized the face in the mirror.

And she'd have to reclaim herself. One cup of coffee at a time.

But by the time Beatrice had risen from the breakfast table and was about to settle in the parlor to write a message to the solicitor, Lady Millbourne was announced by the butler.

For a moment Beatrice felt a sensation akin to relief, but she remembered Charles's warnings when they'd first met. Lady Millbourne was a woman who brokered in favors. Her good opinion was for hire, and as a result, she could not be trusted. But Beatrice could listen to what she had to say. There might be something of use, a small morsel of truth she could glean from the pile of dross Lady Millbourne was sure to spout.

Beatrice had the butler show their uninvited visitor into the parlor and sent Jane to Mrs. Pelham to pull together a modest tea for the guest.

"Oh, my dear. What a horrendous scandal! You've only just been married, and for such a thing to happen . . ." She kissed Beatrice's cheek with an affected air and accepted a place in the plush plum-colored armchair adjacent to the one Beatrice had claimed.

"Thank you so much for your kindness, Lady Millbourne. You can imagine that the late marquess's death came as such a nasty shock to us all. He was such a vibrant man, or so it seemed."

"Well, poison can take down even the most virile of men, can it not?"

Poison. Though the investigation was ongoing, it was the most plausible explanation. To hear it spoken aloud caused a ball of ice to form in Beatrice's gut. Even more concerning was her realization that someone had been gossip-mongering. Either a member of the family or one of the servants.

"How terrible to find out the truth about one's husband in such a violent fashion. How kind of the dowager and Lord John to let you stay on."

"I don't know where you heard that, my dear Lady Millbourne, but nothing is certain. You understand that when a man with the importance of the late Marquess of Northridge passes on, the medical examiners must act with *such* caution. I'm convinced within myself that the doctors will soon come to the consensus that my poor father-in-law died of natural causes before his time.

It's a tragedy, to be sure, but a tragedy of the common sort, I'm afraid."

"But Lord Alnwick is in prison." Lady Millbourne's whisper sounded something more like a hiss. "Surely you can't believe he's innocent in all this. It's all anyone can talk of."

Exactly what Beatrice feared. The scuttlebutt was running rampant, and none of it would paint Charles in a positive light. Beatrice would plant the grain of truth and hope Lady Millbourne would be the vessel to disseminate it.

"You know even better than I how rumors travel in London. By the time they're widely spread, they resemble the truth as closely as a child's nursery room scribbles resemble a Rembrandt. Lord Northridge is *not* in prison. He is merely being questioned. As the heir to the estate, it's his duty to make sure that nothing is in question as he takes over the helm. I expect if the late marquess had been ten years older, none of this would have been necessary."

That Beatrice didn't know where her husband was being kept for his questioning didn't need to enter the conversation, but she used her husband's proper title as Lady Millbourne had failed to do.

"Such a loyal thing you are. I knew the minute you walked into my ballroom that you were too good for the sort of man who was after an American heiress. I'm just so terribly sorry to be proven right."

"Nothing has been proven," Beatrice insisted. "Nor is it likely to be."

"You're new to the way of things here." She patted Beatrice's hand. "This is not the first time Lord Alnwick has been the subject of unflattering gossip, my dear. I hate to have to be the one to tell you."

A bald-faced lie. She was thrilled to be the bearer of such news, and Beatrice knew it.

"I have no idea what you might possibly mean," Beatrice said. "You warned me months ago that *Lord Northridge* was not the most popular bachelor in London, which I was able to surmise for myself.

Since you never gave me a reason for the reticence people felt about him, I attributed it to his quiet and thoughtful nature, which can easily be misconstrued as his being aloof or even forbidding. An understandable mistake."

"Were it merely a taciturn disposition, all would be forgiven with a title and connections such as his. No. It has to do with his time during the war."

"What of it?" Beatrice tried to maintain an appearance of nonchalance. Charles never spoke of the war, other than to tell her it was the reason he walked with a limp and required a cane, especially in foul weather or when walking a significant distance. He offered no exciting tales of his time in India or proud anecdotes of his service. He wasn't the sort to boast, but he wasn't willing to describe his experience at all.

"He wasn't as eager as some young men to serve, but he was proud enough to do his bit. When he returned, however, injured and far less affable than in the years before he'd gone to war, the rumors weren't kind. I wasn't here, but there was talk that his soldier-servant was killed in the accident that damaged his leg."

"Young Francis's death was tragic," Beatrice said, deliberately betraying that she was aware of that part of the rumor at least. "But that doesn't reflect on Lord Northridge at all. Horrible things happen in war. I don't expect this one was any different."

"The rumor is that Lord Alnwick—Northridge, rather—pushed his man in front of him to save his life. What's more, I hear the young man who was sacrificed for his lordship was rather popular in Birchwick and a beloved only son. The village never forgave him."

"I don't believe for one moment that Lord Northridge is capable of such a thing." Beatrice set her cup down with a forceful *clink*. Heat scorched her face. "What a horrid thing to say about a man who has sustained a lifelong injury in service to his queen and country."

"I agree with you, my dear. But the truth is, it set public opinion against him, and it won't help him now."

"Is any of this meant to be helpful, Lady Millbourne? Or are you simply trying to make me feel even worse than I already do?"

"As your friend, I am urging you to protect yourself as much as you can. If things go badly for the marquess, you'll need to minimize the damage. You need to safeguard your own future."

She was beginning to sound like Charles, but not in any sort of way that would give Beatrice comfort.

"I appreciate your concern, Lady Millbourne. I assure you that I will weather this squall just fine."

Lady Millbourne opened her mouth to speak.

"And so will Charles. But I am sure he'll be glad to know that I have such a devoted and caring friend who has our welfare so close to her heart. I'll be sure to tell him this at the nearest opportunity."

"Very well, Lady Northridge. I won't trespass any longer on your hospitality. Have a pleasant day."

Beatrice flashed her a winning smile but did not return the sentiment.

CHAPTER 13 ———————————

~RULE NO. 13~

A good thespian is prepared for anything that
happens onstage, especially the unexpected.

W hat were you able to uncover, Jane?" Beatrice asked before
she'd even had the time to remove her coat and hat. Servants
had the ability to move more stealthily in society than people of rank,
so Beatrice had prevailed upon Jane to wear her best Sunday dress
and to mingle among the women of the aristocracy doing their shop-
ping at Harrods and all the other fashionable places women went.
The hope was that she'd be able to hear what gossip, if any, was being
spread about Charles and how far it had gone.

"I won't insult you by making it less than it is, milady. He was
talked about quite a lot. They speak as though his lordship is going
to be dragged to the gallows at dawn. No matter that he hasn't even
gone to trial yet."

Beatrice sank onto the plush armchair and buried her face in
her hands. She'd expected this, but the reality of it was still hard to
accept.

"I'm sorry, milady, but I thought you needed to know the truth."

"Of course I do, Jane. The problem is what to do with that truth now that you've brought it to my door. My husband is notorious, and all of London would see him hanged. How does one come back from something like this?" she asked no one at all. She nearly had to swallow back a snicker at the realization of how significant the great affair of the spoiled oyster had seemed such a short time before.

"That wasn't quite everything, milady. A number of people seemed to think that Lord Northridge murdering his father wasn't wholly unexpected or out of character."

"What nonsense is this? Lord Northridge is the kindest, most even-tempered man to ever walk the streets of London. They can't have ever spent a moment in his company."

"That I cannot say, but they seem to imply that his time during the war showed a sort of predisposition toward violent behavior. Something to do with the accident that caused his injuries. I heard talk of it in Birchwick but never believed it and have never chosen to dignify the gossip by speaking of it to you before now."

"I heard the same rumor from Lady Millbourne," Beatrice replied. "It has to be a lie, but it doesn't change that the rumors are there."

"I thought it was better you know than not, milady."

"You're absolutely correct, Jane. Take a few hours to yourself. You've earned them."

Her eyes widened for just a moment. She nodded and left.

The solicitor, having received her message, did not respond with a letter in kind, as Beatrice had expected, but came calling midafternoon.

"Where is Lord Northridge being held?" Beatrice asked without preamble when Mr. Delbert Perkins was seated in the parlor.

"I can assure you he's quite comfortable. He's being held in a private home. Under supervision, given the circumstances, but all is being done to preserve the dignity of his station."

Of course. Not Charles's dignity. The dignity of his position.

"Then surely he can be held here as well as anywhere else," Beatrice said. "If it's such a small matter."

"That won't be possible, Lady Northridge. Surely you understand that the police have their security protocols that must be respected."

"Then when may I see him?" Beatrice pressed.

"In due course. We do not wish to interfere with the investigation, you understand. I would not press the authorities for anything unless it was a matter of grave importance. We want to appear compliant and obliging at all times."

"If he were in *prison*, I'd have the right to see him." Beatrice clanked down her teacup. "This all seems so peculiar. They have had my husband in custody for two weeks. Surely the authorities have had time to question him thoroughly by now. What reason can there possibly be for detaining him still?"

"The matter has become complicated, Lady Northridge. The examinations are conclusive for poisoning, so there is no possibility that the late marquess's death can be left unresolved. There is also a more worrying matter. Though I myself was not consulted on the matter, it would seem the late Lord Northridge had been looking into the possibility of making Lord John the heir in lieu of Lord Alnwick. There is correspondence to this effect with another solicitor, who has verified the signatures as genuine. This means your husband would have had a clear motive to dispatch his father before any legalities might have been set in place. Monkshood is the likely culprit, and that is all but impossible to ingest by accident. There is no question that the late Lord Northridge was murdered."

"That cannot be true," Beatrice objected. "The late marquess was not affectionate to my husband, this is true, but he knew how dedicated his elder son is to the estate. Furthermore, he had no grounds to deny Charles the inheritance. I was under the impression these things could not be changed on a whim."

"That much is true. In order for the estate to pass, Lord Alnwick would have had to step aside in favor of his brother. It isn't frequently done, but there are times when a family can exercise their influence over an older son to step aside. Bribes and threats, most often."

Beatrice nodded. Those tactics were not beyond her parents-in-law or brother-in-law. But they wouldn't work on Charles. "My husband would never step aside to see Lord John ruin the estate. But he would not take his father's life. No estate in Christendom would be worth that."

"Lady Northridge, your defense of your husband does you credit. That he was able to secure the hand of one as devoted and kind as you speaks highly to his character. But I'm afraid that even your strident assurances of his innocence won't be of much influence on the courts. And I have to confess to you, it is very likely this will go to trial."

"I see," was all Beatrice could muster.

"Lady Northridge, I do not know you well, but I hope you will accept some well-meaning advice in the manner in which it is intended. Prepare for the worst. I pray that Lord Northridge's innocence will be proven, but the evidence, though still circumstantial, is damning indeed. Brace yourself, dear lady. You are in for challenging weeks ahead."

Mr. Perkins took his leave, and Beatrice had to will herself not to collapse in the parlor. The solicitor, as kind as his intentions might have been, would have her believe that Charles's fate was sealed. He would be found guilty and be hanged for a crime Beatrice was certain he didn't commit, and John would be free to fritter away generations of his family's legacy.

She summoned the strength to climb the stairs to her room, calling to the butler that she would not be in need of her afternoon tea or her supper either. Ignoring custom, she did not ring for Jane to help her change but slipped into a chemise and tried to lose herself under the piles of goose down in the cavernous bed, despite the early hour. She longed for the release of sleep, but the attempt was futile. She would have to find refuge in her books, as she had done at Leedswick.

She returned to the tome of the fifth marchioness. It called her back time and again. There was something alluring about the melancholy in her words. Something that made Beatrice want to comfort the woman who was so unhappy, trapped in a loveless marriage to a man who was more enamored of his plants than of his wife. Even in her copious notes of the plants she grew in her small section of the garden, there was a sadness in the very loops and swirls of the letters she formed on the pages. Beatrice didn't know how long she'd lost herself in the marchioness's journal, but night had fallen when she sat bolt upright in bed and screamed.

Charles hadn't killed the marquess.

It was the dowager.

+———+

Beatrice paced her room until dawn. When the hour seemed decent, she called for Jane, who seemed shocked by her mistress's early summons.

"I need you to dress me at once and take me to Mr. Perkins's office as soon as he's there." Beatrice flung one of her more practical dresses in navy wool on the bed.

"Of course, milady. But that may not be for a few hours yet. It would be best for one of us to go later and fetch him here if it's so urgent."

"It is," Beatrice said, as Jane laced her corset over her chemise. She looked steadfastly at herself in the mirror. "I have proof of Lord Northridge's innocence."

"That's wonderful. But how did such a thing come about in the middle of the night?"

"Bluebells. When Charles and I were walking in the gardens, one of the maids took a great bundle of bluebells to the dowager."

"They were his lordship's favorite," Jane said, her expression solemn as she helped Beatrice into the stiff gown. "She sent them to him often."

"But don't you see, Jane? Bluebells don't bloom in August. They bloom in the spring. There is only one plant in all of Leedswick's gardens resembling bluebells that blooms in August. Do you know what it is?"

"I couldn't say, milady."

"Monkshood. And it's deadly poisonous. The fifth marchioness planted it in the Poison Garden herself. The dowager sent the flowers to the late marquess herself. She must have known what they were. She's been mistress of the gardens for more than twenty years. She did it deliberately."

"I don't know, milady. Just because she sent the flowers doesn't mean she killed him. She even grew bluebells in the hothouse from time to time to please him. I always thought there was an affection between them beyond what is customary in people . . . of your sort."

Beatrice nodded her comprehension. "Those weren't from the hothouse. I saw them harvested from the outdoor gardens with my own eyes. The dowager knowingly sent poisonous flowers to her husband's room, and he died the very next day. Whether they're strong enough to kill through scent, or perhaps through touching the petals, I don't know. But it seems far more suspicious than any evidence they've contrived against Lord Northridge. This has to give them enough doubt to free him."

"Let us hope you're right, your ladyship. But why don't you stay here? If people see you going to the solicitor's office at such an unfashionable hour, there will be talk. I'll go ready myself and go in your place."

"Thank you, Jane. You're a dear. Truly, you've been the closest thing to a friend that I've had since I came to Leedswick."

"Don't mention it, milady. You're a good and kind mistress, and that's a rare enough thing in this world."

Beatrice spent the rest of the morning pacing. First in her rooms, then in the parlor once she'd had breakfast. She tried, and failed, not to peek from the curtains to scan the passersby, hoping to recognize the unmistakable outline of Perkins's bowler hat. By noon she was growing from restless to impatient, and she was on the point of asking Foster to have the carriage readied to go to Perkins's office herself.

But just as she was about to issue the order, there was a flurry of motion as the front door opened.

Jane has come with the solicitor.

Beatrice sprinted to the foyer, the marchioness's book in hand, ready to make the case for her husband's innocence, but it was not Jane and the solicitor.

It was Charles.

Unbothered by the presence of staff and the ability of anyone on the street to see them from the windows, Beatrice launched herself into his arms. She sobbed into his chest, unable to form the words she'd been longing to say for two weeks.

"All is well, my love," he cooed. "I'm here now."

At last, when she was better able to master herself, she took a deep breath. "I knew you were innocent. I know who did it, Charles. We need the authorities in Birchwick to seize your mother as soon as may be."

"There won't be any need of that. The murderer has confessed."

"But if it wasn't your mother . . . ?"

"Your maid, Jane. She signed a confession two hours ago."

"Never. That can't be."

"I wouldn't have thought it, but apparently she overheard John and Mother trying to goad Father into blackmailing me into forfeiting my place more than once. She rummaged through Father's office and found papers drawn up trying to prove me incompetent to inherit. She was terrified they would succeed, and she didn't want to see John as lord and master at Leedswick. She thought the only way to prevent it was to kill Father and ensure that I took over before Mother and John could enact their plans."

"Perish the thought," Beatrice said. "But it doesn't seem likely that she'd go to such lengths just to save *your* birthright."

"It's more personal than that. My brother, like many of his sort, enjoys pressuring women in service to the family to . . . entertain him. It usually ends badly for the maid in question. One of those maids was Maud Kelsey."

"Jane's sister?" Beatrice remembered that Jane had spoken of her sister's employment at the castle.

"Jane's sister," he confirmed. "She was a senior housemaid at Leedswick and fell pregnant with John's child three years ago. The housekeeper sacked her, with Mother's blessing, as is usually the case when this sort of thing happens. Poor Maud spent eighteen months trying to make ends meet, living in workhouses and such with her infant daughter in tow. Both mother and child perished of consumption last winter."

"I had no idea. When Jane mentioned her sister, it always sounded as though she were living."

"Jane clearly took the loss to heart. Maud and the child were the last of her family. She must not have felt like she had much to lose. Though she did express regret about casting any shadow of scandal on you in particular. She was fond of you."

"And I of her," Beatrice said. "You'll forgive me the morbid question, but why kill the marquess and not John? If he were gone, your inheritance would have been safe."

"She worried, and not without reason, that if she failed to act before Father altered his will, then I would be irrevocably cut out from the inheritance, even if John predeceased me. Once disinherited, I could not reinherit. And she didn't trust that some distant cousin would be any better than John."

Beatrice shivered involuntarily. The poor woman had truly been driven by desperation. "Oh, Charles. What will happen to her?"

"She's a confessed murderer, my love. There is only so much leniency they can offer in such cases." He stroked the side of her face with his finger. "She switched his afternoon tea with a cup that had been laced with monkshood and enough sugar so he wouldn't taste it."

"She mentioned he was fond of sugar. She knows so much about us all."

"She was attentive and kind. Just as her sister had been. It's a horrible thing all around."

"We must be able to do something for her," Beatrice urged. "If she confessed, surely a good lawyer can plead her case and have her sentence reduced."

"Perkins is on the case already. I've instructed him to make her seem as sympathetic as he can and hope for leniency from the courts. I fear the best she can hope for is that they offer her a plea on a lesser charge. Transport to Australia isn't an option any longer, but even the strictest courts are loath to hang a woman."

Beatrice shuddered in her husband's arms. "She didn't have to confess. They had no reason to suspect her, but she confessed anyway."

"And that will be her best hope for survival."

EPILOGUE

J ane's trial was one of the most infamous of the decade. The stories of John's cruelties to the women in service to Leedswick went far beyond what even Charles could have imagined. Beatrice stayed in London, and Charles too, in a show of support for their former maid. There could be no doubt she would be found guilty, but the circumstances surrounding the case garnered her so much support from the court that she was sentenced to ten years in a women's penitentiary, almost like a reform school for grown women, rather than execution by hanging.

It still seemed unfair to Beatrice that Jane should be forced to waste such a significant portion of her life in some dank institution, but a chance at life was certainly better than death. Beatrice could not deny that Perkins had done his level best by Jane. He'd shown his skill in the courtroom and become one of the most venerated solicitors in London because of the case.

John's reputation suffered greatly because of the revelations from the trial—his misdeeds with the female staff, his plots against his brother, the rumors he willfully spread, not only about the death of the late marquess but about his brother's injuries in the Indian rebellion. He was decried in the papers, and indeed in every parlor in Mayfair, as the most profligate scoundrel to walk the streets of London. Not a door in polite English society would ever open to him again.

The dowager was tainted as well, for it was well known that she'd always favored John over Charles and did her best to sway the late Lord Northridge against her elder son. Her circle of friends shrank, so she and John decided to try their fortunes in America. Occasionally word got back to Beatrice of her brother-in-law and mother-in-law's exploits, and it seemed that despite the distance and the change in scenery, their characters were very much unchanged by the scandal that enveloped them.

Jane was allowed to write to Beatrice, and indeed they continued a very congenial relationship by correspondence. Jane was able to teach the women of lesser schooling how to read and form their letters and found a good deal of satisfaction in her work. Beatrice was thrilled that her former maid and confidante had found some purpose in her confinement and hoped that Jane's hard work and good behavior would earn her further leniency.

Once the trial had concluded, Beatrice and Charles had eagerly returned to Leedswick, where duty awaited them. The staff met the return of Lord and Lady Northridge with no small amount of enthusiasm. The village, however, did not welcome them home with the warmth they deserved. Their loyalty to the memory of Francis was too steadfast. While Charles's reputation might have been cleared of wrongdoing in the death of his father, it was harder to absolve oneself from the atrocities of war.

As they walked hand in hand through the cavernous front entrance to the castle, Beatrice felt her lungs fill with air more fully than they had in years.

"Happy to be home?" Charles planted a kiss on his wife's cheek.

"More than I could ever express," she said. And it was true. She was home. "Though does the cold welcome in the village bother you, my love? So much of what you worked for was for their protection and benefit."

"And they will know none of it. I wonder if their resentment of me doesn't give them some comfort. If so, I will not try to take that comfort from them. Long before me, the curse of war permeated the very stones of Leedswick, and I fear that it will never be washed clean, even long after the fighting has come to its end. For so it scars the very souls of men. I shall leave the people of Birchwick in peace if it is their wish."

"I hope you'll put these thoughts in your journal, dearest. It will do good for your soul." Beatrice pressed a kiss to his cheek.

"A blessing on good wives who fret for their husbands' souls. But what of yours? Will you be content here tucked out of the way? It may become rather tiresome, especially if we are personae non gratae in the village."

"We shall have the London season for society," Beatrice said. "And a bit of solitude would be just the balm my soul requires when it is over. And one of my first duties as marchioness will be to put a warning sign on that charming section of the gardens."

"You won't rip them out entirely?"

"If you wish it, as a tribute to your father's memory, I will. But I'd hate to undo the fifth marchioness's legacy if you don't."

"Leave it, then. It won't bring him back," Charles said.

"You miss him, don't you?"

"I do. No matter how flawed he was, he was my father."

"And he raised you to be a man of duty and honor. That counts for much in my view." Unabashedly, she kissed her husband gently on the lips in full view of the staff.

"How lucky I am to have married you," Charles said as they climbed the stairs. "Few women would have shown the tenacity you did. The loyalty. I'll never be able to repay you."

"I'm sure you'll think of something, darling," she replied.

"I do believe I owe you a proper wedding night." He lowered his voice to a whisper. "It seems the least I can do . . ."

✦————✦

Despite their best efforts, the village never warmed to them. The tinge of scandal never did wash clean, and with John unable to recant the rumors he'd spread about his brother's war service, there was little Charles or Beatrice could say to endear themselves to the people of Birchwick. Though Charles had hoped that Beatrice would be beloved by those in the marquisate, the belief that Charles had let his soldier-servant take the fall for him was too grave a sin for the villagers to forgive, even with the passage of time.

The shadow of rumors would always loom over them. The whispers would never cease. But Beatrice had found her match in Charles, and that mattered far more to her than any empty words that might be spoken. Their love was not the whirlwind sort like she thought she felt with Thomas. No, it was built on a firm foundation of duty and loyalty—to each other, and to Leedswick. And in this duty, Beatrice found her purpose. And in this purpose, she found solace at last.

Because for once, the only character she had to play was herself.

THE MEMORY KEEPERS —

1917

Love takes off masks that we fear we cannot live without and know we cannot live within.

—JAMES BALDWIN, THE FIRE NEXT TIME

CHAPTER 1 ———————————

LEEDSWICK CASTLE, NORTHUMBERLAND, ENGLAND
JULY 1917

Flinging aside the trailing ends of the paisley scarf twined about her head, Elena Hamilton raised her hand to the polished brass knocker floating dead center on the thick though rather plain oak door and knocked. Why rich folks insisted that simplicity was the key to elegance utterly escaped her mind's comprehension. The "key to boredom" was a better description. A vibrant dash of vermilion—that's what this door needed. A color that beat away the dreariness and boldly declared itself to the world.

The door swung open. "The servants' entrance is around back," intoned a deep voice from the entrance.

Elena centered her attention on the starched penguin blocking the doorway. Smiling brightly, she swept her long, gauzy teal skirt to the side and dipped a curtsy. "Oh, I'm not a servant. My name is Elena Hamilton and I've been"—the door slammed in her face—"commissioned for artist services." Frowning, she straightened. This was the correct address? Oh, balderdash. What if she was at the wrong door?

She took a step back and shielded her eyes against the brilliant light reflecting off the ochre blocks of sandstone for better judgment of the situation. It proved pointless as the walls of the ancient keep

123

blocked out all surrounding landmarks, which more or less proved she was precisely where she ought to be as no other castles of this dimension existed this far north of Windsor.

Stuffing her art box under her arm, she rummaged inside her brocade carpetbag, fingers shuffling over paintbrushes, loose bits of paper, a paint pot with wet paint still clinging to the rim. Aha! Found it. A crisp yet slightly rumpled envelope of the richest cream stamped with the Alnwick crest and a few smudged fingerprints. She quickly smoothed it against her skirt, managing only to smear the prints more. It would have to suffice. Smile dimmed but not diminished, she raised the knocker and let it fall. The door opened.

"My name is Elena Hamilton, the artist. Well, not *the* artist. An artist. Painter really." The door started to shut. She thrust the envelope into the closing gap. "I received an invitation from the Marchioness of Northridge."

The door halted as the penguin stared down at the envelope as if he could deny its existence. Or perhaps it was the paint fingers. Polite society never seemed to appreciate the evidence of hard work. "Is that so?"

"Yes, on behalf of a Major Tobias Alnwick."

The penguin's lips pursed into a flat line as he stuck his sharp nose into the air and opened the door. "Please come in."

The entrance hall was a feast of artistry spun from white marble, red carpets, intricate moldings, arched ceilings, and a cascading staircase. Opulence in the bold strokes of clean lines and geometric trimming.

"Then you must find him immediately. He cannot simply disappear at his pleasure. My son has responsibilities." An older woman with a rope of pearls strung about her neck and corseted perfectly into her expensive floor-sweeping dress descended the marble stairs with a footman but stopped abruptly when she saw Elena. "A visitor."

"Yes, ma'am." Elena shifted the art box under her arm as it grew heavier by the minute. Packing the oils, chalks, *and* pastes was unnecessary in hindsight. The woman continued to stare at her. "Have I come at a bad time? The card did say two o'clock."

"Bad time?" The creases on the woman's forehead immediately ironed themselves to a mask of hospitality as she folded her hands in front of her immaculately cut gown of powder blue that had been the height of fashion before the war. "Of course not, dear. Whatever makes you think so?"

"I . . . um . . ." Elena shook off the less-than-customary welcome. If she could greet a half-clothed Modigliani at the door while fending off Soutine from bringing in another animal carcass for inspiration, she could certainly go along with her new hostess's pretense of serenity. "I'm Elena Hamilton. Thank you so much for extending me an invitation to come to your lovely home."

The woman's polite expression broke into one of elation. "My dear Miss Hamilton! It is we who are indebted to your gracious acceptance. I am Lady Northridge. Please do come in." Motioning the footman on his way, she gathered her skirt in a bejeweled hand and made to retreat back up the stairs. "Stokes, take Miss Hamilton's things to the Painted Room."

Stokes—the penguin—eyed the travel case in question as if it were a poisonous insect in need of a good squashing beneath his well-polished heel. A bug indeed. The bag was a gift to Elena's mama from a highly respected Roma grandmother when they traveled with the caravan around Italy one summer. Mama had sculpted a clay model of the grandmother's wagon and allowed seven-year-old Elena to paint all the decorative colors and designs. A golden season it had been, filled with Tuscan rust, purple grapes, scarves of paisley, and tanned bare feet.

Following Lady Northridge up the stairs, Elena tried her best to keep her eyes from bouncing out of her head as all she truly wished to do was stare agog at the plethora of treasures hanging from the walls. Landscapes rolling, portraits ruminating, monarchs reigning, battlefields weeping. Rembrandt, Raphael, Manet, Botticelli, Rubens, and van Eyck. Priceless works of art in all their glory that were a mere wrapping compared to the sitting room she entered. Red-and-gold-flocked damask wallpaper, black lacquer trim, chandeliers, and gilt frames. Lavishness bidding the masters to shame.

"This is Lord Northridge." Lady Northridge indicated a man sitting in an overstuffed chair by the window.

Placing his newspaper aside, Lord Northridge rose and nodded. "Welcome to Leedswick. I hope you'll find your stay with us short but comfortable."

Never having been in the presence of a marquess, Elena bobbed a quick curtsy. "I'm sure it will be, sir. Comfortable, that is. It's rather difficult to determine the duration as each project requires its own time schedule."

"Yes, well, just so." After harrumphing deep in his throat, he sat and thumbed open his newspaper.

"Won't you sit down?" Lady Northridge settled onto a red-and-gold-striped couch, picked up a silver teapot, and poised its spout over a delicate china cup. "Tea?"

Elena took the seat opposite her on a matching couch. "Thank you." Coffee with milk was her preference, having sipped the strong brew at café tables in Paris and on Italian terraces, but it was hardly considered fashionable in England—tea being the quintessential English drink. When in Rome, as it were.

After scooping a sugar cube into her cup and gently stirring with a spoon, Lady Northridge took a sip. "I cannot begin to tell you how grateful we are that you accepted our invitation. I realize it is customary for the"—she took another sip as if searching for a word—"men to come to your shop in London for their appointments, but Lord Northridge and I wish for this process to go as smoothly as possible.

Tobias—Lord Alnwick—has been through so much already that privacy can only be what's best for him now."

A bit of privacy for the men to grow accustomed to their injuries and the changes they brought about was well and fine, but Elena could recall in her single year of painting masks that not one of her clients benefited from locking themselves away. Then again, unsolicited advice from well-intentioned family members never went over well either. "I can assure you, ma'am, that the Tin Noses Shop respects the privacy of its patrons. Discretion and restoration are our top priorities."

The Masks for Facial Disfigurement Department located within the 3rd London General Hospital was a marvel of its kind. Employing sculptors, casting specialists, plaster mold makers, and painters, the newly established workshop worked tirelessly to recreate missing or mangled facial attributes for the returning Tommies. Poor chaps. Most of them proclaimed it a fate worse than death. That they would rather have an arm or a leg blown off by one of those horrible mortars.

It was one of the reasons Elena had applied for a position at the groundbreaking shop. So many women applied for nursing or driving ambulances, but she wanted to offer her skills in a different way. She now found great pleasure in providing dignity through a new glass eye or molded chin to remind these brave men that life, in all its beauty and despite its offensiveness, was worth living.

"Restoration, yes. Can you guarantee that you will return Lord Alnwick to his . . ." Lady Northridge fluttered her hand as if grasping for the proper word. "To himself?"

Ah, so that was it. Denial by clinging to an emotional response rather than reality. She would do the Expressionists proud. In instances like these it was difficult to decipher who needed to adjust more. The family or the soldier.

Aimie K. Runyan, J'nell Ciesielski, and Rachel McMillan

Elena set down her teacup. "These soldiers have suffered terribly in this war, and they carry home wounds ghastly beyond imagination. Perhaps more so than a missing arm or blindness. We at the shop do our very best to give the men back their dignity. The best sculptors in the country cast and mold the missing piece, and the artist paints it to each man's likeness. Before the war facial reconstruction was unheard of except among surgeons practicing a crude skill. Anna Coleman Ladd and Francis Derwent Wood have refined it in a matter of months out of necessity, allowing these brave men to venture out into society once again without fear of revulsion from those they pass on the street." *Not to mention loved ones.*

"Making them whole again." The woman smiled politely as if she knew what Elena said was true, but belief was having trouble taking root.

"I believe if we can help them to *feel* more like themselves, then that is more important than looking like themselves." Thankfully she was spared another polite remark when a maid glided into the room and bent low to her mistress's ear to whisper.

Lady Northridge jerked away. "He said what?" The maid continued to whisper, but Lady Northridge shooed her away. "Very well. Inform my son, when you find him, that he is expected in the library before dinner for a proper introduction to Miss Hamilton. Greetings are not to be left said over soup."

The maid bobbed a quick curtsy and scuttled off.

Fixing her smile back in place, Lady Northridge rose from the couch. Tea was over. "I believe you might desire a rest. No doubt your journey from London was tiresome."

Delighted to be acquitted of the watery tea brew, Elena stood. "Quite the opposite. I find travel exhilarating to the soul as one shakes off the dust from what has been seen to discover new roads of adventure."

"Ah, well, perhaps you might want to change from your travel

128

costume." Casting her gaze from Elena's unkempt crown to her paint-splotched toes, Lady Northridge's tone shifted upward on the last two words as if she wasn't quite certain they described the outfit appropriately.

Elena could point out the breezy comfort of her Moroccan-inspired kaftan and overlay embroidered vest, but she had the distinct feeling that the word *ease* had yet to slip past the confines of Lady Northridge's corset. "A refreshing splash of water to the face would do me wonders."

Leaving behind the elegant room, Lady Northridge guided her along a labyrinth of corridors and sweeping staircases that bypassed all manner of paintings that begged Elena to linger over the deep shades of indigo, brilliant violets, and warm junipers. Unlike the pristine ones in the entrance hall, the frames here hung crooked with thick dust gathered in the corners.

"I thought you might appreciate this chamber the most: the Painted Room." Her hostess opened a door at the end of another long corridor and stepped into a room of soft pear with painted pink and gold flowers trailing across the walls. Gauzy white covered the bay of windows and four-poster bed while a plush rug of blush and lapis rested on top of a polished walnut floor. "It has the best morning light. I'm told that is ideal for painting."

Elena walked to the center of the room and slowly turned in a circle of awe so as not to miss a single detail. "Shall I be painting in here?"

"Oh no, dear. We would not dream of exposing you to the scandal of a man sitting in your room. My son is very much a gentleman, but the suggestion is highly indecent." The woman's cheeks pinked at the mere thought. "We've set up a studio for you on the third floor in the south wing for complete solitude. You won't be disturbed there."

Quiet or noisy, men or women, Elena had learned long ago to work with all manner of distractions. Mama had run an open salon when they'd lived in Paris. It was a small apartment with two levels propped between a café and a cabaret in the heart of Montmartre, a convenient stopover for artists and musicians and enlightened thinkers after they had coffee and before they took in a show. Edgar Degas would jitter in after four cups to deposit his paintbrushes and lumps of clay on the kitchen table across from Raoul Dufy, while La Goulue perfected her infamous cancan dance in the sitting room to the tune of a scratchy gramophone belting on the stairway. Elena would make her rounds saying hello to the inflow of guests before she meandered to the balcony to lose herself in paint and canvas.

Elena brushed a hand over a delicate frill of petals painted on the wall. "It's beautiful. Monet himself could not have done finer." As Lady Northridge's brow puckered, Elena said, "A brilliant artist with an eye for landscape. I believe you have one hanging on the landing."

The woman's brow smoothed. "Ah. If you have need of anything else at all, do not hesitate to ring. Your stay is to be as comfortable as possible." She stepped for the door, then turned back and grasped Elena's hand. "I am most glad you are here." With a gentle squeeze, she was gone.

Noting her travel case and art case had been delivered, Elena poured a bit of the fresh water from a pitcher into the porcelain basin and splashed it over her face. Then she attempted to poke several escaped frizzy curls back into the confines of the paisley scarf wrapped around them. They refused and she didn't cajole. *"Never force your features to be anything but what they are,"* Mama had often said.

With the late-afternoon sun beckoning her out of doors, Elena spent a good half hour trying to retrace her steps to the main hall. When that failed, she sorted through several rooms that looked a little worse for wear on the ground floor until finding one with a door that led outside. Where outside she didn't precisely know, but the sun was golden, wispy clouds scudded across the sky, and the grass presented a rich emerald that spread happiness through her heart. The best places were often discovered when lost.

She slid her feet down the grassy slope, then hopped off the short drop-off enforced by a stone retaining wall to where the ground evened out to a yawning expanse of unfettered space. At least until it was halted by a towering stone wall with crenellated toppers and watchtowers that served during a bygone time of invading hordes.

Ah, the pleasurable history of these northern lands. Speaking of pleasurable . . . she planted her hands on the ground and turned a cartwheel. Again and again. The lovely blades of grass poked through her fingers and tickled her palms, vibrant lime striking against her pale, freckled skin.

"Trying out for the traveling circus?"

A man's voice rolled down the hill after her. Her long skirt tangled in her feet as they flew over her head, toppling her in a rather inelegant display of surprise. She landed flat on her bottom with the ends of her hair scarf trailing over her face.

"Trying to scare unsuspecting women to death?" Laughing, she flipped the scarf ends over her shoulder and stood to brush bits of grass from her gauzy skirt. The man stood tucked in the shadow of the castle as he leaned against the wall. She must have walked directly by him and not even noticed. "I did try for the cirque once. In Italy when I was six. I was determined to be a juggling unicyclist who balanced on a tightrope."

"Did you fulfill your dream?" His voice was deep and the tone proper to signify an elite boarding school education with just a dash of roughness to root him in this northern territory.

"It turns out that riding a single wheel while juggling requires greater balance than one realizes at first. I've developed a slight fear of spinning ever since."

"Says the lady somersaulting through the air."

"My juggling days might have ended before they ever began,

but it was never my true passion, and a true passion is one you can never walk away from." After hoisting herself over the low wall, she walked back up the slope to where he remained in shadow.

"Not only a lady of daring but one of convictions. Pray tell, what is this passion that has captured you in ways that defying death forty feet above the ground could not hope to achieve?"

"Art."

"The artist. I'd forgotten you were to arrive today." Where before his voice had been a warm blue like sun on the ocean, the clouds set in and colored the blue to gray.

Gray would never do on a day such as this.

"I see my entrance has proven monumentally memorable already." She flourished a curtsy. So many in one day. "Elena Hamilton."

He made no move away from the shadowed wall. "Tobias Alnwick."

"The elusive man himself. Do you know you've a horde of maids out searching for you at this very moment?"

"I've no wish to be found; hence the reason I'm standing outside in a quiet recess of the castle."

"Well, found you I did and glad I am for it, for you are the very gentleman I've come to see. Though it might help if I could see you without all this mysteriousness better suited to a misty moor. Will you not come out from the shadows?"

He hesitated. "I suppose now is as good a time as any to see what you're working with." Briefly touching a dark object at the side of his face, he stepped away from the wall and into the light. "Hope you don't frighten easily, though in that garb something tells me you don't."

She had to look up and up to see the full height of him. He was slender with long legs that looked as if they could cross hilltops in a single stride and broad shoulders that hinted at manual labor uncommon for a nobleman. He possessed a beautiful shade of umber hair with glints of hickory that curled unfashionably over his forehead and below his ears. The left side of his face was lost beneath half a mask that covered his forehead down to his cheek. The skin she could see was a jagged mesh clawing from beneath the mask down to his throat. Yet it was his singular right eye that drew her in with a most delectable shade of brown surrounding a golden center. Her fingers ached for a brush to capture such richness.

She smiled broadly. "I'm delighted to see *who* I am working with."

His lips twisted with condescension as he touched the mask once more. "As flattering as I once might have found it to have a woman visit solely on my behalf, we both know you are here for one reason. To fix me."

"In that you are mistaken. I'm not here to fix you, for that would require you to be broken. Which you are not. A bit scratched and bent, perhaps, but then, who of us isn't?"

"Daring, zealous, and optimistic. A laborious trio of personality characteristics."

"Hardly. It keeps life stimulating."

"I've had all the stimulation I can handle for one lifetime." He moved past her and walked down the slope to stand at the retaining wall she had recently jumped from.

Ignoring his relocation to be alone, she joined him. "I warn you, Lord Northridge—or is it Major? No, Earl something? The entire train ride here I could not determine a conclusive answer as to how to address you—I do not take well to grumps and consider it a personal challenge to raise them from their doldrums. Which is it you prefer?" Standing next to him, she realized her head barely cleared his shoulders.

"I prefer neither grump nor doldrums."

"Lord or Major?"

He sighed with the weight of the world as he offered her only the undamaged half of his profile. "My rank is a reminder of the past four years, which I should very much like to forget. Nor do I care much for the bowing and scraping demanded among the nobler set, though I am titled Lord Alnwick since you care to know."

She studied the handsome bone structure of his face and the way the tanned skin molded perfectly over the planes. The bluish-gray tinge of stubble along the jaw and curving over the top lip, a lip that balanced atop a much fuller bottom one. Once more her fingers itched for a brush to capture the contrasts of shape and color. "To forget our past is to forget a part of ourselves."

"Do you have an adage for every possible point in conversation, or does my pathetic state inspire pithy ideals?"

"'You are only pathetic if you believe to be so.' Franz Kafka told me that once when my mother and I took a trip through Bohemia in the summer of 1911. Or was it Rouault when he came to paint the glass doors of the cabaret next to our Parisian apartment? I, for one, do not believe your state to be so."

The muscles in his jaw flexed. "Then you have not seen darkness."

A chill swept over her. The blood on Mama's lips. The way they moved from place to place. She had not known it as a child, but their frequent travels were to stay one step ahead of *him*. A second chill shivered down her spine. A rope. A man's single leg dangling life-lessly. She pushed the images away. "But I have. I simply choose not to dwell there."

"But you have dwelt other places far less sinister. Bohemia, Paris, London, and now, for a rather short time, Northumberland. Tell me, how did you come by a travel itinerary most only dream about?"

Elena twirled the tails of her scarf, a gift from Mama on her sixteenth birthday. They'd gone to the market after selling one of Mama's sculptures, and she had given Elena free rein to choose from the rainbows of colors. "My mother was a bit of a free spirit. Never in one place for too long, always off on the next adventure seeking love, life, and beauty. She knew everyone of interest, particularly those traveling the fringes of society, for those are the ones living to the fullest without constraints and rules. We always came back to Paris."

"Is she there now, or does she reside with you in London?"

Elena smiled sadly and shook her head, the scarf drooping over her shoulder. "Mama rests in the dappled light of Cimetière du Père-Lachaise. I came to London a few months after she died when war broke out and my art school was closed."

He turned to look at her. The smooth profile expanding into an added half of skin twisted red and white from the survival fight of battle. The gold shone bright from within the brown richness of his eye. "My condolences for your loss."

"Thank you." Though death came as a relief after tuberculosis had ravaged Mama's beautiful soul and Elena's entire world turned topsy-turvy. It never helped to wallow, so she did the only thing she could—she brushed off the sadness like yesterday's dried paint flakes and spread her arms wide. "She would have adored this. Climbing up to those ramparts and staring across the vista. It must offer a stunning view all the way to the North Sea."

His gaze followed hers to the ramparts. "I haven't been up there in some time."

"Whyever not? If I lived here, I would never come down from such a view."

"Gazing over a parapet is too much of a reminder of . . . well, places I'd rather forget."

"That's a shame." She squinted at the wall, imagining burnt orange, rosy red, and butter yellow pouring over it in the mornings. "I bet the sunrise is spectacular to capture. Watercolor, no, oils. Do you know if the studio has stocked turpentine and a portable easel?"

"My mother arranged for all the supplies you might need for the studio, according to the list you provided her when you agreed to come." He gestured to the castle keep behind them. "Would you care to view it now to ensure everything is in order?"

"I'm sure it's lovely. Besides, I enjoy a good surprise."

"Some things are best not left to surprise." He touched his mask as seriousness descended over his expression. "Would you not like to see what you've come all this way for? To gird yourself for the morrow as it were?"

How many times had it taken before he'd learned to brace himself for reactions to his injury? Did he sense right away the disfigurement as he was carried on a stretcher to safety? Or was it a naïve nurse who'd failed to control herself in the operating theater? A well-intentioned hospital visit from a friend gone horribly wrong?

"The only thing I need to gird myself for is breaking in a new brush, as my favorite one snapped a few days ago and I was forced to purchase a new one. Dreadful things with their stiff bristles and smooth handles. I cannot tell you the heartache of losing your favorite filbert brush." She gently touched his arm. "Everything else will keep for now."

The shrill notes of a trumpet blasted the air, bouncing off the stone walls and pinging the ears of all those unfortunate enough to stand in the vicinity.

Elena clapped her hands to her ringing ears. "*Zut alors!* What is that?"

"The dressing alert. Most families employ a simple gong, but the Alnwicks never do anything based on simplicity. Besides that, a trumpet is the only instrument to be heard over the vast grounds." He turned and pointed to the highest turret on the castle. "Vincent, the first footman, stands there and blows his horn into a megaphone. The horn was a gift to my family from King James I for our help in the Union of the Crowns."

"The only heirloom I was gifted was a candlestick holder my mother claimed would summon the fairies when lit."

The trumpet blared again.

"Second warning shot. It would be wise for us to head in. Mother can be temperamental if the starter course is served late." He turned back for the castle. "What time shall we begin on the morrow?"

"Ten o'clock sharp. Midday light is preferable for mask work. It doesn't allow for softening or hiding." He blanched. Elena rushed to cover her thoughtless words. All these months working at the shop ensuring she spoke only comfort to the men, and after finally achieving her first true commission, she inserted her foot directly into her mouth. "What I mean is, it allows me to see the nuances of color and texture that are a requirement for mask painting."

He gripped the door latch, knuckles straining white. "No, Miss Hamilton. I believe you had it correct the first time. After all, what are these masks for if not hiding?"

"Forgive me, I did not . . ."

He opened the door, then stepped aside for her to enter. His gaze strained far away from hers. "Come. Before the dogs are released in pursuit of our whereabouts."

CHAPTER 2 ——————————————————

Opening and snapping closed the gold pocket watch, Tobias paced the art studio. Ten twenty-one. They were to begin at ten o'clock sharp, was that not what the artist had said? Yet she remained missing in action.

He stopped at the bank of windows taking up the length and breadth of the back wall. Situated high on the third floor of the only rounded turrets that weren't crumbling from within, it was easy to gaze well past the keep, lawn, and walls to the rolling hills of green and trees beyond. Places he had not ventured since returning home. Before that he'd not been allowed outside the sterile walls of St. Matthew's in London, and before that it had been a canvas tent in the muds of France.

A canvas tent where another man should have lain and not him.

He ran his thumb methodically over the pocket watch. Oh, the hours, memories, and losses it had counted in the past few years.

Though his memories had been irrevocably tied to nightmares. Could he never look at the watch again without hearing failure ticking its seconds? Could he never sleep again without feeling the bone-shaking cold of the trenches? Could he never gaze at a field again without seeing the bodies mutilated by bullets and mortar shells?

He turned away from the window, snapping open the pocket watch and closing it tight in his fist. Ten twenty-five. This mask could be a way of severing the tie between memories and horror. If not severing, at least loosening the knot by hiding the ugliness marring him that was every day a reminder.

If the woman ever showed up.

Feet raced along the corridor. Miss Hamilton flew into the room like an exotic bird startled from a tree. Dressed in another color-ful array of flowing robes with a silver-studded leather belt cinched around her waist, she reached up to smooth the wild hair clouding around her face in a blaze of unfettered orange.

She sailed straight at him and kissed both his cheeks in turn. "Good morning. My apologies for tardiness. I had the best of inten-tions of rising to paint the early sun, but I forgot I have the dreadful habit of oversleeping. By the time I arrived outside, the sun was well above the horizon. I rushed to capture what I could, but the hour was later than expected and, well, I'm late." Her stream of words cut off. "Whatever is the matter? Are you ill?"

Tobias's muscles refused to move, so shocked was he by the feel of her lips brushing his skin. The last time a woman had come so intimately near was before the war. When Nina had gazed at him in adoration as she tearfully bid him goodbye at the train station. He touched a hand to the puckered skin of his left cheek. "No, I am not ill, merely unaccustomed to being greeted in the European fashion."

"It's ever so much more welcoming, don't you agree? More than a handshake or a stiff bow."

"The whole of England and its stiff-upper-lip occupants might choose to disagree with you. Here, formality is considered welcom-ing as it proves respect for those you are meeting."

"If you don't put them to sleep first." She winked, stunning him further.

He took a step back to put distance between them. Closeness had been the indulgence of youth taken for granted. Receiving an embrace from his mother, slapping friends on the back after a game well played, sitting close to a pretty girl. Shaking the hands of each of his men in the trench before going over the top. The idea now of such intimacies was too raw, too vulnerable. During his months lying in that hospital bed, not knowing if he was to live or die, detachment had become his ally. If one allowed nothing close, people or emotions, one had nothing to lose.

"For one uninterested in formalities," he said, "you executed a rather showy curtsy yesterday upon our meeting. The king himself would be hard-pressed to find fault with it."

"That's because I was taught by a queen. Sinfai Lovell, Queen of the Romani. Mama was serving as an assistant to a great painter at the time who had been commissioned to paint the countryside, and Queen Sinfai was kind enough to tell us the most beautiful spots to seek out. In the evenings she taught me to dance."

"How old were you at the time?"

"Six or seven. I used to practice for hours, imagining myself a princess each time. It's become a habit. The grand curtsy, that is, not imagining myself a princess. A tiara would never sit atop this mane." She combed a hand distractedly through the frizz of orange curls and circled the room. "Now, let's see what we have here. Paints. Good. Easel, brushes, turpentine, water, round palette for paint mixing. Good, good. Your mother has done a marvelous job of collecting all that I need without me needing to use any of the paints I brought. With this magnificent light streaming in through these windows, it will be a pleasure to create in here."

An unexpected bout of nerves hit him. It was the same gut-churning feeling as the first time a mortar had whistled over his head. "Where would you like me to sit?"

Clearly she did not share his anxieties as she waved a hand at him while trying to untangle a paint-splotched satchel slung over her shoulder. "By the window, but not in direct sunlight."

Choosing a straight-backed chair over the more cushioned one available, Tobias carried it to the window and set it down just outside the touch of sunlight.

"I don't see the final cast." She glanced once more over the supplies on the table.

"Mr. Wood sent a note saying the rendering of my face should arrive later today."

"No matter. I prefer to paint once I've thoroughly assessed the area for myself and selected and mixed the appropriate colors. For that I'll need to examine you. Rather closely, I might warn."

"A warning this time yet none for the kiss earlier." The words came out quicker than he could stop them. As if a part of his old, easier self cracked through.

"A bit of cheek lurking beneath the surface. Splendid. I like to be kept on my toes." Turning her back to him, she bent over a box of brushes. "You may remove the mask."

Words more terrifying than the battle cry "Over the top!" ringing down the trenches. One year ago nearly to the month since he'd shouted that command for the last time. A command he'd given countless times before, but on that hot July morning, it had sent all his men—save three—to their deaths on the Somme. One year ago since Tobias had raced to save the life of his company's quartermaster stuck in the quagmire of mud, only he was too late before the mortar fell. The metal struck his face, the sound of crunched bone like a glass bottle dropped into a porcelain bathtub as a barrel of whitewash tipped over his vision.

Phelps had been killed instantly and Tobias had lived. He'd welcomed the monstrous scars and loss of an eye stowed away beneath a mask as a way to hide from his shame of not reaching Phelps in time, of not taking better care of his men. Casualties of war were an ugly truth, but the guilt haunted him. At least here behind the mask and behind his ancestral walls he could remain unseen, without the world staring and whispering, pointing at him in terror and reminding him of his nightmares all over again.

Without the mask there was no hiding.

With shaking hands he reached to untie the bindings from behind his head. They slipped free, exposing his raw skin. He wadded the soft black material in his fist and waited for judgment.

Rattling the brushes in their box one last time, Miss Hamilton turned and crossed the room, pulling the scarf from her neck. Today it was pale green with shots of pink. She gathered her hair into a swirl atop her head, and with a few brisk wraps, the scarf secured the mass in place. Or most of it. Several pieces sprang down her neck and over her ears.

She stopped directly in front of him on a cloud of fragrant wild violets. "Now I see you."

She didn't blink. She didn't frown. Didn't make a disgusted noise or turn away in tears. She merely stared at him as the world once did. Without a mortar shell shredding the entire left side of his face and gouging out his eye. He pressed his fist hard against his thigh as she circled slowly around him. Any second now her revulsion would come.

When she grasped his chin and gently tilted it this way and that, he thought he might actually break his femur from the pressure of his digging fist. The last touch on his face had been from a nurse at St. Matthew's nearly a year before on the day he'd been discharged. He'd returned home and life had resumed. At least for everyone but Tobias.

"The skin has healed nicely," she said at last.

"You must be the one blinded then." His fingers eased against his thigh one by one.

"On the contrary. I've seen a great deal of damage since working at the shop. Some injuries are so twisted and destructive that no mask, no matter how skillfully painted, can hide them entirely."

"Then why do they come into the shop if their case is hopeless?"

"I never used that detestable word. We in the craft prefer the term *challenging.*"

Disgust rumbled in his throat. "Is that what you see now? A socket with some twisted, moist slit? A mere lash or two adhering feebly to all that is traceable of my forfeited eye?"

She leaned back and crossed her arms. "Shall we speak frankly? In such close quarters as we are to be over the next several weeks, I prefer it." At his nod, she continued. "Then know this before we begin, as I will not allow a quarrel to pop up later where I am forced to thoroughly outargue you. You are a tremendously handsome man and not made less so because of the atrocities of war." He opened his mouth for a retort, but she held up a hand to stop him. "We are not creatures made only of appearances. We have minds and souls, and those last far longer than a shapely nose or a twinkling eye. Do not disregard these achievements to mourn the loss of a feature that will only decline in the coming years due to wrinkles and cataracts. A sharp mind never wrinkles."

"If we are to speak frankly, Miss Hamilton, then I shall tell you that's well and good coming from one with all her features intact."

"My features may be intact, but they're hardly enough to recommend me by. Which is why I've developed talents elsewhere." She swept her freckled hand to indicate the paints behind her. "And it's Elena and you will be Tobias. At least in here."

His fingers slowly uncoiled from pressing against his thigh. "Taking advantage of familiarity since that kiss, I see."

"It has a way of cleaving through stiff pretenses."

She wasn't a ravishing beauty by conventional standards. Her clothes were much too eccentric, her hair more orange than a becoming auburn, and freckles dotted nearly every square inch of exposed skin, but she had a fluid manner of moving that was pleasing to the eye and a voice softly accented with the flavors of the Continent.

Interesting would be the closest word he could put his finger on to describe her, and even that didn't quite capture her true spirit.

Not that it mattered to pinpoint her. She was an artist commissioned for work, and in a matter of weeks she would return to London. On to the next hunk of masticated meat they called a soldier, where the war had chewed them up and the world had spat them out.

Wood frames banged together as Miss Hamilton, or Elena as she insisted, riffled through a stack of art material propped against the wall. "Did your mother think I was here to paint your portrait or landscapes perhaps? I haven't seen this much stretched canvas since art school."

"Mother likes to overprepare."

"And your father?"

"Keeps to himself because Mother plans for all of us."

After propping an easel and canvas in front of him, Elena gathered a small round board, paints, and brushes and placed them on a table next to her newly fashioned work area. "Seeing that the mask has yet to be delivered and therefore giving us nothing to work with this morning, I shall use this time to mix paints for your skin tone."

"A thrilling morning you've set for us."

Her eyebrows waggled. "Wait until we sit to watch it dry."

After scooping out a few blobs of paint from their bottles and plopping them onto the thin round board, she began mixing them. A dot of red here, a smear of yellow there. From there she added colored strokes to the canvas and smudged them with her fingers. Observing her method was like watching an illusionist at work. "First, we must use a hard enamel that has a rather dull fleshlike finish for our base. It doesn't chip as easily as oil. We may need to make a few adjustments once the mask arrives, but this will give us a good start."

We. Us. The words settled into him, dashing away the loneliness. "Where did you learn to paint?"

"Where does one learn to breathe?" She smiled with contentment.

"All over and nowhere. From my earliest memory I was surrounded by artists of all types. Painters, sculptors, musicians, actors, singers. I would creep down the stairs at night when I was supposed to be asleep and watch as Mama sat for various paintings. She was a great muse in her day, which she attributed to her dark auburn hair. A trait I seem forever to be waiting for. As with any artist, you pick up your first brush or your first violin and the creation is horrible to the senses, but over time your skill grows, as does your expression of it, and before long—*voilà!*—you have learned and created without realizing it."

Tobias had never created a thing a day in his life. Certainly he appreciated the craftsmanship of a finely aged whiskey or a masterfully designed stained-glass window, but maintaining seemed to be his life's calling. From his days in the nursery, he'd been trained in the expectations of master and lord of Leedswick Castle in preparation for the day Father would pass the stewardship on to him with a firm reminder that his duty was to marry well and maintain what had always been, not to disturb with change. Not even when the castle crumbled with age around his ears. It was a responsibility Tobias did not look forward to.

Tucking away his morose thoughts, Tobias watched as Elena dabbed the tip of her brush into a splotch of yellow and added it to the canvas. "Why do you keep adding yellow?"

"Because your skin has warm undertones. If your tone were more like mine, I would add a cool blue. And then flick on brown spots for the freckles that work to conceal any undertone I might have." Laying aside her tools, she swiped her finger across the paint, then slid it along his jaw. "Close." Cupping his chin, she tilted his face back and forth. "Very close indeed for a foundation color."

"How many layers do you need?"

"Once we have the copper mask, it will be coated in silver and painted with spirit enamel to match your skin tone and then topped with a varnish for complexion texture. The skin is a complex canvas. The blood flowing beneath creates unique dimensions, as does the bone structure and the way the light hits each of these planes. For it to come alive there must be several representations of color at play while accounting for the weather, which turns the hues dull or bright. A tone must be struck for both sun and cloud, while also maintaining a bluish tinge of shaven cheeks. The only thing more complex is the eye. It must be painted on the reverse side of a glass blank or directly onto the plate, which in my opinion never looks as convincing because it's one-dimensional. A glass blank eye offers much more depth and color intricacies." She leaned down until her nose almost touched his. "Browns, nutmegs, ambers, and touches of gold all swirled together in a masterpiece."

A habit of hers, Tobias was learning rather quickly, was her disregard for personal distance. Very un-British-like. It did, however, afford him a close-up of her eyes. One brown and one blue. One more unique feature in the makeup of this unusual woman.

A knock sounded on the door, followed by Stokes's sharp nose poking in. "Forgive the intrusion, sir. There's a package on the receiving table."

Elena leaned away. Her scent of wild violets lingered under Tobias's nose. He turned his head to clear the aroma of it. "I'll be down shortly."

"Very good, sir."

Elena set down her brush and wiped her hands on a rag, leaving streaks of paint on its pristine surface. Excitement danced across her face. "It must be the mask. We should try it on this afternoon before we start painting tomorrow."

Stokes hovered in the doorway, his eyes glued to the window over Tobias's shoulder lest his attention be tainted by the mess in the room.

"Is there something else, Stokes?" Retying his mask in place,

Tobias stood and stretched his legs. His muscles ached from the tension he'd fought while sitting.

"A note was delivered along with the package, sir. Addressed to Miss Hamilton. Both of which were delivered by a rather insistent gentleman."

Gentlemen didn't deliver packages. Such mundane activities were left to the post lads. "Is the gentleman still here?"

Stokes shook his head. "He insisted that Miss Hamilton read the note and reply posthaste."

On the receiving table located in the front hall was the package as promised. Addressed to Major Tobias Alnwick of Leedswick Castle from a Mr. Francis Derwent Wood of Masks for Facial Disfigurement Department, 3rd London General Hospital. His mask. He ran his hand over the carefully wrapped box.

Everything would change with this.

"The man who delivered this, what did he look like?" Elena held the open letter in her hand. She claimed her freckles covered any skin tone to be seen, but they couldn't hide the paleness that swept over her.

Stokes curled his lip. He detested visitors. "A gentleman with a more southernly accent. Kent if I was forced to say. Graying sideburns and a rather large black-stone stickpin in his lapel."

"Polished coal." Elena touched a shaking hand to the base of her throat.

"I begged to know why a gentleman took it upon himself to bring the package rather than utilizing a delivery boy. The man claimed such services are not to be trusted and that he'd plucked the package straight from the boy's hand. I suppose a distrustful mindset is how things are done in the coal region." Stokes cut his gaze at Elena, who was too busy staring at the note as if it might bite her.

Tobias frowned. "Do you know this gentleman?"

"I . . . please excuse me." Crumpling the letter in her hands, she whirled and flew up the stairs.

CHAPTER 3 ———————————————

The mask fit Tobias perfectly, as Elena knew it would. Mr. Wood hired the best plaster-mold makers, sculptors, and casting specialists to ensure these face coverings for the Tommies were nothing short of a miracle of modern ingenuity. First, a plaster cast of the face was made from clay no thicker than a visiting card back at the Tin Noses Shop. Then a copper mask was created from the plaster cast, and that was where her work began by coating it in spirit enamel to match the soldier's skin tone and topping it with a varnish to give the hint of complexion. Texture was added, along with the features needed—painted eyes, eyelashes, eyebrows, mustaches. A step-by-step process of recreation.

Elena had risen early from a night of sleepless tossing and arrived in the studio well before Tobias. She held the copper mask to the light of the gray morning. A finely sculpted replica of the left side of his face and a smooth glass eye waiting for the brilliant strokes of brown and gold to bring it to life. Exhilaration should have filled her as it always did in this, her favorite moment in the process. A blank canvas on which to express a world of new possibilities.

But that note filled with dark-inked words seemed to sear itself across the copper.

Tomorrow. Four o'clock. The White Swan.

"Up early this morning." Tobias's low voice rolled across the room.

Shaking off the gloom, she summoned a smile and turned to greet him. "Eager to begin."

She knew that look, had practiced it often enough herself. He studied her as an artist did his subject before broaching the first brushstroke. With a flip of her scarf, she turned away before he had the chance to capture the layer of unease lurking beneath her surface.

"You disappeared yesterday after the package was delivered," he said. "We were concerned."

The maid had been sent several times to Elena's room, and just before supper the lady of the house herself came to inquire after Elena's welfare, but she had sent them away with reassurances that all was well. "I had a number of things on my mind, seeing as we are to start on your mask today. Checking paints, selecting the right shade of eyebrow hairs. Artist things."

"Is that true, or was it the note accompanying it?"

The man was relentless. Placing the mask carefully on the work-table, Elena fixed him with an even stare. "We agreed to honesty in this room, but there are some things I will keep to myself."

"I understand, Miss Hamilton—Elena. All too well."

Between them passed a sentiment she did not often come across. One of quiet understanding. It was not a feeling she often exchanged with another, at least not beyond art appreciation. This was something that sank deep into her soul, filling the darkened voids with calming blue and a blush of pink. The unease tying itself in knots within her stomach loosened, and the inky black words retreated from the forefront of her mind. "Shall we begin?"

Tobias took his seat from the day before as the light behind him struggled to break free of the gray clouds rolling in from the east, while Elena settled on a low stool in front of her makeshift worktable, arranging the bottle of cream-colored spirit enamel and the concoction she'd mixed yesterday to better match his skin.

"How many of these have you painted before?" he asked after she'd begun.

"I've been employed at Mr. Wood's shop for a year, so I have had the privilege of assisting with nearly thirty masks. Each one as unique as the men who wear them, though my favorite are the eyes. Windows to the soul, they are."

He grunted and turned to the window, hiding the damaged side of his face. "I doubt much is stirring in the souls of those returning from the fight."

"If that were true, they would not be sitting in my chair searching for a way to improve their situation. Nor would I find myself sitting here with you today."

"Don't make many house calls, I take it."

"This is a first, being invited into a private home." Mr. Wood wasn't even sure if it could be done outside the studio, but Elena had volunteered to give it a go after reading the desperation in Lady Northridge's written words. If it didn't work, at least they would have tried.

"Well, the Alnwicks are nothing if not private. For years we've prided ourselves on shutting out the world and keeping to ourselves. Even our tenants, those few remaining who didn't run off because of the murder charges, see precious little of us."

"You didn't shut out the world when the war came to call."

"And look what it got me." He turned to her, his mouth twisted with wry humor as he pointed to his face. "Rising to defend my country was not a cry I could ignore, despite the family proclivity for seclusion."

"I've always heard that blue bloods are eccentric."

"Eccentric is a polite way of putting it. Cursed is another."

The paintbrush dropped from Elena's hand. Cream paint

splattered across her plissé skirt. She grabbed a rag and blotted the paint from the crinkled material as best she could, then gave up. A few smeared dots added character to the cherry color. "Reminds me of my summer traveling with the Romani. They love a good curse story. Tell me all about it."

Standing, Tobias smoothed the straps of his black mask with quick, agitated swipes. "Are we done here?"

"I . . . yes, for the day. The paint needs to dry before we add another layer." She'd overstepped and forgotten the British stiff lip. Again. "I apologize if I've offended you. This may be one of those things you prefer to keep to yourself."

After walking to the door, he paused and stared at her. Elena held her breath. Any second now he would tell her to mind her own business. His shoulders rose and expanded the muscles beneath his jacket. "It's better if I show you."

He led her deep into the northern wing of the castle where the air grew stale and musty. Cracks ran the length of the paint-chipped ceiling, and dust filmed over the windows. Wallpaper peeled from the walls where discolored rectangles and squares marked the homes of once-hanging pictures. Elena was given the impression that all the grandeur was reserved for the front of the castle. This wing, where guests' eyes were not invited, told the true story of a dilapidated legacy. If that was true, how could they afford her specialized house call?

At the end of a corridor, Tobias opened a set of doors on squealing hinges to a small room, bare of anything save half a dozen portraits clinging to the cracked walls for dear life. One of a man in an Elizabethan ruff with a short, pointy beard. A woman in proper Victorian dress with a string of pearls looped around her long neck. The others just as ordinary for their eras. None of whom looked cursed.

"Allow me to introduce you to Charles Alnwick." Tobias stood next to a large oil painting in a faded frame. The subject was a striking man in his twenties with dark hair and large brown eyes. "My grandfather."

Elena studied the portrait. The shading of light and dark, the brushstrokes, the richness of expression. "You have his eyes."

"Better that than the murder on his hands. Or so the rumor goes." Moving to the grimy window, Tobias leaned his shoulder against the casing. "The Alnwick men come from a long line of military service to the Crown since the War of the Roses. Anytime there was a battle to be fought, you could be certain an Alnwick would be there to see duty and honor served. But in the Bhutan War, Charles was rumored to have left his servant-soldier to die after an attack. It wasn't true, but the batman, Francis, was a beloved son of Birchwick. When Charles returned home and Francis did not, the village people never forgave him. They turned against the Alnwicks, and we in turn have distanced ourselves from them. Hiding away as if guilty."

"Your going off to war proves that this guilt is nothing more than humbug."

"Hatred refuses to die so easily. We are pariahs in the very village my ancestors founded nine hundred years ago."

"I don't necessarily agree with the political banality of war where greediness seeks to overpower those who are claimed to be undeserving or weak, but I do believe in people. And people are worth fighting for and forgiving. You are a hero for fighting on behalf of those who cannot defend themselves. Surely they agree by now to let old disagreements rest in the past."

"You have not been in the north country for long, but if there is anything we know how to do in this harsh land, it is to hold a grudge."

"Seems a rather sad way to live. What of the curse you spoke of? Does Francis haunt these halls?" Her gaze darted around as if she half expected to find a ghostly specter watching her. Leedswick's moodiness nearly demanded its own ethereal being.

Tobias glanced over his shoulder, a blue devil of a smile creasing his lips. "We are not in our honesty room now. The less you know of such things, the better."

Shadows sank deep into the cruel gouges on his cheek, his mask a void of black. He had physical scars, but what pain ran the length of his soul? What suffering filled his silence? She hadn't spent much time with people who repressed their feelings, as the circle she had grown up with wore their hearts on their paint-splattered sleeves with abandon. Heartaches were opportunities for sonnets. Tragedy a chorus of lyrics. She had learned that no person, no matter their inclination to outward or inward dramatics, liked to have their feelings forced from them. So she would wait. If he wished to talk, so be it. If not, they were his secrets to keep.

Shifting her attention back to the painting, she noted the cases of books behind Charles, an ornate chair tucked under a scroll-legged desk upon which his hand rested. His other hand was propped against his hip holding a rectangular block.

"What's this in his hand?"

Her question brought Tobias's attention around from the outside gloominess. "His infamous journal. It went missing around the time of his death."

"Have you tried searching for it?"

"Several times, along with my sister, Margaret, my brother, Daniel, and our parents. When I was little I thought if I could find it, I would discover the key to lifting our curse—"

"The one you refuse to tell me about."

He smiled, not giving in to her prodding. "Still, one cannot claim he was entirely without good fortune. He found love with my grandmother, Beatrice. That's her there." He pointed to a portrait next to Charles of a lovely woman with dark brown hair swept atop her head in the height of fashion nearly fifty years ago. She wore a beautiful cream lace dress, with yellow flowers shaped like tiny trumpets adorning an arbor behind her. "One of the 'Dollar Princesses' from America."

She'd heard of those women who came over in droves in the last century with heaps of their fathers' fabulous wealth in order to marry a British title. Their crisp new steel-, oil-, and newspaper-earned dollar bills would bolster the dying estates of noble families and keep them afloat in what was rapidly becoming a lost way of living in excess thanks to the war. What a terrible way to seal a marriage. What was so important about rank and money when love was all that truly mattered? Though she had never experienced it herself, she looked forward to the day she fell headfirst into amour. If any man should take notice, that was.

"She's beautiful," Elena said.

"Yes, they were very much in love and lived happily, even after shutting the doors of the castle."

"What do you mean they shut the doors?"

"With the village blaming Charles for Francis's death, my family found little reason to venture out, so they created their own spot of happiness behind these ancient walls."

"Sounds lonely."

He shrugged and drew a finger across the glass. A bright streak of clarity through the filmy gray. "They weren't as long as they had one another. Soon they had a family, then grandchildren. It was enough for them."

"Would it be for you?" *Zut alors*. Not but a few minutes later and she was breaking her vow to refrain from forcing feelings from others.

He shrugged again and dropped his hand to his side. "I'm not certain what's enough or not anymore. The war has skewed my barometer as to what constitutes happiness."

"I'd say your new mask is a step in that direction. It tells me you don't wish to remain behind these walls forever."

"What we wish for and what we receive are two entirely different matters. As future master of Leedswick, I have responsibilities here. Mask or no, the opportunities that might tempt me elsewhere are simply not attainable."

"Then you must create your own opportunities."

"If only I could bypass realities as you do." He rubbed at the strap behind his ear. Soft as they were, the bands too often irritated the already-tender skin. "You are entirely too cheerful for your own good."

"As you are entirely too gloomy for yours."

"A stalemate."

Considering neither seemed inclined to switch their point of view for the other's sake, only one thing was left to be done. "Then let's break it. We can go in search of this long-lost journal and rid your family name of this supposed curse once and for all. A proper pirate adventure."

Unfortunately, pirating didn't seem to excite him in the least. He pushed away from the window and strode to the door. "Such antics belong in childhood. Come, we've wandered too far from the studio."

She took one last glance around the chamber to appreciate the paintings. Should she desire to view them again, her sense of direction would lead her to a cupboard rather than here. The frames were cracked and dust had settled thickly in the corners. How sad to see family relegated to cobwebs far from the living. Which prompted another thought.

"Why are these portraits so far out of the way in a wing that appears not to have been used for decades?"

"Because these are the black sheep. The ones time has tried to forget and so should we, but now you know what kind of place you've stepped into. The kind that might leave you tainted when you depart."

"Balderdash. I don't believe in a curse and neither should you."

Seriousness burned bright in the mahogany of his eye. "Whether I believe it nonsense is of no consequence to those outside these walls. Some sins never lift, no matter how many years have passed."

A chill ran across her skin as the note's inked words spread in her mind. How true were his words.

＋———————＋

At precisely 3:00 that afternoon, Elena informed Lady Northridge that she was stepping out and would not be back in time for tea. At precisely 3:02 Lady Northridge nearly had an attack of the vapors at such an announcement. By 3:15 the poor woman had been led to a low couch where she wrung her lace hankie. "You simply cannot go without a chaperone. It is unladylike."

"I assure you I have walked many places without a chaperone and managed to return unscathed."

"We can send out for anything you might require in your studio if that is the concern."

Elena scrambled for one of Mama's rambling statements that would be good for throwing off insistent questioning. Aligning artists with whims of illogic, most people didn't probe further into their conjured muses. "An artist craves all mediums of expression. Earth, wind, water, and sky. I must seek these on my own if I am to absorb their possibilities."

By 3:30, Elena had left the protesting lady of the house in the capable hands of Stokes and made her way through the enormous wood-and-iron gates to the small bridge and dirt road to the village beyond. It was a charming place filled with lanes moseying between sandstone cottages and shops with thatched roofs. Bright red geraniums, purple asters, and white roses burst from window boxes as ivy climbed high up to diamond-paned windows and cats slept on stone front steps.

In the town square festive banners and booths were being set up as children chased one another about the green, trying to grab balloons that had been tied up for decoration. It was a well-lived place, like an old man's bones settling after a long day's work. Charming indeed. Then again, Tobias claimed these people would not hesitate to pick up a pitchfork and chase after his family. The devil hid behind an angelic face.

Which was what brought her to the White Swan.

It was a low-slung building with buttery walls and a slate roof. The wrought-iron sign was molded into the shape of a swan taking flight and boasted of existing since 1742. Quite young for England. Clutching her fringe handbag, Elena took a deep breath and pushed open the heavy stained door. Inside, her eyes needed a moment to adjust to the public house's dark wood paneling, high polished counter, and flickering gaslights that barely lit the scattered battered chairs and tables. Patrons who had arrived early for their evening of drinking swiveled to stare over their mugs of warm beer. In her bright flowing skirt and trailing scarf she stood out like a poppy in a snowstorm. Or rather like a poppy in mud, considering the surrounding of earthy browns.

"No birds allowed without an escort," the barman growled from his post behind the counter.

"She has one." A man rose from a booth tucked in the far back corner. With his immaculate suit, polished shoes, trimmed and graying sideburns, and black-stone stickpin, he stood out like a . . . well, like a gentleman among the slops. As he came to stand in front of her, a smile oiled across his face that did little to warm the steel in his eyes. "Welcome, Elena. Won't you join me?"

Her fingers crushed her handbag. "Hello, Mr. Burgess."

"Now, Elena. I have repeatedly asked you to call me Father."

CHAPTER 4 ───────────────────────

The steam had long since evaporated from the chipped cup of tea placed on the sticky table. Elena kept her hands in her lap. In no way would she give this man who called himself her sire the satisfaction of a welcome. "I thought I'd made it clear in London some months ago that I wish nothing to do with you."

Aaron Burgess sipped calmly from his cup of tea, careful to keep the chipped rim from brushing his silver mustache. "As I made it clear that I have no intention of granting your wish."

"You had no right to track me down there, just as you have no right to follow me now."

"As your father I have every right. My contacts at the port in Portsmouth were only too delighted to inform me that your name was spotted on a ship's manifest traveling from Calais, after which you took the train to London. From there I had little difficulty tracking you to the artists' slum off Tottenham Court." He took a quick sip. "I might've known you'd go there. Your mother seemed determined to enmesh you with wastrels of the worst kind."

"Hardly, when she was so determined to escape you."

He dropped his cup in the saucer, rattling the cheap china. "Your wretched mother poisoned you against me all these years. She had no right to leave me and gallivant from country to country with her artist groups."

Elena slapped her hand on the table. She hadn't given this man more than a passing thought in twenty years after Mama told her what kind of monster he was. She wasn't about to allow him to swoop in and twist memories he didn't have ownership to. "You drove her away. What wife would stay under the same roof with a man who strikes her? What mother would leave her child to remain in that environment?"

"Lies," he hissed, that infamous anger rising in his steel-blue eyes. "You were a baby when she absconded with you in the night. There is no way for you to remember what our home was like or who was truly at fault."

"I may have been too young to remember, but Mama never lied about anything. If we were happy, our family would have stayed together."

"Your mother always had a free spirit. One I see she's passed along to you. That stops now."

Pushing her untouched cup aside, Elena leaned forward so he might better hear every single clipped word she had to say. "You have not been a part of my life for twenty-three years. Do not assume to barge in with commands. I've met with you only to tell you—for the final time—that I have no desire for the odious trappings of the Burgess name. Return to Kent and never call at Leedswick again. I am there in a professional capacity and won't have the Alnwick family part of your scheming to woo me back."

Half a dozen patrons had trickled in to sip warm beer at the bar. At the sudden showdown in the back corner booth, they twisted on their barstools with one ear cocked to the commotion, which proved more entertaining than swapping stories of their workday at the mill or the farm.

Burgess must have sensed their audience, for he adjusted in his seat and tempered the anger in his eyes as he took another sip of tea. He returned the cup to its saucer and angled the handle perfectly perpendicular to the table edge. "I require an heir."

His long-lost father-and-daughter act in London had hinted at such, but she much preferred the blunt honesty of the present. One she could reciprocate. "Then find another wife."

"A new wife would not help. After your mother divorced me, my second bride begot only daughters, whom I packed away to boarding school as quickly as I could. She died two years ago, and after a suitable period of mourning, I looked for a third bride, at which time my physician informed me . . . well, suffice it to say children are no longer an option for me."

"A blessing then to prevent ruining any future children."

"A curse." He pushed his cup aside and leaned his forearms on the table, lacing together his long, immaculately kept fingers. The hands of an office manager. "You are my eldest child; however, laws in England require all my holdings to go to my nearest male relation upon my death. A third cousin on my mother's side who is no more than a sniveling weasel. He hates me as much as I loathe him, and he would love nothing more than to break up the company I have built simply to spite me while he rakes in the profits."

"You'll be pushing up daisies by the time he does. What does it matter?"

"Because I have built an empire from the scraps my father left, and I will not allow my legacy to be left in the hands of an imbecile. My shipping company will go on without me and be run according to my specific plans. You remember Simon Mulligan, yes?"

She had been in London less than a month. It had been drizzling that day and she had been longing for the warm fields of southern France when Burgess appeared and offered her the protection of his umbrella. He'd been accompanied by a younger man, a few inches taller than herself with wavy black hair and immaculately tailored clothes that stood out against the wartime gloom when most people were making do with old fashions. He wore a yellow carnation in his buttonhole. "The man you brought along the second time you harassed me. That time I believe it was Piccadilly Circus. I had no lasting opinion of him then, and I certainly don't entertain one now."

"Simon is the man I wish to run things after I'm gone."

Elena smiled, the first and only she would offer this man. "Splendid. Make a note in your will giving this chosen man your empire instead of the weasel cousin and leave me alone."

"It's not nearly as simple as that. My business contracts are obligated to go to a male relative and they are ironclad. Trust me, I have tried to find a way around them, but my father was cunning when he signed the papers over to me on his deathbed. The recipient of Burgess Shipping must be of my blood." The tip of his finger punched the table to emphasize each word that clearly weighed heavily on him.

Unfortunately for him, Elena was in no mood to help lift weights. "I wish I could summon sympathy for your plight, but I have none to give. You will always be the brute who hurt my mother." Holding her handbag, she scooted from the booth and stood. "Now, if you'll excuse me. I'm expected back at the castle."

Showing not the least bit of hurry, Burgess settled farther into the booth and draped one arm over the back of his seat. "Ah yes. Your finger paints for the soldiers who come back blown to bits. Tell me, how is it a girl of your eclectic tastes came to be hired by a reclusive noble family this far north? Pure talent learned from the back of gypsy carts or bordellos across Europe?"

His lip curled beneath the trimmed mustache. "A shame if you were forced to quit before the job was completed. I understand that boy was rather unfortunate with his wounds. So much so that he can't leave the safety of his castle walls for fear of terrifying the local villagers. Not that they want him or his family. Not with that curse hanging over them."

"How do you know about any curse?" She sat back down.

"My friends at the bar were kind enough to tell me the local lore." He nodded in acknowledgment to the men watching her through slitted eyes. "Seems some ancestor got a local boy killed during the

Bhutan War, and no one has been in a forgiving mood since. They cursed the castle and all its inhabitants. It's why the family locked themselves away. From guilt."

Elena cleared the tremble from her voice. "It was an accident."

"So claims your soldier boy, but it wouldn't take more than a match to rekindle the flames of hatred again. Say, a long-lost letter from poor Francis himself stating he was afraid for his life. That this Charles Alnwick threatened to end him once and for all."

"That's a lie."

"Is it when I have the proof right here?" He reached into his pocket and flashed the edge of an envelope. Elena lurched across the table to grab it, but he tucked it away from sight. "Tsk-tsk. That stays with me for now."

"Where did you get such a letter?"

"It's not difficult to dig up dirt in a village like this, and the local yokels have long memories. Especially when the highborn murder one of their own. I'd say it's about time for the deceptive Alnwicks to tumble from their ivory tower."

"Stay away from them." For years she had applied herself to her craft, had allowed art to breathe its colors into her soul. Then the war came, pushing her from her Paris home and into uncertainty on the unfamiliar streets of London, but she'd found her footing again in Mr. Wood's shop where she could use her art to heal and not just to inspire. Men who were devastated by their injuries and could barely summon the will to live. Men like Pierre. She had been too late to help her dear friend and the guilt of it was consuming, but she was determined to make amends for her own failure by not allowing another man in her charge to perish. So she healed the only way she knew how. With paint.

Then came the plea from the far north to help a man who couldn't face the world on his own. She would not fail him, nor would she allow threats to stand against his success. "I won't let you hurt them, nor will I allow you to destroy what I'm trying to create here."

"Create?" He snorted with disgust. "As if that joke of an amputation shop you work at could create anything from the mincemeat dragging themselves in there. They would have been better off left to rot on the battlefield than scaring the rest of society with what's left of their hideous faces."

"You are revolting, and I will not listen to another poisonous word from you." She started to rise, but his arm shot across the table and jerked her back to her seat.

"You'll leave when I'm ready for you to leave."

"Crawl up in a hole and die."

"I will happily flash this letter about town. Or perhaps in front of your employers. No doubt they will relish the attention. Or you can sit like a good girl." He smoothed a hand over the breast pocket where the letter hid. "Either way, you will listen to what I have to say."

Memories of the red welts scarred across Mama's back flashed through Elena's mind. As truly as she saw them, she knew Burgess would make good on his threat. She sat on the edge of the booth seat. "Speak your piece and be gone from this place."

His gaze roamed over her in keen inspection. "It's a shame you're not more of a looker. Despite her flaws in character, your mother was quite beautiful. It seems my traits run stronger in your veins, but you'll learn as I did that looks are not above a sharp mind."

The barb chipped at a spot on her heart that had long since scabbed over, yet the pain still managed to crack through. Her features seemed crafted more for vivid expression than for admiration, which was a difference she never dwelled on for long since beauty was in the eye of the beholder, and as far as she knew, she was beholden to him for nothing. "Nor are they above politeness, and mine is fast waning. You have three seconds."

"Return with me to Kent. Get to know Simon and see the empire that has been built by your family's hands. The empire whose legacy only you can help continue by giving me a grandson."

Surprise gasped from her mouth. She jumped to her feet as all eyes swiveled their direction. "No. Absolutely not. Never will I give a child over to your scheming for some shipping company I have no need for and a family I do not belong to. *If* I have a child one day, it will be a Hamilton, not a Burgess, and you will come nowhere near us."

"Gladly I would have pushed this task onto one of my other brats, but as I will most likely be dead by the time they come of age, to marry you off is my only option." Burgess slid from his seat to stand in front of her. Slowly he buttoned the silver buttons down the front of his dark gray suit. "You haven't had the pleasure of knowing me for very long—your mother saw to that—but one thing you will quickly discover is that I am not a man to be refused."

She met the steel of his eyes with the resolve of her own. "So I learned when Mama showed me the scars on her back. She ran from you as far as she could, so you should recognize the same action as I walk away from you without a backward glance."

He grabbed her arm and hissed in her ear, "I'll give you one opportunity to get the impertinence from your blood, but remember this: I will use this letter to destroy that family sitting high in their castle and any ambitions you have to further your so-called career. No one will hire you once I'm done, and any talent you think you have will wither away. Just like your mother."

He released her so quickly she nearly stumbled into the barstools. Righting herself, she left without giving him the satisfaction of looking back. Only, now what?

+———+

The sun was setting behind a wash of gray clouds, turning the earth to a hazy gloom. A palette of colors infiltrated Tobias's nightmares, painted by the distant firing of guns as they belched mortars and smoke over trenches, suffocating the very air with a thick profusion of death.

He gripped the handrail of the steep stairs leading up to the parapet. This wasn't France. The orange wasn't the burst of a shell, the gray not gunpowder. He moved up the stairs with the memory of mud clinging to his boots and puttees, each step weighted as he'd climbed the trench ladder to the top. Stopping, he squeezed his eye shut.

Next would come the whistle. *1-2-3-tweet!* *"Over the top, lads!"*

A cold sweat tattooed down his spine. He opened his eye. No whistle. No men with bayonets fixed clamoring behind him. This was Leedswick, this was home, and beyond these stone walls were rolling green hills dotted with sheep. Not a battlefield putrefying with muck and bodies.

Muttering and soft slapping came from the top of the stairs and to the left. He took another step up, careful to keep his head below the parapet wall as a breeze ushered in a late-summer chill that permeated the northern air no matter the season.

Wrapped in a thin shawl that slipped over her shoulder, Elena was tucked into the corner where the northern wall dovetailed into the western wall. She had an easel and square canvas before her. Angry red and smudged blacks streaked across the painting as she whipped the brush back and forth, grumbling under her breath.

"Here you are." She didn't hear him. He called out again. "It took me nearly twenty minutes to locate you on this side of the grounds." When she still didn't respond, he gripped the rail and forced himself to the next step. "Miss Hamilton. Elena."

Her brush skidded across the canvas, leaving a blob of red in its wake. Bright as blood. "You're rather making a habit of sneaking up on me unawares." Another gust billowed by, further tugging her shawl from its place about her shoulders.

"I thought the dinner trumpet would have alerted you."

"I'm afraid I didn't hear it."

"I'll have to tell Vincent he's losing his touch. He prides himself on blowing the horn loud enough to be heard in the next county over." Her attention roved over the wall, though by her glazed look she couldn't have seen much beyond whatever occupied her mind. He was intruding, and the last thing he desired was to step into another's emotional tide. Not after fighting so hard to staunch his own after being pulled bloodied and maimed from the battlefield. Tobias turned to go. "Dinner is in half an hour."

"Do you ever find the rhythm of expectation tedious?" Her voice snagged him, holding him to the spot.

"I like to eat, so in this particular case, no, I do not find a scheduled meal wearisome."

A crooked smile tilted her mouth. How easy she made it look when half of her face wasn't shredded off. "On that point we agree. Food is the hallmark of humanity in which we should all take delight, and nothing delights me more than a full stomach."

"Not even painting?"

The smile fell from her face. "Most days."

The tide of involvement tangled about his ankles. He should step out, shake the clinging wet drops from his shoes, but she seemed so small standing there, so forlorn against the world. She'd come so far to help him, the least he could do was not abandon her. "We haven't known one another for very long, but in our short acquaintance I have not found the words *expectation* or *dull* to be part of your sum. Least of all in the colors you choose." He nodded to the painting behind her.

"Ah, this." Her eyebrows slanted down. "At the moment these are the only colors I see."

Earlier that day she had been on the full side of pleasant, despite his proclivity to ignore such enthusiasm. Her lack of cheerfulness now couldn't help but spark his concern. After all, he didn't need a perturbed artist repainting his face. No telling what chaos she might create. "Might it have something to do with your walk to the village? Or that note?"

Her mouth leveled for the briefest of seconds before she shook her head. Grabbing the end of her shawl, she swiped at the latest blob of red streaking to the bottom. "There are things of more importance than that paltry note. Your mask for one. Tomorrow we'll paint the foundation that we crafted today and top it off with a good dash of varnish."

"As long as you don't paint it red." It was a jest, but the humor fell woefully short in the face of reality. The truth was, such vividness had failed to capture him for a long time. The past four years had ground him into the dirt so much that he could barely recognize the open sky as something to be grateful for.

He flattened his hand against the rail, the metal cool under his heated palm. "There are times when I see the world only in certain colors. Gray, brown, khaki. Colors of death and destruction. Sometimes I think it's all I'll ever see."

The admission came out before he realized it. How long had he kept it harbored in the quiet safety of his own keeping? Those who weren't in the trenches couldn't understand, and those who were only wanted to forget it. Her fiery sunset was the first time he'd seen anguish expressed so boldly in a very long time. It prompted courage.

"When my mother died, I could barely pick up a brush, and when I did it wept blacks and grays," Elena said. "In time those grays became soft blues until one day I found myself dipping into the greens and yellows once more. With the occasional crimson when my thoughts become too much and my voice longs to scream."

"This is what you consider screaming?"

"It's the only way I know how to. Voices have a hue to them, did you know? Some are scarlet with fury, others lavender laced with melancholy, or lapis with wisdom. I myself tinge toward yellow, which clashes horridly with this hair, but what can one do but accept and move on?" As if to underscore her point, the wind brushed orange curls across her face. She was so infused with color it was a wonder indeed to pinpoint just one, but yellow seemed a good start.

"What color do you peg me?"

She studied him for a long moment, tapping the end of her brush against her cheek. In the fading light of day her freckles melted into the paleness of her skin. "Pewter. Timeless, sturdy, yet worn. I suspect were you to be polished, we would find traces of green. Life and peace."

He snorted. "You're about four years too late. The war wiped out any peace to be had."

"Balderdash. It's merely sleeping, waiting to blossom again like little blades of grass."

"Says the woman painting a blood sun."

"Yes, well, we all have our moments of relapse when the past comes to call." Her eyebrows slanted once more as she seemed to revert to her thoughts from before his intrusion. Back when she saw only red and gray.

The tide of involvement surged higher. Tobias had stayed long enough. "Dinner is soon. I should go."

"I'll stay here a while longer if you don't mind. Please send my apologies to your mother." Pulling her flimsy shawl tightly about herself, Elena returned her gaze to the ashy horizon. Her paintbrush dangled limply from her fingertips as the fringe ends of the shawl danced about her knees.

"Of course." He started down the steps, then turned back. After shrugging out of his dinner jacket, he placed it over her shoulders and hurried away before he was tempted to look over the wall.

CHAPTER 5

Light poured through the window and danced across the tops of Tobias's boots as he sat quietly in the chair. Just how long could a person rattle on about whatever topic meandered through her mind? And why in this instance didn't it bother him?

"From Prague we traveled to Oberammergau in Bavaria." Elena balanced the copper mask that had been hammered to the thinness of a visiting card on her left hand while she painted on the color of his skin with her other. Perched on a stool, she wore an outfit of bright yellow and green that conjured images of a tropical bird on a branch. "It's a truly magical place and I might adore it more than France. Have you been?"

"To France? Surely you've noticed my souvenir." He gestured halfheartedly to his face.

She batted away his motion with the tip of her brush as if it held no relevance. "I speak only of travels for enjoyment."

How many times as a lad had he gazed over the parapet wall to the seas beyond and imagined himself on a voyage, chronicling each swelling wave, the flocks of seagulls flying to and fro, the shape of distant shores? He wanted the thrill of exploration, but duty to the castle had been ingrained in him since birth. Estate heirs did not wander the earth in search of lands unknown. "Before the war I never traveled farther than the shores of Britain. Unless you count the Isle of Man, where my father took me a few times as a lad for fishing."

"Man is off the mainland, so we'll tally it in your slot for adventure. Should you wish to leave the British Empire behind, where might you go?"

The shiny copper slowly disappeared beneath the brushstrokes, bit by bit becoming more a piece of his skin. He crossed his arms to keep from reaching out to touch it, to determine its realness after living these long months as . . . less. "I haven't much opportunity to dwell on the possibilities of travel. My family tends to prefer the world inside the castle walls."

Hand stilling, her eyebrows inched up at him. "That's well and good for your family, but what about you? Surely a strapping man such as yourself wishes to stretch his legs far beyond Northumberland."

Tobias snorted. "I stretched them all right. Right into a bloody war."

"More of a tumble really. Don't give me that look. If you can be cheeky about souvenirs, then so can I." Winking, she dipped her brush in the paint and swiped it over the mask's cheek.

This was it. This was why he didn't mind her meandering conversations. Because they filled the silences echoing within him like twelve-pound guns. Others prattled on, stretching his nerves taut as barbed wire yet never coming around to greet the obvious, perhaps in hopes of not having to acknowledge his scars. He'd grown accustomed to the quick looks and averted eyes, the desperation to keep to cheerful topics of conversation. They thought they were helping or being kind, but it only served to widen the gap of understanding. Elena acknowledged his injuries head-on with a unique compassion that didn't contort into feeling sorry for him. A refreshing perspective.

"Now, I have a very important question to ask you," she said.

"If it's to inquire whether I consider the right or left my best side, I'm afraid the course has already been set for that."

"Two jests in one sitting. My, my, you are daring. Before long I'll have you bounding out of England and into a whole wide world in need of your wit. My question is: However do you manage to sit for so long without moving? You've barely moved a muscle but to blink since we sat down."

"In the trenches one grows accustomed to stillness. One false move might put a sniper's bullet through your head." His mind summoned the feeling of cramped muscles, stiff joints, and frozen fingers hovering over a trigger. There were times when the peaceful pull of endless sleep became too tempting to ignore, but before giving in to the Reaper's call, he would look down the line of his men, noting their misery, and would vow to carry on for them. Keeping his mind active by recalling stories and calculating arithmetic problems became the savior of his sanity.

"The fear must have been unimaginable."

He pushed the thoughts away, draining his mind of the grays and browns stained with red. "It was."

"As far as I know, we're not under threat of a sniper here, and I'm certain after all that time your legs are impatient to be put to use. Shall we go for a walk?" She hopped off her stool and placed his mask on the table. No trace of copper was left.

"Are you done for the day?"

"Yes, unless you'd like to sit and watch literal paint dry. Tomorrow we'll begin a second coat for texturing. Wrinkles, crow's-feet, warts. You want it, we can add it."

"Has anyone asked you for extra warts to be added? Have we not been mutilated enough?"

"No request for warts, but I did have a chap from Lincolnshire relish a bump on his new nose to make all the girls back home think he'd been in a brawl instead of having it torn off at Verdun. He appeared quite dashing when all was painted and done." She swirled her brush in a jar of clear liquid, then set it aside to dry next to the palette smeared with paint and the mask. "Would you care to take a closer look? The skin tone match is remarkable."

Only once had he summoned the courage to glance in a mirror since his injury. The horror staring back at him was enough to haunt him for the rest of his days. He was not the same man he was in early adulthood, the man he'd settled into the skin of and claimed as his true self. He was something altogether different now, and while the mask would be a gift enabling him to look normal again, it was a stark reminder of the stranger he'd become.

He stood and smoothed the front of his jacket. "It's not the final product. I'll wait until you're done."

"As you wish." Hesitation laced her tone. Without pushing further she removed her smock and draped it over the stool. "I'm eager to explore all the secret nooks of this place and I need a guide. You."

"Actually, I was going to—"

"Think of an excuse to say no so you can avoid listening to me chatter more?"

If only she knew what the silence did to him. "I-I'm afraid I don't have much of interest to contribute to an engaging conversation."

"Allow me to be the judge of that."

In no time at all Tobias found himself strolling the grounds with Elena, explaining the south gatehouse and the part it took in repelling an invading horde of Scots during the Border Wars. "It was from there the defenders poured vats of boiling oil onto the attackers, and the blacksmith, who happened to be a renowned archer, sent flaming arrows into their midst."

An unusual rice-paper umbrella painted with designs from the Orient shielded her face from the afternoon sun as she studied the tower. "Why are castles always so full of tragedy and anger? Where is the beauty?"

"When one is defending one's life, little time is left for beauty."

"Then what sort of life are you fighting for? Where does this lead?" She walked to the wrought-iron gate cut into the base of the tower and pushed it open to reveal a pebbled path winding into a thick swath of trees.

"To the gardens."

Her entire countenance lit up. She grabbed his hand and pulled him down the path before he could protest. Small and cool, her hand fit snugly in his without the slightest hesitation that it was highly improper to be holding hands for longer than it took to hand a lady from an auto. A smile tempted his lips at her enthusiastic innocence. The last time he'd trod this way was before the war when the air was sweet with spring and birds twittered in the branches of the alder trees. A different girl had been on his arm. A girl who had beamed up at him as they made secret plans for the future when he returned from his jaunt to France. His smile curdled.

Everything had changed and that beaming girl quickly became the one running from him in horror.

"Are you all right?"

Elena's soft voice pulled him from his recollections to notice they had come to the entrance of the walled garden nestled in the heart of the woods. The weathered gray stones had lost their straight lines to time and thick patches of lichen, yet they remained resolute in their duty to stand guard over the treasure within.

After releasing Elena's hand, Tobias stopped under the arched entrance as a new well of emotions sprang up. "Yes, only I haven't been here in some time. I almost forgot how green things can be."

Elena brushed by him and stood in a circle where the path diverged in different directions. "I see much more than green. Golden buttercups. Milky peonies. Candy-red poppies. A world of rainbows." Twirling the umbrella over her shoulder, she smiled like one of those dream girls from a painting. The kind that had never caught his attention before but whose fresh simplicity eased the soreness of late. "Take me to your favorite spot."

Pain twisted his heart. Once he thought it to be the bench hidden in the shrub maze where affections and promises had been whispered. Where Nina had promised to wait for him. He pointed in the opposite direction. "The Grand Cascade."

Having come through the northern entrance, they passed through the cherry tree orchard with the soft pink petals long since spent and the ornamental garden with its overgrown rows that had once been cut into precise squares and came to the top of the garden's showpiece. Water tumbled down the twenty-one terraced steps and pooled into a large basin at the bottom due to a clever water system rigged from the nearby river that allowed gravity to do all the work. Dead leaves floated around and mold crept over the ledge, marring the pristine condition that Leedswick's coffers were once funded to maintain. Money seemed to be seeping down the drain quicker with each passing year, and the burden to keep the castle and its grounds afloat grew heavier.

Elena closed her parasol and leaned down to brush her fingers in the gurgling water. "Utterly breathtaking."

"When we were children, Margaret, Daniel, and I would fashion little boats out of leaves and twigs and see whose skiff sailed faster to the bottom."

"Are you close with your siblings?"

He nodded as they descended the chipped brick stairs edging the fountain. "Thick as thieves growing up. Dan is still fighting in France with his regiment. Bit of a quiet one, so we hardly hear from him. Margaret has a family of her own now, but she came to visit me in hospital in France." *The only one.* "Old Peg snuck in a box of honeycomb toffee. The matron wasn't happy when she found the empty wrappers. Do you have siblings?"

"Half sisters ten years younger than I. I've never met them."

A cloud passed over her face. The same kind as when that note arrived with the mask. What in it had caused her to scurry off into the village only to return and commit murder by painted canvas on the parapet? It shouldn't matter to him, this odd woman whom they'd paid a prince's ransom to come to their private home instead of him journeying to the London shop for his new face. Elena had arrived and he'd been determined to get the work done and send her on her way, but instead of keeping a professional distance, she'd kissed him on the cheek and done everything to make him feel . . . normal. Prying into her affairs would only serve to tighten the link she'd woven.

"Perhaps you will now that you've returned to England."

"I doubt that. That man, my father you could presume to call him, tucked them away into a boarding school in the disappointment of not having a son to carry on his legacy. I should like to meet them, these sisters, but only after he's quit this life."

So much for trying not to pry. "Families are complicated."

"Indeed they are."

Reaching the bottom, he guided her to the right where a black metal fence reinforced by thick shrubs enclosed a designated area. "Speaking of which, my own family's morbid pastime of establishing Britain's deadliest plants. I give you the Poison Garden." Barring their way were two massive gates with metal vines curled into them. A large black plate hung on each door with a corroded skull and crossbones and stamped with the warning *These Plants Can Kill*.

"*Zut alors.* If you didn't care for my method of painting, you might have told me rather than resort to this."

"You'll want to cover your mouth and nose. People have fainted due to the toxicity floating in the air."

Rather than being horrified as any proper young lady would, Elena gleefully pulled the scarf from her neck and covered her mouth and nose. Tobias used his handkerchief and pushed open the gate. If not for the sinister gates and menacing skulls to mark this place for what it truly was, one might assume they had stepped into another pleasant English garden filled with bright green plants, gangly bushes, climbing vines, and yellow, purple, pink, and white flowers.

"My several times great-grandfather was a profound botanist, so he created these gardens and allotted this one plot to his wife for her own planting use. Family lore claims she created this out of jealousy for all the time he spent with his plants. He died mysteriously two years after its completion." They walked along the central path as plants and vines of all ominous manner threatened to kill them on either side. "Plants from this very garden were used to kill my great-grandfather. A maid did him in."

"And here most people are led to believe that a garden offers joy, not murder." She stopped next to a rangy plant with pointed leaves and dark round berries. "Do you know all the plants here?"

"Many of them. Don't get too close to that one. Nightshade. One bite of juice will put a child to eternal slumber. Ten or so for an adult."

Careful to keep her distance, she craned her neck to see the berries from all angles. "Remarkable. It looks like a blueberry with the coloring of a blackberry. When pressed, the hue must be incredibly rich."

"Not to mention deadly." He pointed to a tree with branches that appeared to be hanging upside down. Yellow-coned flowers dangled from the ends. "Take a look at this. *Brugmansia*, or Angel's Trumpet. Imported from the wilds of South America. A few decades ago it was fashionable for ladies to keep a flower from the plant to smell and add small amounts of the pollen to their tea to induce a euphoric experience. Or a painless death." One of the many stories the gardeners had told him, Dan, and Margaret when they were children playing hide-and-seek in the hedge maze. They particularly delighted in the more gruesome bits.

Elena gently lifted one of the trumpets with the tip of her umbrella. "They're the same flowers from your grandmother's painting."

"Like I said, my family has an unhealthy fascination with the macabre."

"You say it's your family's, but what is yours?"

Tobias scuffed his boot on the crumbling brick walk. Only in the wee hours of the morning, when time shifted between night and day, did he allow the memories of all that once was. Any other time and the memories became too painful, too painful in his wakeful hours, but here in the garden where the light was hazy, the hurt hesitated.

"As a lad it was adventure and mischief. Within the safe confines of the castle, of course, and as dictated by my parents, who prefer a more sedate life. I had a short reprieve outside the suffocating walls when they sent me off to school and university. Then the war came, and like all the eager lads of the country, I put my name to paper and counted the days until I would finally be shipped off to do my bit for the king. The folly of the inexperienced. Then came the Somme. And this." He touched the black scrap of material covering half his face. "Now adventure belongs to the naïve."

"If that were true, the world would be a dull place indeed. Besides, mistakes are what make us who we are."

"Do you always have a platitude to dole out, or do I bring out the need for silver linings?"

"I simply prefer to see the potential in every situation instead of sulking."

"Grown men do not sulk."

"Then prove it to me when my leaf boat beats yours."

Picking up her skirts, Elena raced out of the garden laughing. A moment of surprise held him rooted to the spot before he shook it off and made after her. If it was a challenge she wanted, his skiff wouldn't disappoint. At the top of the Grand Cascade they both doubled over for breath. Thank goodness she hadn't challenged him to a footrace. His lungs wouldn't have been able to handle it. He'd been idle too long.

"Miss?" Lloyd, the head gardener, appeared holding a rake in one hand and a folded note in the other. He'd lost both sons at Ypres and now tended to the plants and trees by himself as all the other groundskeepers had joined the fighting ranks. "A young man brought this for you a few minutes ago."

Cheeks still pink from exertion, Elena wrinkled her brow as she took the note and unfolded it, revealing its contents to be a flyer for the village's annual Dane Festival. "*Young* man?"

"Aye, miss. Ne'er seen him before, but dressed all shiny and new."

Unease crept along the base of Tobias's skull. The same feeling he got when the Huns started inching from their trenches. How could the woman be summoning this amount of callers in the seventy-two hours since her arrival? "Do you know if this was the same man who brought the package yesterday from Mr. Wood's London shop?"

Lloyd scratched at the patch of gray hair sticking out from under his worn cap. "Don't know, sir. I stick close to me garden. Not much at the castle concerns me."

"It's not the same man," Elena said.

Tobias frowned. More than one mystery caller? "How do you know?"

She plucked a yellow carnation from where it was pinned to the flyer and dropped it, crushing the petals beneath her heel. "Because I do."

CHAPTER 6

The door banged open, startling Tobias from where he stood next to the window, staring across the dusk settling along the ramparts. His mother flew into his chamber with eyes wild. "You must go after her."

"After whom?"

"Miss Hamilton. She's taken it into her head to go to the village. At night, to that festival. Without a chaperone. Heavens above. I knew her to be eccentric coming from"—she dropped her voice to a whisper—"Paris, but I didn't think she would put her own safety at risk. The villagers will not take kindly that she is a guest of the castle. You must return her to the shelter of Leedswick immediately."

He hadn't stepped foot on Birchwick's ancient cobblestone streets since before the war. A distinction he was glad to keep, but necessity called him out to face the fear directly. His mouth twisted with wry humor. Face. The villagers wished to see anything but this mangled mass substituting as his face. That was, if they weren't already throwing stones at him upon learning an Alnwick dared to walk their streets.

Tobias grabbed his discarded jacket from the bed and slipped it on. It hadn't required a great deal of insight to realize that something was wrong the moment Lloyd had given Elena the flyer in the garden that afternoon. The way she'd stamped the flower beneath her heel spoke of an issue more deeply rooted than an aversion to carnations.

One that he would bet held more than a coincidental tie to the first note. And one that did not bode well. Elena Hamilton was a guest in his family's home, and her welfare fell under their purview. If anything should happen to her, he would hold himself fully responsible.

"I'll find her, Mother."

Mother wrung her hands as she paced the threadbare rug. "She has the impulses of Nina. Too carefree for her own good."

The name that once conjured shivers of happiness stabbed him through the heart. "She is nothing like Nina."

+———+

Darkness fell as he crossed the castle bridge, leaving the sanctuary of Leedswick and striding into the uncertainty of the village. When he stepped into the town square, his hands clenched on instinct as he waited for the stares and whispers, the cries of terror as children hid behind their parents. Yet not one disgusted eye turned toward him, and the only shrieks to be heard were from the carnival games, all because the Dane Festival held a tradition of mask wearing. He was but one in a sea of facial guises. He could walk free.

Fairy lights were strung all about from shop roofs and trees, while paper lanterns dangled from poles staked at intervals around the central green. He circled around to the left in search of orange hair yet instead was entangled by the aromas of sweet fried dough, braised pork, and roasted nuts wafting on the cool evening breeze from tables laden with food. Smells difficult to conjure during wartime as most goods were shipped to feed the army.

Game booths boasting a ring toss, darts, and all other manner of cheap feats were set up as the villagers—mostly women, children, and men too old for uniform—milled about in hopes of winning a stuffed bear or a balloon or even a goldfish. In the center of it all was an orange blaze, though not the orange he sought. Demanding a place of pride was a roaring bonfire upon which scraps of paper were tossed for good luck. The fearsome Danes, for whom this entire hurly-burly existed, would be immensely proud that their savage lust to conquer had been reduced to candy floss and wishes thrown into a fire.

No Elena to be found.

A girlish giggle came from the direction of the strongman setup a few yards away, where an officer dressed in the khaki uniform of His Majesty's Royal Army swung a hammer onto a metal disc that spiraled up and pinged a loud bell. The dainty woman next to him giggled again, and the familiar sound pierced Tobias's heart. She was all froth and pink lace with golden curls pinned perfectly beneath her cartwheel hat bedecked with floral roses.

Proving himself the manliest of men according to a rigged carnival game, the officer selected a red rose as his prize and handed it to her with a gallant bow.

Her eyes fluttered in delight over the red petals and landed on Tobias. All vestiges of delight drained from her face.

"Hello, Nina."

"Tobias. I-I didn't think—"

"Think you'd see me here?" He fought to keep his tone polite yet detached. "I decided it was safe enough with all the masks running about. None the wiser to this." He touched his own cover.

She was too well-bred to acknowledge the obvious elephant bellowing between them and fell back to polite introductions instead. As if they were two casual acquaintances without a hundred letters of declarations between them. "Allow me to present Major Theodore Permond. Theo, this is Tobias Alnwick."

"A pleasure to meet you, Major. Long way from home, aren't you?" Tobias nodded to the Oxfordshire and Buckinghamshire Light Infantry insignia on the man's shoulder.

Permond grinned. He was what the women might consider

handsome in a privileged sort of manner. Others with more discerning taste would size him up as a ponce with a taste for beer if the smell rolling off him was any indication. "One travels where one must for one's girl. When we met last year in London for a regimental fundraiser, I could not believe that such an elegant woman could live this far north. I thought the area was reserved for the descendants of barbaric Norsemen."

The admission hit Tobias square in the gut. Last year they'd met. This time last year he'd been lying in a hospital bed begging for death. Wishing that shell had landed smack on him instead of taking only half his face and wanting only a letter from Nina. When the long-awaited letter arrived, it informed him of her cooled affections and assured that he would remain to her a dear friend of fondest memories. The rawness of heartbreak had eased, but a soreness lingered in him still.

Swallowing the rush of bitterness, he glanced to the bonfire, making sure his left side remained hidden by shadow. "As you can see, we still commemorate our Viking history, though we keep it less murderous in this modern age. If you're not too busy sipping champagne in elegant London this new year, perhaps you'd like to experience Yule. That's when the true pagans come out."

"Afraid the delights of London will have to remain in my memory for now." Permond looked meaningfully at Nina, but she kept her gaze firmly on her patent leather shoes, the blaze of pink on her cheeks the only indication that she'd heard him. "I'm only in country for convalescence. Took a round of shrapnel to the chest, but the doctor in Paris patched me up well enough with just enough scarring to prove my heroics."

Tobias shoved his fist in his pocket to keep from slugging the sod on his pretentious nose. "Glad to hear he could accommodate you."

"Saved a bit of the metal as a souvenir to give to Nina, didn't I, sweetheart?"

Nina nodded meekly.

Tobias's other hand balled. He shoved it in its appropriate pocket. "A thoughtful reminder of all you went through to return to her."

Nina's cheeks burned red as she looked everywhere but at him. And why should she? Once had been enough, and it had sent her crying from his presence. She was still beautiful, still poised and demure as all women of noble society were trained to be as the perfect potential wife. He had thought so once, but he saw now the shine had dimmed. Something brighter had streaked into his life. Some*one* brighter who did not care for society's ridiculous outlook.

Oblivious to the torment playing out, Permond looped an arm around Nina's shoulders and beamed like the lucky cur he presumed himself to be. "I'll say. She's been having a right good bawl since I got orders to ship back to France next week." She stiffened as he hugged her close. Patting her shoulder, Permond dropped his arm and swung his attention to Tobias. "Listen to me. Going on about the fighting to you. All I can say is how much we appreciate you civilians working to make the bullets in our guns and knitting those mittens. You don't know how cold it gets in those winter trenches."

"Tobias was in the Royal Northumberland Fusiliers. He was wounded at the Somme," Nina's small voice eked out, though she didn't meet his eye.

Once upon a time Tobias had been thrilled when Nina spoke about him to all who would listen, but now her acknowledgment produced only a hollowness he wished to carve out and toss into the flames of forgetfulness.

"I say, that was a right nasty affair. Lost many an Englishman there." Permond's finely groomed eyebrows drew down as his glassy eyes shifted between Nina and Tobias. "How do you two know each other?"

Nina's lips pressed tightly together while Tobias merely shrugged. "There's a saying that Northumberland is a large area with a small feel. It's difficult not to know all the surrounding families that have lived here for generations. History means a great deal to the people here."

"History belongs to the passing generations." Permond waved a dismissive hand. "As you said, this is the modern age. Time to move things forward, wouldn't you say?"

Tobias uncurled his hands and removed them from his pockets, sloughing off the clinging shreds of bitterness. "On this I think I might agree with you. If you'll excuse me. It was a pleasure meeting you, Major. Nina." He gave a short bow and walked away. "Odd duck," he heard Permond say, but Tobias didn't listen for Nina's response. A response from the girl who had given him the knock held no importance to him. Not anymore.

Striding past the bonfire and a gaggle of children with masks made of leaves and fabric scraps, Tobias searched each booth and food table for the rainbow that would lead him to Elena. He rounded the church's low stone wall that was festooned with banners and there she was, standing behind the goldfish booth. Talking to a strange man in a suit with a yellow carnation in his buttonhole. And she didn't look pleased.

＋———＋

Elena forced her voice to remain polite but firm. The effort gave her a splitting headache. "I will repeat myself one last time so that I am perfectly clear: Mr. Burgess has no control over my decisions or my life. His shipping company and his need for an heir are of no concern to me, and there is certainly no chance of a union between ourselves to benefit him. You've come all this way to woo me in false hopes, Mr. Mulligan."

Simon Mulligan had been waiting for her at the festival as she knew he would be, and he was just as she remembered from their one meeting in London, where he'd presented her with a yellow carnation. He was handsome in a sharp, angular sort of way with coal-black hair slicked back and sharp dark eyes that missed nothing. His manners and speech spoke of a decent education, while his precisely tailored clothes revealed a man accustomed to power. She wanted to rip the yellow carnation from his buttonhole the second she spotted him.

"I understand your hesitation, Miss Hamilton, but allow me to reassure you that I have nothing but the utmost respect for you."

"If you respect me so much, a complete stranger, then why agree to this ridiculous demand of a marriage?"

Mr. Mulligan nodded gravely as if expecting this round of interrogation. "Your father—Mr. Burgess—may have his own plans for proposing a union, but I have my own as well and they are pure and intended for the good of the company. You see, I began working at Burgess Shipping Company when I was only fourteen years old. Slowly I rose through the positions, all of which I know inside and out. While Mr. Burgess may lead a troubled private life, have no doubt that he is a shrewd businessman. He promoted me to his assistant and taught me everything he knows. I love this company as much as he does, and I wish only to keep it in the right hands to watch her prosper."

"The right hands being yours and the only way to ensure that is by marrying the legal heir—me." A chill breeze filled with the scent of salt water from the North Sea ruffled over the village, stirring banners and bumping the paper lanterns into one another from where they dangled on strings. In her haste to put this unpleasant interaction behind her, she hadn't thought beyond grabbing a simple shawl to ward off the night air. She pulled the woven wool closer as the breeze prickled her skin. Perhaps it wasn't only the breeze.

"To put it bluntly, yes." Thoughts and words shifted in his eyes as quickly as the dancing bonfire flames reflected in their dark depths.

At last he settled on a thought that softened the sharp lines of his face. "You don't know me. Allow me the opportunity to change that upon your return to London. I'll show you all the wonderful plans I have for the company, ways to help improve lives around the world, and what we're doing now to help the war effort. I'm a patron at the National Gallery and would consider it the highest of honors if you were to escort me about the paintings with your fountain of knowledge on the subject."

"I cannot and will not be associated with anything that man has touched. It is but dry rot."

He stepped closer, smelling of clove aftershave. She detested clove. "Then do not think of him. Think of what it could be. What we could build together."

"Why are the both of you so persistent in this endeavor? What is the importance in settling this detestable matter with the utmost haste?"

His expression was pained. "It is because your father is not well. His time is limited and he wishes to settle accounts without delay. A year, perhaps two, was the physician's prognosis."

Aaron Burgess was dying. The news should have stricken a daughter's heart, but she had never been his daughter as he had never been deserving of the title *father*. "What he does with his remaining time is not my concern. He has never been a man worthy of sympathy, and deathbed manipulations will not sway my compassion now."

"I understand your reluctance, but know that I am not him. Do not say anything yet, please. Think on what I said. That is all I ask. Good night, Miss Hamilton."

Removing the flower from his lapel, he pressed it into her hand and melted into the crowd of masked revelers before she could outright deny him again. Clever, for she had no intention of accepting, much less thinking on his proposition to become better acquainted. Any man who would associate with her father, no matter his separate dreams of creating a worthwhile cause, was not a man she wished to spend any amount of time with.

"The flower stalker, I take it." Tobias cut through the night like a shadow. He towered over her, angling himself against her side.

"The one and only." Elena resisted the urge to scoot closer to him. She'd dealt with unwanted advances aplenty—after all, it was considered an art form among the *ivrogne* of Montparnasse—but this sudden protection from a gentleman was new and—dare she say?—most welcome.

"Miss Hamilton—"

"Elena."

He took a polite step away and clasped his hands behind his back. "Your personal affairs are none of my business. However, as a guest at Leedswick your safety is my concern. It was utterly careless to slip off into the night to meet a gentleman caller. Any amount of harm might have befallen you, not to mention your reputation."

Yes, she could grow accustomed to a gentleman's concern for her. Particularly one who looked at her as Tobias did, as if she was the only priority before him. It must have cost him dearly to leave his shelter of the castle to come after her. "I have no need of the opinion of others when it comes to my reputation. It remains sterling to me and that is all that matters. As for causing you undue anxiety on my behalf, I wholeheartedly apologize."

Brow furrowing, he rolled his gaze over her face in quick estimate. "Are you quite well? Has he perturbed you in any way?"

Perturbed was one way to put it. Threatening her freedom and Tobias's family's reputation via blackmail defied words.

Handing the carnation to a little girl in passing, Elena looped her arm through Tobias's. He stiffened but didn't pull away, which bumped a small beat of happiness to her heart. "If you allow me to buy you a candy floss, I shall tell you all about it. It's the least I can do for giving you a scare."

A short while later they sat on a bench at the edge of the merriment, tucked deep into the shadow of the church steeple. The town green blazed with the orange brightness of a pagan hall, shimmering off the game booth awnings and swerving between the dozens of people who tossed their wishes into the bonfire's roaring flames.

"So you can understand why I want nothing to do with my father, his company, or this man who promises a shining world of change." Elena's mouth pinched as the rest of the truth bubbled at the back of her throat.

"Is there something more?"

His concerned tone warmed her. She had brought trouble to his door when she only wished to offer hope. Now a letter threatened to ruin the fragile peace he and his family had spun high behind their castle walls. She could not burden him with more. It was her web to untangle from. Pulling off a bit of pink spun sugar, she stuffed it in her mouth and swallowed what she had been about to confess.

"My mother spent her life protecting me from him. I will never sully her unselfishness or love to even consider such a proposal. After all, this is the twentieth century. Women are not meant to be bought and sold for their wombs." She turned at the surprised noise stuck in Tobias's throat. "Apologies. I forget candor should be well disguised under prim manners on this side of the Channel."

"It's quite all right. It's just that I'm unaccustomed to any person speaking so openly about their past." He absently rubbed his palms against his knees. A calming tactic many of the men employed when they came to the shop and the strain of the unfamiliar situation preyed upon their nerves.

She had been open, even about the ugly parts that she preferred to keep hidden, yet with Tobias she had difficulty in differentiating what was best to conceal and what to reveal. Perhaps it was his own vulnerability in allowing her to see the twisted parts of himself that gave her courage to voice her own darkness. No one had prompted that kind of emotional freedom since Mama. Confessing one's burdens was rumored to be cathartic, a release of the pain, but she had never found it so. All it was good for was dredging up old hurts and shames.

Tobias had a way of inflicting neither as he sat quietly listening to each word without judgment or censure. The world at large told her to sit down, remain quiet, and do as she was told—demands she had never been good at following. But Tobias encouraged the opposite from her. He encouraged her to be herself.

"In all honesty, I had no intention of telling you, but as the sordid strings of my life have trailed me here and knocked squarely on your door, I think it only fair you are aware of the seediness blooming around me."

"You hardly seem the seedy sort."

"That's because you don't know me as well as you think you do. I wear yellow with my orange hair. When painting I like to sing bawdy tunes from Moulin Rouge, and worst of all I've been known to stroll the park"—she glanced around to ensure they were alone—"without a chaperone."

A faint smile tugged at the corner of his mouth. It lightened his entire countenance. "Miscreant. However did we allow you under our roof?"

"The question is, how much longer will you allow me to remain, knowing my true nature?" She waggled her eyebrows at him.

"As soon as your task is complete, I shall drop you at the nearest train station and wash my hands of you, returning to the cold walls of my castle to live out the rest of my days as a recluse who feeds the villagers' imaginations for monster tales." His tone was teasing as hers had been, but by the end of his speech, Elena's smile had evaporated.

"Oh, please don't say that. I couldn't bear to think of you hiding behind those walls. The world is too wondrous a place."

"Not the times I've seen it."

"Then you haven't seen the right parts. I could show you the lemon warmth of south France, the crystalline lakes of Bavaria. But why stop there? I've always wanted to experience the Great Pyramid of Giza at sunrise and travel the Orient Express across Siberia." She angled the paper cone topped with the candy floss to him. "Indulge in the beignets of New Orleans, America."

He declined the offered sweet. "I should like to see those very much, but I might prove too great a distraction from the magnificent views. People seek adventure for great architecture and stunning vistas, not deformities."

"Then you must learn to ignore such people. The world was not created for only those perfect in form. It is for all of us. Wounded Tommies and redheads with odd faces too." She bumped his shoulder.

His returning smile sent a pleasant sensation skipping through her. "It's a nice face."

Even more pleasantness twirled through her as she smiled back. "I think you have a nice face too."

"What's left of it."

She cupped his cheek, the puckers of scarred skin warm beneath her fingers. "All of it."

A crisp wind ruffled his hair, teasing a dark curl across his forehead. The strained years of war smoothed into an expression of the lightheartedness that must have once guided him. A lightness that glowed in his eye and reached toward her, inviting her to bask in his company.

"It's nice of you to think so. Not all women do." The light faded into a frown as he took her hand from his face. "Your hands are freezing. We should move closer to the fire."

Hesitation prickled his tone as he looked to the merrymakers gathered around the bonfire, ever careful to keep his wounded side turned to the shadow should a gaze stray his way. Even in the darkness surrounded by other masks, he could not allow his guard of protection to drop. Elena had been surprised to see him. He had made a courageous move in stepping out of his castle tonight, and that was enough to stir a sense of satisfaction in her heart.

"Perhaps we should return to the castle. The hour grows late." The church bells struck the ten o'clock hour as if in agreement.

Standing, Tobias slipped off his jacket and dropped it over her shoulders, then offered his hand to help her stand. She didn't let go, instead nestling her hand into the crook of his elbow as they walked back toward the stone bridge that separated the village from Leedswick.

Two young women wearing face coverings made of feathers and carrying large bull horns filled with cider traipsed past giggling.

"Why do they wear masks?" Elena asked.

"The festival commemorates the Battle of Straw when a band of Vikings landed on our shores. Most of the surrounding villages were pillaged and burned, but the people of Birchwick were clever. While the invaders slept, our people covered themselves in twigs, feathers, and animal skins and surrounded their camp with straw before lighting it on fire. The villagers shrieked terribly with their farming scythes and axes so that the Vikings thought they were being attacked by another band of Danes. The celebrations have tamed down a bit over the centuries."

"A shame. I should like to have seen you in feathers and tree bits. A horned helmet, perhaps."

"Fictitious by the way."

"Still jolly good fun. All things considered, it's been a marvelous evening." She tossed the empty sticky cone into a waste bin, the movement dislodging Tobias's jacket from her shoulder.

He swiftly reached around and adjusted it without breaking stride. "Has it? I thought your ardent beau might have ruined it."

"I never allow bad things to worry me for long. Mr. Mulligan might have been the reason I came tonight, but he also brought you here, inadvertently, and I've had a splendid time talking with you." She slowed to a stop in the middle of the bridge. A river tumbled between rocks beneath the curved stone structure. "I apologize again for the trouble he and my father have brought to your doorstep. They had no right to do so, and I only hope you won't think less of me for not leaving those troubles in Kent where they belong."

"There is no need to apologize. They ambushed you." Gently releasing her arm, he turned to the rail and braced his hands on top. "The truth is, you are not the only one with amorous intent turned sour. The girl I swore to return home to after the war, the girl who proclaimed to wait for me no matter how long the years were, took one look at my face and ran crying from the room. 'Please don't ask me to,' she said."

His long fingers curled over the rail, the knuckles stark white against the gray stone. "She was here tonight with an officer, him and his bloody perfect, unscathed face. While I was being dragged mangled from the field and stitched back together in some casualty-clearing station on the Somme with the guns pounding not two miles away, they were dancing on champagne bubbles in London in the name of fundraising for the troops."

How utterly devastating. Was it any wonder Tobias chose to remain concealed behind his walls when the one person who had promised to guard his heart cut him deeper than any mortar fragment ever could?

Heart aching for him, she placed her hand on top of his and squeezed. "I'm so sorry, Tobias."

He didn't flinch, nor did he move away from her touch. "In a way I'm glad I came here tonight and saw her. Like the closing of a chapter. I once thought her the perfection of womanhood, but now I realize how foolish seeking perfection is. It's not all it's cracked up to be."

"If this was the realization you required, I'm delighted to have wandered off to a clandestine meeting, provoking you into action."

"I was concerned for you."

His simple admission stitched closed the ache of sadness in her heart and sent it pattering along another course entirely. One filled with sunlight and warmth. "Perhaps I should wander away more often if only to incite heroic gallantry. No man has chased after me with romantic intent."

Straightening, he kept hold of her hand, turning it until he was cradling it. "Never? A pity. All ladies deserve at least one romantic chase in their lives." His small finger brushed against hers.

"I quite agree."

"But I should not like to chase you, Miss Hamilton." Her momentary disappointment disappeared as he looped her hand through his arm once again and turned them to the castle, their feet falling in step. "I enjoy far more having you at my side."

CHAPTER 7 ─────────────────────────

The thought of kissing Elena hadn't crossed Tobias's mind until that very moment when she hovered mere inches from his face in an attempt to capture the exact shade of brown of his eye. He'd always considered the color rather ordinary, but she insisted it was more rich mahogany that melted to whiskey in the center. At the moment he was happy not to argue with her.

The night of the festival last week had tilted the world into the unknown. He thought Nina had been the one, but it appeared she was the one only when life was riding high. He needed someone for the valleys as well as the exhilarations. Someone who could look past what he lacked in favor of all he had to give. Since his injury, Elena was the first person to think he still had something worth offering. She saw him as a man, and quite frankly, at times that was all a man needed, but it was more than that. She pulled out his best and gave him hope that good things were still to come.

Rain pattered against the window behind him, bathing the studio in murky gray despite the dozens of candles and lanterns brought in to coax decent lighting for painting. Elena leaned closer, nearly bumping her nose to his. Despite the proximity, her attention remained entirely focused on work without noticing the path on which his thoughts lingered.

"I have never seen a pair of eyes like yours before. One blue and one brown," he said.

She blinked, breaking her professional concentration. "Mama called them lucky. She said there are too many wonderful colors in the world to see its glory through only one shade."

"Perhaps that's why you became an artist. You see more colors than the rest of us."

Settling back on her stool, she dabbed her slender brush into a swirl of brown and yellow paint and brushed it around the center of the glass eye that would soon be joined to his mask. "Now that's an interesting consideration. As if I were perfectly equipped for my passion. To see what others cannot." She fanned the color out, blending it to the darker brown around the rim of the iris.

"What do you see when you look at me?" Before the war he never would have stooped so low with such a pathetic inquiry, but the affliction of battle had a way of carving through the unnecessary. More than anything he needed Elena to find something necessary in him.

"Someone very good at sitting still."

"Is that all?"

"Come now. A lady is allowed her secrets." She winked and his heart did everything but sit still.

If he sat here much longer, he could not be held accountable for his actions with her looking at him in that way. Best to retreat to safer, and more respectable, ground. "Very well, allow me to present another type of secret. A seek-and-find, if you will. We've been at this for most of the morning despite the rain casting a gloom about the studio, and artists require good light for painting, do they not?"

Her hand stilled over the glass pupil. "What do you have in mind?"

"We'll continue the family tradition of searching for my grandfather's journal. It has been lost for far too long, and what better way to spend a rainy day than poking into forgotten castle corners?"

"How positively atmospheric." Hopping off her perch, she placed the wet eye on a soft cloth to dry and rinsed out her brush. "Let's go."

As they twisted down the western corridor, dust rose from their passing footsteps and thickened the air with age. This section had once been the private chambers of his grandparents but had been permanently shuttered when he was a boy. He hadn't returned to search since.

Opening the door to his grandmother's private sitting room, Elena walked in, waving dust motes from her face. "My goodness. Should ever I wish to hide something, it would be in here. No one would ever find it beneath all this dust."

Tobias moved around the chamber, discarding the most obvious hiding places in favor of hidden latches on the wall. "As a boy it was merely a game to be the one to finally find it. Now I feel as if I can relate to Charles's reluctance at the intrusion of the outside world. I want to know if he ever found a way to combat it, if he ever grew restless behind these walls and regretted his choice." He stomped on the floorboards in hopes one would prove hollow for a secret hole.

"If he regretted it, why did he and your grandmother remain? Why did they not try to make amends with the village? He was innocent after all."

"The village did not want them. Guilty or innocent. The damage was done and forgiveness was not an option."

Elena poked her head up the fireplace chimney. Her voice echoed back. "Balderdash. That was two generations ago."

"Believe it or not, my family—this castle—is . . . well, not welcome."

"Cursed, you mean?" At his wince, she shrugged. "When you first told me about it, that day when we looked at your grandparents' portraits, you did not say precisely what the curse is, but clearly it's meant to bring your family misery and fear."

"And so it has."

"Fear lacks good reasoning for why one should not do a thing."

"There are many who would disagree with you."

"Then they are not truly living." She ducked out from under the mantel with aged soot smeared across her temple. "Seclusion might have been your grandparents' happiness, but the answers you seek in a journal may not be the key to yours. Only you can answer that."

The fear gnawing at his peace day and night forced itself to be heard. "What if it's unattainable?"

"You'll never know if you never try."

Tobias crossed the room to her and carefully wiped the soot from her forehead with his thumb. It was the one thing he admired most about her, her fearlessness to find hope in a burning world. She made him want to believe again. "And you? What happiness are you trying for?"

"Right now I'm working in Mr. Wood's shop until this war is over and my services are no longer needed." She could say a great deal about her desire to earn her place rather than having it bought by her devil of a father. "After which I shall raise a glass of champagne to our victory over the Huns." He smiled wryly at her confidence as she tipped an imaginary glass to him. "Then I should like to continue traveling and painting the magnificent sights I see, and if I am very lucky, I will find a patron to fund my quest to capture beauty in paintings."

"Then you will need to find a patron who can keep up, for your feet do not remain in one place for very long."

"No, they gather dust otherwise and leave a doormat where sad memories may come to call."

He searched past her cheerful expression and chipped away at the truth it covered. "You claim that my reluctance to leave these walls is simply a way of avoiding the world. Perhaps you avoid difficulties by running away."

Her smile faltered. "We all do what we must."

"Are you running now?"

"For a man boasting a single eye, you are entirely too perceptive." With a sigh she stepped away from him and leaned against the back of a shrouded settee. "I had a friend in Paris. Pierre. He was a gentle soul who longed to sing on the Garnier stage. When the Germans invaded, he rushed to rescue his mother who lived in the countryside, in the direct path of the marching Huns. They shelled the village one night, destroying homes and killing dozens, including Pierre's mother. He managed to survive but lost his leg. He returned to Paris a broken, guilt-eaten man. I tried to help him, but it wasn't enough. I was so distracted with the invasion and the school closing and Mama that I failed to see the signs. Failed to help him when he needed me most. I found him hanging from a beam in his room with a note that said he could not go on."

Tobias's heart, the one he thought withered and of no use, thumped with sadness for her. "I'm so very sorry, Elena. You cannot blame yourself for another's decision—"

"I should have helped Pierre more, but he's gone and I must find atonement with each mask I paint for a wounded man. If I can bring comfort with brushstrokes, then that is what I will do. It is my only hope of exorcising my shame. With each mask I want to prove that life is indeed worth living no matter our pain."

Drowning in his own pity, he had failed to acknowledge the possible hurts of those around him. Here was this creature before him putting to rest her grief by caring for others while he rambled around like a bear with a thorn in his paw. What an utterly selfish cad he'd been.

Eager to be near her light, he moved to stand next to her. "You are the most extraordinary woman I have ever met. In the rawest and ugliest form of pain, you manage to paint something beautiful. If only I could see things as you do."

"After Pierre and Mama died, I didn't believe I had anything left to offer. My joy was stripped from me. It took time to find it again, to find purpose." Her shoulder brushed his arm as she turned to look up at him. "Your abilities are greater than you allow yourself to believe, Tobias. Tell me what it is that you do see. What ugliness can you transform?"

"I cannot see farther than the completion of this mask. Before the war I was brought up to think only of Leedswick and my coming role as its master. Imagining a life beyond the estate was not tolerated, but her glory is faded, and with the funds—well, this way of life is a relic without the means to support it for much longer. If it were up to me, I should like to hand the reins over to Daniel, strike out, and never look back."

"Strike out for what?"

"I'm not sure." He scuffed his toe against the dusty floorboard as secret longings unlocked themselves from where he'd hidden them deep inside. "See some of those places you talked about. Maybe write down my experiences. A fellow I was in hospital with told me it was cathartic to exorcise the demons."

"Yet you see no further than completing the mask." She bumped his shoulder. He couldn't keep from returning a smile to her knowing one. "It can be difficult to see the next step beyond this war. It was for me after my mother died, and even in the ripeness of grief, deep down I knew I would have to carry on because life could not die with my sadness. At first it was one day at a time, and then it became a boat to England, and now a train to Northumberland."

"With a decrepit soldier who's heir to a failing estate."

"At least you're not being harangued to produce an heir for a legacy you want nothing to do with."

That bull of a father and snake of a suitor. Anger boiled over any rational response. "If that man ever approaches you again, I'll dangle him over the parapets by his ankles."

"Violence for violence is not an act I can condone. Besides, both Mr. Burgess and Mr. Mulligan have long since returned to Kent, where they remain as my burden to bear. Not yours." Her ruddy eyebrows pulled down to a displeased point. "Another thing I do not condone is calling yourself decrepit. You are a man far from it."

"Then perhaps you are the one blinded."

"If you are decaying about the gills, where is your old-man cane or flare-up of gout? Since you have no tufts of white hair poking from your ears, I have no cause to believe you."

"You simply refuse to see what's in front of you, don't you? Forever reimagining things as you wish them to be. Beautiful."

Stepping closer until the hem of her floaty skirt brushed his shoe tops, she tilted her face up with the full solemnity of gray skies manifesting in her unflinching gaze. It both terrified and thrilled him. "An artist's duty is to reveal truth. Not as it is reflected in the world or shown in the fleeting whims of a fickle society, but as it unveils how the subject truly wishes to be seen. I see you, Tobias Alnwick." She placed her hand over his heart. The sensation was without a doubt thrilling.

"And I see you, Elena." Emboldened by her unconcern for propriety, he reached out, grasped one of her curls, and gently pulled the spring straight. "Color of a sunset."

Pink blossomed across her face, brightening the freckles to full effect. "It was darker when I was younger. The color of wet rust. Much prettier."

"I prefer the sunset." He wrapped the strand around his finger, the silkiness cool against his skin. What would it feel like loosed from the scarf that bound it atop her head, its coiled weight heavy in his hands, its copper shimmering like a river over his palms?

Her fingers curved into his chest as he dropped the strand and slipped his hand to the curls tangling at the back of her neck. That intoxicating mixture of terror and thrill drew his gaze to her mouth. He should walk away now, remembering she was a guest in his house and he should not take advantage of his position, but Elena had a way of blurring the lines so that employer and worker, lord and artist, no longer mattered. Society would care if it were to see them together, but society and its opinions had never been of use to him.

A loud throat clearing torpedoed the sunset into tiny bits of obliterated opportunity. "Sir." Stokes stood in the doorway, oblivious to his targeted destruction of romance. So much for the abandoned west wing. The man could find a grain of rice in a snowstorm. "Your mother and father wish to see you in the library."

Dropping his hand to his side, Tobias stepped away from Elena. "I'll be there shortly."

"Very good, sir." Stokes inclined his head and marched away with his beak nose leading the way.

Leaving his grandmother's dusty rooms, Tobias shut the door behind them as he and Elena retraced their steps to the habitable part of the castle. "Looks as if our search will have to continue another day. Allow me to take you back to the studio."

Elena glanced out a bank of grimy windows to the soggy grounds and cluster of roofs beyond the western wall. "No, that's all right. I'll take advantage of the rain stopping and walk to the village. I need to send a telegram to Mr. Wood and update him on our progress. He's quite curious to see how the work gets on outside the workshop to decide if it's a service he might offer to other men finding it difficult to travel to London."

They descended the turret's winding stairs that still bore sword nicks from when an invading lord tried to hack his way to the top. "If you wait until I've attended to the business with my parents, I might escort you partway." Tobias might have strode onto Birchwick's common the night of the festival to find Elena, but he wasn't ready to tackle his demons in the broad light of day without the pretense of masked festivities to conceal him.

"The telegram office closes in half an hour and I don't wish to rush you. How about I meet you on the garden path afterward? A black elderberry tree grows near the roses, and a Romani lady I met once on the road to Seine-et-Marne said the berries create the richest blue-purple color when mashed."

He slowed to a stop at a crossway that would take him left to the library and her down the grand staircase to the front door. Or up another flight of stairs to her chamber. Whichever way she chose, it meant a parting. So he stalled.

"A new painting, I take it?"

"What else?" She didn't move to leave.

"Only elderberries? No carrots, or oak leaves, or cinnamon sticks to drain?"

"Cinnamon sticks?" Her laugh rang off the high ceiling. A sound that had not been heard within these stale walls for some time. "I admit artists are an eccentric bunch, but even we have our limits." She leaned close and dropped her voice. "Besides, I tried once and mostly they leave a terrible mess on your hands. People assume you've been baking all day rather than creating inspired masterpieces."

It was his turn to laugh. "No cinnamon then, which is fortunate. The stuff makes me sneeze."

She grinned and he grinned. And there they were, two grinning fools. Hedging one more minute together.

He needed to leave before the minute stretched into another and then he would be forced to continue this charade talk of carrots or kiss her. Both would require a great deal of courage that he didn't have enough time to summon. He turned left. "Then I shall meet you in half an hour." Seized by spontaneity, he paused and looked back. "Perhaps you'll show me how to use the paint."

Sweeping her skirt aside with dramatic flair, she curtsied. "Nothing would delight me more."

Lighter than he'd felt in weeks, months even, Tobias found his way to the library where his mother and father awaited him in overstuffed chairs with an impressive backdrop collection of books requiring two stories of shelf space to contain vast amounts of knowledge. Heavy damask drapes were tied back to allow the gray light to waver through the diamond-paned windows and cast its dimness across the intricately coffered ceilings. It had been a favorite playroom for him, Dan, and Margaret as children, hiding among the stacks of books and clamoring up the metal stairs to the balcony. Tobias reminisced as the massive fireplace warmed his memories to golden happiness.

Today the library held all the cheer of a tomb as a small flame flickered in the yawning stone hearth, next to which sat a pitiful stack of logs. With most of the footmen gone to fight, Tobias had taken on the task of chopping wood. With over 150 rooms in the castle, he'd been ruthless in deciding which ones necessitated firewood. Never again would this pile of timber and stone bask in the warmth of fortune and abundance as it had before the war. The time of noble families living high in their castles with dozens of servants scurrying about to see to their every need was at an end. Nothing would ever be the same and families such as his could either adapt with the changing world or ruin themselves by clinging to the past.

"Ah, dear. Here you are at last." Mother sat on the edge of her chair with hands primly folded in her lap.

Father sat opposite her ensconced behind his customary newspaper. "Allies Storm Passchendaele" blared the headline in thick black ink. Images of British and French troops advancing on the German lines near the Belgian village sprawled beneath the words.

"We just rang for tea." As if prompted by his mother's announcement, a maid appeared with a tea tray. Mother dismissed the maid and poured the steaming brew into the two provided cups, handing one to Father and placing the other in front of herself. A third glass, this one thicker and bevel sided, she offered to Tobias.

Sitting on a velvet settee that had seen better days, Tobias took the glass and sipped. The tartness hit his tongue and slid down his throat in a pleasant manner. Cranberry juice at room temperature.

He could no longer tolerate hot drinks. Nor anything hot close to his face. It provoked a blackness he'd rather bury. The heat of the mortar shell. A burst of light. Metal shrapnel tearing at his face. Fire all around. His skin flaming with pain. He sipped the juice and pushed away the intrusive memories.

"How are things coming along with Miss Hamilton?"

Tobias choked on the juice. "Pardon?"

Oblivious to the double meaning behind her question, Mother added a splash of milk to her cup. "She's been here nearly three weeks. How go the efforts?"

Composing himself, Tobias placed the glass on the table. The mask. Of course. The reason for Elena, er, Miss Hamilton's visit and not that sudden flip in his chest when she breezed into the room. Or the way she took his arm as if it was the most natural gesture in the world. Or how she— His parents were staring, awaiting a response. "The mask grows more lifelike every day. Or so she tells me. I don't wish to see it until it's complete."

"Whyever not? I think you would be thrilled for the progress as it pertains to your . . . well, you returning to yourself." Mother's cheeks tinged pink as she tiptoed around his supposed fragility. A condition both his parents were determined to ignore for what they assumed was his benefit. Really it was their own discomfort they could not face.

Tobias stared at the condensation gathering on his glass as the dark and light of misery and release battled in his soul. His inner core remained as the man he had always been with values of loyalty and duty, but the exploding mortar shell had done more than carve his face. Its jagged shrapnel had sliced away the frivolous parts of his life before the war until the pieces left behind were sharpened by a survivor's perspective. No one but another survivor would understand. Those at home wished only to have their loved ones returned to them, familiar and in one piece. When they failed to accept the foreign and broken bits, it was enough to make a man doubt his worth.

"Am I not myself now?"

"Certainly you are, dear boy, only we are so eager to see the fin-ished project. Aren't we, Harold?" Mother turned to Father, pleading for support in a conversation that was rapidly turning sour.

The top corner of the newspaper peeled down to reveal Father's eye. "Certainly. What else are we paying that woman for?" The news-paper flicked back to conceal him.

Braving a smile, Mother softened her expression as one did before an unpleasant blow. "What your father means is that Miss Hamilton is a pleasant enough young woman and we certainly value her skills and contribution to the war effort, in particular your welfare. How much longer will her project take? Of course we do not wish to rush her stay, but the cost of entertaining . . ." She spread her hands as if the unfinished sentence might complete itself in comprehension.

Father's newspaper rattled. "What your mother means is that paying a private artist is not cheap and we've spent a great deal in bringing her here to fix you. We have budgeted expenses for the year, and if she stays much longer, we'll be forced to cut back in other areas considerably. Another generation and all of what belongs to you, son, may be gone if we do not conserve resources where they matter most."

"Then sell it," Tobias said. "Grandmother Beatrice's dowry stands on its last legs with no means of replenishing it or affording the upkeep of a castle crumbling around our ears. I seriously doubt the inheritance put aside for me when I reach thirty years old will put a dent in needed repairs."

"It is your birthright to care for this estate."

"It is a weight drowning us. You said yourself that what remains in our coffers may not last beyond the next generation."

Father snapped the paper to the next page. "Certainly true if that woman doesn't hurry up her painting."

"What your father means," Mother rushed in to say, "is that we only wish life to return to normal as quickly as possible. To how it all was before."

Standing, Tobias plunked his half-finished glass on the table and walked to the nearest bookcase. Rows of leather-bound classics in their first editions and more recent additions brought from America were lined up by their matching colors. *"More pleasing to the eye,"* Mother had insisted. She preferred the section on botanicals, which coincidentally were all bound in green cloth. Uniform and pleasant.

He ran his finger down the spine of *Hamlet*. Dust filmed the brown leather and gold-embossed letters. Before the war two maids had cleaned this room daily. Now, one maid remained to care for the entire first floor.

"The eye is nearly complete." Mother gripped her teacup as he spoke. "Miss Hamilton then has only to attach it to the mask and provide any remaining corrections needed once I'm wearing it. By week's end, I imagine. As long as I don't trip down the stairs and damage the other half of my face. Even things out a bit."

The teacup clattered from her fingers to the saucer. "Oh, Tobias. How could you say such a thing?"

"It was only a jest. You remember those, don't you? When humor was once to be found?"

"Of course I do, and I long for those days to return. This addition is only the beginning." Gathering her skirts, she rushed to him. Tears gathered in the corners of her eyes, but the motherly adoration stopped short of reaching out to touch him. "How handsome you'll be. Just like always. Nina will see it, too, and in time return to you. You can be happy again."

"Nina would not take me for the man that I am despite what I meant to her before. I do not want such a woman, nor one with pity or horror in her eyes when she sees me." Despite his missing eye, he was not the one blinded. Before the war he had been a man secure in his position in the world with possibilities strewn at his feet. A mortar on the Somme changed all that, tearing away the old and rebuilding in him a new man from the tatters left behind. "Mother, I'm not handsome. Look at me. I've changed and you're not accepting that."

Father's newspaper crinkled as he lowered it to his lap. "Why else do you think we've hired an artist to come to our private home if not in acknowledgment of your situation?"

"This is not a situation to deal with. I was wounded. On the battlefield in service to king and country. I fell and nearly died." Undoing the strap, he pulled the scrap of material from his face. "Can you not bring yourself to say the words? To look at me as I am?"

A shining tear fell from Mother's eye. "Everything we do is to ensure you never feel different. That no matter what that war has wrought, you will always be our son and we want only the best for you."

"I know you do, and I greatly appreciate it, but what is best for me has changed. I have been forced to retreat behind these walls, to hide from the world until I'm deemed presentable enough for society's weak stomachs. Do not force me to hide further from my own family."

"These walls have protected the Alnwick family for generations," Father said. "We survive because of them."

"These walls are falling down around us without the financial means to support them for much longer, and if we are not careful, we will crumble to dust along with them. It is not a life I want. I tire of lurking in the shadows."

Mother pulled a lace hankie from her sleeve and dabbed her wet eyes. "But, Tobias—"

"I'm sorry." He summoned the words that had knifed into him from Nina's refusal. This time they would not cut but rather set him free. "Please don't ask me to."

CHAPTER 8 ————————————————

Mist crept over the village like a silver veil as Elena left the postmaster's office after having sent off a brief yet encouraging telegram to the Tin Noses Shop. She had every confidence Tobias's mask would be a success as far as artistic ingenuity was concerned, and if their little shop in London were able to provide such in-home services, the number of men helped would double. Men like Tobias, who only wanted to have their confidence as a human being returned to them.

Pulling her shawl over her head, more to keep the wetness from drifting into her eyes than to protect her already-frizzy strands, she hurried down the street and to the bridge that crossed over to Alnwick lands. Leedswick Castle rose solemn and stately from its throne overlooking the village, with mist purling off its turreted corners and crenellated walls like diamond robes. She had been in awe of its majesty at first, but the initial excitement over priceless paintings and silk sheets waned under the impenetrable roots of history holding down its occupants.

Little wonder Tobias felt suffocated. She couldn't fathom planting her roots in one place, not after having been on the move her entire life. She adored the adventures and the changes they offered when life grew too stale. Or too difficult. Was it truly adventuring, or was it running away as he'd said? With him, even standing seemed an adventure. What would it be like to take root in such an adventure?

If the letter got out, none of that would matter.

She turned away from the graying splendor and put her feet to the garden path with its own visions of majesty draped in viridian leaves and golden gorse. While she thought the gardens glorious in the shining sun, rain wrapped them in pure magic. And nothing proved more magical than mixing a new batch of paints, particularly when picked straight from their nature source. Why had she not thought to bring a basket for the berries?

Because Tobias had distracted her beyond all proper thought.

Which he had been doing ever since the night of the festival. Coming to watch her paint on the parapets, entertaining her with stories of Leedswick and his childhood while she worked on his mask, and she in return telling him of the wonders of Europe and the places she hoped to travel one day. He would smile sometimes at that but say nothing as his hand drifted to his face. He was frightened of stepping back into the world, a world he thought would reject him without the painted piece of thin metal shielding him from judgmental views. She longed to take his hand and show him the places of goodness and views that stole one's breath away. She wanted to show him her world of light.

And that started with berry picking. She plucked a leaf from a tree and twirled it in the air overhead as mist gathered on the green points. Would he think to kiss her? Her stomach swooped. Mother had taught her long ago how to decipher between looks of desire that were fueled by *désir* of the heart. Elena knew the lustful leers without doubt, not to mention the proper way of thwarting them that involved a well-aimed glass of water or the end of a paintbrush. But looks of the heart eluded her.

Until Tobias gazed at her with all the warmth of the sun melted into his glorious eye as she tried to catch the exact shades of sienna, umber, and amber mesmerizing the tip of her brush. He saw her. Saw her as no one else ever had. The freckles, the hair, the paint-stained fingers, the failures, the rejections of society—and not once did he judge her. Nor did he ask her to change. She could be her true self with him, and in this critical world that was a rarity of the purest kind. One she did not take for granted, especially coming from such a wonderful man.

Not bothering to stifle a blooming smile, she skipped over a puddle and waited for the air of delight to float her right off the ground.

"Your mother used to adore berry picking."

Elena whirled around. Aaron Burgess stood on the path behind her, immaculate suit and that hunk-of-polished-coal stickpin tacked to his lapel. The air of giddiness crashed in her lungs. "What are you doing here? You are trespassing on private property."

He strolled toward her in spotless shoes that defied the mud soaking the ground. "From your tone I might assume you do not wish me here."

"How observant you are. Leave. Immediately. Or I shall have you thrown out on your ear."

"I don't think you want to do that. Remember?" He reached into his breast pocket and took out the all-too-familiar envelope containing the horrendous letter. "Now I've come for an answer to the question I last posed to you."

"I made myself quite clear and my answer has not changed. I want nothing to do with your shipping company or with you, and I certainly will not be blackmailed into a scheme of heir bearing. If you dare to make any more threats against me or the Alnwicks, I will go straight to the authorities." With no desire to be left alone with this absurd man, she brushed past him and headed in the direction of the castle. The berries could wait.

"And who do you think they will believe? A motherless girl or a powerful businessman with tangible proof? Do not be unreasonable, Elena. Your mother was, and look where it got her."

She halted abruptly, then swung back around to see his

expression that had gone from carefully groomed to sneering. "I beg your pardon?"

"Do you really think you'll be given a better offer than mine? With the paint staining your cheek, your skin spotted like a peasant's in the sun, and your mother's reputation as a muse for hire, no good man of breeding will want you. Unless you're holding out for that waste of scarred flesh up in the castle." His thin lip curled. "Oh. I can see you are. Pathetic."

Shock rippled over her, quickly swallowed by a heated rush of anger. "How dare you!"

"I dare because it's the truth. Come now. This arrangement is in the best interest of all parties. My company will remain intact and my future male heir will stand to inherit all once he comes of age. In the meantime, his father, Mr. Mulligan, will act in his stead, and you, well, once you have served your marital duty, you will be packed off quietly to the country where you may paint to your heart's content to the end of your days. Or to Italy if you prefer. It's quite fashionable for those in marriages of convenience to live separately once their, ah, convenience has been served."

"And Mr. Mulligan is in complete agreement with this vile plan, is he?"

"Certainly. He stands to gain quite the business deal. After all, a wife's property belongs to her husband."

Her fingers curled at her sides. "You disgust me."

"This is your last chance. I won't make this polite offer again."

"If accosting a lady in the broad of day is your idea of politeness, then you have much to learn about manners. I've met drunks in the gutter with more finesse than your ill breeding."

"Lady." He spat the word, grabbing her arm and yanking her to him. "Do not cross me, girl. You will live to regret it. You and your prince from the castle. Some prince. The man is too ghastly to show his face beyond the lurking of night."

Elena wrenched her arm from his grasp. "Tobias Alnwick is twice the man you could ever hope to be. He's kind, and good, and honorable. Qualities your blackened heart will never understand."

"Qualities of the weak. Something you will learn about me soon enough is that I am anything but weak." The unconcealed threat hung in the air like a drop of poison. One second dangling with sinister intent, the next swept behind the gleam of his sharp teeth. "I'll give you a few days more to think on my offer, and it had better be answered to my liking." He tipped his hat in farewell. "Good day to you, Miss Hamilton. For now."

+ —— +

Mud squelching beneath his boots, Tobias hurried down the garden path. He cast a troubled glance to the darkening sky as gray clouds heavy with rain scuttled in for their chance at a downpour. Would there be enough time for berry picking before they released their torrent? Elena had her heart set on new paints, and if he was honest with himself, his hasty remark of learning to paint at her tutelage didn't seem quite as ill-advised as he might have imagined. In fact, standing next to her with nothing before them but a blank canvas and a spectacular view sounded rather perfect.

A raindrop hit his nose. Another his cheek. More pattered across his forehead. He smiled at the sky. Let it rain. They could plan another outing for the morrow.

Rounding a bend of willows weeping next to a stream, he spotted a small figure curled against the trunk of a rowan tree. Hurrying into the grove that was rumored to offer protection and courage to all who entered its sacred realm, he knelt next to Elena, soaked in her clothing. Based on her crumpled expression, she wasn't merely taking shelter from the rain.

He pushed a sodden curl from her forehead. "What's happened?"

"He came back. I told him never to, but he did." A wetness not from the rain filled her mismatched eyes. "He threatened me if I don't agree to marry Mr. Mulligan."

A string of curses hurtled to his tongue, but he bit them back. There would be time enough to deal with that cur later. He needed to get Elena inside. He slipped his arms about her and lifted her, the weight of her drenched skirts clinging to his legs. Her arms came about his neck as her head fell to his shoulder without hesitation. Trusting.

After carrying her back to the castle, he sent her straight to her chambers to change into dry clothing while he arranged a pot of fresh tea in the kitchen. After half an hour of waiting for her to finish whatever women did while changing, Tobias carried the tea tray to her room and knocked.

"You may come in."

Enrobed in a Turkish silk robe with black tassels swaying from the sleeves, Elena sat on the cushioned window seat with rain streaking the glass behind her. Her hair hung loose as the wet curls dragged to her waist like some Pre-Raphaelite titian muse whose painting he saw hanging in Paris during his first leave. His fellow officers had favored the more golden Venus, but the fiery innocent had drawn him. As the one before him did now.

"I brought tea." He set the tray on a table and poured her a cup.

"Thank you." She took the offered cup and sipped. "Mmm. Chamomile. None for you?"

"No."

"It's the heat, isn't it? Many of the men who came into the shop spoke of it. They could no longer tolerate scarves or soup. Fireplaces or blankets pulled up too high." She glanced at the fire, then offered a chair far from its orange flames. "Won't you take a seat?"

He'd never taken a seat in a lady's private chamber before, and he wasn't about to start now. Especially not when anger burned in his bones. Anger and regret that he'd not been there to protect her. "I'd rather you tell me what happened. Did he hurt you in any way?"

"Not in any way that matters." Balancing her cup, she rubbed at the freckles on her hand. "He refuses to take no for an answer. I'm afraid he'll return."

"If he does, I'll have him arrested for harassment and threats."

"Committed against a woman, no court of law will give it a passing concern."

"You cannot leave the castle grounds alone again. Twice he's found you. After today I will not allow him to come near you again. I will keep you safe." He hadn't meant to kneel before her like a knight before battle. Perhaps it was the rain against the medieval stone, or the way the firelight danced in her hair, or the fierce pull to protect those who could not protect themselves, but he wanted nothing more than to slay dragons for her.

"Mama and I always managed to look out for ourselves during our travels, but it's nice to have another person to count on." Leaning forward, she pressed a kiss to his scarred cheek. The warmth of her lips lingered over his skin like sunlight after a long storm. "I'm glad it's you."

He needed to leave before claiming a token. Or a proper kiss. Rising, he turned for the door, but her question caught him.

"Do you think I have too many freckles?"

"If you had any fewer, I wouldn't like you half as much." A boldness took over his would-be knight's heart. "I find you beautiful."

He caught a faint smile touching her lips before she turned to the window, her full expression lost to the scattering of raindrops on the glass pane. She the maiden fair and he with dragons to slay.

CHAPTER 9

obias strode across the library with selected book in hand. *Colors of the Pre-Raphaelite Brotherhood*. Elena had mentioned classical painting techniques the day before as she added the finishing touches to his glass eye, and he'd gone off in search of a volume to pique her interest, making it no coincidence that he chose one with muses much like herself.

"Might you have a moment to spare?" Mother called down to him from where she stood on the bookcases' second-floor balcony. He hadn't noticed her when he entered.

It had been a week since he'd last spoken so frankly with his parents. The air around the castle had been strained ever since. He had been churlish, yet he would not apologize for the truth behind his words. "I'm sorry, Mother, but I'm to meet Miss Hamilton in the studio."

"It won't take but a minute. Please." She hurried down the curling metal staircase to meet him. Shoulders straight as a line, she took a deep breath. "Every man is responsible for his own fate. It's past time we stopped trying to control yours out of our own fears." She looked him full in the face. No blinking, no forced concentration on the unmarred side, but a gaze of respect. "If you can survive this bloody war, I suspect you will conquer what lies outside of Leedswick.

"I'm sorry if we've made you feel like we are less than proud of you. Your father and I have been content to let the world slip by, and the day it came banging on our door with a call to arms, we tried not to hear it, but you answered it and then paid the price. We didn't want to believe that the war could touch us, but you were proof it could. Instead of giving you a hero's welcome, we ignored the truth of what really happened. Will you ever forgive us?" Her chin quivered.

The strain between them broke like a dam, his pain of being ignored and misunderstood flooding out of him on the swift currents of forgiveness. "Only if you will forgive me for being a clot-headed bull when last we spoke. My tone was out of turn."

She placed an unsteady hand over his heart as tears gathered in her eyes. "No, dear. It was precisely what we needed to hear. If not, I fear we may have lost you forever."

"If you could see things half the way I do, you'd realize that could never be true." He pointed to his eye patch. "Get it? See things half the way I do?"

She made a noise caught between a sob and a laugh and pulled a hankie from her sleeve to dab at a slipping tear. "Oh, Tobias. Is it necessary to jest about this?"

"Yes. Laughter is the best medicine, or so the physicians claim. Now, if you'll excuse me. I have a mask fitting." After kissing her satiny cheek, he turned for the door.

"Wait! I've something for you." She pulled out a book wrapped in soft green cloth and handed it to him.

Tobias opened the front cover and read the inscription.

To my darling Beatrice. With all my love, Charles.

With disbelief he flipped through the brown-tinged pages lined with elegant script and dates. "It's Grandmother Beatrice's diary. How did you—?"

"It's been here all along, safely tucked among my gardening books." Mother pointed to where her row of green-bound books sat contently on the shelf behind them. "You and your brother and sister never bothered looking here and always took such joy in searching for Charles's journal like treasure, never imagining Beatrice had one too. Part of me hoped you would never find it, but now I understand it's time you knew the truth. These walls were not meant to be a prison but a refuge."

Gently closing the diary, Tobias tucked it safely next to the art book. He wanted to read it with Elena, for she had wanted to share in the adventure as much as he did. "Thank you."

Mother nodded as if she, too, were relieved of the secrets burdening her. "Now, go to your young lady. I want to see how well she's done with this mask."

Tobias's heart jumped. He quickly tucked it back in place. "She's not my lady."

"She could be. Don't give me that look. The men in the Alnwick family are known to be quite the charmers."

He would decipher that statement later when his mother's eyebrows weren't waggling at him.

The studio was empty when Tobias arrived. Elena's tardiness no longer a surprise, he wandered around the room, riffling through the stack of canvases she worked on in the off hours, until at last he circled with no small amount of trepidation to her worktable.

The left side of his face stared back at him. Smooth cheeked, straight browed, complete with a realistic-looking eye and eyebrow hairs that had been painted on individually.

His chest ached as he remembered the day he'd sat watching her cut thin metallic foil into fine strips, then tint, curl, and solder them into eyelashes. It was as if a mirror had sliced off a piece of him and laid it out for all to see. He reached a trembling hand to touch it, to see if the flesh was warm to his fingertips, and stopped before he could brush a thumb over the delicate eyelid. He wanted Elena here for this moment.

He took out his pocket watch. Twenty minutes late. Longer than she'd taken before. He poked his head out the door. All quiet. He wandered down the corridor. Not a glimpse. He took the stairs to her floor. Empty save a maid carrying linens.

"Have you seen Miss Hamilton?"

The maid cast her gaze to the floor. "Not since the note came."

"What note?"

"The note that came about half an hour ago, sir. She seemed quite upset by it and grabbed her shawl—you know, the one with all the colors."

Fear sliced through him like a poisoned bayonet. He raced out of the castle and down the garden path, lungs burning in desperate pursuit until his hope gave out with the note lying on the ground. He snatched it up and read the boldly stroked words, each one a piercing dagger of anger.

Your answer is required at once. Meet me in the old garden shed or else I will publish the letter in the evening newspaper.

A. B.

The note squished under Tobias's boot as he took off running toward the abandoned garden shed.

CHAPTER 10

Red and black were all Elena could see as she sat on an over-turned bucket in the old garden shed. Red for spitting mad and black for murder. What she could do with those colors on a canvas in that moment would terrify even the bravest of observers, but also she held no brush to paint the fury of her mind. Instead, she was forced to study her surroundings.

The ground was soft dirt with bits of mulch tilled in. Dark green vines crawled through the holes in the walls to wind their way among the missing slates on the roof. Thick cobwebs hung in every corner while the smell of damp earth and decaying leaves moldered in the air. She might have been alarmed at the feel of tiny feet scurrying across her shoe if she weren't so busy glaring at the two men across the small fire from her.

Rats, the both of them.

"I'm glad you've come to your senses," said Burgess from his perch atop a wobbly workbench.

"It seems you give me little choice."

"As I said, I always get my way, but now that the unpleasant part of the business is over, we can move forward with ease."

"Unpleasantness over?" Elena snorted. "You are not the one agreeing to marry this cad."

"Come now, Miss Hamilton. Our union need not be that dis-agreeable." Squatting next to the fire, Mr. Mulligan pulled a dented metal teapot from the heat and poured a fragrant brew into a chipped teacup. "We all get what we want in the end. Your father's legacy carries on"—he handed the filled cup to Burgess—"I gain control of the company by marriage to you, and you paint yourself into oblivion in the countryside. After you provide me with an heir, of course."

"All very tidy." Burgess sipped from his cup and made a face. "A bit stale."

"Apologies. It must be the air in here disrupting the taste. Perhaps a new batch." Mr. Mulligan poured the remaining tea from the pot into a corner. Pouring fresh water from a canteen into the pitcher, he then added scoops of tea leaves from a pouch kept in his pocket. He caught her staring and held the fragrant pouch up to his nose. "Ah! I never leave home without my own fortifications. Business is always more civilized over a generous cuppa, would you not agree?"

Elena shifted on the bucket, trying to find a comfortable position. There wasn't one. "Only if you consider blackmail a civilized endeavor. As it so happens, I do not."

"I told you she was mouthy." Burgess cleared his throat and sipped the tea again. His mouth puckered as he swallowed. "A few husbandly corrections will straighten her out."

Swishing the pot around, Mr. Mulligan set it on a heated stone in the fire. "Now, now, sir. I'm certain Miss Hamilton and I will get along smoothly. After all, she came here, did she not?"

"Only under forced provocation." Burgess patted his jacket pocket. No doubt the letter hid there. The man was completely unimaginative when it came to stashing important documents. Which was to Elena's advantage, for she had no intention of coming to the dank little shed in agreement. She came only to steal the letter and destroy it before it did any harm.

But she hadn't planned on Mr. Mulligan. That man popped up

everywhere like a bad air bubble in a paint can. One man she could likely take by surprise, but taking two would be tricky.

"If I enter into this farce of a marriage"—Elena eyed the gardening hoe and broken shovel leaning against the left wall—"that letter will be destroyed."

Burgess coughed and tugged at his collar. "Certainly."

"I'll have your word on that. If it's worth anything."

"Upon the head of you, my daughter, the damning letter will be destroyed."

"And no harm or threats will come to the Alnwicks."

Burgess held up his hand. "I do so solemnly swear."

"Shall we drink on it?" Pulling the now-heated pot from the fire, Mr. Mulligan poured two fresh cups—did he carry a picnic basket with him?—of tea and offered one to her while keeping the other for himself. "To achieving what one deserves." He sipped his tea, then frowned at Elena. "You're not celebrating, my dear."

Elena held his stare and dumped out her tea. It splashed off the mulch bits and sizzled into the fire. "Do not ever call me your dear."

Coughing again, Burgess yanked at his knotted tie before fumbling for the briefcase lying on the ground next to him. "Now, there are a few"—*cough-cough*—"contracts here to sign. The first"—*cough-cough*—"your marriage agreement, and the second the company and property rights to Mulligan upon my death—" A coughing spasm doubled him over. He gasped for air as red blotched his face, quickly followed by purple.

Elena jumped to her feet. "What's happening? He needs water!" She hadn't meant to care, and truly she didn't, but she could not allow a living creature to suffer so before her very eyes. No matter his vileness.

"I'm afraid water will not save him," Mr. Mulligan calmly replied, sipping his tea.

"Wh-what do you mean?"

"He's dying." Reaching into his pocket, the opposite one from where he'd pulled the tea leaves, he pulled out a second pouch and tossed it into Burgess's lap. Out spilled pointy dark green leaves. "Fresh from the Poison Garden. Do you know, at first I thought it rather macabre that a noble family should tend such a garden, but it turned out to be rather useful."

Burgess fell over, rattling and kicking on the ground as he grabbed at his throat. His eyes rolled up and, with one desperate gasp, he stopped.

Elena's hand flew to her mouth. "He's dead."

Mr. Mulligan peered over the rim of his cup. "So he is. At last. We can finally get down to brass tacks." Setting aside his cup, he rose and stepped over Burgess's body to retrieve the contracts. "A few quick signatures here and all will be in order. But first we take care of you."

Rage and horror collided like a firestorm inside her. "If you think I'm going to sign anything over to you or continue with the marriage, you are sadly mistaken. I'll see you're sentenced for murder."

"My dear girl." He laughed. "As if I need you to do anything."

Looking at her father's body, then at her own discarded cup of tea, the firestorm froze to cold fear. "You were going to poison me too."

"Yes, but your father gave away my game too soon. No matter. I spotted nightshade berries in the garden while I was gathering leaves. Berries are easily enough crammed down your throat. With you finally out of the way, all that's left will be for me to fill in the signatures on these contracts and fake marriage certificate and— voilà!—your father's company is mine without the disgrace and sickening chore of marrying you."

"How can you hope to fill in the signatures if we're dead? Not to mention that petite stipulation in the will stating a male blood relative must inherit? Difficult to have a son from a dead fake wife."

"As it turns out, I'm quite the talented forger." Bending down, he plucked the letter from Burgess's pocket and smiled. "A few samples of handwriting is all it takes and one cannot tell the real from my fake."

"The letter is a fake."

Mr. Mulligan nodded with self-satisfaction. "I paid off a clerk at the War Department to view Francis's enlistment papers. Only took me two attempts to perfect his pathetic scrawl, but it's enough to do damage should I choose to bring this rather convincing letter to light. As for the will, a caveat was easily enough penned stating should there be no male heir to inherit, then all fortunes, estates, and businesses shall be bestowed upon the stated recipient. All rather tidy."

The door crashed open behind her, splintered rotten wood flung aside to reveal Tobias. "Not quite."

Mr. Mulligan's groomed eyebrows lifted in faint surprise. "Lord Alnwick. If I had known you were coming, I would have brewed more tea."

"Another time." Tobias advanced into the shed, his looming presence pushing Elena against the far wall.

"I'm afraid rescheduling is not an option." Reaching behind his back, Mr. Mulligan pulled out a gun. Dull, black, and deadly. "I have paperwork in need of filing that will make me a very wealthy widower. Isn't that right, my dear?" He pointed the gun at Elena.

Her back bumped against the wall, for which she was thankful. Otherwise her legs might have given out, and if she was going to die, it wasn't going to be in a terrified puddle.

"I've sent for the authorities. They'll be here any minute to arrest you. If you hope to flee, your name and wanted photograph will be posted on every corner. There will be a manhunt and nowhere for you to escape." Tobias took a step closer to Mulligan as Elena's fingers brushed against the garden hoe leaning against the wall. "Give up. Now."

"You noble elite think you can bark orders and we'll all jump to obey." Sneering, Mulligan swiveled the gun so it pointed at Tobias. "About time someone finished off what the war was supposed to smite." His finger curled around the trigger.

Latching onto the hoe's handle, Elena jumped forward, screaming like a banshee and brandishing the hoe high. "Iiieee!" She whacked the head of the hoe against Mulligan's hand.

Bang!

The explosion of the gun going off ricocheted around the small shed, ringing in Elena's ears. She shook her head to clear the confusion only to hear the sound of grunting and something heavy pounding against soft flesh. Mr. Mulligan and Tobias grappled on the ground, punching and cursing as they rolled dangerously close to the fire.

Mulligan grabbed the teapot and crashed it against Tobias's head. Howling with pain, Tobias jerked back. Mulligan seized the opportunity, shoving Tobias away and scrambling to his feet, then lurching toward the open door.

Elena swung her hoe and hooked him around the leg, yanking him backward. Tobias threw himself on top of the murderer and pinned him to the ground. "Go find Lloyd!" He panted as Mulligan wriggled beneath him. "Tell him to bring rope."

"Rope? You're going to hang him?" Elena trembled. Her fingers were white around the hoe's handle as she strangled it.

Tobias grinned. Grinned, of all things! "As much as I want to, I'll leave that to the authorities."

Elena glanced to the open door, then back. "They'll be here any minute."

"I didn't have time to summon them." He used his shoulder to shove back a lock of hair from his face. "Once we get this bastard tied up, I'll telephone the police chief promptly."

"Y-you were bluffing."

"Of course. Couldn't have this piece of filth thinking we were all alone. Now go!"

Her fingers went slack and the hoe fell from her hand as she dropped to her knees beside Tobias. She grazed her hands over his arms, shoulders, and face in search of any kind of scratch or blood. His skin was heated beneath her palms. "You're not shot. You're well."

"I'm well. The bullet went wide. Go find Lloyd."

"You're well." Relieved laughter bubbled up inside her, then before she could stop herself, she smooshed his face between her hands and kissed him. A fierce kiss full of every emotion assailing her at the moment, along with a few sizzling new ones. "Stupid man! Don't scare me like that again!"

He let out a shaky breath as a smile curved his mouth. "Promise. Just go find me rope. Please!"

"I'll go find rope. Wait here." She scurried to her feet and grabbed the gun, holding it far away from her as if it might bite. "I'll take this too." She eyed Mulligan's hate-filled expression and glared down at him. "For safekeeping."

Gathering up her skirts, she raced away.

CHAPTER 11

The black edges of the fake letter curled in the orange flames. Bit by bit it crumbled into ash as the last of the remaining threat to Tobias's family withered away. He stood at the library hearth, arm braced against the mantel, staring at the charred logs as they popped and hissed in the heat.

"It's done." Elena's voice drifted to him.

He shook out of his concentration and turned to where she sat curled up on the settee watching him. "It's done."

She patted the cushion next to her and scooted over to make more room for him to sit. "And no one will ever find out."

Tucking the tartan blanket over her bare toes that peeked out, he sat next to her. "About how close my family came to ruination? For the second time?"

"Precisely."

The fire crackled, cozily filling the silence as evening settled outside the library windows. The blues and purples of twilight darkened to indigo that drifted over the gilded book spines and polished wood floors, softening their sharp lines to an indistinguishable haze beyond the pooling light of the fire.

The authorities had arrested Mulligan and hauled him away for questioning before he was to be sent to London to stand trial for murder, attempted murder, blackmail, and forgery. Aaron Burgess's body was to be taken back to Kent and buried on his estate. When the coroner had asked if Elena was to accompany the body, she had politely declined. She and Tobias had been questioned for the better part of the afternoon when Tobias's father had firmly stepped in and requested all further inquiries be brought to him as the incident had happened on his estate. Mother had sobbed over Elena and Tobias before taking to her bed, too upset even to insist they have a chaperone sit with them in the library. If she had insisted, Tobias would have ordered the chosen chaperone away. Burning the letter was a private affair.

Stretching his legs out, he dropped his head to the back of the settee and let the weary bones of his body sink into relaxation. "You should have told me about the letter."

"No, I shouldn't have," she replied without remorse. "Your family has been through enough, and I would never forgive myself for bringing another burden to your door. I couldn't let them hurt you."

He tilted his head to gaze at her. Firelight set her hair aglow as if flame tips flickered among the strands, as the freckles dotting her face and arms seemed to sway across her skin in the shimmering light. She had never looked lovelier, but it was her eyes that held him captive, for they gazed directly back at him. One blue, one brown, both entirely focused on him. Only she dared look fully at him and see beyond the ugliness down deep to who he truly was.

"You didn't consider marrying Mulligan, did you?" His voice came out a touch hoarse, as if he feared the answer.

"Certainly not. He is a monster, cut from the same vile cloth as that man calling himself my father. Though I hate to speak ill of the dead, but nothing good came from him."

"You did."

Her cheeks pinked and she dropped her gaze, lashes fluttering with delicate embarrassment. "Thank you. It's not often I hear compliments."

"You should be complimented every day." The shadows of the room and the warmth of the fire emboldened him to use words that would have sounded brash by day. Here, in the darkened quietness, they could not be more fitting. "About the way your hair blazes like fire in the sun. About the courage you showed today. About the colors you've brought into my dreary world. How I shall never be able to return to the—what color did you call me?—pewter. I see the peace of green now because of you."

"I hope you'll continue to even after I leave Leedswick."

"Leave?" The word hit him like a bucket of cold water.

"Well, yes." The pink embarrassment faded from her cheeks, but her gaze flitted to and from his. "Your mask is complete. We still have a final fitting and any last touches you wish added, but then my work is done and I must return to London."

"Oh yes, I suppose. I hadn't thought of that." The warmth enfolding them from moments before taunted him as it slipped from his grasp. As she was soon to do. What else had he expected? That she take up as resident artist in the castle?

"I do wish we might have continued our adventure in finding your grandfather's journal."

"I have a surprise for you. Wait here." Rising, he crossed to a reading table beneath the windows where Grandmother Beatrice's journal had been neatly stacked atop the art book he'd selected for Elena.

An industrious maid had placed them there when he'd unceremoniously dropped them on the floor and taken off running to find Elena in the garden. Moving back to the couch, he sat once more. This time an inch or two closer to her. "It seems the journal was here in the library all along."

Ignoring personal space and proper distance, she scooted closer until her arm and knees touched him. She'd touched him before, many times in the studio with her fingers skimming his face like the wings of a butterfly. The touch had shocked him at first, after he'd been deprived of the simple gesture for so long, but sitting with her so close now was something else entirely. Here she was not the artist eyeing her subject but a woman who trusted him implicitly.

Resisting the urge to put his arm around her, he settled the journal on his lap and opened it to the front page.

"'To my darling Beatrice. With all my love, Charles,'" Elena said, reading the inscription. "Beautiful."

They flipped through the pages, reading of his grandmother's experience as a Dollar Princess, her time learning to be a countess, a budding interest in gardening, and the murder trial of her husband, Charles.

"He was acquitted of the charges of his father's murder, but he never rebutted the rumors of his batman's." A thin line of frustration formed between Elena's eyebrows as she read the entry. "Whyever not?"

Tobias turned the page, scanning until the last few sentences caught his attention. "She says here that Charles had been through enough and didn't need the added burden of reconciliation with the village." He skimmed his finger over the delicately penned words. "She claims to have been satisfied with his desire to retire away from the rest of the world to a place where they could claim their own happiness. Leedswick is hardly the place for that."

Elena's knee brushed against his thigh as she shifted position. "I know you believe it a prison, but perhaps if you were to try to see the good and not only the bad—"

"At one time there might have been good here, but now these walls do nothing but suffocate. At first I thought it was only me who felt the heaviness, but it's not. Charles felt it too." He dragged his finger back up the journal's page to one of the lines he had skimmed past. "'Charles believes the castle bears a curse. He says war has left its trace on this place, haunting it like a ghost. I won't disagree with a man who has looked in the face of hell itself for king and country, but I, for one, believe war itself is the curse.'"

Leaning his head back against the settee, Tobias scrubbed a hand over his bleary eye, then reached around and untied the scrap of material covering his other side. He slowly worked his fingers around the tight skin that seemed to throb when he read for too long. "At least now I know it's not only me."

Sighing, Elena riffled through the pages to where dried flowers had been pressed against the ink. "It does seem comforting to have that connection through the generations. Too bad it isn't over a love of bird-watching or iced cakes. You people of the northern cliffs have far too morose an outlook."

"How do you suppose we go about changing it?"

"By getting away for a bit. Seeing the world and all its colors and beauty."

He turned his head toward her. "Do you really think that would help?" Feeling her full gaze on him, he realized he'd forgotten to re-cover his face and immediately reached to retie the mask. "Oh, forgive me."

She grasped his hand and pulled it to her lap. "Leave it off. Please. I like to look at all of you."

"I still find that difficult to believe."

"Believe it or not, but it's the truth." She turned his hand over and traced her nails along his palm. Shivers shot up his arm. "As is my suggestion of getting out to explore life and all its magnificent wonders."

"I needn't travel very far to see a wonder." Praying his free hand didn't tremble, he reached up and ran his thumb along her cheek. "Nothing could be more magnificent than you. Only perhaps if you were to show me this world of color yourself. Be my tour guide, my fellow adventurer."

Her eyebrows raised with mischief. "A single lady guiding a young, attractive man about? I would for sure bring a scandal down upon your family, and I think one near blow is quite enough."

The way she looked at him—as if mischief were precisely what she had in mind—sent his heart pounding. He swallowed against all the reasons of logic and pinned his hope to the one thought, the one feeling that made complete sense. "If you're agreeable, I'm certain I could propose an answer that would banish all thought of scandal."

Firelight danced in her eyes. "Hmm. I might need persuading if I'm to consider this supposed proposal of yours."

"Might you indeed." He pulled his hand from hers and gently cupped her face while circling his other hand around her shoulders, drawing her close. Her head nestled against his arm as she turned her face up, awaiting him. He never thought he would hold a woman again, but the creature in his arms now was more than a woman. She was beauty, light, freedom, and pure joy.

Utter happiness filled him, curling his mouth into a smile, as he leaned down and kissed her with all the passion he had to offer.

EPILOGUE

SEYCHELLES
1920

Writing the last line of the day, Tobias closed his moleskin note-book and slipped the pencil in his pocket. It wasn't Tennyson or Hardy, or even that new chap Eliot, but according to his publisher, the people wanted new voices. Ordinary voices that could put into familiar words what the war had done and how life was to move on. He wrote not about the glory found in battle or the fields of pop-pies stained with heroes' blood but of the camaraderie forged in the trenches, the ache of marching feet, the thrill of a care package. He wrote, too, of hospital wards, the nurses' gentle care, the nervousness of going home, and the beginning of life again.

Slipping off the rock, he padded across the white sand to the water's edge. The tiny granules were warm beneath his bare feet as the turquoise water stretched as far as the eye could see, though somewhere out there it bumped into the east African coast. The sun warmed his face and the length of exposed skin from where he'd rolled his shirtsleeves back. He'd not worn a proper jacket and tie in nearly a month, and the freedom was glorious. As was the view before him.

A smile widened across his face as he walked toward his glory. "You've captured it."

His wife stood in the surf, her water-stained skirt tucked up into her waistband. Her long, curling orange hair flowed down her back with a simple strip of cloth tied around her head to keep it from her face. "Not quite." Paintbrush balanced in her hand, she stared at the easel before her, filled with colors of blue, green, and cream, before she swept her gaze to the horizon. "The clouds are determined to defy me."

He dropped his notebook and shoes on a blanket spread in the sand, then waded out to join her. Water lapped around his shins as he planted a kiss on her soft cheek where a new smattering of freckles had bloomed from the sun. "I doubt they do it on purpose."

"So says you. I want this to be perfect. May and Lucille have requested a tropical scene to place next to the one I painted from Norway a few months ago."

After an impromptu marriage, Tobias and Elena had used the money from his small inheritance set up by Grandfather Charles and Grandmother Beatrice to travel the world. If they continued living modestly, the funds would see them through for some time to come, and with additional income from selling Elena's paintings and Tobias's stories, the two were quite comfortable free from the shackles of nobility.

After a brief visit to Leedswick, where Tobias's parents had been forced to close down another wing in the castle to conserve funds, Tobias and Elena traveled to Kent to meet her much younger half sisters. They were delightful girls, though a bit sad to be exiled to a boarding school by a father who had wanted nothing to do with them. Elena promised that as soon as the girls were of age, they could all settle down to be a proper family. Without the likes of Aaron Burgess come to threaten them ever again.

"I'm sure your sisters will be delighted with whatever you send them. They're just as happy to receive your letters as anything else." Slipping his arms around her waist, he nuzzled her neck and inhaled the scent of salt, paint, and wild violets captured in the hollow behind her ear.

She tilted her head so he might gain better access. "They see so little of the world outside their boarding school in Kent. I want to do what I can to broaden their horizons."

"I know, my darling. It's what I love most about you." He kissed her neck, eliciting a sigh from her.

"Is it? Not my charms or unusual good looks?"

"I adore those as well."

She turned in his arms and kissed him, soft as the waves lapping at their feet, deep as the ocean stretching away from them, and as warm as the sun wrapping them in its shining embrace. His love for her swelled inside his heart, filling in the cracks and infusing him with happiness. A feeling he'd once thought lost in the mud of France along with half his face, but she had brought it back to him along with a contentment he'd never known.

She jerked away, scanning the water around their feet. "Oh my! Look. The fish have come for a nibble. They seem to think my toes are a snack." Laughing, she kicked her foot out and the tiny pale fish scattered. "How fares the writing?"

Strange to think he'd become a writer to put his experiences on paper for all to read, but when Elena's artistic friend at the Tin Noses Shop began writing about his work with the wounded, the newspaper was only too eager to hear the soldier's side. Tobias wasn't comfortable opening himself to such vulnerability at first, but he quickly found writing to be a cathartic release of the pain that haunted him and every returning soldier. "Well enough. I'm hoping to have this batch finished before we leave for Egypt. I've read there's a man named Howard Carter who has been doing excavations in the Valley of the Kings."

"How thrilling! Imagine if he were to uncover a spectacular tomb while we're there."

"One can dream." He adjusted the patch over his eye that had somehow become dislodged during their passionate embrace. He'd taken to using the simpler black patch that covered only his eye when they were alone; the rest of his facial scarring he didn't need to hide from his wife. The mask she had painstakingly and reverently painted for him was used only in public, as its fragility would not hold up against constant use. In another year she would have to create a new one for him.

"The post was delivered earlier and I've received a letter from Mother and Father. They're going to consider the offer from English Heritage. The collection usually doesn't accept country houses or estates, but since Leedswick is marked as a site of historic importance dating back to Alfred the Great, they are happy to add it to the conservation efforts. The offer expires in five years, so they have plenty of time to decide and make plans should they accept."

"That's wonderful news!"

"It would hurt to hand over the family legacy after so many generations, but I feel it could be the right thing to do. There simply isn't enough money for upkeep anymore, not even after selling off a few of those master paintings at your suggestion. And besides, after the war, many of the old families are downsizing. They could find happiness living in a smaller house nearby without the burden of castle and keep weighing them down."

"Speaking of weighing down, what is this heat?" Tobias wiped the sweat from his brow.

"It's called humidity, *mon chou*. Don't you remember from Portugal?"

"Yes, but not like this. My lungs feel clamped together."

"Then you should cool off." With a wicked grin she lunged at him. They tumbled back into the water. Surfacing, she pushed the sodden hair from her face and laughed. "Better?"

"Almost." He dove for her. Squealing, she darted away, but he caught her bare foot and dragged her back.

In the end it wasn't about the humidity, or the blue lap of waves, or the tropical setting, or the hours creeping toward sunset, or that for the first time in years he didn't care what others thought should they see him. The entire existence of his life narrowed to this singular brilliant moment and the woman in his arms who made him feel whole and loved.

THE DREAM KEEPERS

1945

One day, in retrospect, the years of struggle
will strike you as the most beautiful.

—Sigmund Freud

CHAPTER 1 ————————————————————

It took the whole of the war for Alec Alnwick to recognize that the silence of Jerry guns was as deafening as the cacophony of open fire. The quiet was as much a statement as the scramble of men holding white-knuckle tight to their rifles as they navigated a Belgian forest far more terrifying than any tale spun on a winter's night. The same men hopeful at the first hum of the Biscuit Bomber plane's engine, promising supplies of bully beef, dried-up biscuits, weak tea for a midtrench brew-up, but also hope.

Hope for a mail call. Hope for an end to the war.

The end came eventually, but not with the climax Alec had anticipated. If this had been a matinee in Leicester Square, the soundtrack would have swelled with the promise of peace and the hero, in full pristine Blighty uniform, would gather the girl in his arms. Instead, England seemed as far away as the day he had first laced his regulation boots.

Belgium surrounded them in a sort of muted beauty from the edges of the Ardennes to the golden squares of Brussels. But despite the scenery, Alec just wanted to return home.

Not yet twenty-five years on the planet and Alec had lived many lifetimes longer at the Front. His friend Evan Laughton had too. Now

239

they lived even *more* lives waiting their turn to ship out in a mix of joy, sorrow, and . . . well, bored lethargy. Too many Tommies to process through the lacy frost of midwinter. With nothing but the danger of their own thoughts to accompany the next chapter of their lives.

Snow brushed over the Belgian steeples and latticed the brown grass and bare twigs as soldiers sat and waited. Alec could almost imagine sketching it. His father once told him that Alec saw everything with the artistic eye he'd inherited from his mother. Drawing made him feel closer to her somehow. But not lately. It was hard enough to hold a sketching pencil steady at all.

His brain had turned through endless nights shrouded by the whistling wind and the long, tapping reach of the bare branches.

"I think you started planning your return home the moment we arrived," Evan told him as they shared a cigarette.

"Everyone plans their return home." Alec's casual tone belied his quickening pulse.

With the night's relief from the absence of gunfire, Alec parried with the limitations of his mind. He refused to be a shell of himself the way the men who'd survived the last war were.

The way Uncle Daniel was.

Lord knew in some ways it would be easier to perish here and now than spend decades wandering through life like a ghost. Daniel hadn't perished during his war, but his death just before the war Alec had recently fought seemed a reprieve for his uncle.

"You really ought to tell me what's going on in that belfry of yours, Alnwick."

It wasn't the first time Evan had asked the question. They had fallen as easily into camaraderie as they had into the first regulation lines.

During the war, when staccato artillery blasts pulsed the gray-green sky as night fell over the far east side of Belgium, his mates whiled away the hours eyeballing pinup girls or reading *True Detective* or *Ellery Queen* magazines, fashioning a semblance of a transient home forged of mud and stone.

Now Laughton pulled a deck of cards from his sleeve and attempted to coax Alec to play. "What are you reading, Alnwick? I have a feeling that if I didn't take the time to pester you, you would open that little book of yours and scribble all the words you have no intention of saying aloud to anyone."

"It's a psychoanalytical column by Dr. Henrik Mayr. About dreams."

Laughton whistled low. "Far too intellectual for me, mate."

"I discovered him ages ago. He wrote about the profound influence of music in combating anxious episodes. The effect of gardening or even of . . . of sketching." Alec scratched his neck.

"You used to sketch. Long before we shipped out here. Maybe that would keep your mind moving if you don't want to play cards." Evan had already laid out a hand of solitaire on an overturned case.

And Alec was leaving out a part of the Mayr story. The part where he'd been corresponding with Herr Doktor Mayr.

When Alec decided to write back, it took many drafts before perfection was achieved. He had a lot of time on his hands (almost as much as he had now, waiting for their ship-out assignment), and he always kept his second-to-last draft before posting it to Vienna:

Dear Herr Doktor Mayr,

As per my last letter I recently reread your essays on the composer Brahms as a significant development in the study of the retention of memory and as a means of sustaining mental faculties even through hardships. During my time at the Front, I have attempted to recall lines of music and the movement of my fingers on the keys from the piano lessons I always enjoyed as a child. In your last letter you asked me if it was enough that I survive.

Truthfully, it is not. See, I come with the burden of duty to my family's legacy.

I am most afraid that I might bloody well survive. Then what will I do with the shell shock and nightmares? The trauma weighs as heavy on my back as a full rucksack. Not just from the burden of this war but also the eventual end of it. Even when I am visited by the most vivid and seemingly normal dreams, none of which have anything to do with the images impressed upon my psyche from the battlefield, I carry it.

My mates here write to their sweethearts in response to letters spritzed with the scents of roses and talcum with berry-red lip prints kissed in the margins, or they play solitaire, and here I am with my mind spiraling to Freud.

"Hold fast, man. And remember who you are!" At least that is what I tell myself. If the world is going to spiral away from sanity, Dr. Mayr, I need to hold fast. *Shell shock. Combat fatigue. Hysterical neurosis.* So many of these terms I read about in your periodicals plague men every day from my layman's diagnosis. My friend Evan Laughton told me he doesn't know how to navigate life again: at his desk with his paperwork, without the shrill roll call to wake him or without the heart-thump of a surprise attack. He told me he wondered if it might be easier just to perish on some remote battlefield in Europe.

I don't have the luxury of wishful thinking. My family's legacy is at stake: a castle haunted by war way up in Northumberland. I'm determined not to become my uncle Daniel, whose war-induced insanity was too often fodder for the wagging tongues of the neighbors and locals who have ostracized my family for generations. I don't know why I hold myself accountable for my uncle, because I live in a way my uncle cannot. He never would have thrown himself into the fray. Would have found, I am sure, some alternative. But conscription cared little beyond paperwork and a few medical tests.

In a previous letter you asked if I would grant permission for a trusted colleague to have access to our correspondence for the purpose of scientific study and in the spirit of goodwill. Please view this response as my written agreement.

Yours sincerely,
Alexander Alnwick

The exchange of letters with Dr. Mayr continued. Most often when Alec found no semblance of sleep. His uncle Daniel had been presented with myriad treatment options, most of which he hid from until he became more and more a ghost of himself. Directly after the last war, there was a resounding decision to sweep the experiences of war under the rug. Stiff upper lip. Daniel had done his bit. Why let it gnaw at him when there was a world to rebuild?

If men were brave enough to admit their ill adjustment, then primitive options were available: a removal of the brain's frontal lobe to hack off the offending part, believed to be the root of the brain's maladies. Or a shock of electricity to startle panic from the body. In both instances the patient was locked far away with little but four imprisoning walls and their own thoughts . . .

Nightmares.

So Uncle Daniel leaned more to the type of medicine he found in the decanters in the study and in the village pub. The more he imbibed, the looser his tongue became to tell Alec all he saw when he closed his eyes.

Alec picked up the next letter.

Aimie K. Runyan, J'nell Ciesielski, and Rachel McMillan

Herr Alnwick,

I write in the spirit of confession and regret, doing so after you have so entrusted me with the candor of your current experiences. Please do not view this letter as dismissive or written in a nature of disrespect. Yet I must clarify something before our correspondence can continue. I am indeed Dr. Mayr, or soon will be, but I am Dr. B. Mayr. My uncle was kind enough to let me read your previous letters as I was the one who did the majority of the research on Brahms as a possible soothing antidote for high-anxiety episodes. My uncle has been my teacher and mentor for a long time. Well, he and Dr. Elisa Bauer, one of the first female psychologists to challenge Freudian views.

But I digress. You are addressing Brigitta Mayr. I apologize for any unintended surprise. I assure you I am as invested in your correspondence as my uncle and as impressed by your utilizing what strikes me as acute self-awareness to acknowledge and respect the unique situation you're experiencing. It is like nothing I have read in my textbooks. How can it be?

I do hope I have not overstepped your kind assertion that your previous letter act as permission for a review of your situation and your very authentic fears and anxieties.

I will speak to your letter of several weeks back and to your fear that some of the men in your situation and with your condition, certainly those who fought in the previous war, would be subjected to some of those rather primitive "treatments."

Obviously, I would never belittle your fears as mercury pills and shock treatments have been a common and well-meaning (if ill-administered) response to the mental catastrophes of war. May I suggest you read another approach? In the Great War Dr. Arthur Hurst, whom I greatly admire, employed nutrition, farming, fresh air, and handiwork to quell and lessen the effects and echoes of No Man's Land. I have attached some of his writings and findings here. Many of the soldiers' experiences of this current conflict are similar to those of the men who endured the previous one and, of course, well before.

Alec set the letter aside to study the enclosed article featuring photographs and illustrations, presumably of Dr. Hurst and his work. If only Uncle Daniel had had access to this man instead of the barbarity of mercury pills and barbiturates that sent men into fits. Alec picked up the missive again to continue reading.

Yes, Arthur Hurst was interested in everything from cultivating vegetable gardens to woodworking and how they gave men an opportunity to bridge the gap between the nightmare of war and the normal lives they wanted to return to.

As for your dreams, Herr Alnwick, they are often a by-product of a mental and physical state and should not be interpreted as anything more than feelings acknowledged.

"Dreams," as Freud said, "represent a disguised fulfillment of a repressed wish."

I will not be so presumptuous in my understanding of you to assume what that wish may be. Rather, I encourage you to begin there to understand that dreams are as much a part of our waking moments as what haunts you when you are asleep, and somehow, then, you can begin to control them.

One shouldn't be nostalgic for war, of course. But he also couldn't have anticipated the way that life before the war—a war that had commandeered years of his life—had sewn itself into his identity. Alec was partly the man who wanted to find a good job and fall in love and shrug out of his family's expectations, even as he confronted what it might mean to live up to the title of marquess—a title he had not given much thought to before he shipped off to war.

CHAPTER 2 ——————————————————

BELGIUM
LATE WINTER 1945

As he and his unit waited to ship out, Alec had plenty of time to reread Dr. Hurst's articles and findings, along with more of Dr. B. Mayr's letters.

The throng of men returning to England withstood lines as interminably slow as molasses, waiting to board the next truck and then train and then take the icy trip across the Channel crowded with Allied ships. Alec, along with so many of his mates, reckoned with the terrifying concept of peace. What was fought for so hard and won so bloodily was a reintroduction to a society that seemed as strange to Alec as his first months of military training and the first blast of gunfire.

"How can I possibly reintegrate into life with a fiancée and a job as a banker?" Evan's voice held frustration, but Alec had seen his steely gray eyes soften with letters from his betrothed, Clara, on several occasions. Evan slapped at a letter from home. "Another one filled with expectation of how everything will go back to the way it was."

The letters Evan received from home terrified rather than soothed him. Alec more than understood. He was in line to inherit a magnificent estate, though the inheritance was complicated by his father's renunciation of the title. And while Alec hadn't given too much mental attention to it during the war, he was stepping into a moment of decision that weighed on his shoulders.

"It's bad enough to imagine sitting at a desk with this blasted gunfire still going off between my ears." Laughton rubbed his hand over his rugged face.

Alec didn't have anyone special waiting for him. At least not of the fairer sex. His parents, Tobias and Elena, had the misfortune of being *stuck* in Corfu. They had ignored the warnings about continental travel, driven by Mother's artistic spirit and her desire to find somewhere to possibly put down roots when "this all blows over."

He knew they felt bad that they'd missed such a crucial part of his life—unable to write to him or send telegrams or packages—but they found it nearly impossible to get back to England. Alec was as worried about them as they doubtless were about him. Especially after learning of Mussolini's occupation.

The happiest moment of the war came from a missive from the family solicitor indicating that he had heard from them. Alec's parents had found a way to help the locals even through the harshest period of the occupation and bombing. Alec knew he would hear a lifetime of stories as they slowly arranged passage home.

Even though his cousin Hal was far closer and the post from him would have come more easily, he didn't take the time to write. The correspondence from *home* was from the solicitor, who wanted to see to estate business as soon as possible.

Then there were Doctors Henrik and Brigitta Mayr. The former provided a whetstone for Alec's thoughts and ideas. The latter? Well, at first he had been mortified that he bared his vulnerable thoughts to a woman. But she was a doctor. Almost. Not some girl tucked beside him in a West End matinee, her perfume lingering on his collar.

No. Brigitta Mayr *happened* to be a woman. But, most importantly, she had been his lifeline.

Alec balanced his notebook on his bended knees cum desk and wrote. He continued to write letters through the long journey homeward. Most often when he was startled from a nap or a short stretch of sleep by a nightmare.

I have acres and an estate. I am not just Alexander Alnwick who has been writing you from a place of muck and dirt. Rather, I am the Marquess of Northridge. So I am burdened with a two-fold expectation: how to be a civilized human being reentering polite society after the greatest hurdle of my existence and how to assume a title that fits me like an oversized suit. The castle I've inherited from a complicated family is said by the villagers to be cursed. High, high in the beautiful terrain of Northumberland, its stones and turrets are regal and beautiful and its gardens filled with dastardly, deadly plants. The curse dates back to my ancestors Charles and Beatrice Alnwick, who lived at Leedswick Castle in the late nineteenth century.

I always supposed the war and Britain's Great Cause would inspire me to do something useful with Leedswick, but how can I imagine another life for a grand estate when it takes me ten minutes to lace up my boots each morning through the fog of another day?

Alec read the letter over. If he had been so coherent with a stranger, couldn't he find a way to meet society's expectations and requirements of him when he reached home?

After an eternity of staring out of the train car, familiar sights emerged against the horizon in a haze of emerald green and chalky white cliffs. He smoothed his sweat-soaked hair from his forehead and attempted to reclaim the patriotism he'd fought for with blood and sweat and sleepless nights.

How strange to see his homeland manifested during the long,

screeching train ride amid men who languished between stops, shoulders drooping and eyes burning with the atrocities seared on them.

Alec finally arrived in London feeling more of an interloper than ever. The city was a snuffed candle, blunted by bombs, with flits of smoke still rising over the confetti of ashes and debris. The train car's window offered a snapshot of the city's slow restoration with scaffolds and cranes brushing a skyline once distinguished by the steeples and towers of its fairy-tale history.

For now the Marquess of Northridge was merely *Alec*, with a pile of dirt-stained, worn letters bound with twine and a future he was as reluctant to embrace as a barrage of gunfire.

Alec settled. His first order of business was to meet with the family solicitor, William Brown, who had seen not only to the preservation of the London house but also to the temporary stewardship of Leedswick Castle while Alec was away.

Alec took a deep breath and walked into the London town house where Brown was waiting.

"So wonderful to see you returned in one piece." Brown extended his hand and motioned for his attendant to see to the kettle and provisions Alec would need. "I understand it has been hard for your parents to get back to Britain. I have the paper detailing your father's desire for you to act as executor in his stead."

Alec felt like half of what he once was, unaccustomed to a civilized world in which he was expected to live. Especially where the ancestral estate was concerned. It had been faltering before he left, and the hardships of war were not the only catalyst of its slow decline. Would it be the same for his mother and father when they finally made their way home?

As for monetary support, for years the estate had tenants, though the community's opinion of the family rendered them fewer and fewer. Then the war came and men were called up. The last Alec heard from Brown there was but one cottage left occupied so far on the edge of the grounds it might have been called adjacent. Still, the tenants who had farmed on the estate for many years continued to call it home.

There was also the income from Father's writing and Mother's artistry. But during Alec's developing years, his parents had allowed for carefully budgeted adventures to Kent and Oxford and the beaches at Cornwall, to Portugal and the French Continent and even Egypt. They had never been as intentional about settling the future of the castle.

"You must have many questions about Leedswick," Brown said once they settled in the sitting room. "I assure you it was taken care of as best as your yearly stipend could afford. Of course, the Alnwick's family account has accrued interest. There are investments and, as I wrote, I was able to repurpose some of this to maintain a skeleton staff at Leedswick."

"The staff?" Alec asked.

With ironic timing Brown's assistant smiled as she poured tea and turned a plate of sandwiches toward him.

"Skeleton." Brown snapped up a sandwich. "But that is to be expected." He took a bite. "You know you could always sell it to the National Trust."

"Would the National Trust truly want a castle burdened by its—*our*—history?"

Brown pressed his lips together. "Your family has never been completely forthcoming about the secrets that I am to believe . . . *haunt* the place. That is the word you use, correct?"

Alec responded with a placating smile. "Yes, the villagers are not quick to dispel said rumors."

Brown nodded. "It is up to you what you decide to do with the estate. Elena and Tobias, as you know, had thought to sell it to the Heritage Foundation years ago."

"It was long their desire." How they had talked about it. Alec's happiest memories were of his daylight explorations around the grounds, running across spans of green grass and watching as the sunshine cast prisms on a small pond. One evening, the night having fallen quickly, he'd known that his long summer days of befriending chickens and mucking out stalls were coming to a close.

"They knew I had a special connection to Leedswick." In fact, his happy childhood inspired his parents to hold tightly to an estate they could ill afford. Even if their gift had borne the brunt of difficult upkeep before the war. Entire wings had been closed off, furniture and antiques sold and regrettably gone as quickly as most of the staff.

"But if you were to sell it, I can guarantee you would be well-set for a comfortable life." Brown unraveled the binding from a business folder and presented it to Alec, who encountered a large sum written on a small piece of paper.

It was enough money to ensure he could keep the London town house running. Enough money to give him the options his parents would want.

Alec cleared his throat. "As I am the heir to Leedswick, I could sell the estate," he interpreted.

Brown kept his composure, but the vehement slurp of his tea conveyed his eagerness. "True." His voice was calculated. "But there is, of course, your cousin. He has been quite forthcoming in his correspondence while you were occupied fighting for king and country." Brown set the cup back in its saucer.

"Oh?"

"Do not be surprised if he expresses a desire to see you. He's written often about making your reacquaintance."

Both knew Alec would never act merely for his own gain, while his cousin was the opposite. While Alec had no intention of passing the estate to the National Trust at this point, he wouldn't pass it to Hal either. Something Brown's tone surmised.

"What if I had something else in mind for Leedswick?" Alec said. "I wouldn't merely want to move in and shuffle stones around—"

"It is yours to do with as you please, Lord Alnwick."

"Alec."

"Well, Alec. What about your studies? Before the war you had planned to go to law school. Indeed, as I recall you were always putting off our meetings. So I was pleased you had entrusted me to continue to handle Leedswick's affairs."

Alec nodded. "And I might still do so. But for now . . ." He stretched. "Let's talk tomorrow after I have tea with my cousin. I believe I'll have a proposition for you."

✦ ——— ✦

Alec welcomed the comfort of the Mayfair town house that evening. He settled on the soft mattress in his bedroom and stretched his arms behind his head. The stark contrast between safety and recent memory tightened Alec's chest. He tried to snatch at sleep in the few moments his brain wasn't beset by all manner of memories, if not of recent wartime experiences then certainly of past times at Leedswick. Though his eyes drifted shut, his brain continued to race ahead so that a blast of artillery fire and the shadows of fallen comrades played in an unending reel.

Sometime later, he startled awake from a nightmare and raked his damp hair back from his face. Steadying his breath, he recalled how his correspondence with Fräulein Mayr helped calm his mind. Or the memory of a game of cards with Evan in a cold, dark forest. Too bad he hadn't been able to sketch since before the war.

Then there was Brown, who hopefully would understand the concept of Alec's plan better than Hal would. But Hal deserved to know nonetheless. When they had been children, a fortnight at Christmas and then through most of the summer, he always felt as if

Harold was eight steps ahead. He was a better shooter, a better boxer, a better equestrian.

Even though Alec had his entire future before him, he was far too often tugged to the past. Especially now that he was faced with the inevitable financial consequences of any action.

Much more than his own whims were at stake. For one, there was Harold. *Hal.* His cousin would doubtless want to be involved in anything that allowed for a portion of the estate. Then, of course, Brown would tactfully let Alec know when some of the family coffers were depleting and his cousin was overdrawn beyond his own stipend.

Alec had barely stepped into the role of marquess before the war. But the war put his responsibility to Leedswick on hold, as indefinite as Alec's future until he could return home. And even though his personality was better suited to books, abandoned castle wings, and secret passages, he knew he cared more about Leedswick than Hal, who hosted hunting parties and expensive soirees the estate could ill afford.

Then came war.

A mortar-shell blast stole the hearing in his cousin's left ear, procuring him an early discharge from the army. Since then, Hal had made easy and quick work of painting the family name, ancient titles, and heritage over Soho clubs and hotels beyond his means with a reckless brush.

Though Alec's war experiences were a far cry from his cousin's, they *were* similar to the experiences of the men who had benefited from what the Mayrs had written to him about. It sounded like utopia to the Alec who remembered wading through the mud.

He no longer wanted to hide in the city. Many estates had been appropriated for the war effort at the height of the devastation: to stand in for hospitals or to oversee training. Leedswick could pay its dues. Late, perhaps, but dues just the same.

In his early correspondence with Dr. Henrik Mayr, Alec was privy to research of American newspapers speaking to the prospective treatments for anxiety and melancholia: frontal-lobe surgery that lobotomized the brain and electroconvulsive therapies that jolted the system through wires and nerves. What he saw on the battlefield when he closed his eyes . . . Sometimes he wished he could be shocked through it.

But he and his men deserved better.

Dear Herr Doktor Mayr,

In the time since my last letter, I have returned home to England, but not without one of your articles where you mentioned how the concept of home had changed significantly during the course of the war. I have been doing some deep research on Arthur Hurst and was hoping to entice you to help me.

Alec smoothed out the creases before he ripped it into pieces and tried again. He would begin this new adventure just as he had begun his connection with this faraway family in their faraway city. It would take a while for him to work up the courage to send it. But when he did, it would read:

Dear Herr Doktor Mayr,

You may think me daft, but I am writing with a proposition nonetheless . . .

CHAPTER 3 ———————————————

VIENNA
SPRING 1946

Brigitta Mayr had never heard her uncle bark as loudly as he did when the *Psychiatrische Zeiten* arrived with the post. Trust a dissension among *Onkel* Henrik's colleagues in the fields of Freud and psychoanalysis amid a crumbling and annexed city to stir his ire. Trust Henrik Mayr to choose a war to focus on slights of psychoanalytical principles.

She couldn't blame him. After all, these days she felt much like a cork ready to pop. She supposed neither of them had anticipated the end of war would seem just *like* the war, with few jobs and little food. Electricity was sparse, and even Vienna's bells were silenced by bombs blasting the city mere months before the last gunfire from the Front.

Even though the *Wohnung* she shared with her aunt and uncle had been spared the Allied bombs over her beloved city, her imagination stretched farther to that kind Brit Alec Alnwick who had corresponded with her and allowed her full access to the vulnerable recesses of his mind.

Especially his dreams.

She hoped that wherever the Marquess of Northridge was, he was feeling more freedom than she was. She hadn't heard from him in a long while. Time meandered slowly now, with little for her to focus on other than how to finish her practicum requirements at university.

Her aunt and uncle had sacrificed so much to pay for extensive studies that far outlasted most degree requirements her friends had attained. And while Brigitta knew she wanted to work in her uncle's field, she needed a more focused plan. It was difficult enough that women in her uncle's profession were few and far between. More still, to reconcile that any small strides she had made in connections in the field were largely due to Uncle Henrik's wide acclaim. During the war, Brigitta couldn't see beyond the blackouts and rations and threat of Allied bombers overhead. In the few moments of reprieve, it was easy to doubt her entire education, her prospects. She couldn't live off her aunt and uncle forever, but neither had she taken the time most young women had to secure a husband.

Not that she had many options left these days, with many of the men of her acquaintance—a few sweet ones she had met at a coffee shop or at a local dance—now lost to the throes of war.

One former student of her uncle's had encouraged her passion. It made Brigitta hopeful that she could find a man who wouldn't mind a woman whose nose was tucked into psychiatry books. But the war had taken him too.

The one reprieve had been corresponding with Herr Alnwick. Her uncle's blessing, when given, had quickened her heartbeat. Not long after, she treasured it as a sign of respect.

As Brigitta stirred watery tea from the twice-steeped pot, she could hear her infinitely patient aunt Pia on the receiving end of another of her uncle's flustered rants about the recent changes to the Viennese School of Psychiatric Thought. Not for the first time her uncle was comparing the warring psychiatric theories printed in the offending paper as being on the same scale as the ancient Roman Triumvirate. He was so loud that he didn't hear the door knocker.

She jumped from her seat on the threadbare chaise lounge in the parlor, teacup barely meeting the cradle of its saucer, then moved through the dining room and to the front door to accept the post. Another letter from A. Alnwick.

She twisted a loose corkscrew curl around her finger.

Your mention of Dr. Hurst in the last war and his methods of treating men who needed some space and rehabilitation before returning to society has been turning over in my mind. And I am prepared to do something about it. I hope I am not being too presumptuous, but as I mentioned in a previous letter, I have a grand estate and not much to do with it . . .

Herr Alnwick had included a list of possible chores and activities recalling Hurst's treatments of handy woodwork and gardening.

There are several gardens throughout the estate. And a barn that, upon my recollection, is home to some animals: horses and cows and chickens.

The longer the letter continued, the rambles reflected his obvious passion for Leedswick. It might have been her psychoanalyst's eye, but she sensed a childhood excitement. One he might not be aware he exuded.

Brigitta had often found ways and means to postulate her own fledgling ideas. And now Herr Alnwick needed help. Brigitta read the note again. *What a mind*, she thought, *to study Freud and Jung while his life was a burning fuse at the end of a snaking wire.*

I have invited four men to stay at Leedswick Castle. The estate is far from its glory days, and I anticipate that men who are still at odds with their brains and their dreams can use the interim for many accomplishments around the grounds before they return home. This is where you—or your uncle, Dr. Mayr, should his schedule prove available—could play a part.

Brigitta bounded across the hall to her uncle's temporary study. The bombs had driven him from his usual office in the Neuer Markt, to her aunt's constant annoyance. *Tante* Pia was clearly intrigued, watching her husband read the letter Brigitta had presented him.

She hid her shaking hands behind her back, carefully studying his slowly spreading smile. "I commend the young man for his industry and for his obvious retention of many of our views, *Liebling.*"

Herr Doktor Henrik Mayr never smiled patronizingly. But he smiled nonetheless even in serious conversations, which irked her. When her own parents had died in a motorcar crash long before the war, she cried in Tante Pia's arms and found an embrace in Onkel Henrik's expression, accompanied by glistening, sympathetic eyes. With her childhood behind her, Brigitta stepped into the studies under her uncle's influence.

"Liebling, it is not appropriate for a young woman to live so far from her family with a strange man."

"But, Onkel, these men . . ." Brigitta rapped her palm on the paper. "I could do something *brilliant.* I could put my research into action and work on my dissertation in a practical way." She stopped for a needed breath and to register any shift in his expression.

She could tell by the way his eyes focused on hers that he understood her. "You know that I have been struggling to decide what stream of psychoanalysis would best suit me. And isn't this a sign? Dreams and subconscious."

She swerved her attention to her aunt. "There will be men everywhere suffering the aftereffects of war on their psyches. This could be a long-lasting pursuit."

She thought of Dr. Elisa Bauer, the revolutionary female

psychiatrist who had found success in a man's profession first in Berlin and of late in America. Brigitta wanted to reach the same level of renown and esteem, attain the same successful career. She just hadn't been sure how to make her research stand out.

"Men, Brigitta!" Onkel Henrik was in a state now, pounding his right fist on his left palm. "In this crumbling old castle."

"Men—" Brigitta didn't make it much further in her explanation. Her uncle was on a rampage. It was almost comical. Blood flushed his neck and rose into his face.

"Here. Herr Alnwick included a photograph of where these *men* will be housed. As you can see . . ." Brigitta presented it to her uncle and stabbed her index finger at the turrets and high roofs and numerous windows. "I can scurry away from all of them. Besides, they're all exhausted from the war." She took a breath. "There is a staff there. *Ein haushälterin!* I will not be the only woman."

The last bit of her sentence was intended for Tante Pia, whose eyes met hers with a challenging twinkle.

Her uncle continued. "I have the burden of your father's expectations for you, Brigitta. I have the burden of his memory. I must take care of you."

"And you will take care of me. By allowing me to go." She gestured to the letter. "He has also invited you—"

"I will not leave your aunt when Vienna is in shambles."

"Precisely!" Brigitta waved her hand across the letter. "Perhaps this is the purpose in our hearing from him."

"Leedswick . . . Castle." Her aunt rolled the words around in her mouth.

Brigitta's imagination sparked. For as much as she loved reading Freud and Elisa Bauer, she also loved reading novels: large gothic novels from the world of Goethe and Stefan Zweig in her native tongue and into the foreign Brontë territory in Herr Alnwick's world. She imagined all of Britain to be the moody moors of *Wuthering Heights*.

Brigitta had always wanted to explore the world beyond her careful circumference. And now? She could stay and face more rations and intermittent electricity and—*blast it*—even the burden of deciding her future. *Or . . .* she could use the time to decide if this was truly her path. She would have men, late of war, to inspire and talk to and hopefully help. Even the titles of the well-worn spines of books she anticipated packing for her trip paraded across her mind.

Leedswick. In the moors of Northumberland. Brigitta always thought weather was a great barometer of madness and passion. She could set off to rainy ol' England and its volatile scenes of Rochester. Heathcliff. Cries into the night heard by overactive minds like her own.

How she would have loved to meet the Brontë sisters and ask them how their imaginations stretched so far out over patchwork-quilt fields when their lives as a poor parson's daughters kept them cloistered near a parish church and an old brick manse. Now Brigitta hoped she might be able to taste a bit of what she had only whet her appetite with between pages.

"Your Tante—"

"Her Tante agrees." Pia Mayr had the rare ability to materialize and punctuate any conversation at the exact moment it needed her. Much as she did now.

"Dearest, this is hardly the time to go traipsing off to an English manor house," her uncle protested.

"Dearest"—Tante Pia's response was emphatic—"if you stay here, the Viennese Psychoanalytic Society is likely to string you up to *Der Steffl*, where the Pummerin bell used to be before the bombs, if only to spite your uncle and his ridiculous feud."

Brigitta's pulse accelerated. An opportunity to leave Austria and the blackouts, the craters, the scaffolds crisscrossing over the Graben and Kärntner Strasse, blemishes of war in a city quartered by Allied domination. A chance to meet a soldier who found her words like armor in the midst of dark moments. It might stall her studies, but then again, it might propel them forward with actual experience.

"Send a telegram to Herr Alnwick," her uncle said over his shoulder as he retreated to his study.

"Be careful, Brigitta." Tante Pia's voice rang out through the small kitchen and Brigitta's excitement. *"Bitte, mein Liebling.* These men are at the precipice of something new. You want to *help* them, and emotions can get out of hand quickly."

"I am not going to fall in love. I am going to help these men find a way back to themselves."

"Schön Brigitta." Her aunt clicked her tongue. Clearly she had no hesitation in referring to Brigitta as beautiful, but her tone contained a soft warning all the same. "It is you who mentioned falling in love. Not me."

CHAPTER 4 ————————————————

LEEDSWICK CASTLE
NORTHUMBERLAND, ENGLAND

Memories of Alec's childhood occupied his brain as quickly as the train cleared London's ravaged skyline and edged toward scenery more familiar to his past. It was an express route to Northumberland, but soon squat little station houses slowed the journey.

Alec tried to read, but his heart and fingertips were thrumming. Still, the more the countryside dipped low under an explosion of golden sky, the more the tension in his shoulders eased. At least he had made a decision. He wasn't sure if it was the right one, but it was a decision nonetheless. It was a risk to confront Leedswick, knowing it would conjure memories of Uncle Daniel just as sure as it would evoke lighter ones of childhood exploration and curiosity. If only he could focus on the happy, safe memories.

A car collected him at the station in Birchwick. Brown apparently had many tricks up his sleeve to anticipate this needed addition to their careful plan.

Leedswick Castle, coming into view, closed the gap between the war he had survived and his childhood shadowed by Hal. *No.* No Hal now. One thing at a time. Alec would slow down, separate one thought from the next. If he let himself think too much, it might lead to the more painful aspects of his last time here: Uncle Daniel.

Alec needed to focus on Leedswick as being as safe as one of those tiny rail houses. He would use his time here to iron out his plans but also to reclaim the joy he'd had as a child. He would decide what he wanted to do next and bide his time until he finally had concrete news from his parents.

Upon their arrival at the castle, Alec found his ten-year-old self in the grandeur of the estate he knew well. The moment he departed the car for the long gravel walkway, he was met by a matronly-looking woman with stringy gray-black hair, who tugged at her patched cardigan, and a stoic-looking fellow who removed his tweed cap and attempted to comb his sparse hair over a growing bald spot.

"Hannigan, milord." He had a burr of an accent native to England's northern tip.

Alec dipped his head at the man.

Hannigan was accompanied by the housekeeper, Magdalen, pronounced *maudlin*, much like the college at Oxford.

Leedswick was still prepossessing, its weathered sandstone clashing against a sky low with clouds perhaps burdened with rain, hanging over the gardens, ramparts, and turrets. He stole as long a look as he could of the grounds before heading toward the castle entrance, knowing his sparse staff was waiting.

But he had a perspective of what it *might* become given his recent experience, and he wanted to take it all in.

It was *his* now, though a little tarnished and worn around the edges.

Magdalen and Hannigan urged him to explore the grounds, and later Alec would at greater length, but first he wanted to take some time inside. The duo Brown had procured clearly were as dedicated to Leedswick as he was, and Alec appreciated it.

The low light filtered through the windows and exposed dust

motes that snowed onto the library's covered furniture. His shoes found every crack in the stone floor. In spite of the room's ominous chill, he was drawn to the broad built-in shelves and the wide grated fireplace and mantel. Alec approached the singed logs, making a note to add chopping wood to the list of rehabilitation chores he had sent to Fräulein Mayr consistent with Dr. Hurst's methodology. Feeding the chickens too. Collecting the eggs. Alec smiled. He had loved collecting eggs when he was a boy.

"I have free rein?" young Alec had said.

"You mean free range," his uncle quipped.

But first Alec wanted to explore the library, its leather and pine scent familiar from childhood when he had stood on tippy-toes, straining to reach a leather tome with words too heavy for his comprehension.

Still, he'd loved the challenge.

He turned to study the wood-paneled wall, stopping, then moving close to a broad canvas with a sprawling battle scene he only vaguely remembered. A plaque underneath it read *The Battle of Culloden.* Alec looked left and right before he stepped closer. He wasn't sure why he felt he needed permission to stand close and even touch the frame, given this was all his. But something in the gravity of the moment stalled him. Startled him. Frightened him.

A battle was a battle, whether immortalized in ripples of oil paints or nipping at Alec's heels and stealing his sleep. What he *did* know was that the depiction of this battle would trigger all manner of dreams in the four men he was hosting, the kind of dreams he wanted them to forget. Uncle Daniel had told him that war still haunted Leedswick—Alec wouldn't tempt any spirit or ghost by welcoming it with a reproduction of a bloody scene.

He pulled at the painting until his fingertips smarted. Wouldn't budge. Years of engaging in prewar fencing and toting his rifle across the Front had made him strong, but apparently not strong enough.

Alec turned at a shuffle in the corridor. "Hannigan! Can you help?"

Hannigan entered the library, and they wrangled and maneuvered the painting to the far corner. The wall behind where the battle scene once hung was faded in a long vertical rectangle.

"It's so bare, milord."

"Not *milord*. Alec. Let's move Charles and Beatrice here." They had been moved once before by his father from the north wing when he'd inherited the title of marquess. Now they could hang directly in view. But Alec had one more favor to ask of Hannigan.

"I know it is probably not customary, but seeing as we are conserving heat and gas, this is the room in which I feel most myself. Could we have Charles's large desk and bureau moved from the old study to the library?"

If he was going to tackle everything from inheritance taxes to outstanding bills and notices, he might as well do it in a room embraced by books. There was something comforting about part of his heritage being moved from a distant wing to a room where he wanted people to feel at home.

A half hour later, after he and Hannigan had moved Charles's and Beatrice's paintings to the library and Hannigan had departed, Alec assessed the portraits from another angle. Alec's notorious ancestors. Were they as uncomfortable with insipid titles as he was?

Charles stood in repose, as vivid and casually elegant as if he were standing across from Alec at that very moment. In his hand was a brown leather book: Charles's elusive journal that Alec's father, Uncle Daniel, and Aunt Peggy had searched for high and low through Leedswick Castle during their childhood.

Beatrice's pose was also relaxed, her full lips and halo of dark brown hair startlingly delicate yet sensual. Gilded frames with slight scallops at the edges snagged the shadows and sliver of moon peering through arched windows. The paintings gave the place a sense of rooted history.

Hannigan reentered the room. "A letter, milord."

"Alec," he said with a smile.

Hannigan merely nodded and bent in a sort of bow. Alec snatched at the missive inscribed with *Mayr*.

His heart set a new pace, excitement building rather than the anxiety he was certain shuddered underneath the surface.

Herr Alnwick,

I look forward to your further acquaintance upon my arrival. I cannot boast to be particularly experienced in your proposal, but your kind tone made me believe that you would allow me to try. I should hope, however, that you would allow me to use this time as an experiment for my own studies. I took the liberty of reaching out to my thesis supervisor and while, of course, I will keep the names of our subjects anonymous, I am quite excited at the prospect of pursuing a new method of cognitive and behavioral therapies.

Alec looked back up at the elegant portraits of his ancestors. Did they ever imagine that Leedswick would be appropriated for rehabilitation? Perhaps they'd be relieved. At least the estate would stay in the family. No National Trust or Heritage Foundation.

For now.

Brigitta took one more glance in the window at her reflection and now-wilted collar. *"The American girls are wearing their hair in Victory Rolls,"* she had told Tante Pia before Brigitta left. Those rolls were long gone now.

Her disheveled reflection in the train car window left a lot to be desired. She did what she could to make herself presentable and smoothed the wrinkled skirt of her light woolen rayon dress where it flared out from its belted waist.

A train to Calais, then the ferry across the Channel where the sea had sparkled and Dover's famous white cliffs rose against the blue sky. By the last leg of the journey, she could barely keep her eyes open, but she had notebooks full of ideas.

The train chugged by the quilted verdant farmland and the stout little brick chapels so different from the onion-bulbed steeples at home. The moors were hilly and almost lugubrious under slanted shadows one moment and sliced through with sunshine another, as if the Creator had yet to make up His mind. The lakes, little bowls of glistening water, contrasted with the green and evoked a feeling of home.

Geduld, Brigitta! She couldn't expect to find patience and fit into the seams of a new place as quickly as the tweed coat Tante Pia had rehemmed from a church bin and tucked around her chin for the cold English nights. *"As cold as the people, my dear."*

Brigitta had kissed her aunt on each cheek. *"Oh, I doubt they'll be cold. Though I'll miss having your Vanillekipferl to warm me up."* The small vanilla crescent cookies were her favorites.

The car sent to collect her from the London station left a lot to be desired. Eventually the manor grounds spread out before her, and the castle came into view in an eruption of turrets and sandstone amid unkempt grass and a garden that might have aspired to the English Country–style if the weeds hadn't swallowed the black wrought-iron gates and covered the metal vines winding around them. There were small hooks and a bit of chain hanging. Perhaps the gates had borne signs at some point, but a quick peek showed nothing.

The car slowed to a stop. "Thank you," Brigitta told the driver. "I can see to my things."

She opened the car door and stretched her limbs only to feel a slight tickle at her ankle. She looked down as a cat looked up with its wide gray-blue eyes. It was a long-haired Persian ball of cotton as soft as a Swansdown powder puff.

Brigitta smiled. *"Kleine Katze. Niedlich."* As she was studying the cute feline's curious little nose, it inched forward and looped around Brigitta's leg.

"Not you again!" a male voice blared. "My sincere apologies. Be gone, mangy critter!"

The figure approached her in a blur of tweed and a long stride before he picked up the now-rebelling, perturbed animal, scolded it a moment, and positioned it in the opposite direction from the castle. Brigitta watched the cat's tail flick before it sauntered off.

"Shoo." The man waved at it even as the cat turned its tiny head over its shoulder to observe him.

Brigitta turned her attention to the stranger. He had dark brown hair just growing out of its regulation length, with several strands falling across his forehead like a light curtain. He had a strong chin . . . so *aristocratic* looking. Perhaps not conventionally handsome, but inching very close to it. Especially, she imagined, when he smiled. His startling amber-gold eyes warmed her, belying his rude treatment of the animal. "What is his name?"

"Pardon?"

"The cat!"

"He has no name." The stranger searched her face. Yes. His eyes were his best feature.

"Everyone should have a name."

"Everyone should, yes, but that is a *cat*." The stranger straightened. "Forgive me, I am new to this lord-of-the-manor bit." He cleared his throat. "Ah. I see your driver was about as attentive to your things as I am to that bloody cat. I paid him well beforehand . . ."

"I told him I was quite capable of handling them myself."

"Well, never mind. I'll have Hannigan out in a minute. No, you really mustn't take the cases. As I said—"

"I got them this far."

The man's mouth eased into a smile. No. His smile was his best feature. *Ja*, definitely his smile.

"Ms. Mayr. Or is it Doctor? Fräulein?" Nerves permeated his words and twitched the muscle beneath his jaw. He leaned slightly forward, rocked a little on the balls of his feet. As if ready for a quick retreat. Interesting.

"Indeed, and you must be . . . ?" Her palm perspired against the handle of her case. "Oh, but how should I address you?" He was a lord. Or a sir. Or a marquess. No . . . *Alexander Alnwick*. The man she'd met through written words. Who'd trusted her with a vulnerability her closest friends hadn't. Surely that bridged a divide.

"Perhaps you should call me Alec?"

"Brigitta Mayr." She forced her hand in his before he had a chance to extend his own. "Brigitta," she repeated. Just as she felt the first patter of raindrops.

＋━━━━＋

Alec didn't notice the drizzle, just a uniquely pretty young woman welcoming herself straight into his home.

"The poor *Katze* will be soaked through."

"He'll survive." A few drops escalated into a typical Northumberland downpour. He enjoyed watching Brigitta's reaction. He, too, was slowly readjusting to weather that turned on a farthing.

Alec retrieved one of her cases despite her protestations, catching a peek of a shapely calf beneath the hem of her skirt.

"No name." She clicked her tongue. Was she truly that interested in the stray? "*Eine Schande.*"

Alec adjusted his collar. "It's not a disgrace, Fräulein, when I don't know the cat."

Brigitta smiled when he spoke German. "Then you must be introduced." She reached for a bag, and the pair toted the luggage to the grand entrance of the manor house, where Alec was startled to see the cat lounging by the front steps. In his short acquaintance with it, it had always retreated to the barn. Its wise little face looked up at Brigitta.

"Sigmund," she christened it. She set down a case and bent to scratch its ears.

"As in Freud?"

She raised to her full height. *"Genau."* She took a step toward him. "It's how we met, isn't it?"

He reconciled his transparent and vulnerable letters with the Brigitta watching him expectantly now: cheeks ruddy with chill, ice-blue eyes tired from the journey but shoulders erect in a bit of a challenge.

She wasn't the woman he'd imagined from their exchanged letters. Or was she? He hadn't known what to envision. After all, he had used her as a lifeline, pouring out his insecurities in hopes of finding some common ground, some answers, some healing.

Now, through sheets of rain, she rebalanced her cases and seemed to be admiring the surroundings, was perhaps even a little intimidated by them.

"Just wait until you get lost in a maze of overgrown shrubs," Alec said dryly, trying and failing to hide the smile pulling at his lips.

"Oh, truly?"

"You sound almost excited. I wasn't expecting that from you."

Brigitta raised her chin a little. "Well, I wasn't expecting *you* to understand my native tongue, Herr Alnwick." She smiled. "I am greatly looking forward to seeing how else we can surprise each other."

CHAPTER 5 ————————————

Brigitta couldn't blame Alec for seeming nervous and as change-able as a sky that couldn't decide on rain or sunshine. At times a shadow darkened his face and his golden eyes turned downward or looked everywhere but at her while he clasped his hands behind his back. He had introduced himself to her in vulnerable thoughts and questions through paper and ink, had allowed Brigitta and her uncle to peer into his every weakness. Now when he did look at her, it was with the keen awareness that her understanding of him went far deeper than any veneer he might don or role he might hope to play.

Hannigan took Brigitta's luggage upstairs to a room not too far from the office space Alec had arranged for her. She was so over-taken by the estate—but also the courtesy of someone seeing to her needs—she couldn't help but give a little curtsy.

Alec chuckled, probably in spite of himself. Their eyes met, and he continued on with the informal tour.

She gestured around the room. "All of this is yours?"

"My family's. Even my parents would be hard pressed to call it theirs. More something we've inherited. If she were here, my mother would say it was a ball and chain. You can never truly be free, she told me, when you're the custodians of something so splendid."

Still, as they began to wander at a recreational pace, he seemed to admire it as she did.

"Is this your first time welcoming guests here since you've returned?"

"Yes. It is." Alec stopped a moment. "It's odd talking to someone who knows so many of my limitations."

"Limitations?" She was delighted their trains of thought were seemingly riding the same rail. "No. I see potential." She followed his lead when he started walking again. The high arches and long corridors breathed a reverence into her, as if she were attending church.

"You know more about me these days than my own family."

"You will tell them. In your own time."

He led her to the second floor via a stone staircase. "Magdalen made up your room," Alec said. "I haven't had much time to get everything ready." He stopped at a large bedchamber in a cold, dimly lit hallway.

"It looks like a palace."

He nodded. Brigitta noticed that his eyes lit up. Perhaps he was embracing the compliment. This was the first thing he had shown her that wasn't burdened by experience: a beautiful, historical place whose stories he was explaining with the air of a tour guide.

"Magdalen will have everything you need. We're understaffed here, and as you can see, the castle and its grounds are a little run-down. But I suppose that serves our purpose here." He turned to leave, then stopped. "Join me in the library? Perhaps in a half hour?"

"That would be lovely."

"I've decided that is where my office will be. Ha! It sounds so official. My *office*. For correspondence and to receive callers." He raked his fingers through his brown hair, stalling in the doorframe. "I'd decided I would pretend to have things in order and controlled. But I figure you already know that my head hasn't been screwed on straight for a long while." He glanced away. "I really don't know what I'm doing. Maybe I'm just hiding away."

"The brave thing about what you are doing is allowing yourself to show other people what you're most afraid of."

He looked at her with those startling eyes of his. "Yes."

A dimple creased the right side of a smile she wished she could smooth out. And when combined with his rich speaking voice, strong hands, and kind demeanor, every last word from the letters and plans Brigitta had read served to paint a full picture. Even as Alec straightened his shoulders and tried to mold himself into this world of arches, turrets, and long-abandoned castle wings, the slightly crooked smile betrayed him. He was not completely at ease. But he would be, she decided, and soon.

"I'll leave you to get settled. I'll have tea waiting for us downstairs."

Ja. This was certainly the solicitous man who had written her.

✦————✦

Brigitta Mayr rocked on her oxford shoes, her hands tucked behind her back. She was surveying the library much as she had the corners of the estate: with unbridled curiosity. Alec almost wondered if she would have properly introduced herself to that mangy stray cat if he had not intercepted their meeting.

After years of being around the dead, Alec was startled that Brigitta was so . . . so . . . *alive*. For one, he could drown in those light blue eyes of hers. For another, she couldn't seem to stand still. The only steadying thing about her was when she focused on him.

Alec assumed she was turning the first pages of the current chapter of his life with silent observation. She was a medical professional. Her uncle was a renowned scholar of Freud. Could she see into his soul and detect his uncertainty?

"The men should arrive tomorrow morning." He broke her careful study of his person. "See, I've worked further on the basic plan I had sent you based on institutions that helped men in the previous war." Alec smoothed his trousers.

"The men need to embrace the last stage between their war years and their lives now. As you said in your letter."

"We need them to associate their surnames not with barked orders but with the freedom they have to transition from their old lives to the new."

"Your plans and your letter, Alec . . . they were so detailed. Not perfect, but this is an experiment, ja?"

"Yes. Which is why I can't help but think I have no right to propose it. My barrister in London and my friend Evan Laughton and I found some willing participants, but that doesn't mean . . ." He stopped, took a breath. "I think there was a reason for me to learn about Dr. Hurst. I don't want you to think this is just a whim."

"Not a whim, Alec. You want a sense of permanence, and on some level you want to heal your uncle Daniel by proxy."

She saw through him so clearly. Startled, he cleared his throat to maintain a semblance of control. "Dreams are repressed wishes. Isn't that right? According to Freud, that is."

"See?" Her eyes glistened. "That is why I named the cat for him." She rose a little on her tiptoes, defining long legs in beige stockings. The sun streaming through the arched window backlit her profile. He was about to speak when he heard a crash that startled him far more than it should have.

He looked over to where Magdalen was picking up toppled tea trays.

Alec's breath hitched, his chest pounded, and his ears rang with a familiar buzz. "I-I'm . . ." He didn't get through his apology, merely nodded and splayed his right hand over his heartbeat.

Brigitta was watching him with compassion. "Startling easily is to be expected." She set her hand over his wrist, doubtless feeling the accelerated pulse. "I guarantee it will get easier. Just like your uncle

Daniel you speak of, my uncle remembers the last war. And in every story he told me, he never saw an end to the reminders. To the horrors he had seen when he got back to Vienna. You never forget, but it lessens. You find you can live again."

"Brigitta, I—"

"Alec—"

They verbally tripped over each other a moment.

"Brigitta, I need someone to speak to on a . . . a professional and psychoanalytic level. About my dreams and what I am thinking."

"Of course. That is why you wrote to my uncle."

"Indeed. I don't want you to take offense." Alec took a beat. He had so little control over his dreams or the spirals of anxiety that assaulted his brain, catapulting him back to the war.

Yes, he wanted to redeem the estate and make amends for the riches afforded him while so many slogged back to prefab housing and long commutes on the Tube.

Still, he wanted to carve out a bit of care and attention for himself.

"I want you to be available to speak to the men arriving here. But I also need someone to talk to." He stopped. Let the sentence hang in the air for a while, resisting the urge to justify it.

Waiting for her to catch up.

"I would like to make a proposal of my own, Alec." Her smile spread slowly so he didn't have to take his sentence a step further. "I will meet with the men you've invited here and offer them what help I can, given the limitations of my own education. But I would also like to propose that you continue to write to my uncle. Uninhibited."

Alec raised an eyebrow. "Uninhibited?"

"And most especially if a nightmare startles you awake. You do not worry about sleep; you write my uncle instead."

Alec exhaled his relief, then chuckled. "Is it going to be a problem that you know me as well as I know myself?"

"A problem?" She smiled. "Or an advantage?"

CHAPTER 6 ─────────────────────────

The portraits of Alec's ancestors watched them closely with a severity that tamed even the Culloden battle painting. The latter was looking a little like a slouched ghost in the corner, shrouded by a sheet, ready to be moved.

"It's odd to be back here." Alec watched the portraits back a moment. "When I was a child, I thought if I stared at them long enough, I would know their stories. I've heard snippets, of course. One cannot have such a magnanimous family and not hear snippets. There was a court case. A trial for murder . . ."

Brigitta's eyes widened with interest.

"Beatrice there"—he nodded to her portrait—"was what was known as a 'Dollar Princess.' Her fortune saved Leedswick from financial ruin in 1870. She kept a journal of her experiences at Leedswick. It's around here somewhere."

"A Dollar Princess?"

"Women who were sold off by greedy mothers in New York to marry English aristocracy." It was a crass way to put it, but that's how his spirited mother had framed it.

"She found a new home?"

"I get the sense it took a long time for my great-grandmother to find home."

"And your mother, Elena?"

"Sometimes I think she was most at home when we were off on

adventure. My *father* is her home. Her paintings are her home too. She can find home anywhere."

"Have these men, the ones who will be joining us, already been home?" Brigitta traced her finger around the rim of her empty teacup.

"Yes. And judging by their quick responses, they haven't fared too well." Alec stretched in his chair. "My friend Evan Laughton has been in contact with them. And I assume their stories are not so different from Evan's own. According to his letter he told his fiancée that he was helping a friend, and he is of course. I don't want anyone to feel that what he's doing here has to be kept secret. But I also want the men to have the privacy that I want." He sighed. "I'm just as lost as I assume they are." He looked at her for a moment.

"You seem pretty found here."

"I don't want to play lord of the manor. But I wouldn't mind attempting something that aligns with my conscience. Especially since I have such a large place at my disposal. And I thought that since my letters with your uncle—and you—were so meaningful to me . . ."

The very *real* fact was that she was a very *real* woman, whose slight curves and band of freckles on her nose he never could have captured in ink and paper. "Then maybe I could translate some of that and some of what Hurst did to my experience here."

Brigitta smiled and swept up a strand of hair. Each hairpin safe in place.

For now.

Brigitta waited for Alec to rise before she abandoned the matched, if chipped, tea service. Alec centered on one cup without any wear or break. "When I was a child, I liked the chipped cups. I thought they had character. Maybe now I deserve the one whole cup."

They explored the books and files around them. The slightest movement or touch of a spine sent a puff of dust in flight.

"I really should be consulting with Hannigan. I haven't even shown you your office yet."

Brigitta raised a shoulder in a shrug. Then held her finger under her nose to stifle a sneeze. Alec was immediately apologetic.

"It's just the book's way of saying hello," she said.

"And telling us it needs a dusting."

"We can see to that." She ran her finger over the spines. "But I want some light bedtime reading and a . . . what was the word you used? Dollar? Yes. A Dollar Princess just might be it."

Brigitta followed his sight line up over rows of tomes about psychiatry when a particularly fragile copy of Robert Burton's *The Anatomy of Melancholy* caught her eye. She met Alec's eyes with a slight *May I?* tilt of her chin.

"This library is as much yours as mine." He helped her extract the weighty tome from its place, and she carried it over to the large mahogany desk, scalloped and elaborate and most likely from the previous century.

Would this be one of the valuable pieces he might have to sell to keep the castle? She imagined his ancestor Charles seeing to his business affairs from behind it. "This is one of the first treatises ever published on mental illness." Brigitta had recognized it immediately. "Before they even knew it was an ailment. Burton thought that idleness was the root of melancholy."

She turned to the opening page and smelled the stale seventeenth-century sheets of paper, near translucent with wear. "My uncle would love to see this." She looked at the book rather than at Alec, though she felt his eyes closely on her.

He unfastened the buttons on his shirtsleeves. He stopped to examine the cuffs before folding each sleeve back and pushing the fabric up to his elbows. It wasn't particularly warm. Was he just finding something to do with his hands? Not for the first time she noticed how they were at odds with the rest of him: always tucked in his pockets or behind his back.

Brigitta noted the strong, sinewy muscles in his forearms, then, at her observation, he pressed his long fingers on the desk blotter. The casual motion seemed a sign of his comfort with her. Not just a gentleman squire cloistered in this ancestral seat in the moors a breath away from Mr. Lockwood assessing his new tenancy at Wuthering Heights. Rather, a man assuming a new role at the coalescing of instinct and inspiration.

Names written in Alec's hand scrolled evenly across a sheet at the top of the desk blotter: *Jones, Clarington, Adamson, Laughton.* Underneath, a scratch pad listed chores and ideas alongside bullet points, some of which were struck through and marred with inkblots.

When Brigitta's eyes met Alec's, he retreated a little. "I hope I know what I'm doing." He rose and pushed back his chair, sighed. "I have to reconcile someone I put on paper—a faceless person—with a live human being."

"Better than an *unliving* human being." She nudged his shoulder.

"I must be off to prepare for my—*our*—guests." Alec gave a small bow. "Please, stay. This room is as much yours as mine."

"I should help too. I can help Magdalen prepare food for the week."

"Yes, but I am sure she can spare you for a few moments. I have set up a makeshift office of your own and perhaps you can select a few books to take with you." He smiled and Brigitta retreated to the bookshelves.

As a child she believed her uncle's library possessed the answers to everything. Often she would pull down a random book and run her index finger under paragraphs of content that was far beyond her limited understanding.

Now she hoped that the general perusing of pages would give her an increased understanding. Another level on which she could meet Alec.

Brigitta's attention narrowed on a small and narrow volume covered in green cloth, and she bent to retrieve it, leaving a cloud of dust in its wake.

Taking care because of its obvious age, she gingerly opened the book to a woman's handwriting on pages stained with wear, and just near the crease of the spine was a pressed flower. It was worn and yellow, in the shape of a horn with sharp, rigid petals almost untouched by time. She read the words *Charles* and *Leedswick*.

Beatrice Alnwick.

Brigitta looked over to the portraits: An elegant woman preserved in pearls and pompadour. A man with a brown leather journal in his hand, poised to inherit the magnificent grounds around him. His wife in the portrait beside his, a gilded lily frame and elegant. A Dollar Princess. She looked to be worth far more.

Brigitta leafed through a few pages. She was holding a careful map to the estate as seen through the eyes of a woman who loved gardening and her husband but was trying to step into a new world she didn't understand. Who used the diary not only as a way to understand the world around her but to impress memories and ask questions and write reminders that would later help her in the garden and even in her new social circumstance.

She carefully set the diary atop *The Anatomy of Melancholy* and took it up to her room. Even with the presence of Magdalen, Brigitta couldn't help but feel like the only woman in the whole of Leedswick. With Beatrice's thoughtful guidance on the bedside table, Brigitta was certain that would no longer be the case.

+ —— +

Leedswick was cursed, all right. By Alec's stupidity.

His heartbeat accelerated. He wasn't certain if that was on account of three strangers and Laughton about to arrive or the fact that Alec had invited a woman—a living, breathing woman—into his house.

"Better than an unliving one."

He smiled thinking of her kind attempt at banter. She was going above and beyond to put him at ease.

He focused on scribbling a rudimentary schedule that included everything he could think of for distraction. For wasn't that at the heart of all this? Distraction? He had to ensure that the time the men spent here wasn't merely what he worried his own time would become: a means of making the time tick by in between nightmares.

Hours awake delaying the time before he had to close his eyes again.

It is terrifying . . .

Alec shook his head and refocused. Hannigan would see to a session on chopping wood and introduce the garden, shrubs, and other landscaping to the men. Magdalen would ensure that the meals were made with what was gathered and collected from their labors. Brigitta would present the men with a small introduction to her role here.

Hannigan brought the post: a telegram from Laughton about train schedules and arrivals and a telegram from Brown. Apparently Cousin Hal had been using the Mayfair town house quite a lot recently. Perhaps throwing elaborate parties beneath the Swarovski crystals of the dining room's grand chandelier and making use of the wine cellars, dusty and untouched from before the war.

Alec couldn't decipher if this was a warning or just a piece of information doled out pragmatically.

✦ —— ✦

Alec was almost relieved when he rose the next morning. He had a feeling that the longer he, Brigitta, Hannigan, and Magdalen spent in the castle, the smaller it would seem. Mostly because of Brigitta. Even when she was not in view, he sensed her. He was well aware of her presence in the castle and the ease with which he was able to talk to her. Far more, she had become a friend as well as a confidante.

Alec strolled toward the barn—not too fast, not too slow—noting the moodiness of the clouds over the thatched roof and the incomparable stillness of dawn, his boots melting into a grass misted with morning dew.

He smiled when he saw Brigitta's profile at the mouth of the barn. So much for solitariness. "I would think you're hard at work." He appraised her overalls, her blonde hair carefully braided and tucked under a gingham kerchief. Her arms were full of Sigmund Freud. The cat's wise little face was scrunched—whether in annoyance or fond introspection, Alec couldn't be sure.

Brigitta, apparently, had the same idea judging by the basket at her feet, likely for egg collecting.

She set the cat down and picked up a pitchfork. She scooped hay with rudimentary aptitude but impressive fervor.

"Give me that." He nudged her aside and took up her chore.

"Look at you . . ." Brigitta studied him.

Alec smoothed his trousers, raked his fingers through his hair, and balanced the pitchfork again. Brigitta moved to the side and he continued clearing hay from the path to the chicken coops. Overhead a few raindrops evaded the makeshift board he and Hannigan had nailed earlier in hopes that when the men arrived, they might see to the waterproofing of the roof altogether.

Alec threw his weight into his task, fully conscious of Brigitta in his periphery: watching him with little care as she knelt in the hay, running her hand over the now-arched back of the languid cat.

"My mother would josh me about wanting to be out here instead of fulfilling my station as a proper heir of Leedswick. She rarely meant anything malicious by it," he explained. "It was her brand of sarcasm. She was as suited to fulfilling her station as marchioness as I am to fulfilling my role as marquess."

Alec smiled softly at the memory.

"You need to own every bit of who you are, Alec Alnwick," she said after a moment. "And that means you will have to own the fact that you chose to come to a place where your family has been ostracized for years." She smoothed the wrinkles in her old dungarees, hand-me-downs she must've gotten from Magdalen.

"How did . . . ?"

"I talked to Magdalen and to Hannigan. But I also know that there has been no visitor here save myself since before the war. Certainly, if you were the lauded and returned marquess, heralded by your recent service in battle, they would be lining up to put their cards on a silver platter and await your reception of them. But no one."

Sigmund circled Alec's leg in a casual loop as if making a statement, rubbing his soft little head against Alec's calf.

"He likes you." Brigitta chuckled.

"More's the pity for him." Alec took him in. He had to give the creature some credit for his persistence. Sigmund was determined to belong.

"Not even the vicar has been here." Brigitta picked up her earlier theme. "Magdalen was saying that she thought it would be a good idea to at least invite the vicar. Perhaps he doesn't think he is welcome."

Alec set the pitchfork next to the wall, opened the latch on the chickens' cage with a bit of trepidation, and fell back a step the moment one of the fowl squawked into animated view.

Brigitta laughed.

"Hey there," Alec cooed at the bird while performing the careful choreography of dodging flapping wings and a curious cat in pursuit of the eggs.

Brigitta lunged to help and scooped up Sigmund before he could playfully swat at a chicken. *When in Rome*, Alec thought.

He picked up and soothed a chicken, speaking to it with a low, rumbling voice. With the bird controlled, Brigitta slowly lowered Sigmund to the barn floor and reached for the egg basket from the ground.

"I used to do this as a boy." Alec turned to face her and gingerly arranged the eggs from the cage into the basket she extended to him. "But I don't remember it being so difficult."

Alec startled at a squawk behind him. "Ow!" The bird pecked at his pant leg. Another ruffled past him.

"The Marquess of Northridge." Brigitta clicked her tongue. "Fighting chickens."

Alec got hold of the bird with a choice word. He held it tight and let out a slow exhale.

What Alec might have lacked in brawn needed for farm chores, he compensated for with sheer determination. He realized that he had gone the whole of the morning without a flash of memory or a recollection of a battle scene. An explosion or a loud cry in the night.

Alec brushed a wisp of hay from his trousers. It could work. Arthur Hurst was on to something.

"You missed one." Brigitta pointed to a stray egg that had rolled near his foot.

"I miss a lot." Alec swept it up and held the egg out to her. It was smooth and round, not speckled or somewhat brown like some of the others. "I clearly missed that I should have invited the vicar around for tea." He shook a clump of hay from his shoe. "I am not a particularly religious person, but it must mean something to Magdalen."

"Nor am I particularly well versed in English customs. But I can see it would mean a lot to Magdalen, who *is* a religious person. And it just might nudge a door of communication open to the villagers a little bit. I've read enough Jane Austen to know that the vicar is the key to the heart of an English village." She smiled. "So it is a good thing that I had Magdalen ring him round for tea *before* the men arrive."

"Are you in charge now?" He meant for his tone to be challenging, but his smile ruined it.

"I am helping. It is a big castle. You need all the allies you can get."

They now had a full basket of eggs.

Alec inspected it. "I think this just might work."

✦————✦

Vicar Richard Montmouth introduced himself with meek propriety when he met Alec in the faded parlor room. Alec had only had a short break in which to bathe away the scent of chicken coop.

"Lord Alnwick." The vicar settled and folded his hands in his lap. "I remember when you were a boy."

"You have a good memory then, Vicar." Alec settled into a wing-back chair across from him. "I was only here in the summers, mostly when my parents weren't traveling. And you may call me Alec."

"But always inquisitive," Montmouth recalled. "And well behaved. Especially in contrast to your cousin Harold."

"Would you care for tea?"

The vicar smoothed his cassock over his chest with a nod. "Alec. Doubtless you have seen a lot during the war. M-many men have been to visit me about their experiences. But Magdalen and that kind young lady thought you might want some reinforcements of a . . . ah . . . *spiritual* nature before your guests arrive."

Brigitta had been thorough. Magdalen arrived to set a tray of tea between them.

For a moment they were silent. The vicar put a biscuit on his plate. Alec sipped tea. "You don't think Leedswick is cursed though, do you? Surely your parishioners have mentioned the castle at some point. I am not so blind as to think my family is not a part of village gossip and probably has been for years."

"Are you so superstitious, Alec? You always seemed too pragmatic for that sort of thing."

"I don't know what to believe. All I know is that if there is a curse or a haunting, then wouldn't it be better to face it straight on before I try to help anyone else?"

The vicar took a moment. "And then there was your uncle. I know he was a favorite of yours."

"Everyone has a sad history." Especially because tragedy rippled through time with his great-grandfather Charles's alleged involvement in the death of his batman, Francis Dawson. War had never truly left the castle. It was in the walls, in his nightmares, and now would traipse in with the men he had invited.

"Yes, everyone *does* have a sad history. I know no one in the parish who has not experienced great loss. I will say a prayer for you and for Leedswick, Alec, but not because I think it is cursed, but rather because what you are doing deserves a blessing."

Later, after the vicar left with a promise to call again once the men were settled and with a reminder of the parish hours for Sunday service and Communion, Alec crossed to the library only to see Brigitta holding their basket of eggs. "What are you doing with those?" He nodded toward the eggs.

"I am taking them to Magdalen. I know from your letters that there are rations here—especially on grain, sugar, and clothing." She looked out in the direction of the gardens that could soon produce fruit and vegetables to supplement the eggs. "It's even worse in Vienna where our Reichsmarks mean nothing now, and many Allied attempts at aid are commandeered or cut off by the Soviets."

She blew a strand of blonde hair from her forehead and lightened her tone. "So? How was the vicar? Was he the heart and soul of the English village?"

Alec smiled. "He was very reassuring."

Alec mused a moment as Brigitta walked away, a light bounce in her step that eased his leftover tension about the imminent arrival of their guests. *The heart and soul of the English village?* Perhaps. What might be the heart and soul of Leedswick? The men arriving and falling into the rhythm of his designed chores with ease? The return of his parents and whatever canvas onto which his mother had impressed her wartime experience on a Greek island? Sigmund the cat? Or perhaps (and Alec was getting ahead of himself) the light laugh of a bookish girl who was as enamored with chickens as she was with Freud? Time would tell.

The last option kept his brain turning for the rest of the day.

CHAPTER 7

Brigitta took little time in bringing the basket of eggs to Magdalen. A nervous energy began the moment she untied the kerchief in her hair and kicked a strand of hay from her boot.

"My, you were successful!" Magdalen assessed her small bounty. "Nice to see some life around the place again."

"I think that will become a morning habit."

"It will have to be. I suspect these new men will have quite the appetite for all Hannigan anticipates putting them to work."

"I can help you." Brigitta watched the woman roll out dough with strong forearms. The kitchen was not as modern even as her aunt's, what with a woodstove and even a dated icebox, but Magdalen didn't seem to mind. Indeed, she had full command of it. Brigitta flicked flour over the worn wooden counter and started on her own kneading.

"You are very swift and strong at this, Brigitta."

Brigitta put more elbow grease into it. Just as her aunt had taught her. "Just earning my keep."

They worked in relative silence for a few moments until Magdalen inspected the vegetables she had chopped for soup and Brigitta stopped at a loud chime that reverberated over the tiles.

It emanated from beyond the kitchen and through the corridors. It sounded like a doorbell. Having not heard it before, she was surprised at how it filled the entirety of the castle wing with sound.

288

Brigitta nervously ran her fingers through her hair and wiped her hands on a discarded dish towel. "Wish me luck!"

She controlled the urge to run to join Alec in the front hallway to greet their guests. Instead, she took the increasingly familiar route with a buoyant stride. Four men now stood in the foyer, holding their sparse and worn luggage. One man had a canvas rucksack slung over his shoulder, perhaps tugging his recent war experience with him.

Alec edged slightly in front of Brigitta: a protective gesture that tugged at her heart.

The men seemed immediately curious upon seeing her but also well mannered, tipping their hats and, in the case of one with tawny hair and a long gait, giving a small bow to accompany a shy smile. This, she soon learned, was Adamson. Then another man with dark hair had a more confident air. Alec wrung his hand and cupped his elbow in greeting.

This must be Evan Laughton, Alec's best friend mentioned in a few of his letters. Then Clarington and Jones, who were decidedly more studious of Brigitta. Knowing how few men returned at all from the war, she was determined to treat them as best she could. She tried to read the tilt of the head, the way a suitcase was set on the floor, the way a man took in the new surroundings. Clarington was overly content; Jones wasn't sure what to make of it all.

Hopefully she would be able to write Onkel Henrik shortly with her observations. They were all ordinary young men. She couldn't begin to imagine what horrors they had seen. But with the exception of tired eyes and lines at their eyes and mouths, which she was certain stood as testament to what they had witnessed, they looked like regular men. British, of course, and so different from her countrymen in some ways, but regular nonetheless.

"Just leave it there for a moment." Alec motioned to their luggage. "Hannigan will see to it. Come take a tour of the place."

Alec commanded the small procession. Then, for a slight

moment, he raised his eyes to her. She gave him a quick smile, after which his shoulders relaxed and he continued.

On the battlefield he wrote that Dr. Mayr held him fast with words. Now she merely had to lock eyes with him in a dusty corridor to help him gain his confidence.

It seemed like she was not alone, though. Evan Laughton interrupted a growing silence with his booming voice, testing out the rafters. "Well, now I can see why I made fast friends with you, mate." He looked up and over the grand hallway, arms theatrically outstretched in a small semicircle around the luggage. "Look at this load of stones!"

"Leedswick has seen a few years that have made it the worse for wear," Alec said pragmatically.

"Haven't we all?" Laughton chuckled.

Alec stole a look at Brigitta. She was carefully assessing their added quartet. Since she'd arrived, he sensed when she was reading him like a book, and he tried to exercise the same careful and cautious appraisal of the new dynamic. It was easy enough to do during a tour of the castle.

"Here in the village of Birchwick, my family's history casts a bit of a dark shadow," Alec explained as they reached another of the castle's broad wings. The furniture was sparse, and heavy wood-paneled doors and walls were offset with a few tapestries. "So if you go into town at all, you might hear some disturbing things. I think it best to ignore it. But there is a rumor of a curse."

"Ghost stories already?" Adamson said as they stopped outside the door Alec told him would be his bedroom.

What with the sun stabbing through the arched window to warm the wooden boards below, the wing was already thawing from years of unuse. Really, Alec had to thank Hannigan and Magdalen for adapting so quickly. Brigitta too.

Something about her presence settled him enough that he could address what he had hoped might be contained within the walls of the estate. "You can help me understand myself a little bit better but also redeem the use of this place."

"Redeem," Laughton said from just behind him, his gaze taking in the tapestries and portraits. "I like that thought."

Alec took a moment. "Fräulein Brigitta Mayr is especially interested in observing us and providing cognitive therapy. And in studying dreams." Alec turned emphatically at the last word. A few of the men shuffled. Laughton cleared his throat, but Alec continued. "I know that when we dream it's wretched. Sometimes not even a dream at all, is it? They're just scenes reenacting over and over across the battlefields of our minds. Every horrific thing we saw. That's why Fräulein Mayr is here." He lifted his chin a little. "Her research at the university for her doctorate is almost complete."

"Fräulein sounds Jerry to me," Clarington added.

Brigitta was still and silent. Alec took a moment to read the temperature of the room. Adamson was merely interested, Jones was studying his shoe, and Clarington's brow was furrowed.

"Fräulein Mayr is Austrian, the niece of renowned psychoanalyst Herr Doktor Henrik Mayr. I was fortunate enough to write to them during the war."

"He was always writing them," Laughton attested.

Alec shot him a grateful look. Evan was a good ally to have.

"Always writing a woman? Weren't we all?" Clarington quipped.

"For a slightly different purpose." Alec cleared his throat. "As Evan mentioned in his letter inviting you here, there will be no weapons on the premises. There are some relics of rifles and hunting paraphernalia around, but we will adhere to an honor code. This should be the first step to trying to find something normal. We will be so preoccupied with our work around the manor house that we'll feel too exhausted to think much of anything else."

"And that is Alec's wishful thinking." Laughton smiled.

"Don't get me wrong—I was happy to get away from my mother-in-law for a spell," Jones said. "But the letter did little but say it was an escape, that some bloke in the last war had done something similar, and that someone would listen to me talk about my nightmares."

"It's a stepping-stone," Brigitta said. "Between your old lives *in* the war and the lives you will settle back into."

"Sounds a lot like that chap in the American book about a boy who doesn't want to paint his fence so he gets we lot to do it for him," Adamson said.

"We are used to routine," Alec said. "Roll calls and reporting for duty and training and then . . . well . . . the rest of it. We are used to answering to our ranks and surnames. And if you're anything like I am, the instant you have two moments to rub your thoughts together, it ends badly."

Clarington ran his hand over the worn banister. "So we test out our work ethic here?" He flicked a bit of dust from his fingers.

"With a safe landing space. Brigitta will be here, and she'll have access to her uncle. The local vicar will be on hand . . ."

"And we can hunt ghosts and figure out why the villagers hate the Alnwick family so much!" Laughton added.

There were a half dozen rooms spread out through the wings still salvageable and warmed by Magdalen lighting the fires in each hearth grate and assuring that the bedding was clean and carafes of water were fresh. Thus, it was easy for each man to have his own room and plenty of space in between. A couple of the men would work on restoring the corners and crannies of the castle, repairing and detailing. There were boards to paint and doorknobs to be reaffixed.

When their luggage had been distributed, they assembled in the dining room for lunch, the ominous long table seeming shorter given its new occupants. The arched windows and high, beamed ceiling and stained, wood panels were familiar to Alec, but something altogether refined and new to the guests.

He cast a look at Brigitta, who smiled encouragingly in turn. It had been her idea to use mealtimes as a sort of *Gruppentherapie* (he loved how the term sounded in her accent). It would become a safe and easy way to scratch the surface of common experiences while they both hoped time with her would chip away at further barriers.

Even so, the conversation didn't begin easily even after Magdalen arrived with freshly baked bread and a large pot of soup. But it wasn't the prospect of discussing the war or mental faculties, Alec suspected. More that table manners and polite conversation after years of scrounging and placing a makeshift plate on folded knees or an overturned rucksack were as hard to resume as adjusting to a dry, warm bed.

Clarington inspected his water goblet, Laughton tucked directly into the food, and Adamson studied the monogrammed silver spoon by his place setting.

Brigitta cleared her throat and told the men that she would be happy to discuss anything with them. "Dreams. Memories. Anything you cannot hold off."

Laughton swished the water in his goblet. "But of our own volition, correct?" Alec knew he was asking this on behalf of the table and not just himself.

"And you will be in my complete confidence. But I have done enough study to know that dreams can mean something strong enough that they can change *everything*." Brigitta put her napkin in her lap. "How you approach your family, your work. And how you will be able to . . . what is the English word? Acc . . ."

"Acclimate?" Jones asked with a kind smile.

"Yes, acclimate." Brigitta smiled back. "Back to your old life. And

Aimie K. Runyan, J'nell Ciesielski, and Rachel McMillan

when you understand why you see the things you do, we can help you see them less or at least comprehend them."

Clarington still seemed skeptical. He was leaning away from the table. "All while fixing barn doors and feeding the cows?"

Alec moved his soup tureen aside in favor of a notebook. "Ms. Mayr and I have seen to a sort of schedule for your activities. Hannigan has helped. He has run of the place. Knows a sight more than I do."

"And then what?" Adamson broke the long silence.

"Yes," Clarington added. "What?"

"I'm not sure," Alec responded with equal austerity. "I just hope."

"Hope for what?" Laughton asked.

Alec looked over them with a grimace. He hadn't intended to speak about his own past so soon. "To not be a shell of myself. Any closeness I had with my uncle Daniel was always disrupted by what the war had left on him. He was cursed by his inability to stay above water before his memories dragged him down. I can't help thinking that if someone had thrown him a rope . . ."

Brigitta leaned over the table, eyes sparkling. "This is *your* rope." She turned and gave Alec an affirming wink.

And for all of Alec's attempts to be cool, casual, and in control, it was then he dropped his spoon so it clattered into his bowl of soup, the splash liberally spraying his chin.

"Ha!" Clarington said.

So the skeptic could smile after all.

CHAPTER 8

Onkel Henrik had once told Brigitta that the hardest part of his psychology profession was moving from theory to practice. It was one thing to read about a case study or evidence at a distance, in clinical terms, over a nice cup of tea. But it was quite another to see a case study embodied in a living, breathing human.

Alec had spoken about these men's arrival, she had seen their surnames and recent ranks, but now she saw they were living and breathing humans, pale and still in need of fattening up a little, perhaps missing their families or jobs. Unsure of the space they were wading into.

After their meal, Brigitta watched Alec point his guests in the direction of the parlor. He was truly committed to his venture, even as she read a slight rigidity in his back and his propensity to dig his hands deep into his pockets when nervous or stressed. She supposed they trembled a little. She'd seen him flex his fingers open and closed into fists, apparently in hopes of steadying them.

She didn't blame the new arrivals for stealing a furtive, speculative look at her now and then. She was a *woman* in a male-dominated profession and they were under a strange roof not long after reacclimating to their home country. Still, they were gracious enough to smile at her. If distantly. She sensed they were with her in person but partly somewhere else: straddling two worlds. Like Alec.

Now, as they sat around the parlor fashioned with dark

mahogany paneling and furniture that must have been fashionable in the earlier half of the century, Brigitta surveyed the room. Her uncle was fairly prosperous before the war had worn Vienna at its seams. And even though she was fortunate to enjoy suites in a grand Baroque building overlooking a courtyard, this opulence was different: wooden beams and a Tudoresque fireplace that overtook half of the room. If Vienna's formal palette was too much whipped cream, then Northumberland finery was of a more rustic flavor.

This morning collecting eggs had been so different from writing papers and studying and reading Dr. Elisa Bauer's most recent research. Shoulders back, Brigitta spoke slowly. "You must have many questions for me."

Silence.

She looked in Alec's direction. His amber-gold eyes were steady and calming, and he gave her a small encouraging smile.

"You are here because you can help with our dreams, is that correct?" Evan Laughton's eyes were kind. No wonder he and Alec were good friends.

It was something mentioned before, of course, but she had an inkling the men were too preoccupied imagining their lives here, her place here, and the new surroundings to truly respond to it.

Brigitta nodded. "My research has been on dreams and their meanings. Their interpretation. My studies in psychoanalysis as well as my uncle's experience have always made that a subject of fascination to me."

Laughton had broken the ice.

"Just like Freud?" Adamson asked quietly.

"Precisely."

"I never sleep." Clarington's arms were folded across his chest. From the moment he arrived he had tried to put up barrier after barrier. Even now he didn't look directly at her, rather just past her shoulder.

Then Jones chimed in, stretching long legs out in front of him from his end seat on a rolled-arm settee. "If I do, it is only for a few hours before I'm blasted awake with a thought or a scene or . . . I don't think a lady should hear this."

"She is not a lady," Clarington blurted, sitting in a russet wingback chair. "Look at her clothes!"

"She *is* a lady," Alec interjected. "And as I mentioned in my initial letter, she will have her uncle's assistance, isn't that right, Dr. Mayr?"

No more Fräulein, Brigitta noticed. He was establishing a rapport but also a divide. The moniker, she could hope, would earn their respect. My, how softly he did it. She was seeing his lord-of-the-manor traits enter in, even as his collar wore a stain of soup from an earlier faux pas.

"Yes. My uncle, Herr Doktor Henrik Mayr, is merely a phone call or letter or telegram away." Brigitta sipped her tea. "Combat fatigue isn't any different from other illnesses. As far back as Hippocrates, soldiers spoke of battle dreams."

"What if I don't have combat fatigue?" Clarington said.

"I know that you're here because you are unsure about what life holds for you. You were dealt a serious blow." Her eyes met Alec's. "That's the term, isn't it? A blow?" He subtly inclined his chin. "In the previous war, a Dr. Arthur Hurst helped men recent of battle to find healing and a chance at normalcy by allowing them the space they needed while providing a listening ear. As long as they were working toward a communal effort, they could find a bit of who they were before."

Alec interjected. "I know Laughton helped to persuade you to come. I know you were in the mindset that allowed you to take a chance on anything that would keep you from confronting your daily lives. I know because I am the same. But I own this huge house for the time being before my family decides whether to turn it over to the National Trust. As long as we're here, why not work? Why not occupy ourselves with chores around these halls and in the gardens, see if it helps? There's even a chicken coop!"

He paused and waited for slow-coming smiles. "And if you feel that all of the . . . pictures or images or memories are crowding your mind as they do mine . . . then Dr. Mayr will have, at the very least, a listening ear."

Laughton had procured a deck of cards, perhaps from his pocket or a side table, and he began laying them on the empty seat beside him. Clarington was picking at a random thread on his trousers. Jones was invested in a ceramic vase that might have been of great financial value. Brigitta, now familiar with many sun-faded blocks of walls where great paintings might once have hung and worn circles of tables and mantels where great artifacts might once have sat, wondered *how* great its financial value.

"I know you want to become the men you were before. I understand that. Everything must have seemed so simple . . . *must* seem so simple when viewed through the . . . What is the English word? *Film*? Yes. The film of what happened before." They were tentative around her. She didn't anticipate that would change overnight. But her uncle had once told her that sometimes the greatest asset a person had was the strength to admit fragility. She could turn the tables so the men who met her at their weakest were momentarily given the upper hand.

"I will not be using any of you as an experiment, of course. But I would like to put more of the theory of my research into practice. I am inspired—as was my uncle—by how Dr. Hurst was able to find ways to help men without grilling them or forcing them into a chair to talk to him. I want to do the same." Brigitta blinked.

The men's eyes had shifted from a moment ago and were now settled on her, waiting. Hopeful.

"I won't ever take advantage of your position here or your confidence. But merely by living here, you might be able to help *me*."

That was the magic right there. A little shudder of chivalry begun in a few throats clearing was now refined into a need to rise to help *her*.

A few moments later, Alec proceeded to give directions to the makeshift office he had established for Brigitta, close enough to their individual rooms that they would find it without difficulty but removed enough that they could maintain privacy.

Brigitta smiled throughout his explanation—and hoped she could live up to the role they needed her to fill.

✦———✦

Lieber Onkel,

By the time you read this, it may seem like I am repeating myself, since we have talked on the telephone. It was Alec's brilliant idea to see if I could use the vicar's telephone, and it gives me a ramble of a walk into the village—as long as Elizabeth Bennet strolling to Netherfield—or a chance to sit next to Hannigan in the motorcar. He is largely silent, but he has started to tell me more about his love of the castle and to teach me about some of its history! How wonderful, too, that you are able to use the telephone at the Universität given the haphazard state Vienna is still in. I seem a million miles away from it here. So I will save my private musings for our written correspondence and the observation journal I have started. I have decided I will, without breaking the men's confidence, include some of what I observe here. For one, it all starts with dreams, doesn't it? Sleeping or waking is always the center of our subconscious. If we dream vividly, we try to interpret it. If we awaken with a jolt, we are plagued by it the next day. If we fail to fall asleep, we worry about the hours lost in slumber. But for now, they are settling.

Evan Laughton, Charles Jones, Giles Clarington, and Thomas Adamson. Laughton is most comfortable assessing the value of the leftover antiques in this broad estate, Clarington enjoys experimenting in the kitchen, Jones is our woodsman and jack-of-all-trades who has impressed Hannigan with his ability to fix the chicken coop and the fences, and Adamson couldn't wait to get a rake and hoe in hand. He likes to be away from the castle whenever possible and away from the other men. Laughton mentioned in confidence he believed the man was mercilessly bullied by a particular soldier during basic training. Odd to think that the trauma of war so often attributed to the enemy could be caused by an enemy on your own side.

Over the past several days, I have found their resistance thawing. Alnwick's guests were perhaps wary at first, but are now interested. Settling into the peace found here, I suppose. For there is peace aplenty. Jones recalls shooting with a precision that could take the wind gauge off the roof of the barn, and yet his hand shakes in the night when he wakes at what he feels is the first rippled shot.

Clarington can recall the nickname of a lorry engine but not the name of his cousin or childhood pet fish or mother's maiden name (selective memory, I think?).

Alexander Alnwick speaks at length about a family curse, which, horrid as it might seem, is (at best) the reason the townspeople and villagers keep clear. His talk of a curse has offered our small group something to keep their minds busy. Alnwick also has created a sort of schedule for the men to help them gain skills that evaded them before the war. During these first days, though, it feels merely as if they are whiling through the days in hopes of finally sleeping through the night.

Dreams are repressed wishes, as we both know from our research.

But perhaps the wishes themselves are dreams.

Things that may have been completely foreign to them before—doing farm chores, making bread, planting a vegetable garden—

On the subject of gardens, the grounds here are like a maze of greenery and shrubs. Just like Schönbrunn Palace in the summertime. There is one garden set apart like a children's story, guarded by two rickety old gates. I can tell the gates used to bear signs, for the clasps are still intact, but I have no clue for whom it was named. Within the garden are beautiful yellow flowers much like a pressed flower I found in the diary of the woman who once lived here. Far from the double doors of the main house, the garden as it stands is little worthy of that name. Adamson, however, believes we can tame it. He took several moments to consider what he wanted to say.

"Perhaps while we're seeing to the garden, you might be able to . . ."

I smiled and interpreted precisely what he meant. He wanted to talk. Away from the corridors of the castle, away from the other men.

So I merely said, "Of course."

That is what I will say to all the men, whether they finish their sentences or not.

Natürlich

CHAPTER 9 ———————————————————

O ver the next several days Alec found Brigitta startlingly suited
to Leedswick, despite her city upbringing and her oxford
shoes. Alec sometimes thought of Klimt, the Viennese painter of her
home city whose paintings were often threaded with gold.

Every morning before the men arrived downstairs, he and Brigitta
gathered eggs before chatting casually in the dining room at breakfast.
One morning as the fog began to rise like a curtain, Brigitta tugged
Alec across the grounds from the barn to the overrun, fenced garden
with a now-familiar enthusiasm. Alec consulted his wristwatch.

"There's new life to the place after a few days." Alec watched the
damp grass make patterns on his shoes.

"Perhaps we are breaking the curse?" Brigitta didn't turn or look
at him. He watched her peer through the gate posts with the same
slightly wrinkled nose as when she settled eggs into the basket with
a few terms of endearment in German for the chickens.

Alec shoved his hands deep in his pockets. Something about
the garden made him sad, as it had when he was a kid. So much so
he avoided it altogether. He somewhat recalled a history of it that
his mother told: perhaps more in illustration than in word. She was
always sketching it. Even the portrait of Beatrice in the library fea-
tured the yellow flowers found within the garden.

Alec didn't know a lot about curses, but he *did* know that Uncle
Daniel had seemed to be possessed by one now and then. Glassy eyes

and a slight shudder trembling through him. And more so just before his uncle passed.

"Are you sad because the garden looks so forlorn?" Brigitta asked. He hadn't noticed her eyes so intent on his profile.

"No." He flicked a few blades of grass from his shoes. "I was thinking about my uncle Daniel. He once told me about the term *basket case.* Now we all use it to talk about someone who is just . . . overcome. Distressed. But Uncle Daniel knew its origin as American slang for a man in the Great War who had lost all his limbs and needed to be carried in a basket." It could have been him. Could have been *any* of them.

Vines sneaked haphazardly up the gate posts and over the sides of the fence. Hannigan and Adamson had their work cut out for them with shears and a hoe and determination.

"I suppose you can be cursed by a physical ailment or horrible limitations. Though I am not sure what is worse . . ." Brigitta's voice trailed off, her fingers tracing up a vine.

"Even physically, your mind might still allow you to be yourself." Something his uncle completely lost. Something Alec worried about losing.

"A bit like a curse, then." Brigitta was prodding in that soft way she had. He was learning how she spoke and how intentionally. Often to drive the conversation or turn it in a compassionate and gentle way intended to help him find the safety he needed to speak what was truly on his mind.

"I never really thought the place was *actually* cursed." Alec reconfigured the conversation. He had already shown so much. "Other than by a bit of sadness and a series of unfortunate circumstances."

"Such as?" Brigitta still had the egg basket hanging on the crook of her arm. Just under the cheesecloth she used to cover them, he noted an irregular egg. Noticing his interest, she handed it to him. Perhaps anticipating he needed something to focus on and turn in his palm. It wasn't smooth and light brown like the others.

"Most of the curse stems from my great-grandfather, Charles. He was blamed for the death of his batman during his time in service over eight decades ago." *Long before Uncle Daniel.*

"Do you believe it?" Brigitta turned and her wide eyes met his.

"No. You've seen his portrait. Hanging in the library with his wife, Beatrice. The occupants of this estate have seen so much death, and most of it not even within these walls. No. In the way that the brutality of war carries over from the battlefield." He thought of the *Battle of Culloden* portrait. It was removed from the library, but not far from mind.

Basket case.

He handed Brigitta the spotted egg for safe return in the nest of her basket. "So hopefully by the end of your time here, you'll go back to Vienna knowing what your thesis will be and I will at least have *tried* to redeem this place."

"To break the curse?"

Before he could respond, he heard a slight rumble. Brigitta was hungry. He stifled a smile, certain she would be mortified if she knew he'd heard it.

But she laughed outright without ladylike pretense. "I have certainly . . . How would you put it?"

"Worked up an appetite?" Alec hadn't slept well the night before. Had begun to dread nighttime for the tossing and turning and harried snatches of shut-eye. Had cursed the morning light through the window and the flashbacks that truncated what little rest he'd gotten.

But if all mornings started like this, he might not dread night so much after all.

———————

The little food provided by ration cards and the bread shortage was supplemented by the gardens: radishes, carrots, and cabbages. Herbs and plants were boiled for tea, mint added flavor to tea and some of the cold salads, and even the fish from the nearby creek provided sustenance. Alec had never paid attention to what was served before. Not with his parents' skeletal staff and certainly not with the bully beef tins parachuted to the Front.

Indeed, throughout the war, the farther you moved from the city, the better chance you had at procuring provisions. He could believe it wandering around the estate grounds. And here now a cornucopia of breakfast dishes with an eruption of verdant green and color.

Yes, the dining room was most often where he saw his guests—mealtimes were a sure way to spark conversation as well as ensure the whole of their small crew occupied the same space. Even though the previous sleepless night stung his eyes and a yawn tightened his smile, every morning he woke at Leedswick, he felt more promise wherever he was in the castle that this could be his full-time home.

He felt the promise more so on a morning when Brigitta showed him a particularly enticing passage of Beatrice's journal. He never tired of these little snippets into his family history, especially from such a beguiling source. Nor when Brigitta apprised him proudly, chin tipped slightly upward.

It was one of the things he admired about her: she didn't furrow her brow or expect that they recall a previous conversation. He knew he could confide in her. *A basket case.* She was a locked vault.

He certainly felt more focused. After all, there were so many things that required his attention. There was William Brown in London handling the estate from the city. Brown had heard from Alec's cousin Harold a few times, but only for an emergency bank draft now and then. Brown was also the one who kept Alec informed about his parents. There was no word of late, but that was to be expected (at least according to Brown). The world was in chaos, and with it wires were crisscrossed into an elaborate maze.

Magdalen and Hannigan and the four guests were doing wonders occupying their days with cleanup and repairs around the castle. And Adamson smiled for the first time, truly, when Alec mentioned how the lawn directly in front of the manor was looking far better than when he had arrived.

"My grandfather was a landscaper," Adamson said proudly. "But we never had access to grounds like this."

Brigitta's role might have been a bit startling. Still, he admired how she persisted in engaging them. But she always persisted: in learning Northumberland dishes in the kitchen with Magdalen, even in befriending the cat.

The men clearly noticed her as a young, attractive woman, but every conversation he overheard between one of the men and her was respectful. Her curiosity and intelligence were a welcome change from several years of long periods deprived of female company.

How long would it take before they saw her as a prospective anti-dote to too many lonely nights far from the company of women—? *No.* He wouldn't be so cynical. Nor so base. Perhaps he had every right to be. But these were *good* men. Still, there were large spans of the day when he didn't see them . . . or her.

Certainly, Laughton's easy personality could wade into flirta-tion. And Alec had happened upon Adamson and Brigitta talking quietly while Adamson aided her in the application of a hoe and rake. From Brigitta's enthusiasm throughout the morning, reciting the names of different weeds and plants, she was learning a fair bit about gardening.

He wasn't jealous. He couldn't be. Not when he had invited her and she so clearly treated everyone equally here, her personality an alchemy of a bright disposition that contrasted with the esoteric research she cited from the dusty books in Leedswick's library.

Alec was foolish enough to think they all might have gone on as they were—even after four short days—learning to be comfortable in the company of each other. But it was more than that. The term *comfortable* did a poor job of defining the way his heart rose a little when he first saw Brigitta or explaining how he wanted to gather up what he saw throughout the day so he could tell her about it and see her reaction. Indeed, he had never known from his previous experiences with the opposite sex that even conversation about a cat could resemble flirtation.

Was it flirtation? Or friendship? Perhaps, for them, flirtation was amplified friendship.

Interrupting Alec's musing, Hannigan peered into the library and announced a visitor, prompting Alec to follow him to the foyer.

It wouldn't be someone from the village. It was unlikely to be a tenant.

Alec wasn't fit to meet any guest with a semblance of decorum. He was attired in worn canvas trousers and a homespun shirt. Still, he raked his overlong hair from his eyes and straightened his shoulders as he stepped to the door Hannigan opened.

"Well, look at *you!*" The boisterous voice echoed beyond the double doors.

And Alec had little choice but to welcome his cousin Harold. Hal.

Who didn't merely enter but rather pushed through.

Hal was halfway through the corridor, swiping a look up and around the broad walls and beams, not so different from the boy who had chased Alec around with a threat of a dunk in the nearby pond in previous summers. "Having a party then, Alec?"

Clearly his cousin had heard voices from the dining room. His eyes swept over Alec's unkempt hair to his scuffed shoes. Alec shoved his slightly shaking hands deep in his pockets.

His brain pounded until two words tightened in his throat:
Basket case.

This time, Hal wouldn't win.

CHAPTER 10 ——————————————

Onkel,

I am absolutely fascinated not merely by Herr Alnwick but also by the castle itself. It seems to tell a story of its own. Some of the furniture is in the aged Italian Renaissance–style that still exists alongside the Victorian period pieces that remind me of Alec's ancestor Beatrice's time. I have spent so much time in the pages of her journal lately. I have met Leedswick twice: once through my own experiences and then through her observations. Unfortunately, a lot of the wings and rooms have been closed off due to the cost of lighting, heating, and cleaning them.

My observations:

Adamson acts as if he hasn't been in the company of women in a long time. Or, at least, as if he never found a lasting friendship during the war. Said the war was almost a reprieve from basic training before they shipped out. Knows everything about mushrooms and fungi. When something in the garden strikes his fancy, he talks for hours on end, even as if I am not there. He knows which plants are edible and which are dangerous. As deadly as many of the plants that grow here are, they can also be used for medicine. Odd how a plant can be both useful and lethal. Fortunately, I have found several books on plants in the library.

The information therein has helped me reconcile how something can be used for good or ill.

Jones, our jack-of-all-trades, found a beaten, worn sign in the potting shed. He is endlessly curious and is always searching for something. He told me his dreams look a lot like this—searching for something.

If the castle truly is cursed by war (as Alec's family believes), then maybe I'll find the answer just by being here.

Alnwick said he has slowly been sleeping through the night.

All the men are more animated during the day and more introspective at night.

As for Tante Pia's postscript, tell her not to read too much into my time spent gathering eggs with the lord of the manor. After all, the men need to eat.

+———+

For good or ill. The dichotomy was never so pronounced as when explored through the arrival of Alec's cousin Harold.

Of course, with his appearance, Brigitta noticed Alec freeze while the others seated swerved around in surprise. Perhaps hastily recalling his manners, Alec forced a smile.

She assumed he was nervous because this was a new variable. Not because Hal had a way of dominating every situation, as Alec had once mentioned.

"And even at the head seat!" Hal exclaimed.

"Everyone, this is my cousin, Harold Alnwick-Wilcox," Alec said. "He is visiting quite unexpectedly from London." Alec's response to Hal was focusing on careful enunciation.

Harold nodded around the room. There was a familial resemblance between the cousins, but only when one looked closely.

"One of these things isn't quite like the others," Hal said appreciatively, his eyes assessing her.

She could see Alec out of the corner of her eye, watching his cousin closely. As for Brigitta, she refused to bow to his clearly intended hold on her. Alec sought her out as an ally. *Yes.* His lip curved slightly in an attempt to lure her into admitting that this was a laughable ruse of which they were but victims.

"Hal, this is Fräulein Brigitta Mayr." Alec's voice was granite. "Her uncle is renowned for his experimental studies in psychoanalysis."

Hal's eyes stayed on Brigitta even as he addressed Alec. "What in hades have you done with Leedswick?"

"I've done nothing with it. Other than make it a little bit more habitable! These are a few of my friends. Clarington, Jones, Adamson, and Laughton." Alec's voice was a tightwire as he motioned to the gentlemen.

After a long, lingering moment Hal's eyes snapped away from her to the half dozen men around the table.

"We are addressing each other mostly by our surnames but not our ranks as we became accustomed to. During service." Alec's voice assumed a clinical air. "Old habit. Laughton there served in my unit."

The men nodded at Hal in turn, as if hearing an inaudible command.

Hal surveyed the table and settled on something at his cousin's careful setting. "My cousin used to prefer the odd teacup. The chipped one. Now here he is with a perfect specimen from a set that, gentlemen, has seen more than its share of wear."

Brigitta studied him a moment. Why would Alec's cousin focus on that? What power did Hal yield? But more importantly, *why*? From her vantage he was little but an impostor.

Adamson didn't look up from his plate or mumble a "pleased to meet you" as the other men had done. Odd, because despite his shy ways, he was always unfailingly polite. A bashful young man still raised with the manners of a country gentleman. Brigitta wanted to brush the slight smudge of dirt from his temple and smooth out the weariness that lined his eyes and mouth: a man tattooed by age long before he had lived out its years.

The more Hal talked, the tighter Adamson gripped his fork. Was it that a stranger interrupted a world he was slowly settling into?

Certainly she could understand if the men were caught unawares by Hal's presence, having trusted Alec that their time here was of a private nature and only recently finding her here. But what words didn't reach Adamson's lips manifested in his body language. He swallowed hard. The fork held in midbite when Hal announced himself was now clutched in a white-knuckled hand.

Brigitta didn't want to draw attention to Adamson, so she lowered her lashes before casting a quick look at Alec, who commanded the room, his chin slightly raised.

"I suppose I came at the right time." Hal settled at the table, and Magdalen brought another place setting from the kitchen along with a large jug of ale.

He's a buffoon. Brigitta didn't enjoy sizing people up so quickly, but if the shoe fit . . .

"Unlike you lot, I didn't get much past basic training. Shell landed right by my ear before much action happened and I was home in a flash. Missed all the guts and glory." Hal tugged at the collar sloppily opened above his creased jacket. "Pity. I could have been right at home here."

Alec slowly sat again. Harold's effect rippled through some of the men: a spoon accidentally hit the side of a bowl with a *clang*, and Jones developed a sudden cough. She studied the friction between them. She had supposed it would serve as the intersection of their similar experiences, a response to someone who spoke a different language merely by not serving time at the Front. From what Alec had told her, they had all been conscripted and expected to fight for king and country.

Hal's outlier status became more amplified the more he attempted to gain common ground. He had trained, from the threads she'd sewn together from his mumbles and asides, but he had not served, at least not according to Laughton, who defined it differently.

"I think there are two levels to service: the willingness and training to fight shows great determination, like Alec's cousin, but the service that unites those of us here implies that we saw action."

Alec, of course, attempted to ameliorate the situation. When he reached for his water goblet, his fingers trembled slightly. For all that he teased about not being lord of the manor, he certainly fit into the role, whether consciously or not.

Brigitta tore apart the last heel of her roll but did little more than separate the crumbs with her fingers. When she looked up, her gaze met Adamson's. Just a flash of something glinted in his eyes: Anger? Confusion?

Hal evidently noticed how intently she was watching him. "Are you avoiding me, *Fräulein*?"

"*Entschuldigung?*" She begged his pardon.

"Nosy little kr—"

"Stop that!" Alec stepped on what was doubtless the beginning of his cousin's derogatory utterance.

The word was left behind, but Hal's derisive stare still unnerved her. She focused back on the meal at hand, a smile forming at how quickly Alec had defended her.

Once dinner had finished, Brigitta helped Magdalen dry dishes in the kitchen. "Have you met Harold before, Magdalen?"

"Not in many years." She wrung the last drop from the dishcloth, tightening her arms and emphasizing the veins through her wiry fingers. "But you would do well to always choose Alec's side. Harold will try to make his voice the loudest. But it's often not the loudest voice that has anything to say, is it?"

A short time later, Magdalen was rolling out dough in the

kitchen while Brigitta was making a subpar attempt at reproducing *Vanillekipferl* on a tray when Hannigan arrived in the doorway to deliver the post.

Brigitta snatched the small pile in hopes of receiving a letter from home. She fanned through the papers until she stumbled upon a telegraph clearly addressed for one Harold Alnwick-Wilcox at his alternate residence from William Brown, Solicitor.

Brigitta stole a peripheral look at Magdalen, hunched over her dough, arm muscles flexing and contracting with each careful, intentional movement. She returned her attention to the telegram. Hal was overdrafted at Barclays bank. In the amount of ten thousand pounds.

✦———✦

"Not right now." Alec shrugged Hal off. His cousin had followed him from the dining room to the library, and Alec needed a few moments without him . . . without *anyone*. Especially the someone who had all but insulted Brigitta at the dining table.

"Cousin," Hal persisted, his footfall close behind Alec's own, "still think this old place is cursed? We could go find a ghost or two."

"Later!" Alec folded his fingers into his palm and tightened his fist. Hal was calm, but after his recent rudeness toward Brigitta, Alec wanted to be alone and find some occupation to keep him from challenging his cousin. "Go . . . go find a guest room. Hannigan will help you. Or go explore the grounds."

"You sure know how to make a chap feel welcome. Fine! You needn't stab me with that look. I'll get out of your way." Hal gave a mock salute and turned.

Alec ensured Hal's presence was far gone before he sat at Charles's desk. Other than the pen and blotter and telephone, Alec hadn't really explored the desk since its relocation to the library from a forgotten wing. He was in no mood to do anything other than escape, but he finally had a few moments to peek inside.

He opened the top drawer on the right side. There was little that held value and yet a mountain of sentiment. A few lists and ledgers. Soon he discovered a few pocket-size pictures of his mother's drawings and a framed and grainy picture of Leedswick captured in sepia: its turrets and stones etched in his mind's eye much as they were captured here. He was happy he'd had the foresight not to topple everything into the rubbish bin before the relocation of the desk: a true antique and a piece of rare value.

He opened the center drawer. Its dust puffed up like an exhaled breath and tickled Alec's nose. Inside were several coins engraved with the date 1871: currency from the time of Beatrice and Charles. Triangular paper clips, a wax seal Alec imagined imprinted on his correspondence, a few letters he tucked in his pocket for later review, and even a smart monogrammed fountain pen bearing the initials RHA: Reginald Heathcliff Alnwick. Charles's father. Alec's great-great-grandfather.

Alec's pursuit was oddly calming. No one else was part of this exploration—just himself and this meeting of the past. No Hal. No Brigitta. Nothing but wood and worn varnish. But just as Alec stretched his hand to the back of the drawer, it stopped. A barrier. He reached again until his knuckles scraped against a backboard.

Still . . . he continued. Back, back, until his fingers slipped and the bottom of the drawer gave way. Alec cursed a moment, thinking he had damaged an antique. But he hadn't. The drawer had just given way to a false bottom.

A smile tugged his cheek when his fingerpads made out a rectangular shape. Was this what his father could never find?

Alec bit his lip in concentration and squeezed his eyes shut as he pursued its recovery.

And then it was there.

In his hand.

Alec raked his fingers through his hair and surveyed a small, creased leather book. His accelerating heart rate identified it before his curious brain caught up. More so when he gently riffled the pages and saw a straight, slanted hand in dark ink splayed across every page with dates and occasions.

Charles's journal.

Opening the brown leather front cover released the scent of dust and ink. The journal, long hidden from the elements or wear of a half century, was remarkably well preserved. Down to the dried flower pressed in the front page: from the boutonniere on Charles's wedding day, or so a small note said.

Alec closed it for later perusal and gingerly placed it on the desk blotter. He would treat it as gold.

This was the key to his past. But perhaps also his future? He was too excited to read it now.

The contents of the leather-bound journal had, for all intents and purposes, skipped a generation since his father, though he had searched, had never found it. And how timely for it to reappear as Leedswick's fate hovered between their avoidance of its history and a promise from the National Trust. Perhaps Tobias hadn't found it not only because of the desk's secret compartment but because Alec was meant to.

Now, Alec had the time, the will, and the determination.

And with Charles's journal: a start.

CHAPTER 11 ——————————————————————

This nightmare was different from the others Alec had experienced during his return. It was but four nights after Hal had
returned, and yet when Alec startled awake, the four-poster bed that
had seemed a safe retreat was now a prison.

Odd, since his sleep had been much better since his arrival at the
castle. The intense reaction he experienced from a vivid dream was
not one he fancied. No. Not when he had jolted awake with a sound
so shrieking and real it was as if it directly pierced his eardrums. This
particular evening, he had fallen asleep much faster than of late. His
first excited perusal of Charles's journal had kept his eyes pried open.
He was torn between racing through it for answers that had evaded
his family for decades and savoring it.

Now he looked around while catching his breath. His bedroom,
the same he had slept in as a child, was dead quiet save for the wind
and an overgrown branch tapping like a long finger on the window.
Beside him, Charles's journal he had abandoned when sleep overtook
him sat with a small envelope as a place marker. He reread the lines
he had encountered earlier.

> Before the war sleep was a friend. Rarely elusive; reliable and
> true. But in the time since I served, it is fickle and cruel as a lover
> scorned, though the face that keeps me abed isn't that of a lady but
> of Francis, my soldier-servant who stood by me through the war.

And the face that kept Alec abed was a phantom. The lone figure of a piper.

He slowly slid into his leather mule slippers and glanced around the room, steadying himself by clutching the bedpost. Odd, the noises that had bumped in the night when he was an imaginative little boy were not what chilled him now. Nor what roused him. Instead, he heard bagpipes so loud and close that he was startled they weren't in the room with him.

Alec smoothed his hands over his trousers again and again until his heart found a resting rate. His breathing slowed, and he focused on how different this experience was from his now-customary dreams of the battlefield, the reliving of scenes from the war. Brigitta had often paraphrased a quote from Freud (sometimes even to Sigmund the cat, pliant in her arms): *"The interpretation of dreams is the royal road to knowledge . . ."*

The road to knowledge would start with Alec's recognition of *how* this nightmare was different from others since his return from war.

Soon the day came back to Alec when Uncle Daniel, between sips from a monogrammed flask once belonging to Charles Alnwick, had first told Alec and his parents of the lone piper rumored to have paced the beach at the Somme. Many thought the piper was insane, but his insanity recalled, at least to Daniel, the age-old belief that bagpipes were not just a sign of mental incapacity but also a signal that reinforcements were coming in the war—the way the Scottish scared the encircling British centuries before.

"As soon as they heard the shriek of the pipes," Daniel explained, his glassy eyes momentarily focused, *"the English shuddered with terror."*

Alec could almost hear the mournful wail of pipes rumbling from the walls. He figured his uncle had used the story as a way of explaining his own mental incapacity. Surely it was Hal's recent appearance that brought this specific nightmare and the recollection of Uncle Daniel's story.

Aimie K. Runyan, J'nell Ciesielski, and Rachel McMillan

Over the past four days his cousin had kept mostly to himself and asked few questions about the state of the manor and the whereabouts of Alec's parents. Still, Alec needed to learn why his cousin was at Leedswick and what he had been doing at the Mayfair house. Or more precisely, what money on the family accounts was slipping through his cousin's fingers?

A few late breakfasts with Hal should be easy. Alec was usually so invigorated from early mornings spent working with Brigitta that he was in a moderately pleasant mood. Pleasant enough that he wouldn't shove his cousin into the wall in front of their guests should he discover the man's motive for being here was nefarious.

Brigitta had offhandedly mentioned she would do what she could for Hal.

Brigitta.

Too many scenes played across his now-level head: Brigitta with that darned cat. Brigitta leaning over his great-grandmother's diary with wide eyes befitting a porcelain doll.

He reached for his robe and stepped quietly into the corridor, using a torch to navigate past the broad stone walls, feeling calmer as the ghosts of sheets over unused furniture and a warm, flickering light in the level below came into view.

Alec followed the ribbon of light to the library, where he found Laughton alone, aligning a game of solitaire, the soft strands of music playing on the Victrola. Brahms. One of the pieces Alec recalled discussing from his early correspondence with the Mayrs.

Laughton's cards fanned out like an accordion across the worn carpet. Evan's shaking hands placed them in descending sequence with a melancholy proficiency Alec recalled from their time hunched in a trench.

"Couldn't sleep?" Alec tugged the belt of his dressing gown and carefully sidestepped the cards on the floor. He continued when

318

Evan didn't respond. "Neither could I. Anything in particular?" Alec hoped Evan would tug at this thread of conversation.

When he still didn't, Alec expounded. "My uncle used to dream about a lone piper on the beach. He told me about it when I was young."

"The one who went barmy?" Laughton started, then coughed. "Daft?"

Alec didn't qualify his comment. Merely continued. "Tonight I saw a long stretch of sand and horizon and blue ocean and the piper trolled up and down. Piping. He played but I never saw his face. And just as the artillery and cannons began, I woke up."

Brahms scratched on the phonograph in the silence. Then Evan said, "Doesn't sound too scary to me. We saw far worse together."

Alec nodded. "That's just it. It frightened me because it was so eerily calm. And it reminded me so much of my uncle." Why was the beach far scarier than the shrill whine of shells or the prospect of bombs bursting?

"You wrote Dr. Mayr about this piece." Laughton didn't look up from his cards. "But never mind that. Tell me about the piper."

"Uncle Daniel used to say that the piper is one of the castle's curses. I believed him." Alec exhaled.

"I somehow hear this song." Evan waved at the phonograph of the same walnut veneer as the matching cabinets. The Brahms song dipped against the shrieking wind outside. "And I recalled seeing this record earlier."

"Did it help?" Alec approached the cabinet and saw to a dram of whiskey for both Evan and himself. *"Slainté."* He passed the drink and affixed the crystal topper to the decanter. The liquid burned down Alec's throat to slowly settle in his chest and spread through his arms and fingers.

"Not as such. But having someone else helps." Evan was expecting Alec to share.

Alec could be vulnerable to a point. He'd keep more about his uncle tucked away for now.

"I see black on black." Evan swirled the amber liquid until it sloshed the sides of his beveled glass. "The Brahms is a little more soothing than nothingness. You talked of this curse a lot when we were over there. I remember. At first a few bits and pieces." He studied his glass. "Then you decided to write letters instead."

"Pardon?"

"I was right there, Alnwick. Right there all along and you gave me bits and pieces, but then you would retreat into pen and paper and reread about Arthur Hurst." Evan exhaled. "I needed you to talk to me. I was *hoping* you would talk to me."

Alec wasn't sure what to say. "You know."

"We were in such close quarters. I snatched at that magazine with the Hurst article. You just didn't notice. And I thought I needed this as much as you. A few weeks to screw my head on straight. And if you had *truly* opened up to any of us . . ."

"I'm sorry, Evan."

"I'm more sorry for *you*. You have everything here, yes. And I respect and clearly benefit from how you've opened up this space for us." He flicked at a card. "But we saw the same things, Alec. We lived in the same world. Maybe I can get to know you here in a way I couldn't there. But I hear this song"—he inclined his head toward the phonograph—"because I read about it in one of your magazines about music and psychoanalysis."

The needle turned and scratched to an end, then a slow rotation of the cylinder spun to a halt. Slowly, Laughton dismantled his game of solitaire, and Alec realized this was their first conversation without shots ricocheting off objects or mud squelching under boots. The only sounds in the silence were the rain's rhythm against the windowpane and the slap of cards being rearranged.

"Good night, Alec."

"I'm sorry, Evan. I truly am."

"How can you be sorry for something you didn't know you had done wrong?"

Still, once Laughton left, the unanswered question sat with Alec. He crossed to the phonograph and returned the record to its sleeve.

"What's this then?"

Alec glanced over his shoulder to the doorway. "Hal."

"Saving the good stuff, eh?" Hal beelined for the decanter. "Want a top-up, cousin? A nightcap?" He ripped the glass from Alec's hand before he could decline.

"Tell me what the problem is, Alec." Hal downed his drink. Poured another. "Up in the middle of the night? Bad dreams? Is that why you have this little charade here? To make yourself feel better?"

"I wanted to find something useful for Leedswick." Alec sloshed the amber liquid around in his glass. Perhaps his tongue was loosened by the drink. He was more inclined to think it was from Laughton's candid assessment. "My friends are here to restore parts of the estate. Dr. Mayr is doing some work on her thesis and research, and it helps to have men who struggle with sleep and dreams."

He met Hal's gaze. Something flickered in his eyes: a look Alec recognized from when they were kids. Then again when they were adults and Hal was challenging him. *Why do you follow the lines, Alec? Why don't you try to wring out every opportunity from our connections?*

Hal assumed a look of nonchalance. He didn't even look tired. Didn't look as if he registered it was three o'clock in the morning.

"Cousin," Hal started smoothly, "doesn't this take a trip down a road of memory? Let's see—"

"Do you need money, Hal?" Alec cut him off. His brain had already trod well down the road of memory. It was little help to be accompanied by his cousin. "Is that why you're here?"

"Doesn't everyone?" Hal sloshed a liberal pour of scotch into his just-drained glass.

Alec curled the fingers of his right hand into his palm, now wide-awake, the nightmare long washed away by his interactions with Evan and Hal.

"Then there's the matter of that assistant of yours. She could psychoanalyze me."

Alec wanted to do something entirely different to him. A common theme every time his cousin referred to Brigitta in a tone that made Alec want to demand a duel of fisticuffs or swords. "I won't hesitate to ask you to leave if you interfere for one moment in what I am doing here."

Hal drained his drink. "The war changed you, Alec. Somewhere along the line you grew a backbone. Tell you what: I need a bit of routine. Why don't we have breakfast tomorrow morning."

"I highly doubt you'll be awake when I eat, Hal."

"We can discuss estate business."

Alec raised an eyebrow. "Estate business?"

"I saw Brown in London. We can talk about how you could sell Leedswick to the National Trust." Hal shifted. "We can discuss it over tea. Just like when we were children. You take the chipped cup and I'll take the most refined china."

"I don't—" But it wasn't worth it.

"Don't tell me you're thinking of keeping this blasted, cursed pile of stones. Just because some of your friends are here. Think of it!"

"It's becoming more than a pile of stones." Mornings retrieving eggs with Brigitta. Evenings lingering over dinner, conversing with the men, slowly thawing their inhibitions. Laughton carving his way into the conversation Alec held with himself on so many occasions regarding what the castle was, what it meant, and how two people who had spent so much time in the same place diverged and followed two completely different paths.

"There is enough here to sell off. That Culloden painting in the library should be worth a pretty penny. Hannigan said you'd moved it."

"You want me to sell Leedswick piece by piece? Our family's history so you can what? Dine at The Savoy? Impress a girl? Don't you *dare* give me that look you used when we were children. I know from Brown that your finances are a mess. I didn't ask to be in the line of succession!"

Hal nodded. "Precisely. No one would give a fig if we bury the blasted place. No one was happy here. Not Uncle Daniel. Not even my mother! There's those stories about Great-Grandfather Charles. Dragging cowardice and our family name into the same sentence." He stabbed Alec with a warning look. "Certainly you don't want the same fate. Right now your friends are here. A pretty girl in the bargain. But when they leave, you will be left with Hannigan and Magdalen and fires you can barely keep burning in wings that are overrun by cobwebs. And if you want to nip out for a pint at the local, not only will it take you a trek as long as a Jules Verne story, you'll be met by the disdain of all Birchwick that has wanted our family off of this land for seventy-five years. Why win one war just to fight another?"

"You didn't fight in the war."

"I fought enough." Hal smiled. "Sometimes the men I see here, they almost look familiar. Just like the same poor sods I saw in training. Like lambs to the slaughter, probably wouldn't stay upright the moment they got over there."

Alec was happy for the glass in his hand. He squeezed his anger into it until his knuckles were white. It was too late for a row with Hal. "I wager you treated them as such. High and mighty."

Hal laughed bitterly. "I've always had a bit of fun. Especially with the chaps who didn't know I was joking. One poor runt was terrified of me: lanky sort, straight off the bus from that family farm. Literally shook in his boots. Told the others he could take anything from the earth and tell if it was food or foe. If a mushroom would poison or nourish a man. Thought it was how he could help on the battlefield." Hal shook his head. "As if that would help in the middle of a war. I told myself that I was prepping him for Jerry. What chance did he have staring down the barrel of a gun in the mud and rain if he didn't stand up for himself?"

Alec bit his response through gritted teeth. "What chance indeed?"

Then a yawn started in his throat and stretched through him. A positive sign. Hopeful for sleep, Alec set his empty glass on the table. "For all that Leedswick is cursed, I *did* have good memories here. Even with you, Harold. With or without my parents, I won't sell off our heritage so quickly."

Hal shifted. "*Our*? So you will share it?"

"I already am, aren't I?" He supposed the drowsiness of the last sip was on account of the late hour.

Hal eyed the decanter. "Perhaps I am here partly because I want to reconnect."

"You truly mean that?"

"For all our differences before and during the war, we always had this old place, didn't we?"

"Yes."

"Sleep well, Alec."

Alec nodded. "'Sleep was a friend.'"

And hopefully it would be again.

CHAPTER 12 ⸻

A Fortnight Later

Dear Herr Doktor Mayr,

In regard to your last letter, your niece is quite astute. She often talks about Dr. Elisa Bauer, but I am beginning to think Brigitta is equally as skilled. When the other guests speak to her, there has been a ruminative smile on her face and a propensity to scribble in her notebook. Sigmund Freud (the doctor, not the cat of whom I have written before) has often taken her full concentration, the periodical open to columns on dreaming and wakefulness, the id and the psyche and all manner of words in German and English that she sometimes speaks under her breath . . .

A lec held the unfinished letter so the ink of his slanted writing could dry. Truthfully, he was surprised his brain had been able to wring out these thoughts at all. It had been faulty of late. Perhaps tired given the expectation of work and the balance of his duties with the vivid dreams that had continued since he first saw the piper and talked to Evan about it. That particular dream had tipped something over.

This very morning Alec had downed two cups of tea before he wrote the first part of the letter. Tea leaves were still rationed, but

Hal had been kind enough to shove his own cup in Alec's direction. When Alec returned to the blotter later that morning to finish it, he was surprised he didn't recall scribbling the letter at all. It had been several days since his last letter, but in those several days, the piper had returned each night. And in those several days, things had been shifting. He read over the words he had previously scribbled. Small talk.

Brigitta would want him to be completely transparent: if not with her, then with the person next best to her. He began the letter again, flexing his hand and his mind. Was he imagining the changes happening around him, or were they as real as the bloody, chaotic scenes he saw whenever he pressed his eyelids closed?

> Dear Herr Doktor Mayr,
>
> I am beginning to believe there is something about the hour of 3:00 a.m. that tricks a man into believing that everything he has fashioned in his mind is a lie. But what can explain away the daylight hours? There is little other explanation for the fact that a painting that I had removed from the library and put in storage has reappeared.
>
> Then there is the music. A Brahms piece from the time of our first correspondence. I most recently heard it when I encountered my friend playing a game of solitaire and listening to it on the phonograph. Now it has followed me throughout the corridor.
>
> You might chalk this up to a prank, but the men have solemnly sworn on our collective experience that they would not be so cruel. Since we are undertaking this venture together and I have developed a respect and admiration for her, I have been too proud to tell your niece. Doubtless your response will tell me that she is the perfect person to confide in . . .

Alec held up the new pages until the ink dried his confession. At first he had believed he was just groggy. But it was when the grogginess bled through the daylight hours beyond a compulsive yawn that he began to worry about a divisive split between sleeping and waking. It continued throughout the day and muddled the way he navigated the odd incidents he relayed in his letter to Brigitta's uncle.

The matter of the Culloden painting, for instance. He had covered and moved it only to find it in the dining room and then in the library again. Hannigan knew nothing of its reappearance, and none of the men so much as blinked when he asked about it, not for the first time, at dinner that evening.

"There's no trouble at all if you found and moved it for whatever purpose," Alec said in a tired but aware moment.

He tried to stay lucid and focused for Brigitta. An invisible thread had been pulling him toward her since she had arrived, and it was tightening the longer they shared space, even as their eyes met as if conducting a conversation without words. But there was something else in her gaze. It held his longer and the spark he felt in his lucid moments was replaced with his awareness of her concern. As if it were a palpable thing he could feel.

As Hal now prowled the halls and corridors doing little but making noise and assessing what was left in the bare wings, Alec was often awake as the sun rose to part the sky and flush the turrets and stones with yellow and pink. Then as he made his way to breakfast, Hal would intercept him and tag along. Often Adamson and any of the other men not assigned to the early morning farm chores would stroll in and join them for the meal.

Alec tried spending more time in the library behind the grand desk with its false bottom. He focused the best he could on any business with Brown the solicitor, who wanted to know if there was anything else from the estate he could anticipate selling. Bills were piling up. Alec saw to what business he could and regularly checked in with Laughton for an account of how things were going with the men. His friend couldn't hide his concern any more than Brigitta could.

"You're sure you're all right?"

He mentioned Charles's journal, always near him, as a distraction, but Laughton looked unconvinced. Lately Brigitta had been joining him with the counterpoint of Beatrice's journal. She didn't take it to her room at night but rather left it in the library near the portrait of the woman who was as fascinating to him as she was to Brigitta, but even more so when the two artifacts were set side by side, opposing sides of the same coin.

Alec sat alone as afternoon spilled into evening. He blinked away the perspiration stinging his eyes. When had the library grown so warm? He certainly didn't recall lighting a fire, yet he blinked to find the mantel dancing with ruddy light. He didn't remember Brigitta leaving. He did remember her talking about the gardens and how when she was out there she felt closest to Beatrice. His ancestor was a foreigner just like Brigitta was.

Suddenly suffocated, Alec pressed his hand to his throat. As dry and scratchy as a night with the whiskey decanter, though he was certain he had only partaken of water today. Not to mention the tea that had fortified him as he wrote to Brigitta's uncle. The books in the library reached out from their shelves in his peripheral vision.

Alec pressed his fingers to his temples. He took a deep breath. He would forgo his bed. Doubtless he had missed the dinner hour, given the darkness outside the windows. And he wasn't surprised that no one had roused him. It had been his own rule that mealtimes were not as perfunctory as some of the other leftovers from their army training days. And why head where he wouldn't sleep anyway? Lately, the longer he stared at the ceiling in his room, the more his mind festered with doubt until he couldn't tell if he was imagining the amplified symptoms he felt or was really experiencing them.

He supposed his imagination had been wrapped up in Brigitta rather than the shadows vanishing under the brush of his torch, his footfall hopefully silent as he attempted to iron out the anxiety of the day with one of his nightly journeys. Sometimes things went bump in the night and startled him in the shadows. Sometimes he discovered something on his aimless wanderings, like a phonograph of a slightly older model than the one Evan had used while playing solitaire.

It was tucked away atop a stack of chairs his torchlight only brushed over when he heard a mouse scurry in the corner. Alongside it was a series of records, including a Brahms recording. He hadn't realized Brahms was such a part of the Leedswick music library. Perhaps that was why it stood out when Brigitta's journal article had mentioned him.

His eyes adjusted to find himself in a broad, grand room he assumed must have hosted balls and soirees at the pinnacle of the castle's elegance. But didn't he *know*? Shouldn't he have remembered? His memory flickered in the corners of his mind like the candles he found in a dusty desk and lit.

The room was frozen in time. He set down his torch, retrieved the Brahms from its case, and fixed the needle. The record landed not at the place of the symphony so familiar of late but with the steady three-quarter time of one of the composer's waltzes.

A few notes and swells of music rumbled out and he felt relaxed. Finding a moment of serenity in a secret bower.

"Hiding in here?"

Alec startled, hand still on the phonograph arm.

Not so secret.

Brigitta smiled, her blonde hair, not in its daytime braids, catching in the low light.

"What are you doing here?"

"I followed you. I went to the kitchen to get milk for the cat and saw your torchlight." She surveyed the room, took a wide spin, then tilted her head a little, listening to the Brahms, studying him.

She frowned. "Alec, are you quite well?"

"I've not been sleeping well. Dreams."

"Nightmares? My room is far enough from yours that I don't hear you. You're in the other corridor, ja? Eastward? But I've certainly heard my fair share of names and shouts."

"So many things not in the places they should be." Himself, for one. Standing here on a floor dusty and scratched but that had once, he was sure, been graced by chandelier light. "Today I have been drifting in and out."

He slid his gaze up to the sighing crystals of chandeliers whose illumination had long sputtered out. Another corner of the castle still broken. Without veneer or shine. He and the men focused on the parts that served a purpose, that needed immediate repair, so that which was grand and beautiful but useless fell by the wayside.

Too many rooms. A maze and a puzzle. Too many for any human to need. Too many for a man fresh from mud and foxholes. Who needed this much space?

Why was this space so *small*? But it wasn't; it was spacious. She was close and far.

Alec pinched the bridge of his nose to slow the carousel of his mind. Then he looked up and noticed Brigitta retrieving several candles from her pockets.

Something in her presence grounded him. Alec refocused. *Focus on her.* The candlelight backlit her figure. It snagged in her hair and shadowed her high cheekbones. The fluttering flames outlined the curves just visible under a day dress of light cotton, its sleeves like an upside-down lily of the valley or Angel's Trumpet. The latter was a flower that grew in Leedswick's gated garden and one whose illustration he recognized from Beatrice's sketches.

"You're watching me rather closely." He felt more than saw her eyes pan over him in the dark light.

She scratched matches and lit the remaining candles until there was a dance of thumbprint shadows against the threadbare tapestries on the paneled walls. Now, together with his handiwork, the room was aglow with warmth.

"Just assuring myself that you are truly all right. You've been quieter lately, but I assumed you were deep in your own thoughts: About the castle. About your ancestors' diaries." She stepped closer. "About the fact that this experiment of ours will be ending soon and everyone will disperse back to their lives and *you* will be the sole guardian of a massive garden, several chickens, and a cat." Her tone was playful; her eyes were not.

Alec tried to steady his pulse at how blue they glistened in the semidarkness. "About the fact that you can talk to me."

They watched each other a minute before she spoke again. "Do you ever feel you are connected to generations? And an entire past?" She settled into the Brahms a few beats. "I think music can do that. That we are just one link in a long chain of people and history."

"It is a little overwhelming."

"Careful there, Alec." She placed a steadying hand on his forearm.

"What?"

"You didn't feel that? You swayed a little." Confusion crossed her features, but she quickly smoothed out her expression. "If you're going to move involuntarily like that, it may as well be for a better purpose." She smiled.

Static crackled until the familiar three-quarter notes of a slow waltz filled their silence. She had changed the record from Brahms to Strauss. "Reminds me of home," she said, noting the change of composer.

She moved with perfect rhythm and a preternatural grace to the wordless time signature of a waltz. Her gaze was warm as the flickering candles.

Then she boldly grasped his left hand, moving it to the scoop of her waist before gently placing her own left hand in his right. Poised and at the precipice of a rhythm she expressed with the sudden narrowing of her eyes rather than the movement of her feet.

On Alec's end there was no fear of movement when he was feeling off-kilter. He just saw *her*. A wonderful, beautiful brain framed by tousled blonde hair and a pretty, interesting face. Alec's chest constricted in a moment so present and full of affection. Hope too. It spread over his shoulders and apparently directed his stride to close the space between them.

The music's meandering rhythm was even and safe somehow. It grounded him. At least momentarily.

"Say, if we were in Vienna right now and this song began to play, how would I ask you to dance?" She smiled coyly.

"I would say that the way I've been feeling today, you might find me a poor dancing partner. But I'd be kind enough to offer to fetch you a glass of punch and ask if you wanted to take a turn in the courtyard."

And here, on the balls of his feet, he anticipated her tempo. Wherever the bars led. The music played on and Alec felt secure, tucked into his bower of wood-paneled walls and scalloped wall sconces and flickering candles, with a woman tentative in his arms. For the moment his feet knew the way. And if they faltered, Brigitta had him.

He spun her slowly as he was taught in First Form classes at school, and he compensated for his lack of proficiency and practice with sheer determination. With one turn he was wholly with her, and then he fell back. The room was light. His head was light. For a few moments it was a whipped frenzy of music and *Brigitta*.

But that didn't last. The room was warm—*too* warm—just as the library had been earlier. He steadied himself a moment by grabbing her arm instinctively. And with the movement and his widened eyes meeting hers, Alec spun in the reckless web of a waltz.

Her lips were so close they trembled a little. His heart was a ramming drum, and try as he might, the moment he surrendered her hand, he moved his free hand in a long line down the hair tumbling over her shoulder. He wanted to be vulnerable with her. Tell her that the room was hazy at the corners and not just from the candlelight. "Your hairpins."

"What about them?"

"They never stay. And yet you try to keep your hair up. It's a losing battle. Why fight a battle you can't win?"

"I keep wanting to look a certain way so I can be taken seriously." She seemed a little puzzled at the switch in conversation. Yet she didn't disengage from him.

"I'm sorry." He let his hand drop to his side. "I shouldn't have taken the liberty."

"I took the liberty of putting your hand at my waist and forcing you into a waltz. And you lost yourself when you gave into the buoyant rhythm of it. You didn't feel you had to run it through your mind first or through a letter or an article. You waltzed with me because we were *here* and it felt *right*."

"I . . ."

"You are different than I am." Brigitta crossed the room and removed the needle from the phonograph. "Because I have the gift of recognizing when a moment that may not seem to mean anything has the potential to mean *everything*. You are trapped between wanting to live up to your family's legacy here and wanting to reconcile the horror you experienced at the Front. But there is *no life* in the middle."

Her voice stilled, and he focused on her face.

He could feel his fingertips pulsing and his heartbeat accelerating, and not just from her company. "You are being so open with me. You always are."

"I sense a change in you. That's why I came to find you." Her eyes pored over his face. "I feel something, Alec, and it stretches beyond our camaraderie and whatever is going on in your mind. I want you to know that I am *here*."

She squeezed his forearm. She wouldn't let him falter. But he read something else in her eyes. A flicker of something he wondered if she could see in his own. Something more than camaraderie. *Attraction.*

"Just because you are now overseer of these . . . these stones and these walls and windows, do not—do *not*—become just another link in the chain of your heritage." The last words she spoke in carefully enunciated German, which accentuated their meaning far more when they vibrated through his nerves to settle and tighten in his chest.

She took in the grand room. "You can take the good and the bad. Same with your memories of your uncle Daniel."

The candles dripped low.

"Y-you think that's what is happening to me?"

"What I think of you, Alec, is that part of you might be terrified of your own heart. Of a kiss, even."

A kiss. She had said it like a shrug, or perhaps a sigh. He hoped a sigh.

Any response Alec wanted to make was scalded in his throat. *I'm not ready. I don't want to kiss you when I'm not feeling like I have complete control over my feelings.*

"May I take the liberty, Alec?" Brigitta whispered as her fingertips smoothed his hair from his forehead. Her stare singed him: over his temples and down, down to his mouth before meeting his gaze.

Alec leaned in a little, took a long breath, and set to claim a liberty right back. He pursued her delicate landscape with his lips. He started at her temple, then down over the slope of her high cheekbone and into the dimple that pressed a corner of her mouth.

And for just a moment the world became clear.

But just a moment. Then there were two of her, then one again. Then shadows pressing in and flickering light. He hated himself for giving in to this moment when he wasn't sure who he was. When more and more he was doubting things. Was she even here with him?

"Alec!"

His name pierced the tunnel narrowing his vision of the ball-room. He got away, falteringly, as fast as he could.

CHAPTER 13 ——————————————————

Dear Onkel,

I am still putting touches on my observation journals for this week. It has been a week since I found Alec in an empty ballroom all but scared to go to sleep. It is no wonder his dreams seem so real to him that he believes he is living through them even when awake. There have been other odd symptoms that indicate far more than a mental malady: his pupils dilate and he flushes quite often, even when a room is cold. I beg him to talk to me, but nothing comes out. Laughton, his closest ally and confidant during the war, said that Alec has always been tight-lipped. The more he has regressed into his symptoms, the more he fails to open up as he did when we first met.

When I first came here he was exhausted but still animated and perhaps excited about the prospect of helping men like himself. But his condition has worsened at the most unfortunate time. He was on the brink of talking to me, really talking to me about some of the symptoms, but then he seemed to slip out of himself. I would interpret this as an episode of panic since other times he is completely lucid.

All clinical, as you would say. Expected given what they've endured. During the day they have become more animated, and a camaraderie exists that only men of a similar experience can share. At night, as I've previously written, things are different. Alec hallucinates. He is nervous. He continues to drinks pots of tea or ring for water as if it is the middle of summer and he is constantly parched.

Of course you know Hal arrived with the subtlety of a hurricane. But I cannot place the sole blame on him. Though I have rarely seen two people from the same family so vastly different. But how can it be that someone who was slowly getting better suddenly exhibits more symptoms than before? Could it be a result of poor, disturbed sleep?

As for Tante Pia's postscript, I do not believe I am showing an inordinate amount of attention to Herr Alnwick beyond strict professionalism. Then again, he has begun taking a greater liking to Sigmund, and I believe the slight quickening of my breath when seeing him swerve his hand over the cat's head is merely another salient observation which, doubtless, will yield some clinical relevance . . .

After Brigitta signed off with a fond greeting, she corrected her letter with the stealth hand of an army officer blacking out anything that might be intercepted by the enemy during the war. No mention of how Alec's hand fit like a glove in the curve of her waist or how his breath on her cheek startled her heart into a rising thump. Lately, his symptoms had accelerated beyond what she'd confided to her uncle. Her uncle would advise her to seek local medical attention. *"The physical and mental are so closely intertwined,"* he would remind her. She wanted to. It was the professional thing to do. But it did little to compensate for the *personal* feelings she had.

The sun blasted over the desk in the temporary office space where the door was kept open as their guests came to talk to her.

For several hours she listened to Clarington's attempt to quell the sound of gunshot blasting even when there was silence around him:

a psychosomatic symptom alleviated when he was occupied in the kitchen. On his way out he playfully nudged her shoulder. Just like she was one of his mates. She would have smiled more widely if her thoughts didn't spring back to Alec. He had been listless at breakfast that morning.

When Laughton sank into the chair across from her a few moments later, it was to admit that he missed home. "But I am puzzled that when I had the opportunity to be home after so long, I immediately wanted to come here."

"You said to escape the expectations of your home and your fiancée."

"Yes. But don't you think it selfish of me? To be burdened by someone who just wants to *help* me? To love me?"

Brigitta shifted. Wasn't that what she was trying to do with Alec? Trying to help him rather than allowing someone else to?

"Write a few letters, perhaps. And start thinking of everything that will happen when you go back."

"Yes." He seemed happier by the end of their conversation than when he entered the room.

"And tell your fiancée. Tell her what you've confided in Alec and in me."

Laughton rose. But before he left, he turned to Brigitta.

"I hope Alnwick will be all right. I thought he was the one of us most likely to have it all sorted. Especially since he read those articles from your uncle."

Brigitta merely nodded.

Not long after Laughton's departure, she successfully convinced Jones that the tremor in his left hand that disappeared when he was busy with a recent woodworking creation was his brain's way of letting him know that he would be okay. It just hadn't caught up with the rest of his body. "You will get there."

In the absence of gathering eggs with Alec, tending to the

garden—Beatrice's garden—with Adamson had become a favorite part of Brigitta's day. He was reticent to sit across from her desk, and she never minded losing herself in the plants and soil. Beatrice's diaries helped her understand the intricacies and joy of gardening, while Adamson helped to deepen her passion. The longer they spent in the garden, the more Adamson felt at ease talking about his experience.

"People say war is a common experience. And it is, to some extent. But for me, Miss Mayr, I was still an outsider. Even if an outsider experiencing what everyone else did."

His words gave her pause. The other men spoke along similar lines: their worry about their sleepless nights and the trauma they saw. Their worry that they wouldn't fit seamlessly back into the world they'd left. Adamson believed he hadn't fit in to begin with.

Brigitta took a break from raking over weeds and used the crook of her hand as a visor from the sun, only to make out a figure in the distance walking toward the iron gate. The closer the figure approached, the more easily recognizable he was.

Adamson pulled a plant to show her. "One bad weed can overtake a whole garden."

"Indeed." Brigitta wiped soil on her trousers as Hal joined them through the gate.

"What have we here?" Hal patronized. "Gardening lessons?"

Adamson stiffened.

Brigitta shrugged off Hal's derision. "And if it is? Thomas is a genius with these plants."

"Half of this garden is poison," Adamson gritted out through his teeth. "Lethal gardening lessons."

Hal didn't flinch at the threat in Adamson's tone. "Miss Mayr, I have just taken a far-from-pleasant tea with my cousin."

His eyes were undercut with purple and his unwashed hair gleamed with a layer of pomade. The scent of liquor lingered on his open collar. "I would like to talk to you about how mentally unfit he is."

Adamson removed the knit cap that half hid his profile and smoothed back his hair before studying the toes of his shoes.

"*Sir . . .* ," Brigitta said, noting Adamson's discomfort.

"Hal," he corrected.

"*Hal*, I would prefer not to speak about Herr Alnwick's perceived limitations unless we are alone."

"It was one of the conditions of being here," Adamson interjected.

"Very well, then perhaps we can find ourselves alone." He shot a look at Adamson, who slowly gathered his tools. The confidence he had shown while helping her navigate the garden was replaced by a deflation through his shoulders and slightly bent spine.

"Thank you for your time, Adamson," she called after his retreating back.

"Now, Miss Mayr." Hal fell into step with Brigitta once Adamson was a fair stride ahead. "As mentioned, do you truly think my cousin is fit to host these men? Look at Adamson there!"

They both watched Adamson swing the rake haphazardly over the grass, cutting into swaths of land in the process.

"I took his response to be from *your* sudden appearance and not anything to do with your cousin," Brigitta said.

"Alec couldn't even see fit to brew a fresh pot of tea!" Hal's labored breath was sour at her ear.

"I don't see how a pot of tea has anything to do with this. Besides, if you were so concerned about the freshness of the leaves, you could have attended to breakfast."

"He didn't bother to ring Hannigan. Even when I asked. His eyes were vacant. You'd think *he* was the one with the late evening out and not myself."

"At least you have the decency to admit your vices." Brigitta smirked.

"Is he truly fit to use Leedswick for this purpose? I loathe to talk family business with you, but his parents are going to come back from Lord knows where and face a son who has not bothered to keep up even the slightest traditions. Have you spoken to Alec recently? Has he made *any* sense to you?"

Brigitta stopped and conjured her composure. Hal didn't *loathe* talking family business at all. He was frenetic as they continued their fast walk. She would choose her next words carefully. "Herr Alnwick is merely doing his best. As we all are."

"Well, I, for one, believe your best would be to ring a *real* doctor."

"*Wie bitte!*" she exclaimed. "I beg your pardon!"

"If you don't, then I will. Truly, my cousin is very ill. You don't want to be responsible if the situation declines any more than it already has."

"I am going to *help* him."

Just as they approached the entrance, he cupped her elbow. Brigitta pulled her arm back.

"I sent a telegram to Brown, his solicitor, to ring for the family's trusted London physician. He should be here by tomorrow evening at the very latest."

"There was no need to do so!" she blurted, hoping her own guilt didn't show through. She felt more defensive than she ought because she realized *she* should have been the one to make the call in the first place.

<hr />

Alec's hand still burned with the feel of her fingers in his as he recalled the way she'd looked with her hair down her back when they'd danced the other night. He had slept poorly . . . *again*. Had avoided Brigitta that morning . . . *again*. He sat to tea with the guests and then barely remembered a conversation with Hal.

The sight and smell and nearness of Brigitta invoked Brahms and a waltz. His breath on her cheek.

The kiss they'd shared.

But one memory melded into another, and he couldn't quite differentiate what was real and what was not. The sleepless nights, the inability to stomach more than a few bites. He grabbed Brigitta's arm to steady himself, to keep him upright. He was seeing things. The striped light casting shadows materialized into overbearing leviathans ready to pounce from the built-in library shelves whose walls seemed to close in.

She was speaking to him and trying to steady him. "I think your cousin Hal is right about a doctor." Her voice came in and out of focus.

"Alec." His name caught in her throat. In the distant part of himself that was still Alec, he heard her whimper and then heard the *clack* of her oxford heels as she slid with his weight. But the voice wasn't enough to keep him from falling and taking her with him.

＋━━━＋

Brigitta's shoulder throbbed with a sudden sting under his weight. She wriggled out from underneath him, frantic when his weight was limp even as she caught her breath and her bearings.

Once she disengaged, he fell back with his eyes closed, his breath light. She quickly ran her fingers over his forehead, under his hairline, and over his neck and shoulders. Had he hurt his head?

She shook him slightly, upsetting a swath of rusty-brown hair from his forehead with her left hand. Her shoulder throbbed something fierce, as did her right wrist.

With her gentle gesture Alec finally stirred. He blinked up at her, his eyes less glazed than they had been before. He slowly seemed to register her, his gaze noticing the way she held her arm.

"Brigitta . . ." His voice was tentative, then grew stronger. "I hurt you."

She shook her head. The pain in his eyes caused her own to sting, and her first tears started to fall. He was clearly mortified, and every last professional instinct she harbored dissolved.

She was taught never to show emotion against a patient's obvious trauma. But he wasn't a patient when confused and unsettled like this; he was just Alec.

You'll have to work on this. It smacks of favoritism. You'll have to call a doctor—this is far beyond your reach. Yet you still want to help him.

Dazed, Alec averted his eyes, smoothed out his trousers, and slowly got to his feet. He extended a slightly shaking hand to her, and she used her left hand to take it.

He very gingerly assisted her to her feet. "You should sit."

He could use a chair himself, she thought, as he led her to one of the two wingback chairs on the opposite side of the large mahogany desk. They sat together, under the watchful eyes of Charles and Beatrice. Alec's eyes were even clearer than they were a moment ago, as if he had stepped back into himself.

Alec ran the back of his hand over his mouth. "I don't know how else to describe it. And then I make up things that seem so real. I see them *so* clearly."

"My uncle was a way you felt safe when you were in the war." She theorized aloud. "His articles and his correspondence. We don't have time for any other Alec than the one who was brave enough to write to me. And we don't have time for your pride. If you are keeping anything from me, I wish you would tell me." Her exhale blew a strand of hair from her forehead. "And I think that is why you left the other night. After we danced. I am *right here*. I am going to find a way to solve this."

She was so determined to hold fast and keep what she could of him before he slipped from her as so many of the patients in her textbook studies and her uncle's articles had. The agony of his realization that he'd hurt her still wrinkled the lines in his brow and pressed into the brackets bordering his long-absent smile.

His eyes focused on the wrist she held in her lap. "Let me see," he said quietly, leaning forward and gingerly touching the tips of the fingers she had curled into her palm.

She would bring him back to himself. But here, now, when his demons were replaced by his attention to her safety. The man she saw clinging to life and the present was the man so winningly vulnerable in their first correspondence.

―――――――

Alec leaned forward, meaning to take her hand, but first he inhaled sharply and shoved his hands through his hair. The moment gave him the courage to reach out and gently transfer her hand from her lap to his hand. She shifted a little closer. The brush of his finger over the whisper of a line separating her palm from her wrist was, he hoped, tender. "All right?"

"Yes, Alec. I am. But *you* are not."

He placed his thumb and index finger on either side of her delicate wrist. Under his thumbpad he felt her pulse, a light throb that quickened the longer his finger remained on the point like a second heartbeat.

"Tomorrow we should ring for a medical doctor."

He shook his head. "You can't get a doctor to help someone who is cursed. Just like my uncle Daniel. Sometimes he was like himself. Sometimes not. Ask Hal. What doctor would understand that this house is cursed?" Paintings moved mysteriously. Music played automatically. He was fine in the morning and then half unable to remember his name by noon.

"Leedswick is timber and stone. It is not blood and all of the intricate neural pathways of which the human mind is comprised." Her voice was weary and resigned. "You are far more yourself now, and yet just moments earlier . . ." She motioned to the place where he had fallen.

He couldn't keep the plea from his voice. "I have no right to continue to host men here if I cannot keep control of myself."

She gave a decisive nod. "I am going to help."

CHAPTER 14 ──────────────────────────

How could a man so determined to maintain his sanity and himself during the onslaught of war slowly lose what he was so determined to protect in the midst of rebuilding his family estate?

She had underlined it in the portion of her observation journal she hadn't shared with her uncle. Probably because it was a question too personal, especially given her growing attraction to Alec. But that didn't matter now. What *did* matter was that Hal was going to fetch a doctor.

Of course, the thought of a medical doctor had crossed Brigitta's mind before. She'd just finally placed Alec's well-being ahead of her pride. Now, long after he had abandoned the library in pursuit of a midday rest, Brigitta ran her knuckles over the crick in her neck.

Her uncle had taught her to treat psychoanalysis like a detective novel: It took a long study of a patient's surroundings and history, their dreams and future plans. The little clues and red herrings that populated the German translations of Poe and Doyle her father read to her as a little girl. Some of the little clues were confidently recorded in her observations as she leafed through her quickly jotted notes:

Alec's movements slower.
Hal often breaking his fast at noon hour, nursing his head

and spreading his fingers over the table in hopes of some
remedy for the previous night's scotch.

Alec sipping from the perfect teacup somedays and other days
allowing Hal to grab it first.

Sometimes they are joined by Adamson or Clarington.

Alec is always awake and thriving in the morning, even after a
poor night's rest.

At least she'd thought so. At least it *had* been so as the men filtered in and out of the dining room.

Mind racing, Brigitta thought of Beatrice: she represented words
tucked in a diary so old yet so easily surging through Brigitta's brain
as her memory augmented the past. She often was surprised to
look up and around and not see the woman sitting across from her.
The pompadour, full lips, and delicate lace that courted her throat.
Brigitta was almost as familiar with Beatrice's features at this point as
her own for the amount of time she'd spent looking at her.

Clarington once told her that in Beatrice's time, subjects were
painted alongside emblems and symbols of their lives as the optimal
way to secure preservation. Brigitta looked closer at the painting,
then closer still. A frame around a gilded memory.

Oil-painted shadows and contours.

A small green diary in her ivory hand, much like Brigitta's own
observation journal.

Then the arbor behind her, draped with yellow flowers, each one
like a small trumpet.

Brigitta sat back a moment. She knew this flower from the garden she and Adamson spent time in, exploring the medicinal and the
poisonous, the bitter and the sweet. The dangerous. But this trumpet
flower . . . definitely dangerous. Her breath caught a little and she
set to verify what she found in the pages of a favorite library book:
Historia Plantarum.

There, carefully indexed. *A deadly plant.*

"Never jump to the first conclusion." Her uncle had taught her as much.

She consulted her observation journal. Alec's entries were taking up more space than the others.

By the time she revisited the chapter in the book, dusk kissed the horizon outside the arched windows.

Brigitta retrieved the torch Alec kept on the desk near the far bookshelf. She left the library, crossed the long corridor, and carefully opened and closed the broad front doors with a delicate hand, hoping Hannigan wouldn't hear and follow her. Soon Brigitta found the familiar path to the garden in a careful stride lit by torchlight. Moonlight painted the lattice of ivy growing up the sides of the estate, crawling and stretching with raspy fingers that tapped on the windowpanes. She continued across the now-manicured lawn until she reached the gated entrance of the garden.

Illuminating the illustrations from the book into focus with her torch, she found the Angel's Trumpet while shining the light over the garden at large. Together she and Adamson had done wonders to the overrun country garden so that even with just her low torch-light, she made out color and composition. Still, the horn-like flower so innocently distinguished by its unique shape stood pronounced against the darkness. *Brugmansia* was its proper name according to the book. With just a low dose it could greatly affect the person consuming it. With a high enough dose or over a prolonged period of time it was lethal.

Brigitta brushed her finger over one of the flowers, its petals like silk. It was unique and oh-so-small. How could something so seemingly insignificant wield such danger? She snapped off the head and placed it between the pages of the dusty book.

She ribboned the torch over the dark path back to the house. Such a different beauty than the gardens and cobbles that met her in

Vienna. Perhaps that was on account of trying to see Leedswick as Alec might—with the potential to be something beyond what it was.

Just as she saw him.

When Brigitta reached the castle and slipped back inside, the foyer was quiet and dark with the exception of a small *pat-pat-pat* on the floor.

Sigmund.

He looped around her ankle and followed her in.

"Just you and me, eh, Sigmund? We need to tell your master something."

Alec deserved to know. As soon as possible.

His bedroom couldn't be too difficult to find. She was familiar with the stretch of the eastern wing where the men had their lodgings, a few safe corridors away from where she stayed, Alec respecting propriety.

She pressed her fingers into the cat's fur. Alec had mentioned his room faced the sun: it blasted through when his curtains were drawn shut and acted as an alarm for him to begin their morning egg-collecting ritual.

She moved to the eastward hallway, steadied herself, and buried her nose in the cat's welcoming fur. She hadn't been to a man's bedroom before. After her light knock, she intensely awaited movement behind the door. The house creaked and sighed much as it did every night.

She heard slight movement before Alec appeared on the other side of the doorframe: bleary eyed, pale, shaking a little. Watching her intently, hardly catching his breath. She set the torch and the cat on the floor, then gripped Alec's elbow and tugged him inside his room and shut the door behind her.

Alec tied his robe with trembling fingers.

"I was worried about you." Brigitta gestured to the sofa in the corner just beyond the still-made four-poster bed. Then she bent over to pick up Sigmund again. "N-no, no . . . *sit*, Alec. Don't get up on my account." She placed Sigmund in his lap.

Alec studied Sigmund a long moment through heavy-lidded eyes. He ran his finger over the cat's ear. Sigmund's answering purr seemed to settle him.

A sheen of perspiration glistened on his forehead, even as he enfolded the cat in his arms. He was clearly in a state. There was no quip about Sigmund. No retort.

"Brigitta." His eyes were glazed beyond mere tiredness, but they focused a little on her and she took it as a promising sign.

She took his shaking hand.

"I don't think you're going mad." She watched the wheels turn in his mind. "I found something in the garden. It's a plant that when meted out slowly can cause debilitating symptoms in humans."

"Wh-what kind of symptoms?"

She held out the crumpled specimen she'd found in the garden. She scratched Sigmund's ears for a moment, then showed Alec the chapter. "Intense thirst."

He was tired. Fading. She set the book down and poured him a glass of water from his side table.

"Confusion. Nervousness. Hallucinations."

"It would most likely have to be in a beverage easily concealed," she said emphatically. "Your cousin has motive, Alec. It wasn't my business, but I accidentally saw an outstanding bill for a phenomenal amount of money he had lost."

"Hal is always losing money. That doesn't change anything."

"Maybe he wanted to find something of value here and needed to keep you from learning about it."

The more Alec talked and sipped water, the more lucid he became. As if this smashing through to his secret gave him the brainpower to continue. He shook his head. "But he wouldn't try to kill me. Would he? He told me he wanted things to change between us."

Brigitta tipped her head back, staring at the ceiling, searching for an idea or solution.

"You hallucinate. You are delusional at times. You tremble. This is far more than what I noticed in you when I first came here."

They both stopped at a knock on the door. Brigitta shot up at attention. Alec set the empty water glass on the side table.

"Sir . . ." It was Hannigan's voice.

Alec was unsteady on the way to the door. Brigitta attempted to blend in with the wallpaper as best she could in case Hannigan made her out. Outside, the long branches tapped against the windowpane like overlong fingers.

Sigmund mewed and retreated. Alec held the door open merely a sliver, hiding Brigitta from Hannigan's view.

"Sir," Hannigan repeated from the door. "There's a commotion downstairs."

"What sort of commotion?"

"Your cousin . . ."

From her vantage, she could see Alec shift uncomfortably.

"He's moved the Culloden painting and Adamson has confronted him about it."

Alec and Brigitta approached the library and slowly entered. *No need for Hannigan. No need to make a scene.*

"What is happening here?" Brigitta asked.

Alec fought through his own haze of fatigue to make out the tired lines on her face. Yes, his lucid thoughts flickered in and out like a waning candle, but *this* was real enough. Her reaction made it so.

Alec *knew* he was watching Adamson confront his cousin, who held the Culloden painting in his arms. Alec *knew* there was a phonograph on the table where it hadn't been earlier. Adamson had a poker fixed in his white-knuckled grip.

"I am not *stealing* it! I am moving it."

"Why?" Alec's head pounded and his throat felt dry.

"Because he is a thief!"

Hal ignored Adamson's interjection. "Because I knew it would *bother* you." He sniffed. "You might not remember, but as a child you told Uncle Daniel that it bothered you. All those men led to slaughter."

Alec couldn't conjure a response.

Hal forged ahead. "Because it is a prank."

"And is part of the *prank* poisoning him?" Brigitta asked.

Hal shook his head, frowning. "I beg your pardon?"

"You as much as told me . . . you as much as gave me a . . . a . . ."
She searched for the word. Her second language was longer in

coming when she was flustered. "An *ultimatum*. That you would find a medical doctor. But wouldn't you be sure that he would discover what I have—that you have been *poisoning* him!"

Hal stepped back. Adamson was still in view, strong and ready to pounce. With the exception of his breath moving in and out, he was silent.

"I haven't *poisoned* anyone," Hal sputtered.

"You were not at all flustered when you encountered Adamson and me in the garden. When I told you that there were dangerous plants there. Most people would be set off by something like that."

"Because it *is* dangerous. It's just the bloody signs have gone missing. I figured you lot knew that much."

Alec blinked. He assumed his cousin had a million and one faces for a gaming table or to spin a yarn. But there was no tic or identifiable sign on his visage. More still, he had a hunch.

"He's telling the truth," Alec told Brigitta.

"I could get what I wanted," Hal explained. "Elena and Tobias never cared about the estate either way, and if Alec were shipped off, then they might be willing to let me have a crack at it. I just needed enough evidence to convince him he was unstable. It was a prank."

"Your unpaid debt," Brigitta said.

"Unpaid debt?" Alec prodded.

"I would never *poison* you."

"No," Brigitta interjected. "But you would have him sent away. You would humiliate him. If not you, then . . . who?" She turned to Adamson, whose palms instinctively rose the moment she looked up.

Alec strangled a breath. This was it. He was in control. He could steady two mercurial tempers and waylay the effects. If only he could keep his eyes peeled and his heartbeat steady. If only he could overcome the obvious effects of the poison running through his veins and tingling his fingertips, swelling his tongue.

"I only meant to set him off," Adamson spat, stabbing a look at Hal. "I never slept when he was around. Never knew when he would wake me up. Torture me with his stupid need to act like he was commander. Because I was weaker! He browbeat everyone. I didn't think I was doling out a strong enough dose, and I never imagined that I was hurting Alec!"

Alec's head buzzed.

Brigitta cursed in her native tongue. "The soldier . . . the one you talked about. The abuse you suffered . . ."

"The only enemy I truly fought was from my own *country!*" Adamson's eyes glared daggers at Hal. "I recognized the Angel's Trumpet the moment I arrived. Low doses are not lethal. They *shouldn't* be."

"But low doses over time?" Brigitta said.

"There was no sign that it was affecting him at all!"

"But how would you . . . ?" Brigitta's voice trailed into German. But Alec knew enough of the language to make out some semblance of her question. "How would you dispense it . . . when we were all so far apart except for . . ." She pressed her right hand to her temple. "Tea!"

Alec followed her train of thought. It was the only time they were together. Hal making a public comment about the chipped cup his cousin used. Oftentimes Alec forgot which cup belonged to whom. Adamson's plan had this advantage.

"I knew I could always find them together in the morning," Adamson explained. "I was *so* angry."

Perspiration stung Alec's eyes. He had to hold out. Be it poison or another malady.

Brigitta stepped from behind Alec so they stood side by side.

"Look what you made me do!" Adamson said, glaring at Hal's face. His breath was sawing in and out, his swallows harsh and panicked.

"No." Alec chose his words carefully. Certainly, time and water had diluted the poison's effects, but he wanted to sound steady and strong. "Don't let him do that. Don't give him the opportunity. I don't want to be Daniel. I don't want the curse to be here. To be what we remember. Hal . . . whatever Adamson did, I . . . I will understand him more than you. Because *you* . . . you will never know what it is like to s-speak . . ." He slowed his words until they were enunciated precisely. "To speak our language."

"Are you calling me a coward, Alec?" Hal spat out.

"I am calling you a *bully*, Hal," Alec rasped. He looked to his cousin and then to Adamson. A sheen of sweat glazed his forehead. He pressed his two forefingers to his temples and tried to breathe through an accelerating heartbeat.

"He didn't even recognize me!" Adamson's voice was cold. The blood drained from his face as he confronted Hal. "How could you not even *recognize* me!" He raised the poker high above his head just as Hal reached into his jacket pocket and produced a gun.

"You don't look like you did then. You're older."

"And you didn't care," Brigitta offered. "Because he was nothing to you but an easy target."

Alec wasn't sure if he could trust what he was seeing. Worse, scanning the room for Brigitta made everything seem closer. He reached for her. Adamson was unrecognizable right now, and Alec didn't trust the man at all, wielding a fire poker as he would a sword. Alec was standing in the middle of two hostile men, wanting to determine Brigitta's proximity and how he could best protect her.

But he was seeing everything through a slow haze. He was off-kilter again after a few clear moments. Was this what it was to be like them: in and out? He wasn't sure if he could save Brigitta in a dangerous situation like the one unfolding before him. How could he, when he couldn't even see the confrontation in front of him clearly? He could see nothing clearly now. Just the shape of the petals from that flower, the edge of the table, and the marble of the mantel all becoming one.

Then a flash of blonde intruded and that poker again. A swing—a stark, swift motion he hoped didn't catch Brigitta in its wake.

Just as the latter shoved him out of the way.

CHAPTER 16 ———————————————————

B rigitta pressed a glass of water into Alec's shaking hand, and the perspiration from the glass was a welcome cool against his palm. His eyes were wild on hers. "Where . . . What . . . ?"

"That's what happens when you sleep for a full day and a half." She smiled. "But the poison should all be out of your system, and the doctor is coming back tomorrow to make sure that physically you are *richtig wie Regen.*" Right as rain.

"You're not hurt?" The scene rushed back to Alec and he sat up with a jolt.

"No. But Adamson was taken to a facility that will hopefully help him in a way you could not. That I could not."

"And Hal?"

Brigitta shifted, smoothed her hands over her skirt. "He's fine. But gone."

Moments later, Alec nodded, registering the past day and what it meant for all of them. His experiment and the fact that someone could have been killed.

"And me?" he added, his voice a rumble.

"That's where I come in." She smiled and gave a low whistle. The cat appeared at her call and jumped into Alec's lap. "And Sigmund Freud, of course."

Alec saw the library through a new repository of stories breathing through Leedswick's history. A composition of recent memories:

Laughton playing card games with him. Jones presenting him with a batch of misshapen cookies attempting to pass as baking. Clarington fixing the hidden drawer in Charles's old desk and adding another secret compartment.

He accepted both as he accepted Brigitta flitting in from retrieving eggs or walking into a room with Sigmund at her side, the cat's long tail snaking up the hem of her skirt. Each little moment connecting the dots that explained why his heart was thrumming and from no symptom other than this new one.

"I wish I could prove I could have saved you," Alec said.

"It's rather fortunate for you that I could save myself." She cast him a look. "Besides, it truly needed to be Adamson who intervened."

"Why do you say that?"

"Because he needed to clear the past with your cousin. Just like you need to make your peace with the piper. And with this curse."

Alec mulled this over. "Uncle Daniel never recovered from the war. He drank. He amplified all the rumors about my family. But . . ." Alec's memories softened. "He also played chess with me. Talked to me. When I was a little boy, I didn't care about . . . I didn't understand *how* I fit until I met Daniel." Alec pushed his hair back, shook his head at the carpet. Yet he saw far more clearly than he had the last several days. "Hal took advantage of the weakest parts of myself."

"Seems he took advantage of the weakest parts of everyone." Her fingers moved over the shelves. "The curse is not cowardice, Alec."

"Your clinical voice, Brigitta." Alec laughed.

She rolled her eyes playfully. "You are *not* destined to follow, because you have a connection that the rest of your family did not when they lived here."

"Oh?" Alec raised an eyebrow.

"There is nothing about your retaining Leedswick that is for your own interests." To demonstrate, she opened Charles's journal. He had long abandoned it when his mind had closed in.

A part of my soul was left behind on that battlefield, and I hadn't enough left to set things straight. There is nothing I can say to squelch the rumors now that they're so well seeded. Short of dear Francis coming back from the great beyond to clear my name, there are those who think ill of me, and there is nothing to be done to sway them. I'd not spare it a second thought were it not for Beatrice. She is the embodiment of all that is good in human nature. She deserves to be loved as the most benevolent marchioness ever to hold the seat. But the people will, I'm afraid, always look at her askance because of her connection to me. I can only pray they will temper their disdain long enough to see how remarkable she is. But if nothing else, I will shelter her in Leedswick and create for her a haven so resplendent that the outside world will hold little appeal for her. It's not enough, but I will do everything in my power to make sure that each day she lives, she knows she is loved.

"He let himself be fettered to that horrible rumor," Alec exclaimed. "Even if he wasn't on trial for his batman Dawson's death, that is what he was convicted for. At least by the community."

"I suppose we cannot compensate for the people we are when under the influence of something far greater than ourselves. Adamson was just fighting another war."

"Hal was just fighting Leedswick and me."

Her shoulders relaxed as she rose. "Don't attempt to wrap Leedswick around your shoulders, Alec. It won't fit. It certainly didn't fit the men who came before you. But it can help the men here now. And the men in the future."

"Future?"

She nodded, then was silent a long moment. "I should have called the doctor. I knew what was happening to you was out of my hands, but *I* wanted to be the one to help. I wanted to prove to myself that I could take care of you. That it was *my* job. It was rather selfish of me, and I apologize."

Alec studied her. "Only selfish dependent on your motive, I would say."

Brigitta ran her finger down the line of his arm. "What if the motive was that I wanted to take care of you for the same reason you wanted to take care of me?"

For the same reason my heartbeat is a ramming drum right now?

Alec focused and returned to the journal. Charles's batman—Francis Dawson—was the harbinger of the curse because he was so beloved by a village willing to allow Leedswick to crumble into disrepair or be appropriated for war. Tenants long flown from the vast grounds. A poison garden overrun with weeds. Uncle Daniel's inability to escape from what he had seen, all because of a perceived madness. And then Alec, who had experienced a madness far removed from the horrors of war.

Brigitta continued to go back to the part of the letter that made a plea for Charles's marchioness. "Another experiment marrying one old world and a new," she whispered.

Connecting dots. Sometimes with a waltz, sometimes with a slight touch or an interpretation of a sigh. There was an entire future in which to connect more.

"When I first came here"—her finger traced circles on his forearm—"I thought that this entire world would be a Brontë novel." Expectation simmered in her voice and shone through her eyes. "It's almost *sinking* in romance, isn't it?"

Alec loved this contradiction in her: brain wrangling logic and analysis, heart thrumming at Beatrice and Charles's love story. *Wait,* he thought, *until you meet my parents.*

Dear Onkel,

It is too early for any observations on the men who will be returning to their homes soon. We experimented, but I think we made headway. If all of this results in Alec having found a way to live with his past, then I like to think it is worth it. Observation: when Alec told me William Brown, his solicitor, anticipated a return of his parents, I immediately believed this was a new starting point. The missive suggests they had a trying time of it. But Alec has seen through his own challenges, just as they will see through theirs.

As for the Brahms, Alec still hears the phonograph, still cites your article from the battlefield. "F—Ab—F," as it would read in musical notation. I did a little reading up on the sequence from the Brahms symphony in your research. And found that without your intention, it produced a message for a man poisoned more by the aftereffects of war than by anything a poison garden could produce.

"F—Ab—F." For Alec the notes represented a message to many listeners of the composer. Free but happy. *Frei aber froh.*

Free of the last bits of the effects of his illness the town doctor saw to.

But free and happy didn't need to mean free from danger or tears or memories. It might even mean shadowed moments in an impoverished castle.

Per Tante Pia's postscript: She did warn me about love. And I confess that it is of a far stronger diagnosis than I might have anticipated. And according to her postscript in your last letter, as to a remedy, I can only speak to how it starts in small doses with symptoms heightened first by a quick smile and glance, then by the recurrence of small moments and by a steady starting ground. Sometimes a symptom reveals itself earlier, long before you look for it: as far back as initiated trust in letters. I wonder if Elisa Bauer has ever studied the consequences of falling in slow motion for someone who was brave enough to be vulnerable.

If she has felt anything similar to the way your heart jumps when he brings you a (nonpoisonous) flower from the garden or hums the music that guides the first steps of a waltz when you're in the library sans gramophone, then she would discover it's a quite different kind of mental malady. And one she might not mind one bit.

CHAPTER 17 ————————————

LEEDSWICK TO REMAIN A CONVALESCENT HOME FOR TRANSITIONING SOLDIERS

The Marquess of Northridge, Alexander Alnwick, has retained the psychological expertise of Viennese doctoral student Brigitta Mayr. Temporarily, the two will continue to supervise a convalescent home.

Unbeknownst to many, for the past several weeks, the marquess has opened Leedswick to several men in an effort to bridge the gap between their war experiences and their return to their daily lives.

The return of Alnwick's parents adds to the magnanimity of the estate long supposed cursed and obsolete due to the nature of the mystery surrounding its former marquess Charles Alnwick. But his great-grandson is adamant that the castle has been redeemed and will continue to be so as long as new men find a few weeks' reprieve and a haven in which to share their experiences.

Brigitta leaned over Alec's shoulder to read the paper Magdalen proudly provided with the tea tray. "You could still clear Charles's name."

The previous evening Brigitta had read his name aloud in a far more intimate context, a few choice paragraphs from her recent correspondence with her uncle and aunt.

"For what purpose? Just to let the community know that he was wounded trying to save his batman? The rumors got it backward, and he was forced to fight to clear his name when he did nothing wrong. Charles found exoneration in memory the way he hadn't in life. It was enough that he forgave himself." Alec shook his head. "How do you clear the name of a man who was really a hero? And merely to pander to village gossip? Then there's the irony. Charles *was* a hero. But he still couldn't save Francis."

Laughton, Clarington, Jones, and Adamson exchanged their time on the grounds for letters that brimmed with anecdotes of progress and personal news. Brigitta showed him a paper she had written on symbols and symptoms of shell shock and recent research on dreams arising from war experience. He was happy the slowly recovering postal system allowed her to continue her studies in Vienna. Later, she recited a few choice lines from her letters in postscripts to her aunt. The longer she continued to read, the more eager Alec was to find her pliant in his arms, his earlier resolution to regard her on a strictly professional level having dissolved completely.

He was no longer her employer, nor the Alec whose words appeared in those letters so long ago. If Leedswick crumbled or the Angel's Trumpet took over the fields and moors beyond, he probably wouldn't notice. He just saw *her*.

On the morning Alec received Brown's telegram that he anticipated Mother and Father to arrive at Leedswick the very next day, Alec was more elated than nervous. He could convince his father that Leedswick belonged and they belonged in it. Then he could ask his mother about the whisper of a memory of a family heirloom. A blood-red garnet set in diamonds: a ring severe but elegant. A perfect wedding ring. An emblem. A *promise*.

At least for the meantime as he sought Brigitta's company and laughter and conversation. As they grew ever closer to each other, often spending hours in the garden that had proven so dangerous to him and so fascinating to her. Much as they prepared to do now, finding their way to the old metal gates.

"They will have so many stories," Brigitta whispered over the wrought iron, peering into the chaos only recently crafted into careful order. Weeded and arranged, the colorful floral horns of the Angel's Trumpet were easily distinguishable from the hemlock and ragwort. Brigitta held tightly to one of the gate posts. The signs were affixed again and she ensured they were straight.

"Do you still hear the piper?" Brigitta looked over the plants.

"The odd shrieking sound would startle away the approaching English and the enemy would be afeared of a great bellowing monster." Alec smiled. "Funny how I often thought of my uncle."

He watched as she nodded to the strange, unfurling flowers, the shoots of grass between, a dichotomy of death and beauty.

Spring yawned over the estate and crocuses had fought through the brown thaw of the land. The warming sun shone on turrets and gables, its spreading rays turning them golden, and Alec knew the castle would never be a burden because now it was home. Some of the wings were still closed off, and others were undergoing renovation. But because of the newspaper article, the villagers provided donations that supplemented the men's work.

"I like to believe that this is their attempt at reconciliation," Brigitta said. "For all that they avoided your family these many years."

And what a time to reconcile, Alec thought. For Leedswick was far from dilapidated as he continued to work on his plan. Hiring a medical doctor and another therapist for when Brigitta returned for her final semester in Vienna.

Any day now. Any day the new men would come for eight-week intervals, trading their ranks for names as needed, trusting their new ability to smooth their fingers over wood and to wrangle weeds from a poison garden, turning up soil and roots and deadly misshapen bulbs.

Any day now. His parents would arrive by train tomorrow and look him and the castle over and cherish both. Just as Alec had come to cherish that little ball of curious fur with its scrunched-up face and knowing eyes. The creature who now easily answered to Sigmund. No longer a stray but rather as much a part of the stones and arched windows as Alec or Brigitta.

Life bloomed even as transient guests returned to their homes to reclaim the small corners of their worn lives. And even as wars were waged and fought and never truly won, Alec wore the past like a medal.

He restored the *Battle of Culloden* painting to the library, if at an angle slightly out of view and well away from Charles's and Beatrice's portraits, which took center stage visually.

On the day before Brigitta's planned departure, he found her best suited as a subject to his careful touch, caress, and the press of his lips.

He remembered the first time their fingers had met over the transfer of a teacup. The first time their eyes had laughed over the collection of eggs.

"We could stroll into town without having a curse hurled on our heads." Brigitta's voice rose with optimism, her breath stolen by his romantic pursuit. "With the vicar acknowledging us. With a stop for tea."

"We could stay here without a curse on our heads too," he said drily, nose falling to her shoulder. He made long work of her profile and steady chin with his eyes and then his lips.

She ran her fingers through his hair to cut off his train of thought. Imagine! Leaving him and their lethal garden and endless corridors. The library and portraits. He was certain Northumberland wasn't drained of Austria's color; it was merely a different palette. He would shade and contour the corners of its new portrait.

"If you need to go back to Vienna, then I need you to go back," he said. "But if you need to be here . . ."

"Mein *Liebling*." Brigitta kissed him hard and full. "I would never do that to our cat."

AUTHORS' NOTES

From Aimie K. Runyan

This project was one conceived in the dark hours of lockdown and proved to be a bright light when I most needed it. I loved losing myself in Beatrice's story and found great comfort in her pluck and spirit. *The Truth Keepers* takes place in the early days of what we now refer to as the Gilded Age. America was well into recovery from the Civil War, and we were seeing the dawn of an age that would see unprecedented riches for the elite in society, as well as an unprecedented disparity of wealth between that elite and the working classes. It would be ten or more years before it was in full swing, but the wheels of this movement were in motion. Lina Astor was already the undisputed Queen of New York.

My hope was to show the social machinations were often built on the backs of those who served them. How the happiness of the working class was often dependent on the whims of their employers. The injustice of a system where women had little recourse for the harms committed against them. I hope I have, in some measure, been successful in those efforts.

From J'nell Ciesielski

The Masks for Facial Disfigurement Department, otherwise known as Tin Noses Shop, was opened in 1917 after British sculptor Francis Derwent Wood saw the devastating effects of facial injuries on the soldiers returning from war. Wood, along with several other sculptors and specialists, began creating copper masks that would look as natural as possible and would offer the lost sense of dignity back to the soldiers. These returning men had become strangers to themselves, unable to look at mirrors and causing their own loved ones to turn away in horror, which could often prove more harmful than the physical wounds. Men who had signed up to protect king and country were suddenly a blight on civilized society, unable to walk down the street without being screamed at. In Sidcup, England, near a hospital specializing in facial injuries, park benches were painted blue as a code to warn townsfolk that any man sitting on one of these blue benches might be distressful to view. Heartbreaking!

If reconstructive surgery was not possible to repair shrapnel wounds, fractured jaws, or ripped off noses, Wood and his team worked endlessly with molds and paints to recreate what had been lost. "My work begins where the work of the surgeon is complete," Wood stated in an article to *The Lancet* in 1917. A task he and his team took with great pride for two years until just after the end of the Great War. Wood's innovative task inspired the American sculptor Anna Coleman Ladd to open the Studio for Portrait Masks in Paris on behalf of the American Red Cross, where thousands more soldiers were offered hope in becoming themselves once again.

Being extremely fragile, these masks did not last longer than a few years and the wearer would have to commission a new mask to be made. For this reason, not many masks survive to this day, though a few appear on display at the Imperial War Museum in London.

From Rachel McMillan

While we took liberties in our fictional estate of Leedswick, the mention of Arthur Hurst and the transition of the estate for men suffering from shell shock are rooted in fact. Hurst was a noted figure in the practical treatment of patients after the First World War and in recognizing that experiences at the Front in battle scarred men not only in body but in mind.

Vienna, Brigitta's hometown, is fondly called the City of Dreams, due to the influence of psychoanalytical discovery and being the home of many brilliant minds in the pursuit of treating mental illness: including Sigmund Freud. While now we are more aware of anxiety disorders and panic attacks and PTSD (post-traumatic stress disorder), many men of Alec's time chose to tuck their experiences away.

Female students of psychiatry and psychoanalysis in Brigitta's field were slowly and surely establishing themselves by the middle of the twentieth century. Anna Freud and Karen Horney are two real-life figures who, in composite, I used to create Elisa Bauer: the doctor Brigitta holds in such high esteem.

ACKNOWLEDGMENTS ─────────────

From Aimie K. Runyan

With many thanks to:

My agent, the incomparable Kevan Lyon, for her constant support.

Our amazing editor, Kim Carlton, for her insightful edits and creative vision.

The entire team at Harper Muse for their warm welcome and bringing this project to life.

My wonderful writing support teams: the Tall Poppy Writers and the Lyonesses. We are better together!

My family, especially Jeremy, Aria, Ciaran, Maureen, and Jay, for dealing with me on a daily basis while I'm a harried mess from deadlines.

The Trumbly and Vetter clans for their unwavering support.

Rachel and J'nell for being incredible colleagues and friends.

Readers everywhere—I appreciate you!

From J'nell Ciesielski

First and foremost I must thank Rachel McMillan for asking me to be a part of this project. The woman knows every writer in the business and had her choice of picking any person in the biz, so you can imagine my utter astonishment and giggling delight when she asked me if I wanted to collaborate with her. Rachel is simply the most generous, kindhearted, enthusiastic, hard-working, and every other positive character trait nameable in the entire world. It's why everyone trusts her, why people love working with her, and why I'm so incredibly lucky to call her friend.

Aimie Runyan, you are the ultimate professional and I'm so delighted that Rachel pulled you into this snug little trio. You bring a polish to any project and our work is elevated beyond recognition thanks to your awesomeness. I can't wait to continue working together, mainly so I can see daily pictures of your cat and whatever deliciousness you're baking.

Thank you so much to Kim Carlton, Julee Schwarzburg, Jodi Hughes, and all the other wonderful team members at Harper Muse who have helped polish this lump of coal into a diamond. And a special shout-out for the design team who gave us this amazing cover to represent each of our ladies and the parts they came to play in an extraordinary castle.

Of course, no story would be complete without the key players in its creation. My family. Somehow you still don't think I'm weird for talking to imaginary people. Love y'all!

From Rachel McMillan

I would like to thank my friends and coauthors Aimie and J'nell, who are the best partners and supporters ever! And I am so thankful we are friends. I would also like to thank the wonderful Kim Carlton, who believed in this project. You are such a wonderful editor and friend. Julee Schwarzburg, thank you for showing us again how detailed you are in seeing our visions come to life. My thanks to Jodi Hughes and the wonderful editorial team at Harper Muse.

My thanks to my incredible family: Gerald and Kathleen

Acknowledgments

McMillan, my siblings, Leah and Jared, and their families. And a special shout-out to my new nephew, Roman: the first time of (inevitably) many shout-outs in my books.

I would also like to thank Linton and my pals at my other "office": Union Social at Yonge and St. Clair. *So* many words of this project came to life there.

And a special thanks to my Opa, Thomas Bruce Cann, who served as a stretcher-bearer for the Fifth Division of the Royal Canadian Army. This is the second time I have been able to memorialize the post-war experience in fiction and I am so proud of and grateful for his legacy and dedication to our country through his service.

DISCUSSION QUESTIONS ─────────────

For *The Truth Keepers*

1. An important theme of *The Truth Keepers* is how the household staff is treated. What differences do you notice about how each of the characters treat staff and their personalities in general? Is there a correlation between how the characters interact with staff and their moral code?

2. What do you think Beatrice wants for her future? Why does she enmesh herself in the theater and the world of theatrics?

3. What are your thoughts on the fifth marchioness? Why do you think she became so obsessed with her gardens? Do you think they represent anything larger? Why do you think she decided to create a poison garden specifically?

For *The Memory Keepers*

1. During the Great War so many soldiers returned home with terrible injuries and disfigurements and often became outcasts among the citizens they fought to protect. What might it feel like to look in a mirror and find yourself unrecognizable, and perhaps less accepted by society for your new appearance?

2. Elena views the world through a unique lens that's more akin to a kaleidoscope, allowing her to see others as they truly are and not simply the face they present to the world. Has there

ever been a time in your life where you viewed something differently than everyone else? Why do you think that was? Were you judged for it? Did you second-guess yourself?

3. Guardianship of Leedswick Castle is a sore topic in each of the stories. The Alnwicks face the same problem as many titled families did after the war: Save their centuries-old estate or face the inevitable and sell? Do you think Elena and Tobias should have fought harder to save the castle for the sake of its history and help it to become more a part of the local community once more, or were they right in shedding what they considered a burdensome weight?

For *The Dream Keepers*

1. Though from very different backgrounds, Alec and Brigitta have an immediate rapport: thanks to their having corresponded while Alec was at the Front. In the age of social media and online connections, can you think of a time when you were able to connect with someone in words before you met them in person? How did that experience influence your friendship?

2. Brigitta left Vienna and her uncle's house to live at Leedswick, and if ever she thought she was in a "man's profession" before, she certainly felt it then: especially given her interest in psychoanalysis. Can you think of an instance where you fought to fit into a world determined to see you as different?

3. In *The Castle Keepers*, the legacies of those who lived in the castle were not always positive. In fact, the belief that the castle was cursed is a major motif in the novellas. Does your family history involve a threat or a curse? Has this superstition— possibly built through generations of stories and belief—have a more logical explanation?

ABOUT THE AUTHORS

PHOTO BY AIMIE K. RUNYAN

Internationally bestselling author **Aimie K. Runyan** writes to celebrate unsung heroines. She has written six historical novels (and counting!) and is delving into the exciting world of contemporary women's fiction. She has been a finalist for the Colorado Book Award three times, a nominee for the Rocky Mountain Fiction Writers' "Writer of the Year," and a Historical Novel Society's Editors' Choice selection. Aimie is active as a speaker and educator in the writing community in Colorado and beyond. She lives in the beautiful Rocky Mountains with her wonderful husband, two adorable (usually) children, two very sweet cats, and a pet dragon.

Visit her online at aimiekrunyan.com
Instagram: @bookishaimie
Facebook: @aimie.runyan.author
Twitter: @aimiekrunyan

Bestselling author with a passion for heart-stopping adventure and sweeping love stories, **J'nell Ciesielski** weaves fresh takes into romances of times gone by. When not creating dashing heroes and daring heroines, she can be found dreaming of Scotland, indulging in chocolate of any kind, or watching old black-and-white movies. She is a Florida native who now lives in Virginia with her husband, daughter, and lazy beagle.

PHOTO BY BRYAN CIESIELSKI

Visit her online at jnellciesielski.com
Instagram: @jnellciesielski
Pinterest: @jnellciesielski

Rachel McMillan is the author of The Herringford and Watts Mysteries, The Van Buren and DeLuca Mysteries, and The Three Quarter Time series of contemporary Viennese romances. She is also the author of *Dream, Plan, Go: A Travel Guide to Inspire Independent Adventure*, *The London Restoration*, and *The Mozart Code*. Rachel lives in Toronto, Canada.

PHOTO BY AGNIESZKA SMYRSKA

Visit her online at rachelmcmillan.net
Instagram: @rachkmc
Facebook: @rachkmc1
Twitter: @rachkmc
Pinterest: @rachkmc